John Harding was born in a sm... ... ...age ...th ... of Ely in 1951. After local village and grammar schools, he read English at St Catherine's College, Oxford, where he once sat next to Martin Amis during a lecture and discovered gross moral turpitude (the two events are unconnected). He worked as a newspaper reporter, then as a writer and editor in magazines, before becoming a freelance writer. His first novel, *What We Did On Our Holiday*, was a bestseller and was shortlisted for the WH Smith Book Award for best first work of fiction. He lives in Richmond upon Thames with his wife and two children.

Acclaim for John Harding's *What We Did On Our Holiday*:

'A wonderful novel about filial love and primal fear, written with great humour and a rare generosity of spirit. Truly original and beautifully controlled, right up to its gripping and painfully moving denouement'
Deborah Moggach

'At times so moving it's painful to read, this book is beautifully written and very funny'
Woman's Own

'A wonderfully funny, original and moving novel . . . Harding has knife-sharp observation, immaculate timing, and the guts to take his story as far as it will go'
Helen Dunmore

'The rite of passage that occurs when the roles of parent and child are reversed has been well covered in fiction, but rarely as movingly as here. Harding tackles a difficult subject with a light touch, great humour and a complete lack of mawkishness. What really makes the book special, however, is its lack of blame or rancour. For all his characters' annoyances, jealousies and power struggles, the relationships Harding explores . . . are underpinned with great love and humanity. A really wonderful book'
The Times

Also by John Harding
WHAT WE DID ON OUR HOLIDAY
and published by Black Swan

WHILE THE SUN SHINES

John Harding

BLACK SWAN

WHILE THE SUN SHINES
A BLACK SWAN BOOK : 0 552 99966 0

First publication in Great Britain

PRINTING HISTORY
Black Swan edition published 2002

1 3 5 7 9 10 8 6 4 2

Copyright © John Harding 2002

Set in 11/13pt Melior by
Kestrel Data, Exeter, Devon.

Black Swan Books are published by Transworld Publishers,
61–63 Uxbridge Road, London W5 5SA,
a division of The Random House Group Ltd,
in Australia by Random House Australia (Pty) Ltd,
20 Alfred Street, Milsons Point, Sydney, NSW 2061, Australia,
in New Zealand by Random House New Zealand Ltd,
18 Poland Road, Glenfield, Auckland 10, New Zealand
and in South Africa by Random House (Pty) Ltd,
Endulini, 5a Jubilee Road, Parktown 2193, South Africa.

Printed and bound in Great Britain by
Clays Ltd, St Ives plc.

Make hay while the sun shines
Proverb

To make hay of something – to throw into disorder,
to confuse, to make a mess of
Penguin Dictionary of English Idioms

ACKNOWLEDGEMENTS

Anyone who has read John Carey's *John Donne: Life, Mind and Art* (Oxford University Press, 1990) will recognize it as the source of Michael Cole's understanding of the psyche of his favourite poet. For this I am deeply indebted to Professor Carey – not to mention his thrilling lectures on Dickens more than thirty years ago. Cocaine users should note, however, that it is useless as a chopping board. I have also found invaluable Professor Carey's edition of Donne's works, *John Donne: The Major Works* (Oxford University Press, 2000) – but, again, only for its original purpose.

Other works on Donne that I have found useful are *John Donne: A Life* by R. C. Bald (Oxford University Press, 1970), the most detailed biography; *John Donne Coterie Poet* by Arthur Marotti (University of Wisconsin Press, 1986) and *John Donne: Man of Flesh and Spirit* by David L. Edwards (Continuum, 2001).

Definitely less colourful than Alfred Baretta's *Silent Killer, How to Lower High Blood Pressure* by Dr Caroline Shreeve (Thorsons, 1994), *100 Questions and Answers About Hypertension* by William M. Manger and Ray W. Gifford (Blackwell Science, 2000) and *The Essential Guide to Hypertension* by the American Medical Association, edited by Angela R. Perry (Pocket Books, 2000), are, for that very reason, safer recommendations for those who already have the condition and are seeking information on the subject.

For information on cocaine, I have relied on *Cocaine: The Drug and the Addiction* by Arthur G. Herscovitch (Gardner, 1996), *Adverse Health Consequences of Cocaine Abuse* (World Health Organization, 1987), and especially *The Face Magazine Cocaine Special* (May, 2001).

For Jack and Edmund

AUTHOR'S NOTE

The quotations at the head of each chapter are
from the works of John Donne.

ONE

Full nakedness, all joys are due to thee.
As souls unbodied, bodies unclothed must be
To taste whole joys.

To his Mistress Going to Bed

When my doctor, a Croatian with the unlikely name Branko Stanic, suggested I wear a blood-pressure monitor for a day, I could see his heart wasn't really in it. The pale full moon of his face, with its livid, strawberry-red birthmark right where the Sea of Tranquillity would be, had a resigned look to it. It was the look of a father who, having tried unsuccessfully to helmet his small son with the lessons of his own experiences, watches him pedal off bare-headed across unyielding asphalt. 'Well,' it says. 'I tried.'

Moments earlier Branko had shaken his head as his sphygmomanometer exhaled. He noted the height of the red line on its column of figures and let out a world-weary sigh of his own which duetted with the air escaping from the rubber bulb in his hand.

'What is it?' I asked.

His brow creased. '170 over 120.'

'That's bad?'

He broke into a smile and a chuckle dribbled from between his thin lips. He nodded enthusiastically. 'It's

11

bad. We should get you started on medication straight away.'

'But I feel all right,' I protested. He stared at me wordlessly. 'OK, a little dizzy sometimes, maybe, but generally all right. It's only when I come in here and you strap that thing around my arm that my blood starts pounding.'

'White-coat hypertension. When the blood pressure is only raised in the doctor's surgery. It's a known phenomenon. But in your case, my friend, I think not. You have a long history of high blood pressure.'

'I don't want to be on medication if I don't have to.'

'All right, my friend, we'll monitor it for a day.' When he said 'my friend' it was not as if by rote; he managed to inject a bubble of shared humanity into it. 'But it will be the same in the end. Now, you need to come in first thing on a typical day. How about tomorrow? Is that a typical day? Oh, and wear a baggy shirt.'

So, this morning I went to see the practice nurse. She made me strip naked to the waist and taped a blood-pressure cuff around the upper part of my left arm, just above the elbow. She had me put on my shirt and threaded the rubber tube up my sleeve and down inside my shirt front. She told me to fasten my buttons and tuck my shirt tails into my Levi's. She took a small but weighty plastic box, around the size of a fat Walkman, with two loops on the back and asked me to undo my belt, pass it through the loops then do up the belt again, so that the box was on my left side. She snaked the rubber tube through the gap between the bottom two visible shirt buttons and round to my side where she plugged it into the machine.

'The cuff will inflate every ten minutes,' she said.

'You'll hear it bleeping as it deflates. The computer on your belt will record the readings. Sleep on your back or your right side tonight.' She droned on some more, but I wasn't listening, not listening being something I do rather well. Instead I was contemplating the ingenuity of my new armlet, hoping its ability to computerize the rotten fruits of a lifetime's debauchery would somehow protect me. But at last the nurse got a winding-up tone to her voice which drew my attention back to her. 'Bring it back tomorrow and make an appointment to see Dr Stanic for the results.'

'That's it?'

'That's it. Put your sweater back on and no one will know a thing about it. Not even you.'

In contradiction, as I lifted my right hand to pull down the other sleeve of my sweater over the thickened left arm, the rubber tube abraded my nipple in a cruel parody of a lover's caress.

That's how come I start beeping as I drive around the city ring road in the late afternoon. In itself this wouldn't matter. I have long since grown accustomed to the sudden inflation of the cuff – as if some night-club bouncer is gripping my upper arm in his massive paw, squeezing out the blood until, just as it goes numb, he eases off and the beeping begins, signalling the rapid return to normality. After the first few times, when the beeping was fast and insistent, my heart sounding wildly its tom toms of distress, I grew accustomed to it. And during the morning it settled down gradually from that early, strident beep-beep-beep-beep into a slower, more relaxed beep . . . beep . . . beep . . . mimicking the rhythm of a life-support machine on some TV medical soap.

It has caused me no problems. Throughout my one lecture of the morning I managed to conceal the sound

13

with bravura fits of bronchial coughing. That it is now back on panicky beep-beep-beep almost certainly has less to do with the parlous state of my cardiovascular system than the presence beside me of Tamsin Graves and my intention of fucking her senseless. She has the eyes of a doe, big and soft and brown, and I have been stalking her ever since she transferred to my class on Elizabethan and Jacobean poets at the beginning of term. I finally pounced, with the opportunism of a serial killer, when I surprised her crossing the university car park a few minutes ago. 'On your way home?' I asked. 'Like a lift?'

'Oh, it's OK. I wouldn't want to put you out.'

'You're not. It's on my way.'

'Where are you going?'

'Where do you live?'

'Riverside.'

'How lucky. That's just where I'm going.'

We'd been walking side by side, edging through the parked cars and I stopped, pulled out my keys and indicated the battered silver heap before us.

'My car.'

'Well, I don't know . . .'

I raised the book I was carrying under my arm. *John Donne – Poetical Works*. 'We could carry on the discussion of Donne we were having in class yesterday. You've missed two whole terms. I could give you some – ah – pointers.'

I had the car's passenger door open. She tossed me a smile and ducked inside. I closed the door with a satisfying slam.

It's a seduction technique that has served me better than any other over the years, the combination of a ride home and a seemingly impromptu tutorial on Donne. Notoriously so, on one occasion prompting a colleague to nod at a particularly lovely young student and remark, with an envious sneer, 'Been there, *Donne* that, I suppose?'

Once on the ring road I shifted up the gears to cruise and my left hand to Tamsin's knee. She let it lie there, unmoving like a sleeping toad, and stared straight ahead, pretending to stifle a smile. It is this moment the cuff chooses to inflate, and the shock causes my hand to grip her leg like a clamp. As tightly, in fact, as the cuff is gripping me.

'Sorry,' I say, but she isn't listening. She's staring at my upper arm as it swells and bulges beneath my cotton jumper.

An image of Popeye jumps into my mind, his arm held aloft, the muscle inflating after he inhales a can of spinach through his pipe.

'Jesus, that's amazing!' Tamsin gasps. 'Do you work out a lot?'

I've got my mouth working on a dismissive, macho smile when the muscle starts to subside.

BEEP-BEEP-BEEP-BEEP-BEEP-BEEP-BEEP.

I move my hand back to the gearstick and look at the road ahead as though preoccupied by the traffic. How can I confess to this twenty-year-old girl that I'm hooked up to a machine designed to measure and report back on the frailty of my worn-out old body? As yet she sees only the advantages of my extra thirty years. She thinks me mature. Ripe, not gone to seed. She imagines I know arcane corners of sexual behaviour, secrets gleaned from long years at the coal-face. For Christ's sake, she even thinks I have muscles! I do the only thing possible. I act as if nothing is happening. Well, most of me does. But not my traitor heart.

BEEP-BEEP-BEEP-BEEP-BEEP-BEEP-BEEP.

The beeps accelerate with the quickening of my agitated pulse. I stare straight ahead and, with great deliberation, overtake a lorry.

'Professor Cole? I think that's your mobile,' she says.

'I know. I'm ignoring it. It'll stop in a minute.'

And, of course, when my biceps goes flaccid again, it does.

Tamsin's bedsit is typical student habitat. The usual neutral-coloured carpet, some kind of beige or cream or brown, impossible to pin down. The walls, painted a noisy yellow, are decorated with a few pictures of pop stars, most of whom – sadly, it strikes me – I fail to recognize, and three fine art prints. These are disappointingly over-familiar – Hopper's *Nighthawks*, Millais' *Ophelia* and Munch's *The Scream*. Their strangeness as bedroom fellows suggest that their selection has been based more upon Tamsin's liking for them than on any decorative master plan. That said, by revolving one's gaze around the room in a clockwise direction it is possible for a tortured mind (mine, for instance!) to construct a kind of narrative from them. A lonely girl spends a dispiriting evening with other losers in a late-night bar. She returns home and, for reasons best known to herself but possibly due to her disturbed psychological state, lets down her hair, assumes nineteenth-century dress, bedecks herself fantastically with flowers then ends it all by throwing herself in the local river, where the discovery of her body provokes – on the third wall – the eponymous scream.

After this triptych, it is a relief to turn to the fourth wall and find it occupied by a large mirror in which are reflected the humble contents of the room: against one wall a small pine coffee table, home to a minuscule hi-fi with a few CDs stacked neatly beside it; a low wicker armchair squatting in one corner; a desk and chair, with a laptop and some books; and, occupying most of the remaining space, a (regrettably single) bed, with African print fabric thrown over it and matching cushions leaning against the wall at the head end, in a futile attempt to disguise it as a sofa. Reclining against these cushions is a balding and battered teddy bear, taking it all in through his solitary glass eye. Anyway, there you have it. You know the place, I'm sure: we've all been there. And if you don't, well, I'm not the man to make it any more real to you. I am usually too distracted by doing and thinking to notice what's around me. One of the things that drew me to Donne perhaps, a poet famously unappreciative of the visual world.

We sit side by side on what is not yet (but, if my scheme prospers, soon will be) a bed and drink coffee. I make sure Tamsin is seated on my right, so she'll be unable to see the engorging cuff when the thing goes off and, also, so she's nearer the head of the bed, conveniently positioned for the African pillows when I eventually make my lunge. I read, as is my custom on these occasions, Donne's poem 'The Flea' in which his seduction technique is to argue that since he and the woman he's addressing have been bitten by the same flea their blood is already commingled so what can be the harm in fucking, which involves a lot less mixing of bodily fluids? As I read the first stanza, which of course I know by heart, I lift my eyes briefly from the book to dart Tamsin a look that acknowledges her appreciation of its subtlety and draws her thereby into the conceit. So engrossed am I that I ignore the cramp in my arm and am as jolted as Tamsin by the rude interruption of the monitor.

'There goes your mobile again,' says Tamsin. 'Don't you ever answer it?'

'No,' I say. 'It will only be something important.'

'Funny ring your phone has,' she says, as we wait for the beeping to end. 'It's like those bleeps on a pedestrian crossing. I bet if you're out on the street it makes you want to run across the road before the traffic starts up again.'

'That's amazing,' I say, with a smile. 'How did you know that?'

'Better be careful, Professor Cole. I mean, what if you were waiting at a pelican crossing and your phone went off, and you thought it was the crossing signal and walked across the road and a car was coming, or a huge truck and . . .'

'Gulp.'

'Better make sure you always wait for the green man,' she says, wagging a playful finger at me, her eyes wide with mock concern and I realize the monitor has not hindered my plans at all but, rather, acted as a seduction aid. A twenty-first-century flea.

I resume the poem and as I read the penultimate lines,

> ' 'Tis true, then learn how false fears be;
> Just so much honour, when thou yield'st to me . . .'

I turn my face towards her. 'Don't suppose you happen to have a flea about you?' I say.

'Oh,' she replies, taking the book from my hand and tossing it across the room on to the seat of the wicker chair, 'I don't think we need a flea.' She pulls me down upon the African print pillows and our lips meet under the furry Cyclops' accusing glassy stare.

After a minute or so of this, Tamsin pries herself away from me and rises. 'Listen, I'm just popping to the bathroom. Why don't you take your clothes off and get into bed?' she says, and disappears.

I glance at my watch and calculate it must be some seven or eight minutes since the monitor last went off. As I take off my shoes, socks, jeans – carefully unlooping the computer from the belt first – and under-pants, I wonder how to explain the monitor to Tamsin. For a man so lacking in empathy with others, I am able nevertheless to see how it will look to someone standing in Tamsin's shoes (not, I hope, that she'll be wearing any). The ultimate accessory for the past-it generation, more damning even than matching denim shirt and jeans. In a glance I will find myself transformed from man-of-the-world older lover to fifty-year-old (in a couple of weeks or so) dirty old man. At this moment the cuff begins to swell once more, and a few seconds later the beeping begins, bleating out my age in its treacherous Morse. There is no way I can tell her about all this. I decide to do what I have often done in my long career as a serial adulterer. To chance it.

Still wearing my shirt and sweater I position myself on the right edge of the bed. I run the tube from the bottom of my shirt and tuck the monitor between mattress and bed base. The first place a burglar would look, of course, but otherwise safe. I lie on my left side, facing the centre of the bed, arm and tube pinned safely beneath me. If I can maintain this position and perform single-handed, as it were, all will yet be well. After a muffled protest, the beeping at last subsides. I have just ten minutes to do the deed before it starts again. I map out a timetable: one minute for kissing, perhaps, to re-establish mood, five maybe for foreplay – or would that be over-egging things? – say thirty seconds to put on a condom, allowing for the fact I'll have only one hand, perhaps another minute to effect an entry . . . The door from the bathroom opens and Tamsin emerges, naked save for a pair of very brief knickers.

'Somebody certainly wants to get hold of you—' She stops and stares at me. 'Do you always keep your jumper on?'

19

'Not always, no. But quite often. It's . . . er . . . unconventional, I know, but there's something about it – you know, one half being clothed and respectable the other naked – that makes me feel, well, so dirty, I guess. Do you have a problem with that?'

'No, I don't think so. Would you like me to put a sweater on too? I have a really nice Arran. I mean, if it turns you on . . .'

'No, no, it's just for me.' I nod approvingly at her body. 'I prefer you to be naked. The nakeder the better, in fact.' She peels off her underwear and lies down beside me. As she puts her arms around me, I stroke her with my only available hand moving it fast in the hope she won't notice its singularity, and steal a glance at the digital clock on her hi-fi. All this talk has already wasted a minute. I revise my schedule, allotting four minutes to foreplay. By the end of two, I'm already massaging her clitoris.

'Fuck me! Fuck me! Fuck me!'

Tamsin's urgent demand wakes me from the temporary reverie I've slipped into, prompted by the glimpse I was permitted of her bush before she took her place beside me, which was fleeting, but enough to register its autumnal russet tinge. I am minded for a moment of Donne's image of a wreath of hair remaining upon the bone of a long-dead body. I quickly bury this uncomfortable thought under a consideration of the infinite variety of the private parts of women. I begin to catalogue the various thatches I have seen. Black. Brunette. Blonde. Red. Grey (yes, even that when more tender meat was not available!). Cave-woman wild. Tangled. Combed. Soft. Coarse. Wiry. Shaved (a whole sub-species this including the so-called landing strip, the Mohican, the neat little triangle and now, according to a magazine article I read the other day, elaborate designs, geometric shapes, letters, pictures of animals – dear God people are going in for topiary down there!) At which point my reverie is rudely – very – interrupted once more.

'Fuck me, Professor Cole, fuck me!' pants Tamsin, seemingly more desperate than ever – though I sense this is more histrionic than hysterical. I would like to believe her enthusiasm genuine, that it stems from an inability to resist my overwhelming sexual magnetism. That she doesn't only want me for my mind. And I do believe it, I do! With every inch of my engorged ego as I attempt to lever it into her (not easy whilst lying on my side, but I have, as you know, my reasons for not altering my position). But – and there is always a 'but' where questions of sex and honesty are concerned – another part of me recognizes Tamsin for what she is: a twenty-year-old attempting to evince the wild passion she feels my experience of so many women over so many years will lead me to expect from her. Any failure in her arousal – her clawing, biting, gasping foreplay suggests – will be an admission of short-coming in herself and nothing to do with me.

'Call me Michael,' I tell her.

'Fuck me, Michael, fuck me!' she pleads.

I peep down at the Old Soldier, who has served me so well during the long years of campaigning that have brought me to this time, this place, this bed. There he is, dependable as ever, standing to attention, eager dolphin smile indicating his readiness to do battle, though dimly seen at this moment, his magnificent purple sou'wester being shrink-wrapped in a plastic mac.

Of course all these thoughts, so wordily and yet inadequately expressed here, even my sly southward glance, have taken nano seconds in reality, but even so this is way too long given the matter in hand (and not in Tamsin). I am – as so often lately – thinking rather than doing, my dithering threatening to turn this into the very Hamlet of a fuck. And this despite my tight schedule. I sneak a look at the hi-fi clock. Five minutes gone and still not in!

As if in acknowledgement of this, Tamsin's hand reaches down, flicks mine aside and seizes the Old Soldier, showing scant regard for his years. She begins rubbing his head unceremoniously up and down her cleft, though whether to increase her pleasure or the flow of lubrication, I can't be sure. Perhaps both, since there's now a great deal of moaning on her part and it's certainly getting slippery down there. There's something so rapacious in the utterly self-absorbed way she does this that I cannot find it pleasurable. My heart goes out to the Old Soldier in his suffering, the indignity of his being treated as a dildo.

But, like everything else, the moment comes to an end and, as the digital clock changes to indicate four minutes left, Tamsin lifts her top leg and braces her hips. She tugs the Old Soldier towards her and is just about to insert him when a chill shudders through me, leaving me momentarily frozen, all the hairs on my considerably hairy back standing on end. In the fraction of a moment it takes me to pull back my penis neurones whiz along dopamine paths in my cerebral cortex, chemical gears whir and click, flicking through the database of primitive responses in my brain. And come up with this: not a known reaction to copulation (indeed another, simultaneous, message from elsewhere informs me that the Old Soldier is now somewhat at ease) but a primeval awareness of being watched. Not only that, but direction-finding as to the source of observation and possible attack is included in the report: behind me and to the left, in the corner where sits the wicker chair.

I turn my head as well as I can to look over my shoulder, and for the merest fraction of a moment have a sense of someone sitting in the chair. I blink and there's nothing there. The chair is empty. I have half turned back when my mind replays a little video to me. Tamsin's nonchalant throw. *John Donne – Poetical Works* sailing through the air and landing upon the seat of the chair. I recall it because of my momentary flutter of anxiety that the book might be damaged. I make the half-turn back again. *Donne* is lying on the floor beside the chair.

'What?' says Tamsin, as I continue to gaze over my shoulder, my cheek resting on her uppermost breast.

'It's nothing,' I stammer, turning to offer her a weak smile. 'I was . . .'

'Oh, I get it.' She smiles. 'You want to suck my breast and you can't get at it, is that it?'

She puts her hand under her left breast, lifts it and thrusts the nipple between my open lips.

'How's that?' She presses herself against me. 'Is that what you like?'

'Urrrrmmff!' Not only is my mouth full of nipple but my nose is buried in her breast, which may be small, but is nevertheless sufficient to cut off my oxygen supply. I'm suffocating here. 'Urrrrmmff!'

'Hey, you really like that, don't you? It's funny, I never had you figured for a tit man. Why didn't you just grab it? I can't believe you're shy.'

She lets go of the breast and I unplug my face from it and come up gasping for air. I look at the clock. Three minutes to detonation. I peep back at the chair. Nothing there. My hackles are going down. It was just my guilty imagination, after all. A wild speculation that I might somehow find a private detective hired by my wife sitting there.

'So why didn't you just grab it?'

I tap-dance. 'I wasn't sure you'd had enough arousal time. You know, there's research indicating that on average it takes thirteen minutes of foreplay for a woman to be sufficiently aroused to bear having her nipples touched and I wasn't sure we'd been, you know . . .'

'Well, we did get down to it pretty fast, didn't we?' She runs her fingers through the rug on my back. 'One minute we were having this, like, really intense discussion about John Donne and the next we had our clothes off.'

'Exactly. We got from the metaphysical to the physical pretty damn quick.'

Her body arches as she laughs at this. It is a joke that embodies all the naughtiness of our situation: the book closed and abandoned, the pupil's legs opened and the teacher between them, abandoned too, but in a different way, the relationship subtly subverted. It is also a joke that, of course, I have cracked many times before and the freshness I manage to bring to it – never failing to elicit a laugh – is a mark of the consideration I award each new lover.

Again my thoughts are interrupted as Tamsin once more seizes the initiative and the Old Soldier in her left hand. She registers that he is not quite fit for duty, drops him for a moment and uses her hand to thrust her left nipple back into my mouth. She presses my head against her breast thereby making sure I can no longer breathe, much less talk. Her right hand takes hold of the Old Soldier and strokes him as gently as it is possible to do through rubber while still retaining any point in the action. Trooper that he is, he immediatedly stiffens and prepares to go over the top.

And then, with me poised once more on the threshold between adultery and . . . what? Not innocence exactly, but the greater innocence of one

24

less adultery, grant me that at least. And then, and then . . . an icy-toed spider tiptoes along my spine, the hairs there erect and ready for a different kind of action. Fight or flight, perhaps.

Slowly – it has to be slowly, with Tamsin's nipple between my teeth and her hand pressing down on my head – I slide my face round to look behind me.

'Ow, that hurts!' cries Tamsin. 'Do it again.'

But I don't. The nipple is released as I lift my head and my jaw drops open. I am looking again at the wicker chair, which seems now to contain a largish shape. A shadow the size of a man. I can't make out what it is. I blink hard and in that moment the shape takes on light, colour and form. A woman. An old woman. The room is suddenly as cold and quiet as death.

I lift my head still further.

'What?' says Tamsin again. 'What's the matter?'

I scarcely hear, much less reply. In a flash I understand for the first time the concept of flesh creeping. The figure in the chair is now as distinct as the body of the girl next to me. I know this woman. My grandmother, my father's mother, Agnes Ada Cole. There is no mistaking her. Even though she is sitting one can still appreciate the massive frame. Her height of course, which must be six two or even six three, but not just that. Her solidity. Not an ounce of fat on her. Hard, hard muscle every inch.

She looks back at me and at the precise moment our eyes make contact I feel the cuff tourniquet my left arm. She holds my gaze as it begins to deflate and I barely notice the absence of beeping from the monitor, signalling the lack of a pulse. I could swear a smile flickers across Agnes Ada's lips, as though she's pleased to have shocked me, the child whose restless adolescence so often shocked her. And she has. Why wouldn't I be shocked? Why wouldn't my heart stop beating? After all, the woman has been dead for twenty-five years.

Tamsin is sitting up now, tracking my gaze to the corner of the room, scanning the chair and the walls for explanation. 'What is it? My posters? You noticed my pop posters and that made you think about my age? You think I'm too young for you, is that what this is?'

I feel my pulse kick in again and snatch some air into my stricken lungs.

'What are you doing here?' croaks a strangulated voice, and I realize it's mine.

'What?' says Tamsin. 'What do you mean? Why shouldn't I be here? I live here, this is my flat. And you know very well what we're doing here! What's the matter? Are you having a bad trip or something?'

Agnes Ada sits motionless, that ghost of a smile still in possession of her lips. Or is it in her eyes? The same blue as my own. I never noticed when she was alive.

I turn to Tamsin. 'It's my grandmother. She's dead.'

It's a startled deer who stares back at me. Is it fear I see in those eyes?

'Listen,' she says, kneeling on the bed beside me and pulling a sheet modestly over her breasts, though not before I notice the left nipple appears strangely different from the right, elongated and sore, and catch myself wondering why. 'It's the drugs. Oh, don't worry, Professor, everyone knows about you and drugs. It's cool. But right now you're having some kind of bad drug reaction. You need to keep calm.'

I look back at Grandma. She puts a hand into the pocket of her pinafore, which she is wearing over a simple cotton dress patterned with blue cornflowers that I seem to remember well. Her hand reappears holding her spectacles case. She removes the rubber band used to keep it closed, takes out her glasses. She blows on each lens in turn, rubs them on her apron, holds them up to the light to inspect them, puts the glasses on. She shuffles in the chair, settling herself. She nods at me. 'Carry on,' she says. 'I seen pigs at it more times than I care to recall but I int never seen hoomans doing it.' She gives a chuckle and nods at Tamsin. 'Though I reckon it won't be much different. You can tell that one's going to squeal like a stuck pig.'

That does it. I'm out of my catatonia and the bed in one leap, almost falling over as the tube from my arm to the monitor wedged under the mattress jerks me back, like a cartoon dog on a lead. I tug the tube and the monitor shoots out from its hiding place.

'Hey, what's that?' I hear Tamsin cry. 'What's that you've got wired to you?'

My legs are as rubbery as the tube and scarce able to support me. Trembling, I forage among the tangled bed-linen for my underpants, and hurriedly pull them on, in my terror not even bothering to disrobe the Old Soldier, who dangles limp in his now several-sizes-too-big raincoat. Besides, I am overwhelmed with shame at the idea of Grandma seeing him. To remove the condom would only emphasize his adulterous intent. I tug on my trousers. The monitor flaps against my thigh. I zip them up and stuff it in my pocket.

'What's that thing?' Tamsin springs from the bed, trying to grab my pocket. 'You were *taping* me, weren't you, you sick bastard? What's the idea? Were you planning to play that to your sicko friends?'

I push her away and continue dressing. My socks not making themselves evident, I slip on my shoes without them. I don't bother tying the laces.

Tamsin is trying to pull on her underwear. It's a black lacy thong, so sexy fifteen minutes earlier, so pathetically inadequate as practical underwear now, its flimsy nature emphasizing the difference between that earlier time and this. In her haste, thighs clamped together, standing on one leg, trying not to lift the other too revealingly high, she gets the strip designed to cleave apart the twin hemispheres of her buttocks caught between her toes and almost tumbles over. She looks so pathetic it would bring tears to another man's eyes. I know I should embrace her, but I don't, and not just because of my state of terror, but mainly because when I was compiling my list of cunts just now there was one I forgot to mention. Myself. The biggest of them all.

I sneak a sidelong glance at the corner, half convinced that the hallucination must have dissipated, and meet Agnes Ada's macabre grin. Pain grips my chest like a vice. A sixteenth-century description of the execution of a Catholic martyr, like those Donne himself might have witnessed as a child, springs into my mind. The executioner cutting open his prey, plunging his fist into the chest cavity, pulling out the still beating heart and waving it before his amazed victim's eyes. I am brutally reminded of my own precarious bodily condition, the present frailty of my heart.

'Look, Tamsin, I wish I could explain. I – I have to go. I . . . er . . . I'm due for drinks at the Dean's. I'm – I'm sorry.'

'Sorry?' Tamsin seems unaware of her naked breasts, which wobble as she shakes with rage, and I am ashamed to confess that even now, under such circum-stances, my eyes cannot help following their movement. 'Sorry doesn't even begin to cover what you've done to me today. They warned me to stay away from you! They told me what would happen! But I wouldn't listen. Oh, no. I thought it would be different with me. And it was! You tr-tried to t-tape me!' She sobs and buries her face in her hands.

I glance into the corner. Agnes Ada raises her eyebrows comically.

'Sorry,' I mutter again, though whether to the crying girl or my deceased grandmother – or both – it's hard to say and I open the door and slip out. The door slams behind me. I race down the six flights of stairs from Tamsin's top-floor flat, my sockless, unlaced shoes loose on my bare feet, slipping and clip-clopping down every step.

Half-way down the final flight a door opens somewhere above. Tamsin's furious voice echoes down, 'You forgot your book!' followed by the noise of John Donne bouncing off banisters and clattering downstairs, a fall that will surely break his spine.

I clip-clop back up to the landing above and find him where he has finally come to rest, open, spine up, tented over the banister rail. Tenderly, fearful of adding to his injuries, I retrieve my torn-jacketed and broken-backed long-time companion in the art of seduction. Who knows when I may have need of him again?

TWO

Here needs no marble tomb, since he is gone,
He, and all about him, his, are turned to stone.

Elegy on Sir Thomas Egerton

My first encounter with Death. I don't count the demise
of my father who took an end-of-furrow turn too fast
on the Massey Ferguson and tipped himself and the
tractor into the twenty-foot wide drain edging the field
he was ploughing. The exact cause of his passing was
never determined. Whether he was drowned or
crushed to death was a matter of debate. Whatever,
I don't remember anything about it, although perhaps I
should, since I was four years old at the time. The same
age, coincidentally, as Donne when his father died. A
psychoanalyst or third-rate novelist might want to
make something of that, of my later fascination with
him, but I don't buy into it. For one thing, the fall-
out from these events was so different: Donne found
himself with a stepfather six months later; my mother
never remarried and the paternal role in my life was
played by Agnes Ada. For another, I was in thrall to
Donne's poetry long before I knew any of the details of
his life.

No, my father's death left little impression on me, as
did his life. I recall him only as a shadowy presence,

looming out of the mist of my early memory, indistinctly viewed, a tall, heavy-set man with no face, wearing an overcoat tied with string, in itself no big deal since everyone in my childhood fastened their coats that way. I was probably unaware of the existence of coat belts until my teens.

And although I dimly recall Granddad as someone small and bent, whose face was mainly teeth and who followed his elder son to the cemetery in Ely a year later, I have no recollection of his dying or funeral either. Is it normal for a child not to record such traumatic early events as these two deaths should surely have been? Did I bury them somewhere as too painful to contemplate? Does one represent the moment when Death walked over to me, bowed, smiled and offered his bony hand to begin our lifelong dance together? Who can know? So, let's return to the first death I do remember.

It was a wintry Saturday evening. I was probably seven. A pitch black night, the stars chased from the sky by a ferocious north-easterly down from the Arctic, bringing with it a stench of matted fur from some tundra-dwelling beast. Polar bear? Walrus? Reindeer? Who can say? It mingled with the oily tang of mackerel, picked up en route as the storm screamed in over the North Sea. So different from our normal Fenland scents: the rotten-wood mustiness of peat; the mouth-watering smell of celery, which assailed the nostrils everywhere in season, as though someone were permanently making a stew. (I have read that ninety per cent of the celery produced in the British Isles is grown within a thirteen-mile radius of Ely Cathedral, a statistic I have always had my doubts about, thirteen being such an odd figure that it can only have been selected for maximum sensationalism, suggesting perhaps that ten would yield far less and fifty no more).

And on foggy November nights, when the sugarbeet factory near Ely was going full blast, long chimneys spouting its infernal flames into the sky, a fetid, sour-sweet smell hung in the air, staining the mist brown, corroding the lining of your throat until your eyes watered, and stinking up your clothes.

But not that night when the wind was battering the house and rattling the window-panes so hard that at first Mum didn't notice the hammering on the back door.

'Open up, Lizzie! I'm freezing my arse off out here!' At the roar of Agnes Ada's voice my mother leaped from her fireside chair and scuttled in her frightened-mouse way to the door. Agnes Ada was banging so hard it was difficult for Mum to slide back the bolt and her fumbling seemed to take for ever. Finally the door burst open and Agnes Ada came in, a gust of winter, scratchy woollen coat grey as her hair, a touch of drab in our cheery kitchen where the fire was already weaving its red-net patterns on my bare legs.

'Cup of tea, Mum?' asked my mother. She always called her mother-in-law 'Mum' as an acknowledgement of her position as clan chief.

'No, I int stopping and no more are you, so git your coat on, gal. Old Tom Duffield's gone.'

'No, he never has!'

'Yes. Come on, now.'

'What about Michael? I can't leave him here alone.'

'Bring him along. Tom dint hev no one so there's no one to mind.'

Mum hurried us into our coats. 'Come *on*, Michael, don't keep Grandma waiting,' she said, as I doubled back from the door to grab a book.

Then we were off, Agnes Ada turning her head as we scurried along behind her to toss a few words over her shoulder for the wind to blow back to us. 'It's a filthy night, Lizzie, but I got to hev you along. He's a Sitter.'

I was puzzled by that but the wind was around my head and there was no chance to think. We tucked our heads into our chests and trekked off in single file along the Ely Road. In our village it didn't much matter which path you chose in life, the straight and narrow, or the other, easier way. It was all one in the end. When you died, you left by the Ely Road, Ely being where the nearest cemetery was. There was no burial ground in the village. Something to do with Fen shrinkage, the continuing contraction of the black peat soil. You could see it at work. Every year ground level went down, exposing another fraction of the foundations of the vicarage, the oldest and most imposing building in the village. Every decade or so another step would have to be added to the long flight stretching up to its front door as the foundations of the red-brick building rose out of the earth. On Sundays, when we passed it on the way to the Baptist Chapel, we speculated about when it would finally collapse.

Each week the vicar's wife would visit the village school, a Church of England primary, and tell us a Bible story. I could never look at the vicarage without remembering the morning she had read, with, it seemed to me, more energy and emotion than her usual style, the parable of the foolish man who built his house upon sand. If we had had a cemetery, the gravestones would have grown out of the ground little by little, like great stone teeth, first wobbling and finally toppling over. Perhaps, my macabre young imagination conjectured, the coffins would have floated to the surface without their occupants having to wait for the blast of the Last Trumpet.

It was only two miles to Tom's house but it must have taken us the best part of an hour, the wind

33

pausing for breath every so often then gusting to fling a handful of hailstones, like grapeshot, into our frozen faces. Shit! It was a hard dragging-up I had. When I look back on it now it's like coming across a formerly much-loved but now old and unfashionable jacket in the back of the wardrobe. Did I really wear that? Did I really live like that and survive? A lonely only child, fussed over by the two women, and occasionally beaten by my uncle Frank, deprived of material comforts. The landscape of my memory is always bleak, windswept and cold. And you know what? I'd give an arm or a leg, even my eyes, to be back there now. I'm not talking about regret, or doing anything different with the often miserable intervening years that got me from then to now. Just to have it all ahead of me, money in the bank, every penny still unspent.

Be that as it may, our journey ended eventually, as all journeys must, and Agnes Ada's shaking fingers scratched the key to Old Tom's back door against the lock until they drove it home. We staggered inside, a few dead leaves scuttling in with us for shelter. First thing I noticed was the smell, a mixture of the cold damp of a house that's uninhabited and the extra malodorousness of the unliving, a combination of decay and effluent whose recipe is known only to corpses.

Agnes Ada put the lights on. The kitchen was small and dominated by a large table with an oilcloth cover, orginally green check, bleached almost white in many places now by sunlight and scrubbing. A cast-iron cooking range, bearing the rusty evidence of a single man's neglect, filled the chimney breast, with a few battered pans hanging above it. Under the window was a worn enamelled sink, grey-veined with age and use, a wooden draining-board and a couple of cupboards below. The walls were painted in pale green gloss, and bare except for a simple wooden mirror, a calender with a picture of a Shire horse and the legend BOWDEN'S FOR ALL YOUR ANIMAL FEEDS AND NEEDS gilt embossed upon it, and a few horse brasses on their leather tackle, placed by someone with no eye for balance or more than a perfunctory interest in the result.

Agnes Ada parted the thin blue wool curtains that separated the kitchen from the front parlour with a harsh grating of brass curtain rings on unpolished metal pole that set my teeth on edge.

At first I thought there had been some mistake and that Old Tom was still alive. There he was, sitting in one of the two armchairs, eyes wide open, staring at the television set in the corner. But then I noticed his skin had a greenish lustre to it, like algae on the surface of a stagnant dyke and at the same moment I realized his eyes had no shine. The light was out in them. I saw then that the TV was not switched on and suddenly knew Old Tom to be as lifeless as the dead grey screen.

'That blessed neighbour of his dint even see fit to close the poor bugger's eyes,' snapped Agnes Ada. 'If there's anything I hate it's that. Coming into a place and finding the bloody thing staring at you. Come on, Lizzie, let's git him on the kitchen table.'

'What about . . . ?' Mum rolled her eyes in my direction.

'Well, he can stay in here. You'll be all right, won't you, Michael?'

'Can I watch telly?' I asked.

They looked at one another.

'I'm not sure,' said Agnes Ada, perhaps the only time in her life I ever knew her not absolutely certain of everything. 'I don't know as it seems quite right, somehow.'

If my mother hadn't interfered, the set would have remained off, but fortunately she weighed in. 'It'll hev to stay off,' she told me. 'It's disrespectful to the dead.'

Now that Agnes Ada had a point of view to oppose, she started to find her feet. 'Bugger that! Bugger respect! The old sod won't know nothing about it. He int never gunna see nothing no more.'

'Is it OK, then, Mum?'

Mum shrugged that if it was all right with Agnes Ada, who was she to argue? but got enough disapproval into the shrug to resurrect Agnes Ada's doubts.

'He can watch it,' my grandmother pronounced, after a moment or two's deliberation, 'so long as he don't hev the sound on.'

Mum traced two leads sprouting from the back of the set to their respective plugs, located the electric and aerial sockets and plugged them in. She stood in front of the set and studied it, as though its two knobs were the complex console of an alien spaceship.

'Turn the big knob, Lizzie, that's the on–off,' said Agnes Ada, with what I detected to be more than a little enthusiasm. She'd had her own set for about a year and was devoted to it. She loved to watch Westerns and – unusually for those unenlightened days and with typical perversity – always wanted the Indians to win.

There was the usual dusty crack as the set signalled the arrival of power but, of course, as yet, no picture. Mum shifted her attention to the other knob, which was helpfully marked 'VOLUME' and turned it anticlockwise as far as it would go.

I sat myself in the armchair that wasn't occupied by a corpse and waited eagerly for the set to warm up, rubbing my hands and blowing on them to speed the same process in myself.

Meanwhile Mum and Agnes Ada had their coats off and stood either side of Old Tom. They joined hands under his knees and around his shoulders.

'One, two, *three*!' said Agnes Ada, and they lifted him, still sitting, and carried him into the kitchen whence came a loud thump as they deposited him on the table.

My teeth were on edge again as the curtains closed but I didn't care because the TV picture had appeared. The trouble was it was rolling from top to bottom, with flashes of people between fast-moving, striped horizontal lines. With a year's worth of television already under my young belt I knew enough to fear that this might be due to the way the wind was playing with the huge H of the aerial, springing it back and forth on the rooftop. But, with the admirable optimisim of youth, I went on watching in the hope that the picture might come good, as Agnes Ada's sometimes did once the set was properly warmed up.

As I waited, I listened to the whispered conversation from the other side of the curtain.

'Phew! He don't half stink.' My mother's voice.

'Well, that's only to be expected.' Agnes Ada was breathing heavily as if from exertion, although the accompanying small bumps and thumps I heard offered me no clue as to what her efforts might involve. 'Old Tom didn't smell too good when he was alive. To tell the truth he don't smell much worse dead. Help me off with this vest.'

The picture was still rolling and from the old clock on the mantelpiece I saw I had been watching the striped lines endlessly unfurling for five minutes. We were at the outer edge of reasonable warm-up time. Experience taught me that if the lines hadn't settled themselves into something like a picture by now, they weren't likely to.

'Is that pan boiling yet, Lizzie? I'm gunna use this shirt of hisn for rags. It int none too clean but it'll git the worst off him.'

'I dunno, Mum, thass a good shirt, that is.'

'Do *you* want it, then? Is that what you're saying?'

'I'm not saying anything. I'm just saying it's a good shirt. It'd likely wash up all right.'

'Might do for Michael when he's bigger, I suppose.'

My momentary alarm at the idea of wearing Old Tom's stinking shirt was dissolved by the lines in front of me, which suddenly stopped rolling and were replaced by a picture. Foggy perhaps, but a picture nevertheless. Pirates! A pirate captain was making a speech to his men, clinging to the rigging as he exhorted them to bravery. I screwed up my eyes and concentrated hard but it was no use. I couldn't tell whether he was Tyrone Power or Errol Flynn. *That's* how bad the picture was.

'Now you mention it, Mum, it might. P'raps I should keep it, then, if you think that would be all right.'

'Yes, all right. We'll use his vest for the rags.' The sound of ripping cloth. 'Git that water over here.'

A Spanish galleon filled the screen, and behind her another ship, to which the camera panned, focusing on the top of the mast where a flag was being run up. The Jolly Roger! Cut to the whole ship, turning to port, waves lashing her bows, to a fitting soundtrack from the neighbouring room of water sloshing in a pan.

And then the lines started up again. From the next room came the sound of something being dipped in water and the pit-pat of it dripping on oilcloth as the women busied themselves at their task, not speaking.

I looked at the curtains. No movement. I looked at the television. Lines scrolling crazily. I knew that somewhere on the back of the set would be two knobs, one of which might end my misery.

I held my breath and listened to the sound of rag being dipped into pan. After a couple of minutes I could identify the alternating rhythms of my mother and Agnes Ada at work. My mother's dip was delicate and followed by a gentle wringing out of her cloth, as though she were afraid too much noise might waken the dead man before her. Agnes Ada's was a swift in-and-out sort of dip, a slosh-it-about, let's-get-it-done-and-mop-up-later kind of action. Dip, slosh. Dip, slosh. Dip, slosh. It was as regular as the clock ticking on the mantelpiece. Now I became aware of it, that sound, too, went into the equation. Tick-tock. Dip-slosh. Tick-tock. Dip-slosh.

I lifted myself from the chair, alarmed at the sudden creaking of its springs. I paused and held my breath. Tick-tock. Dip-slosh. Tick-tock. Dip-slosh. I tiptoed across the room to the set, which was inconveniently angled across the corner. Without moving it, it was impossible to look at the back. I glanced at the curtain. Dip-slosh. Tick-tock. I bent and reached my hand around the set, patting the cardboard backing material like a blind man. The knobs were not in the top right-hand corner, as they were on ours – not that I had ever been allowed to touch them, of course, but I had seen Mum do it. I felt lower and my fingers touched one, then the other of the tiny plastic pro-truberances. I tried to remember how they were on our set. Was 'VERTICAL HOLD' on top or 'HORIZONTAL'? There was nothing for it but to take a chance. I was so scared of doing damage that I held the knob between my finger and thumb as tenderly as later I would touch a woman's nipple. If I turned it, everything might, just might, come right. Just as likely, everything might get a whole lot worse. I held my breath. Tick-tock. Dip-slosh. Gingerly I rubbed finger against thumb, caressing the plastic nipple between.

Suddenly the striped lines shifted from straight across the set, turned to a forty-five-degree angle, tore up into a corner and immediately reappeared, this time ranged up and down and moving sideways across the screen.

Tick-tock. Dip-slosh. Tick-tock. Dip—

My arm shot out from behind the set. I stumbled backwards, recovered, and made a dive for my chair. The curtains parted, Agnes Ada's head poked through the gap and she stared at me, her hooked nose at its most hawk-like, beady bird eyes staring hungrily at me as if I were roadkill.

'All right, Michael?'

I nodded. She turned her head and looked at the TV, eyes blinking with the moving lines. You could just make out Flynn/Power for a split second in the interval between the lines scooting across the screen.

'No cowboy film on tonight?' There was a sliver of regret in her voice, and losing interest, she pulled her head back through the curtains.

I exhaled and took a breath for what seemed like the first time in hours. My heart was drumming in my chest. For a moment the sliding lines before my eyes seemed a reasonable price to pay for the narrow escape I'd just had. But, of course, for a child, one moment and the next are different lifetimes, and before another minute had passed the frustration of watching a naval battle sliced up so that two men engaged in face-to-face combat found themselves transposed to opposite sides of the screen, battling it out bizarrely back-to-back, got to me. I became aware that the fight was now being carried on in an eerie silence. The dipping and sloshing from next door had ceased.

My fingers itched to get at the knobs again. But first I had to know if the coast was clear.

The old chair creaked gratefully again as I stood up. I tiptoed over to the curtain, and found a patch which was worn so thin it amounted to a hole. Certainly large enough for a boy's eye, even one that grew wide with what it saw.

Old Tom was naked, which in itself was of interest to me, as I had no father or brothers and had been brought up almost entirely by women. A late developer, I hadn't yet reached the stage of comparing penises with other boys. As luck would have it, at that very moment, Agnes Ada gave a derisive nod at the curled pink prawn lying on its hairy pubic cushion.

'Good thing the old bugger never got himself a wife,' she said. 'She'd a hed the devil of a time finding that in the dark.'

Mum put her hand over her mouth, stifling a laugh. 'Oh, Mum!' she remonstrated. But I could tell she was pleased at this rare moment of conspiracy between them.

Tom's penis, though, was of only momentary interest to me, because much more sensational was the shape of the corpse, which was more or less as it had been in the front parlour. Tom was lying on his back, but his thighs were pointing vertically at the ceiling, which is why his penis was resting on his pubic hair. His knees made a right angle and below them his legs returned to the horizontal, parallel to his back and the table beneath it.

At that moment I knew what a Sitter was. Although I'd never heard of rigor mortis, I was a country boy and had seen enough small animal corpses to recognize the stiffness death brings. Indeed, my best friend Owen and I had once found a black cat that Death seemed to have caught in the running position, tail flying out behind him, stiff as a board. We took it in turns to use the tail as a handle and terrify small children by making him run at them. Old Tom had died in his armchair and not been found until his body had set like concrete. I was about to find out why a woman as

41

heavy-boned and powerful as my grandmother had extra cachet as a layer-out of the dead.

Agnes Ada dragged a kitchen chair to the bottom end of the table, its back against the table's edge. She raised one foot to it, then stopped and muttered, 'No, wait a jiffy.' She looked around the kitchen, spotted a tea towel hanging on the range, and draped it over Old Tom's groin.

'I may be hard up,' she said, 'but I int doing it with no corpse.'

'Oh, Mum, I think he's way past anything like that.'

'Well, you never know. If hair can keep growing on a man's chin after he's gone, who's to say what else can keep going?'

She put her foot on the seat of the chair again. 'Keep a hold of him, Lizzie, don't let him roll off.'

My mother was at Old Tom's head, and pressed her hands down firmly on his shoulders, her face uncomfortably close to his. He seemed to be grinning, lips peeled back over long yellow teeth, although I felt sure they hadn't been before, as though amused at the difficulty he was causing them. Or perhaps I hadn't noticed and he'd died laughing at something funny on the television. *I Love Lucy* perhaps. For a moment I worried about the phrase 'I could die laughing' and wondered if I should maybe not watch comedy shows again.

Agnes Ada pressed down hard on the chair, testing its strength and stability, then hoisted herself up and stood on it. Then she climbed on to the table. 'Good job he's got a good strong table. I don't know what I'm going to do with this flimsy little Formica-topped gate-leg rubbish people are getting nowadays,' she muttered. 'Formica! Bugger that!'

Mum looked down intently at Old Tom and remained silent in the way of a woman who's recently dipped into her husband's insurance money and bought herself a Formica-topped gate-legged table.

Kneeling at Old Tom's feet, Agnes Ada tugged at them with one hand, as I'd seen her do to a Christmas turkey, and pressed the other down on his knees. The legs lengthened slightly as the knees went down. Immediately Tom's head and shoulders bobbed up.

'Hold him down, Lizzie, hold him down! I don't want that old bugger laughing in my face.'

Murmuring an apology, Mum pushed the upper torso down, which caused the legs to shoot up again, and leaned over the dead man's head, grinding her elbows into his shoulders.

'Humpf, there's only one thing for it.' Agnes Ada stretched her arms across Old Tom's legs and planted her hands on the far side of the table. Then she craned herself up until her knees were above Tom's thighs. Slowly she let herself down on the dead limbs, and when they had all her weight, began to rock up and down on them, pushing his knees with her hand. Pearls of sweat stood out on her brow. She grunted with effort. 'You old bugger,' she spat. 'You was an old bugger when you was alive and you're an old bugger now.' Tom smiled back defiantly. 'But you won't get the better of me.'

She tugged at his ankles and the knees dipped again. She lifted her huge frame right off him, quivering from the effort. Then she dropped down on to his knees and began bouncing up and down on them again. The table shook each time she landed with a resounding crash. At the head end Mum was holding on for dear life, knuckles white, teeth gritted, tears in her eyes as each bounce threatened to resurrect Old Tom again.

'Come on, you old sod, come on!' hissed my grandmother. 'You're dead and it's time to lie down!' And then suddenly, there was a crack like ice breaking on the village pond when the first thaw came, or Uncle Frank's axe splitting a log. Loud enough surely to wake the dead. Loud enough to make me cry out from my hiding-place behind the curtains. The knees broke, Old Tom's legs collapsed and he lay on the table as flat as a Fen field.

At my cry, Mum's eyes had shot towards the curtains and seemed to bore right into the hole through which I was peeping. I scurried back to my chair.

The curtains screeched open. 'You all right, Michael?'

I proffered a weak smile.

'Good film?' She nodded at the TV.

I looked at it for the first time since I'd fled from the curtain. The rolling lines had disappeared, the fog had dissipated. A perfect picture showed the stern of a pirate schooner sailing off into the sunset. Across the screen the words 'The End' were being scrawled in antique script as if by an invisible quill. I batted my eyelids, fighting back tears. It was over. I had missed it all.

THREE

I stand on the Dean's doorstep, late, haunted by an hallucination of my dead grandmother and sockless. Not the best state in which to arrive at an important social function. I've repaired my appearance as best I can. I check one last time as I ring the bell. Hair no longer raised, brushed flat by my hands and an emergency application of spit. Shirt buttoned. Blood-pressure monitor once again attached to belt and concealed by jumper. Shoes laced as tightly as possible, although still slipping in the absence of socks. It can't be helped: I will have to do.

A cold wind tickles my exposed ankles and I stick both hands into the front pockets of my Levi's to work them down my legs a bit, so that they all but touch the tops of my shoes. Quite presentable. I take out my hands. My trouser bottoms shoot up again. Of course, naked feet would raise not an eyebrow in summer – or even now, in May, were I shod in sandals, espadrilles, plimsolls or even trainers. But not brown brogues.

There is nothing else for it: my hands will have to remain firmly pocketed. I attempt to incorporate this into the casual air I affect as the Dean herself, Jane Yeats, answers the door, wine-glass in hand. 'Michael! So glad you could come.'

I find this a strange greeting, as if I might somehow not have. This is, after all, an English faculty drinks party. I am, as is surely universally acknowledged, the head-of-department-elect, my appointment awaiting only the formality of the board's ratification later this term. In such a situation how could the party take place without me?

The Dean bends towards me, automatically proffering a cheek for the standard social-situation greeting among colleagues. Hands in pockets, arms rigid, it's impossible for me to bend forward and get any sort of contact between my lips and her cheek – she is not a tall woman – and there's an awkward moment while the cheek remains in place, on offer, as it were, but unkissed. In the end I solve the problem by leaning backward as far as I can and limbo-dancing – the shuffling style happily obviating the need to lift my feet and any consequent clip-clopping – towards her until I can brush my lips against her downy skin. There's no way I can lean round her without showing an ankle so she has to make do with an old-fashioned, Europhobic, mono kiss.

'Come in, make yourself at home. Everyone else is here.'

I can't work out whether or not this is a rebuke for my unpunctuality – which matters, because Jane is head of the appointments board. I follow her, admiring nostalgically en route the alluring swing her buttocks gain from her high-heeled shoes, into the drawing room, which is full to its ornately corniced high ceilings with the hum of conversation, cigarette smoke and soft jazz. It's only now that I realize just how late I am: the crowd is so dense that it surely already includes all the teaching staff and research graduates, and the one or two more promising students who are usually honoured with invitations to this kind of bash. As we enter, Jane's husband, Jonathan, waves to her from the other side of the room and she excuses herself, saying, 'Get yourself a drink,' and is swallowed by the throng.

Briefly I crane my neck, a flutter of hope taking wing in my breast as I search for Harriet. When I can't see her – and, given her small dark form, this is hardly surprising in such a crowd – I push through the press, nodding away attempts at conversation in my desperation, after my recent fright, to reach the drinks table, positioned, as usual, next to the fireplace, which is aglow with red-hot logs on this unseasonably cold May evening. I remove my hands from my pockets to pour myself a glass of wine and warm my ankles.

Once holding the wine-glass, of course, I can keep only one hand pocketed. Disturbingly, as I raise my right hand to lift the glass to my lips, I discover that exerting too much pressure with the left causes the opposite trouser leg to rise. The obvious solution is to alternate glass and trouser hand so as to keep shoving both legs down, but taking care to maintain a sober expression to avoid any suggestion I may be playing with my genitals. I am just getting into a nice rhythm with this when, above the sea of people, I spot the shark's fin of Brady Tait's black quiff cutting its way through, heading straight for me. A moment later he stands before me, a large smile taped across his face. 'Michael,' he says.

'Brady.'

He surveys the room with the attitude of an anthropologist observing an especially primitive tribe. He sips his drink. He turns back to me. 'Donne done?' he says. Of course, he could equally well be saying, 'Done Donne?' but I feel not, since the latter lacks the elegance of the former and anything that comes out of Brady's mouth has already been to finishing school.

Silently I promise myself that my next area of study – if I am ever done with Donne, that is – will be a writer who is less punnable – or, at least, less pertinently so. Donne! It rhymes with pun!

'It's – ah – coming along,' I lie. 'I'm on the home straight. No sense rushing it. That's one thing I don't believe in.'

This is my own bitter dig at Tait's prolific publishing record. Articles and papers issue from his word-processor seemingly without him writing them. Since he crossed the Atlantic to inflict himself upon us at the beginning of the academic year he has already delivered to his publisher a thousand-page-long study of the role of drugs in punk novels.

He takes another sip of his drink, which looks suspiciously like unadulterated orange juice. 'Well, we're all looking forward to it.'

'Thank you. That's nice to know.'

'So, do you have any idea of a publishing date?'

'I am – ah – hoping to have it done, er, finished, by the end of the academic year. Given that, well, I'm expecting an increase in my workload here after that.'

'Really?' He looks genuinely surprised. 'I don't think so, Michael. I don't think you need worry about that.'

I'm about to ask him what he means when a bottle of burgundy is thrust between us and tipped to fill my already empty glass. The short, plump, bespectacled form of Karen Epstein follows the bottle. As always, I cannot help looking down on the black curly tea-cosy of her hair without feeling sorry for her. Why doesn't she just shave it all off? I wonder for the hundredth time. Why wouldn't you?

'You guys talking about Donne?' she asks, pouring the rest of the bottle into her own glass, filling it to such an extent the liquid is held in only by surface tension, requiring her to lean and slurp it so it doesn't overflow the brim.

'For our sins,' says Brady.

'You know what I don't get about that guy?' She beams her owl eyes first at one and then the other of us. (Why doesn't she get smaller spectacles?) We don't answer because we know she's going to tell us anyhow. 'The way he's always trying to get some woman into bed. He doesn't do any of the real love stuff, does he? I mean, there's nothing erotic about Donne. He thinks of a nice philosophical conceit and expects it to get him into a woman's knickers.'

Sometime while I am looking at Karen, Brady takes off his smile and sticks on a bigger one, which he's wearing when I look back at him.

'I mean, "The Flea". Come *on*! This flea took your blood and what I'm going to take won't even do you that much harm so why not get them off? It sucks. And you know why it sucks? Because if I were in some guy's bed and fleas started hopping about all over me I'd be out of there so fast you wouldn't even have time to say metaphysical. I'm going to screw some bloke who has bed-bugs? Give me a break.'

Karen's accent is an odd mixture of soft Midlands burr and staccato clipped New York. Although she's only ever spent one week in that city – and, indeed, in the whole of the United States – a love of all things American and her being half Jewish lead her to think of herself as some kind of honorary New Yorker. She actually sounds more American than Tait who, in his preppy way, is constantly trying to move his accent the

49

other direction across the Atlantic. I can never see them together without recalling the first time they met. The conversation went like this:

Tait: 'What part are you from?'

Karen: 'Birmingham.'

Tait: 'You don't have a Southern accent.'

Karen: 'No, why would I?'

Tait: 'Well, coming from Birmingham and all.'

Karen (sighing exasperatedly): 'Birmingham is not in the south. But seeing as it's only the second largest city in England you can't possibly be expected to know that.'

Tait: 'Uh-huh, I get it. I thought we were talking Alabama.'

Karen: 'As if!'

Karen is one of the few women in my life at present whom I haven't fucked. More, she is actually one of a much smaller and still more select band: the women I haven't even tried to fuck. I would like to chalk up a few moral Brownie points here, to pat myself on the back for this meagre demonstration of restraint. But, sadly, the only reason sex has not reared its ugly head – nor the Old Soldier his handsome one – between us, is that I am not attracted to her. Although, of course, that in itself has not always been sufficient reason to stop me. It is just that with Karen, I am *very* not attracted to her. My not having fucked her means I have also not fucked her around, or up, or over, or off, with the result that, unlike most of the other women I know, she is – her attitude to Donne notwithstanding – a good friend.

Karen and Tait are soon engaged in a deep discussion about the new collection of poems by a post-punk performance artist he is particularly keen to promote, so I slip off in search of Harriet. I catch sight of her dark bob among a crowd of graduate students over near the window. This glimpse of her occasions, as it always does, a bout of tachycardia in my unruly heart and I am on my way over to her when I hear my name called from another direction. I swivel to find the head of the English faculty, Stanley Horgan, waving at me from his armchair. Although only around sixty, Stan has suffered two strokes and a concomitant diminution of brain power. At the rate he is losing brain cells, I reflect, as I sashay over to him, hand pushing down hard in pocket, in another year or two he'll be able to talk to Tait as an equal.

'Michael, my boy,' he says, raising a feeble hand in greeting, the epithet reflecting more our perceived relative states of health than our ages, since he has little more than a decade over me. And also because our relationship has always been father–son. I've never resented him, even though ten years ago he sneaked head of faculty by being next-in-line, when many had expected the prize to come to me as bright young (although not *that* young even then) thing. Well, I have less reason than ever to resent him now. I've hung on and on, missing one or two good opportunities elsewhere, mainly through a combination of my depression and being rooted in my dissolute life here. And now he is retiring because of his ill-health and, by the same reckoning that appointed him, it is, at last, my turn.

His corpulent figure is ensconced in an armchair and he is holding a large glass of wine, stoking up another stroke by the look of him; his face so red it looks like he is wearing his blood on the outside of his cheeks. He indicates the chair opposite. I plonk myself into it and find my trouser cuffs immediately rise up, so I put down my glass, slip my hands into my pockets, stretch out my legs and slide down in the chair until my body is rigid and at forty-five degrees to it. I must look the very opposite of a Sitter, like someone who has died in his bed and is now waiting for Agnes Ada to come and break a bone or two and mould him into a chair.

'How goes it, Stan?'

'Oh, well, can't complain. Doctors tell me not to drink but, then, what do they know? Anyway, you look very relaxed.' A reference to my head being almost on the seat of the chair.

'Yes, pretty well.'

'Must say, Michael, I feel a lot better knowing I won't be doing the Kappelheim this year.'

This reference to the annual lecture, traditionally given by the head of the department to the whole university, or as many as can cram into the Great Hall, gives me a warm glow. The unusual circumstance of my being invited to deliver it in the light of Stan's ill health is nothing more than an acknowledgement of my position as his heir apparent.

'I'm sure.'

'Yes, I'm very grateful to you. Both of you.'

'Both?'

'Yes. You and young Tait. I'm looking forward to it. What are you doing yours on?'

'Donne and . . .' I say distractedly. 'Tait? I think you're mistaken about this, Stan.' I wonder if he's been taking his medication or if he is simply pissed again, but then the worm of doubt that has been burrowing towards my heart ever since I spoke to Tait breaks through to the left chamber with an accompanying stab of pain.

'No, no mistake, Michael. At least, I don't think so. The Dean told me. Time to break with tradition, she says, have two shorter lectures.'

'I don't understand.'

'Something about concentration spans. She says thirty minutes is all anybody is able to spend in the sixteenth century these days. Meaning Donne, of course. Then they get Brady to talk about one of his American poets. Bit of colourful language. Very cutting edge for the sponsors, she reckons.'

He tips his head back, draining his glass, flecks of burgundy anointing his white shirt. He reaches towards the side table by his armchair on which stands a half-empty wine bottle, refills his glass, settles himself once more in his seat and looks at me again.

'Stan, when did this—'

'Christ!'

I follow his gaze and realize he's staring at my arm, which has just inflated. His eyes bulge and he turns – impossibly, I would have said a moment earlier – a deeper shade of red.

'Bloody hell, I can cope with the small animals but this is—' He screws up his eyes as though fighting back tears. Fortunately by the time he opens them again, the cuff is deflating.

Beep-beep-beep-beep-beep-beep-beep.

He heaves a sigh of relief. 'That your phone, Michael? Aren't you going to answer it?'

'No, anybody I need to talk to is probably right here in this room.'

Stan is still watching my arm, which has now returned to normal, as if fearful it may explode again. After a second or two, at last reassured, he takes a sizable gulp of wine.

'Hello again, Michael. You're looking very relaxed.'

It's Jane.

'Well, actually I'm not, Jane. Not at all relaxed. Stan's just been telling me about the Kappelheim. Or should I say Kappelheims?'

She smiles and there is something so intimate in it, so just meant for me, that I am reminded of the smile on her face as I rolled off her naked body – was it five or six years ago – and told her that this, of course, had

53

been a period, a whole term even, of madness, which had to end because I was happily married and so was she, etc., etc. The smile then said, 'OK, but not OK.' The smile now says, 'Payback time.' I curse my lack of foresight. She was not Dean then, but there was a ruthlessness about her in the sack that should have alerted me to her ambition. I recall how Donne was, well, undone by a woman. How his burgeoning civil-service career was ruined by an ill-advised marriage.

'Yes, we're having two lectures.'

'But I thought when you asked me . . . I mean, I naturally assumed . . .'

'Ah, well, Michael, my old love. These days, you can't assume anything.' She ruffles my hair, turns and struts off, a whiff of Chanel and menace left suspended in the air behind her.

'Hello, Michael, you're looking very relaxed.'

It's Harriet. Harriet Bright, youngest member of the teaching staff and my own Dark Lady. What a poem Donne might have made of that! The contrast between her name and appearance. Bright, as in sharply intelligent and also as in sunny disposition, her full, ripe lips always ready to loose a smile on this dull world. Dark in her looks, hair black as coal, eyes some shade beyond even that. Looking into them (how could I have found Tamsin's attractive?) brings to mind those sleek limousines whose blacked-out windows make one long to know who is inside.

'Well, I'm not. I just heard Tait and I are sharing the Kappelheim.'

'Yes, he told me.'

'What do you think?'

'I think you'll blow him off the lectern. Now, stop worrying about it, get up out of that chair and come next door. Jonathan is putting some old disco music on. Some of us youngsters want to dance. Seventies stuff. Come on, you can tell me what it was like being alive then.'

'Ha bloody ha.'

She reaches down, takes hold of my wrists, tugging my not unwilling hands from my pockets, and pulls me out of my chair.

''Bye, Stan,' I say, glancing across at him. His chin is on his chest and he is fast asleep. Unless, of course, he's had another stroke, which I don't want to think about.

Harriet leads me by the hand through the open doorway into the next room, where above a disco beat a woman's voice intones the words 'I feel love', ironically, I think, since Harriet shows no signs of registering the electricity coursing from my fingers to hers. Like Karen, she belongs to that exclusive club of women I have not fucked but her membership derives from an entirely different cause: I love her. The moment I first saw her she seemed to personify the vague abstraction to which my love has always hopelessly adhered. She is the one I had always known was out there somewhere. That I have never attempted to consummate my desire is down to the knowledge that, should I ever do so, and fail, I would have to live the rest of my life without the possibility; it is not a prospect I have so far been able to face.

We begin to dance and she gifts me her biggest smile.

'Hey, no socks,' she says. 'Cool.'

I don't remember a whole lot more about the evening. I know I danced a great deal, and how difficult it was to prevent anyone else finding out about my socks so that some of the students present thought I was the ultimate in nonchalance and by the end of the evening two or three of the men were dancing with both hands in their trouser pockets too. (I suspect they admired, too, the cavalier way in which I ignored the regular – very – summonses from my mobile phone.) I know an awful lot of marijuana got itself smoked and an awful lot of it by me. And I know I walked up and down the broad suburban street, ankles ghostly white in the unforgiving light of a big old moon, thinking about my grandmother and getting myself straight enough to pilot my battered Golf home. But mostly I just remember the bits that matter. The conversation with Tait. The grenade old Stan tossed in. The Dean's raking smile. And then the bit of my brain that isn't addled with drink and drugs wakes me up and tells me I'm home.

I park some distance from the house and wait for the monitor to go off. When its beeping has subsided I haul my tired old body out of the car. I have ten minutes to get into the house without Alison knowing. There are two reasons I need to do this. First, later when she finds me in my study, I can pretend to have been in much longer than I actually have, enabling me to shift the party at the Dean's an hour or so earlier thereby establishing an alibi for the stolen couple of hours when I was driving Tamsin home, seducing her (almost) and driving back to campus. This is necessary because Alison will almost certainly have telephoned my office during this period and will want to know why I wasn't there. The second – and possibly more pressing – reason for subterfuge is my urgent need for socks. Any excuse I can come up with for their absence is likely to be a lot less likely than the real reason, namely adultery. I don't feel I can bear the injustice of being accused of something I haven't managed to do.

I can easily explain the total lack of a greeting to Alison on my return by saying she was on the phone when I came in and I didn't want to disturb her. She spends so much time on the phone that this is entirely feasible and involves little risk of exposure, as my successful use of the strategy countless times before has proved.

I turn my key slowly and silently in the front-door lock. Being caught sneaking around is not a problem in itself: I can plead not wishing to wake the children – I am, after all, a considerate father. I open the door. The hall is in darkness, with only the light leaking under the sitting-room door permitting me to see anything at all. I step inside, turn and begin to close the door very slowly because it has a tendency to slam if you just let it go. And then I feel it again: my hackles rising. The hairs on my neck are lifting, as though someone is stroking them the wrong way. I pause, the door still open. I turn suddenly, just in time to see something dark, the size of a child of about ten – so too old to be either of mine, and anyway not upright enough to be human, almost, but not quite, on all fours, hands practically dragging on the floor, more like in fact a chimpanzee – scuttle away into the darkness at the other end of the corridor. I am so startled I let go the door.

Crash! It swings shut, making the birds in the Victorian stained-glass window in its top half tremble on their perches with the impact. As so often happens in life, no sooner does one door close than another opens, and light floods into the hall from the sitting room. Alison stands in the doorway, her long blonde-streaked hair shot through with bolts of gold from the back-lighting, creating, as it were, highlights on her highlights.

'I thought I heard you sneaking about,' she says.

'I wasn't sneaking about. I'd hardly slam the door if I were sneaking about, would I?'

'Well, you shouldn't slam it, you'll wake the boys.'

'Damned if I slam and damned if I don't, eh?' I'm trying to be jocular, but there's an edge I can't keep out of my voice. What *was* the thing that disappeared down the corridor?

'Where have you been?'

'What do you mean, where have I been? Don't start all that again. Working, of course.'

'I called your office earlier. I got the machine.'

'What time was that?'

'Don't you know? Haven't you checked your answer-phone?'

'You know me, I always forget.' I'm trying to edge past her to make for the stairs and the safety of my study, but she bars the way.

'Yes, I know you.'

A brief silence while we both chew this over.

'Where were you?'

'Drinks with the Dean, I reminded you of that this morning.'

'Yes, but that was at seven, wasn't it?'

'Six. It got shifted earlier.'

'OK, so where were you at five when I phoned?'

'In the cafeteria. Thought I'd better not go to Jane's on an empty stomach.'

'I was calling on the mobile. I was driving past with the boys.'

'What a shame. If only I'd known, you could have dropped in, had tea with me.'

'We did. Drop in, that is. For tea. We didn't quite manage the "with you" bit because you weren't there.'

'I was probably in the library. Checking a few references for the book.' My Donne book.

'Ah, yes, of course. The book. The one that's not *done* yet.'

The emphasis she puts on the word makes me

wonder if she's heard campus gossip, but then, I reassure myself, it's an obvious joke. And then I realize that if she's not making so direct a reference to my infidelity she may perhaps be attacking it obliquely, making a dig at the wastefulness of my life and its role in my failure to produce the promised work. For half a second I wonder which is worse.

'Listen,' I say, trying to push past her. 'I have work to do. I don't want to stand here talking in the dark.'

She moves to block my passage and stretches out an arm. A click as she switches on the light. For the thousandth time I wonder why, as a man who has always preferred small women, I picked someone as tall as Alison. Her legginess excited me, I suppose. There seemed then to be so much more you could do with long legs. Now her height intimidates me.

She studies my face. 'You're pale. You look as if you've seen a ghost.'

The aptness of the expression brings back the hallucination in Tamsin's room. I shudder and wonder if Alison can see it, this involuntary tremor running through me. 'Just tired,' I mumble. This time I manage to push past her. 'Now, if there's nothing else . . .' I'm on the stairs now, taking them two at a time.

'Just one thing.'

'Yes?'

'Why aren't you wearing any socks?'

I freeze, mid-bound. 'I had to take them off. My feet were itching. Athlete's foot, I think.' Shit! Why did I say that?

'I wonder who you caught *that* from?'

'Probably the showers at the gym. Now I think of it, they had a notice up about it. Been an outbreak.'

'I'll wash them for you.'

'My feet?'

'Your socks. Give them to me, I'll wash them.'

59

'I – uh – threw them away. Thought they might be full of – you know – spores.'

I start off up the stairs again.

'Yes, and you're full of bullshit.'

I bound up the rest of the way and make for our bedroom. I need to shower, to get Tamsin's scent off me, because Alison will need only a whiff of evidence to make our life even more of a misery.

I turn on the shower in the en suite, wander back into the bedroom and begin to pull off my clothes. I am just taking off my jumper when the monitor kicks off again and I am forced to consider the logistics of showering with it on. I unloop it from my belt, and decide I can hold my left arm aloft, with the monitor in my hand, thereby keeping both it and the cuff dry. It will mean showering one-handed but, hell, I'm getting used to doing things that way. I take off the rest of my things and am down to my underpants, monitor dangling from its cuff, when Alison walks in. She steadfastly ignores it, knowing any reference to it may be interpreted as the opening of negotiations for a ceasefire.

'You're having a shower?'

'Well, as you pointed out, I'm half undressed anyway.'

She ignores the joke. 'Who is she? Another fresher?'

'What on earth are you talking about?'

'I don't know how you can. They all seem so young to me. I looked at them in the cafeteria today and they're like schoolgirls. And that's to me and I'm only thirty-seven. What must they seem like to you? Or is that the attraction? Is that what it is? You like little girls?'

'I don't have to listen to this. I'm sick and tired of your paranoia.'

'Paranoia is when you're worried about something that isn't happening. That isn't the case here.'

60

I stride across the room towards her, aware of the psychological disadvantage of being clad only in my underpants, but balancing this somewhat by clutching the monitor martyrishly in my hand. I thrust my face into hers. She flinches. 'Get a life, woman! That's the only problem here. You were intelligent when I met you—'

'I was one of your students. I can't have been so bright or that would have told me something.'

'Just shut up and let me talk for once, will you? That's another of your problems. You starve yourself of intelligent adult company. You spend all your time with the kids so you can't even observe normal conversational etiquette any more. You have to jump in with whatever you've got to say before the next poo, or fight or—'

'OK. I looked at your diary in your office. You're free tomorrow afternoon. You look after them then, you're such a wonderful father. I'd like to get my hair cut.'

'Fine. No problem. I like being with my kids, I don't spend my life moaning about it. Now, if you'll kindly just SHUT UP a moment, JUST SHUT UP!'

'Adult company, huh!'

I ignore her and begin to march back and forth across the bedroom, ranting. 'You just have no idea what it takes to keep all this going, do you? The shit I have to wade through every day to keep this household afloat. The lectures to boorish kids who are too busy checking their text messages to listen, the hours of meetings in which I and other academics as innumerate as myself waste our fine brains in vain attempts to save money on gardeners or central-heating engineers, the political chicanery, the things I have to endure to try to get a better job to feed us all, the sucking up to people I don't like, the backstabbing of people I do. And why don't you know? Because you never ask me about it, you don't *want* to know. And even when I try telling you, you don't listen. You *can't* listen. Your memory-banks are full to bursting. Your mind is in overload with trivia about the sale of windcheaters in Children's Gap, how much you saved on toys in Argos, the amount of iron there is in spinach, how you can persuade a two-and-a-half-year-old to eat spinach, how Jake behaved in someone else's house, the price of Lego. THE PRICE OF FUCKING LEGO! What to put in party bags because their birthdays are only six months away and you need to be thinking about it now, spare underwear in case of accidents, are they accidents? Is there a psychological cause? Would a pet cat cause asthma? I could go on and on and on! But what would be the bloody point?'

I tear off my underpants with a magnificent flourish and wave them at Alison. 'What happened to things like poetry and music and philosophy? What happened to the big questions? How have you let worrying about the psychological implications of constipation replace worrying about why we're here? It's the demise of a once fine brain that makes me mad.' I toss the underpants at her head, their uselessness as a missile emphasizing the hopelessness of it all. 'Oh, what's the use?'

Alison beats away the flying Y-fronts with her hand. 'So you didn't fuck a student today?'

'No, nor anyone else. And I resent your fucking groundless suspicions.'

'You didn't have sex?'

'I just fucking told you, didn't I?'

'What's that, then?' Mouth half open, I am about to hurl more righteous resentment after the underpants when I see she is looking at the Old Soldier.

All too late realization dawns as I glance down and see him dangling there, all dressed up and nowhere to go, a disgusting old flasher in his plastic mac.

*   *   *

Shamed and showered, an hour later, in the warm refuge of my study, I read Donne's sermon on married love in which he says a man should love his wife because she is his wife, not because she is a woman. 'A man may be a drunkard at home, with his own wine, and never go to taverns,' he says. 'A man may be an adulterer in his wife's bosom, though he seek not strange women.'

I move on to his sermon 'On Where the Dead Are' where he talks of the soul remaining in the room where it separated from its body. 'Those whom I call dead, are alive,' he avers. It's a speculation that greatly occupied him, that the dead might be all around us. I think of my vision of Agnes Ada. I keep going back to that image of the book on the chair.

Musing on this, I pick up the phone. 'Tommo, about that last delivery.'

'Yeah?'

'Could there have been something wrong with it?'

'What do you mean? That was top-class stuff. You know that. You tried it. You were flying.'

'Have any of your other customers said anything about it?'

'Not a word – except can they score some more. What's the problem, Michael?'

'It's just that I've been having these – uh – hallucinations. Could it have done that?'

'Hallucinations? Michael, I don't think so. What else have you been taking? You been dropping some acid? Or maybe overdoing the drink? Alcohol will do that to you, you know. It's called the DTs. You start seeing small furry animals. Is that what's happening, Michael? Are you getting small furry animals?'

'Well, quite big ones, actually. You know, like a chimpanzee.'

I have to hold the phone away from my ear as an eardrum-bursting guffaw erupts from it. Finally Tommo calms down. 'Michael, it's not the coke, believe me. Now, you still want that delivery tomorrow?'

'Yes, of course, but I can't come to the gym in the afternoon. I have to look after my children. Can you come to my office in the morning?'

'That might not be such a good idea. I'm attracting a lot of interest from the boys in blue at the moment.'

I tell Tommo where I'll be in the afternoon and he says he'll drop in to see me.

'Oh, and Tommo,' I say, as he is about to hang up.

'Yes, Michael?'

'Bring double.'

I sneak into the bedroom but needlessly since Alison is still awake, sniffing into a tissue. Her back is resolutely to the door, anger having given way to withdrawal.

'Listen, Alison, now you've calmed down, there's a perfectly simple explanation for all this.'

'I catch you wearing a condom and you think you can explain it away?'

'I put it on because I was going to see the Dean.'

She sits bolt upright. 'That fat cow! I couldn't stand it if you've been screwing her again! Oh, God, the humiliation . . .' And she's off, nose buried in the tissue once more.

'I haven't been screwing her or anybody else,' I say truthfully. 'That's what I'm trying to tell you. There's a good reason for that condom that has nothing to do with sex.'

'Which is?'

'Prostate trouble.'

'*Prostate trouble?* I thought that was something old men got.'

'Well, yes, most people do but you don't have to be

that old. Don't forget I'm fifty soon. That's well within the range.' My voice is a mixture of sadness and embarrassment now. As luck would have it, the cuff puffs up around my arm. We listen as the beeping reinforces my argument.

'That's one reason I didn't want to tell you. I'm already conscious of the age difference between us. How do you think it feels to find you've joined the ranks of the living dead?'

She is looking at me now with a softer light in her eyes. She wants to believe this. But an edge of cynicism, born of long years of marriage to me, which creeps in ever more frequently these days, is there now too. 'Listen, if all this is true—'

'True? Of course it's true. You think I'd humiliate myself like this if it wasn't? Jesus, I'd rather be caught with a girl – at least it would show I'm not on the scrapheap.'

'Well, I don't see what this has to do with the condom.'

'The prostate is situated next to the bladder. In middle-aged men it has a tendency to swelling. Branko found this at my annual health check, along with the hypertension. The enlarged prostate presses on the bladder and interferes with the flow of urine. Sometimes it's impossible for me to piss when I want to. Others, the stuff just dribbles out without me knowing. I was attending a social function vital to my career. I didn't want to wet my pants. So I took the precaution of sticking a condom over the end of my willy to catch any dribbles.' Even as I'm coming out with all this I find myself thinking, Hang on, the fact that I was still wearing the condom when I arrived home means I can't have had a pee all evening. An awful thought follows. Maybe I do have prostate trouble! Maybe I'm telling the truth!

Alison stares at me, pity and disbelief fighting a battle in her eyes. 'Is this true?'

I wipe the back of my hand over my eyes, quickly, as though I don't want her to notice. I nod as though I can't speak for emotion, not entirely a fake gesture now I have my prostate to worry about as well as my BP. Her hand reaches out and lays itself on mine. A little gentle patting. Her other arm comes around my neck and pulls my head down to her breast. 'Oh, Michael, Michael, Michael,' she sighs, wearily but not without affection.

Down in my loins the Old Soldier stirs, and I wonder where I've put the rest of his plastic macs.

FOUR

. . . all our life is but a going out to the place of execution, to death. Now was there ever any man seen to sleep in the cart, between Newgate, and Tyburn? between the prison, and the place of execution, does any man sleep?

Sermon preached to the Lords,
28 March 1619

On 25 February 1631, at the age of fifty-eight or fifty-nine (his exact date of birth is uncertain), Donne dragged his ravaged body from his sick bed and into the pulpit of the chapel at Whitehall where he preached for the last time. That it was to be so was apparent to the whole congregation, which included King Charles I, not merely from his gaunt appearance and strained voice but from the nature of his sermon, the justly celebrated and magnificently macabre 'Death's Duel'. As the tears streamed down Donne's cheeks and he struggled to make his voice heard, none there doubted but that they were listening to him delivering his own funeral oration.

The actual event, though, didn't take place until some time after Donne had arranged a bizarre rehearsal. He obtained a large urn and a big wooden plank. A portrait painter was sent for. Donne had fires lit in his study, stripped off his clothes and put on his burial shroud. A servant knotted it, head and foot, parting the top to reveal his face, and Donne clambered on to the urn, where, eyes closed, he squatted, like a homunculus in a jar on a laboratory shelf, while the artist drew him, full-size upon the wood. The finished portrait was then hung by its subject's bed as a constant reminder of what he had coming. When the time came for him to die, he lay down upon his bed and carefully positioned body and hands so as to be ready for burial. No messy laying-out for him! No bouncing up and down on *his* legs after he was gone!

Weird? Yes. Obsessive? Without doubt. And yet, that said, Donne was only attempting to exercise some control over the one bit of life where no matter how rich or talented or well dressed or beautiful or con-nected you may be, you don't get to call the shots: the end. He sought to conquer his fear of Death by trying it out while he was still alive. This endeavour tugs at my heartstrings, not least for its futility. For which of us hasn't lain upon his bed and pretended to be dead? Who has not envisaged his own funeral and imagined himself lying in his coffin, straining to hear through the wooden walls of that capsule what the muffled voices of those left behind have to say about him? But that's missing the point. We won't be listening! We won't be there! We won't even be someplace else! We won't be anywhere at all! We won't be!

I lie in the darkness thinking about Donne and listening to the faint whistle of Alison's breathing. Every ten minutes the cuff squeezes my arm to remind me that another chunk of my time has passed. As it detumesces I listen to the beeping of my pulse measuring out smaller morsels of my mortality.

All my life I have been doing this. From the early age at which I first grasped the relentlessness of time. How this moment is merely a stepping stone to the next and then is gone, to be revisited no more. How moments add together to make minutes, and so hours, years, decades and centuries. How Christmas will not only come, but be unwrapped and over too. I have lain in the dark suffocating in my panic, wanting to scream, 'It's not fair! I don't want to die! Stop the clock!' I have sometimes got out of bed, stolen downstairs and paced around, unable to sit still with my fear. Or tossed on some clothes and fled through the sleeping streets, hoping to leave the horror behind, only to find, of course, that it stalked me, a malevolent shadow.

Sometimes, when my head swims with the inevitability, I even consider doing away with myself as a means of escape, and then allow myself a wry chuckle at the irony of thereby accomplishing the very thing I seek to avoid.

And, of course, my panic has worsened as the years have flown by. Not having the buttress of religion with which Donne shored himself up, I have relied upon the ostrich method: I put my head in the sand and fill it with other thoughts. There's no need to think about that now, I've told myself, you still have sixty, fifty, forty, thirty years of life expectancy ahead. But, lately, I don't seem able to talk myself round any more. Death impinges on my every waking hour.

I read a bedtime story to my children and when it finishes, 'And they lived happily ever after,' I long to add a screaming codicil: 'And then they died!'

In Dorset once we took the boys to a fossil museum. As they clambered over plaster models of ichthyosaurs and the like, I felt myself going dizzy in my attempt to cope with the time frame we had entered when we paid our admission fee: these creatures were around for forty million years, this species a hundred and fifty million. And I have some seventy years if I'm lucky. At the end of the exhibition a sign said:

It is easy to view the rise and fall of the dinosaurs and the eventual emergence of man as a progression, with ourselves as the apex of evolution, the point it was all aiming towards. Nothing could be further from the truth. Rather, man's appearance is due to an extraordinary series of chances, without any one of which he would not have developed. Dinosaurs ruled the earth for three hundred million years. Compared to that man's existence here is but a blip in time. As the dinosaurs gave way to something else, so will we.

I showed the curator a fossil Edward had found on the beach. He said it was around forty million years old. Forty million years since this thing was alive! Donne hated the idea of being dead for centuries while he awaited the resurrection. What would he have thought of forty million years? Or three hundred? To not be here for so long. Or, as Agnes Ada used to put it, 'You're a long time dead.'

Now, I can no longer tuck my boys into bed without stroking their smooth limbs and envisaging the old men they will become, these same limbs gnarled with veins and twisted by arthritis, until they, too, succumb to time and any memory of me is consigned to death with them.

I lie here thinking about my Donne book and how pointless its completion is. Few people today read his poetry. Soon, in another thousand years or two, no one will understand a word of Shakespeare. And, anyway, I heard a man say on television the other day that in a billion years or so the sun will burn out and the earth left spinning in icy darkness. Who will read Donne then?

When I open my newspaper over breakfast each morning, I turn first to the obituary page, seeking comfort there. I look eagerly for the ages of those newly deceased. If I come across someone of, say, ninety-two, I make a quick calculation that such an age will give me another forty-two years. Then I deduct that amount from my current age (which I always round up to fifty) and, arriving at the result (in this case eight) will tell myself, 'Well, it seems like for ever since I was that age. It's a whole lifetime away. No need to worry yet.' (Of course I don't let myself think about what I'll do if and when I reach ninety-two. Hope to be gaga so I won't know? Take comfort from someone who has made it to a hundred, perhaps? Even though the extra few years would seem a mere snap of the fingers by then?)

If, on the other hand, the subject of the obituary has died young, say at thirty-eight, I immediately draw satisfaction from having beaten him. In spite of his achievements, I have the drop on him: I'm still alive! I listen to *The Marriage of Figaro* and taunt Mozart: 'OK, your genius produced this, one of the great wonders of our civilization, but by the time you were my age you'd been dead fifteen years! Maybe you did write the Jupiter symphony, the clarinet concerto and *The Magic Flute*, but you're gone and I'm still alive!'

Sometimes I find people whose ages are similar to my own, people in their late forties or early fifties, and in these cases I seek reasons for their early demise that may not apply to me. For example, a heart damaged through rheumatic fever as a child or a deadly disease contracted in a tropical country that I would never be foolhardy enough to visit. Lately Death has cut whole swathes through those people who achieved celebrity as rock musicians in the sixties and seventies, mowing down the icons of a generation.

At first I took comfort from their profession. 'It's their lifestyle,' I told myself smugly. 'No wonder they burned out, all the sex and alcohol and drugs.' And then, one day, it hit me: 'Wait a minute! That's *my* lifestyle too!'

I understand the inextricable links between my morbid fears and my appetite for sex. 'I'm tired of your never-ending mid-life crisis,' Alison once said to me. She has the mistaken belief I fuck around to cling on to my vanishing youth. How can she know I do it to forget? In this priapic quest for oblivion must lie the origin of the overworked Elizabethan pun (naturally used by Donne himself) *to die* meaning to copulate or, more particularly, to experience orgasm. For only in this fragment of a moment do we taste the nothingness of death while still alive. In the chase, in foreplay, we're so focused on our goal we're able to push our fears aside. And in the split second of its achievement we embrace a transitory, blissful emptiness. As we come, we go. To a place beyond thought and fear.

It's no surprise that Donne, in his early life, was a libertine, or that conceits of love and death are so intertwined in his poems.

Donne's particular horror was the corruption of the flesh. He couldn't bear to think of his body rotting or being devoured by worms. Partly this was sheer physical disgust. But mainly he was haunted by the idea that God might not be able to find him when the Last Trumpet blew time for resurrection. What if he'd turned to dust and the dust been blown all over the place? he wondered. He obsessed about whether God would need the whole body to resurrect someone. And in that case what if a man had lost a leg? What if he'd lost the leg in Africa, but himself been buried in England? Would God be able to trace the leg's rightful owner? What if someone were eaten by cannibals? How could God ressurect him when he'd also be part of the cannibals' corpses? What this tells me about Donne was that here was a man struggling to understand the practicalities of the resurrection because he desperately wanted to believe it could happen and at heart felt it could not. This is what draws me to Donne. I recognize in him someone whose fear of the void to come matches my own. A like mind.

I look for other like minds in the world around me. Occasionally someone makes a remark or does something that allows me a glimpse of their dark secret. 'As a child I used to lie in bed unable to sleep for thinking about the vastness of space,' a friend of Alison's said to me one day. Our eyes met and signalled our mutual terror. But, of course, the one thing you don't do with a like mind is voice your fear. For if we all did that, how could we go on living?

The beeping of the monitor and the thoughts it stirs up makes sleep impossible. I take it in my hand and pad softly to my study, intending to do some work. *John Donne – Poetical Works* lies where I dropped it on my desk. I see it again on the floor by the wicker chair. How could an hallucination move an object? What, I ask myself, if what I saw was not an hallucination after all? Once again, terror pricks my skin, but this time I embrace its icy touch. For with it comes the trembling into life of something else. Call it hope, perhaps.

FIVE

And that this place may thoroughly be thought
True paradise, I have the serpent brought.
                                      Twickenham Garden

'FUCK OFF, YOU, I DON'T WANT YOU! YOU GO
AWAY! YOU FUCK OFF!'

I drop my book and I'm out of my seat like a bullet.
Where is he? What's happening? What's the problem
now? I scan the concrete apron in front of the single-
storey brick building. It's a fine spring afternoon and
the place is heaving. Like when I was a child myself
and I'd dig up an ants' nest. Little bodies scurry to and
fro, weaving around one another, sometimes missing
by a hair's breadth or, more often, colliding, bouncing
off each other like dodgem cars before carrying on to
wherever they're going. If that's anywhere at all, that is
– it looks so random. With ants you understand it just
appears that way, but that they know what they're
doing really. With kids, I'm not so sure. Suddenly I
spot Jake, about to mount a tricycle, and make a mental
note I'll have to deal with that, and preferably sooner
rather than later, but first I need to find Edward. I can't
even remember what he's wearing. Is it his red jumper?
Or his little blue jacket? In my mind's eye I see him in
the red, but I can't be sure. I catch a flash of red

disappearing round the side of the building. I'm after it, fast as I can, which is not very fast since I have to avoid tripping over the little missiles hurling themselves at my feet. I don't want to crush a child. And I've no wish to kiss the concrete.

I reach the corner of the building in time to spot a red blur rounding the next corner to the back. I head after it, catch my foot on the wheel of a tricycle and nearly go over but manage to keep my balance. Around the back of the building it's a little quieter but not much. As I turn the corner I come face to face with a small girl in a bright red dress. She looks up at me, bristling with hostility. 'Why are you chasing me, mister? I'll tell my mummy of you.'

I offer her a weak smile by way of apology and, I hope, to show her I'm not some kind of pervert. She folds her arms and stares back so hard it hurts and I have to turn away.

The plastic climbing frame is teeming. I poke my head inside and look along the tunnel. There's a child in there. Not Edward. I go round to the other side of the building. In the sandpit one small boy is beating the shit out of another with a plastic spade, raining blow after blow down on his head. Momentarily I wonder which child I'd prefer to be mine. I decide the victim, not the perpetrator. But neither of them is. Close by, their mothers stand deep in conversation, oblivious to the mayhem a few feet away, plastic against head not making a lot of noise. As I pass, I reach down, snatch the spade from the boy's hand and toss it twenty feet or so away. The boy looks up at me in shock, then the corners of his mouth melt downwards before it opens and a huge wail erupts from it. Immediately the women stop talking and are down in the sandpit. As I walk away I hear the mother of the one who was getting the bashing saying to her son, 'Did

you make Jonathan cry? Did you hurt him? Did you?'
His first lesson in justice, I think.

I'm round the front of the building again now, and
still no Ed.

'YOU! I DON'T WANT YOU! YOU FUCK OFF!'

It's right behind me. I swivel and see my two-and-a-
half-year-old son just inside the open-fronted building,
sitting at the table with the little wooden train set on it.
His face, apoplectic with rage, is upturned to a woman
standing beside him who bends away from him, as if
scared he is about to bite her.

I'm there in a second. I pick Edward up and hug him.
His cheek burns against mine, his little body overheating with anger. He shakes a finger at the woman
like a Chelsea boot-boy at a visiting supporter.

'YOU GO AWAY! I TOLD YOU TO FUCK OFF!'

'It's all right! It's all right,' I tell him. 'Daddy's here.'

The woman holds up a chocolate digestive. 'I – I only
offered him a biscuit,' she stammers. 'I didn't mean to
upset him.' She sports a badge saying 'Jennifer'. I've
seen her here before. One of the crowd who run the
playgroup.

'It's OK,' I say. 'He's shy with people he doesn't
know. It's just his way of handling it.'

'Oh, is that what it is? You don't expect it from such
a beautiful child. He looks so – so, well, angelic.' As
she puts the biscuit on a plate on the table, she risks
a sideways look at Edward who glowers back, then
buries his face in my jacket. 'How interesting.' She
gives me a little smile so patronizing I suddenly want
to tell her to fuck off myself – but of course I don't –
and retreats to the other side of the room, tiptoeing
away as if the floor might be mined, fearful of another
explosion from Edward.

I take a biscuit from the plate and hold it out to him.
There is a meekness in the tentative way he takes it

from me and in the catch of catarrh in his throat, from all the crying, as he whispers, 'Thank you, Daddy,' that is about as near as a child his age can get to remorse. I fumble in my pocket for a tissue and wipe his eyes.

'Please may you put me down now. I want to eat my biscuit on a chair,' he says, as though nothing has happened. I set him down and he scrambles into his seat again and, holding the biscuit to his mouth in both hands, begins nibbling its edge like a hamster. I look at him and wonder where all the fury has gone, wishing I could get rid of my own as easily.

Of course, Edward doesn't actually say 'fuck'. He doesn't know any swear words. His mother doesn't use them and neither do I, at least not in front of him or Jake, at least not very often. But although he doesn't swear, when Edward goes ballistic, it somehow seems as if he is. When he screams, 'YOU! YOU GO AWAY! I DON'T WANT YOU! I SAID GO AWAY!' the words may be innocent, but the venom with which he spits them out is pure four-letter. I don't hear his actual words any more. All I hear is 'YOU! YOU FUCK OFF!' And the effect it has on the people he screams at – an old lady who chucks him under the chin in Tesco, a kindly shopkeeper who asks him how he is today – is the same. As if they, too, are hearing a string of obscenities.

It's amazing Edward doesn't know any swear words. They're the only words missing from his vocabulary. He started talking when he was about ten months old. One day as I was pushing him along in his buggy he suddenly pointed at an Alsatian and said, 'Dog!' Even the dog pricked its ears and looked surprised. That's how it began. By the time he was a year, he could say any word you could think of. By fifteen months he was speaking in whole sentences, making rhymes and generally coming on like a three-year-old. You'd be pushing him on a swing and he'd come out with something and the other people there would stop pushing their kids and say, '*How* old is he?' Old before his time, I usually tell them.

I'm standing watching him and thinking about all this, when a finger digs me hard in the kidneys and a voice says, 'Here, I want a word with you, mate.'

As I turn round I find myself thinking it's a good thing I handed in the BP monitor at the doctor's this morning. God knows what an afternoon at a children's playgroup would do to the readings. A woman is standing about two inches from me. She is hard-faced, her head shaved and skin so red it looks like someone's taken a cheese grater to it. She has a child attached to one hand. The little girl in the red dress.

'That's him, Mummy. That's the nasty man who chased me.'

'What's your game, then?' says the woman, pushing her face forward so that my nose and her nose jewellery are practically touching. Her breath stinks of cannabis. 'What you doing chasing little girls? You some kind of pervert, mate? Hey? Hey? What's your problem, then? I know your sort, mate. You want your dick cutting off, you do.'

Just my luck. One of the swamp people. My hands drift towards the free-kick position.

'Excuse me, is something the matter?'

I'd never have expected to be relieved to see Jennifer, with her neat little bob and her designer jumper.

Edward immediately jabs his finger at her. 'YOU! YOU GO AWAY! I DON'T WANT YOU!'

'Language!' shrieks the swamp woman, looking at him in amazement. She turns to Jennifer. 'I never heard nothing like it from a kid his age.'

'Apparently it's a defence mechanism. He's shy,' says Jennifer, raising a doubtful eyebrow to her.

'Huh, that's a good one,' retorts Swamp Woman. 'Shy or not he had to learn the words somewhere, didn't he? It doesn't surprise me one bit he's using language like that with a pervert like him for a father.'

'Has something happened?' asks Jennifer.

'He's only been chasing my little girl all round the building, that's all. I've read about people like him. They'll try it anywhere.'

Both women stare at me accusingly.

'It's all a mistake,' I say. 'I didn't realize I was chasing your daughter. I thought it was my son. They're wearing the same colour, see?'

I point to Edward and we all turn to look at him, sitting at the table finishing off his biscuit in his bright blue jacket and grey trousers.

The two women turn their heads and stare at me again.

'Well, I – uh – thought he was wearing red.'

Swamp Woman picks up her little girl, in what seems to me an unnecessarily protective manner, and carries her off, saying over her shoulder to Jennifer, 'You see? You want to watch him, you do.'

Jennifer smiles at me in a way that manages to say she knows I'm not a pervert, just another incompetent man who can't cope with a small child. I'm just thinking she doesn't know the half of it, that I can't cope with *two* small children when, right on cue, the other one streaks past the open front of the building, head bent over the handlebars of his trike, legs whirring round hell for leather. I abandon Edward and rush outside. Jake really shouldn't be allowed on a trike, not when there are innocent bystanders around, especially when some of them are so little they haven't been bystanding that long. Jake is the worst kind of cyclist. He can pedal but he can't steer. By the time I'm outside he is already disappearing round the corner of the building. No way am I playing that game again. I'll never catch him up, he's moving so fast. I turn and look to where he will eventually reappear when he completes his circuit. I hold my breath. It's like when someone dives into a swimming-pool and you wait for them to resurface. There's always a little bit of you that panics that they won't. Especially when you can't swim yourself. By the time I have to breathe out, there's still no Jake. I suck in another deep breath and head for the corner he should be coming round.

At first sight it's a massacre, small bodies strewn everywhere on the concrete path, women running to comfort their injured progeny, a great deal of wailing and bawling. At the end of the path is the upended trike from which Jake is in the act of untangling his long legs.

Dispensing apologies, I make my way over to him. He finishes picking himself up. He rubs a nasty-looking graze on his knee, standing on one leg to do it. He doesn't cry. This sort of thing happens so often to Jake that it's no big deal.

He looks up at me, biting his bottom lip, trying to gauge my reaction. 'Sorry, Daddy, but it really wasn't my fault. These little kids should have got out of my way.'

'OK.' I pick up the tricycle. 'But maybe it's not such a good idea to ride this today when it's so crowded, all right?'

'All right, Daddy.' He gazes at the trail of mayhem he's left and the toddling wounded. Suddenly he breaks into a run and trots over to a small boy whose mother is trying to stop him crying. Jake puts his arm around the child's shoulders and says, 'I'm sorry, I didn't mean to run you over.' The kid looks up, as if Jake were a pop star or something, which is probably how a four-year-old looks to a toddler, and starts laughing. His mother ruffles Jake's long blond curls and leads the child off towards her seat under the tree.

I notice a guy dusting down a toddler of about two, obviously another of Jake's victims. 'Sorry about that,' I say to him.

'What? Oh, don't worry. Nothing broken. Heads hard as concrete these little chaps, haven't they?' I look at his kid, whose face is so pasty white it *looks* like concrete.

The man holds out a hand to me. 'Tim.' His middle-class accent goes with his Timberland boots and Gap sweatshirt. He is probably in his late thirties, one of those people who work from home, a journalist or software writer.

'First time here?' I ask, shaking his hand limply, wanting to avoid striking up any kind of acquaintance which will prevent me working while at the same time feeling obliged to make conversation – as you do when your child has nearly killed someone else's.

'Yes.' He smiles. 'Must say, it's nice to see another chap here. Felt a bit awkward, just me and all these women.'

'Yes, well. They're OK. Just look helpless and they'll sort you out. You can get a cup of tea inside the building.' This last bit is to get rid of him. I know the type. Bring their kids here because they can't stand to be shut inside four walls with them, except if the kids are watching a video and then they feel bad about that. I know because I'm one myself. 'You'll have to hurry, though, they stop serving at quarter to and it's nearly that now.'

'Oh, righto. Thanks.'

'Pleasure. Sorry about the hit-and-run.'

He stomps off in his Timberlands and I pick up Jake, carry him to the front of the building, grab Edward and take them to the sandpit, where I get them settled down building a castle. Then I head back to my chair and my book.

I've only read half a page when Timberlands is back, carrying two mugs of tea. He hands me one.

'Oh, that's kind.' I let my book fall shut and stick it on the empty chair next to me. I'm obviously not going to get much work done this afternoon. It's shaping up to be one of those days. Anyway, I'm not finding it easy to concentrate. I need Tommo. I'm feeling twitchy. In the absence of anything else I imbibe tannin. Tim sits down on the chair the other side of me.

'Don't suppose you've heard the cricket score?' he asks.

'Can't say that I have.'

It's going to be a very long afternoon. I consider collecting the boys and leaving, but that means definitely no possibility of getting any work done because at home I'd have to entertain them and, besides, I have to wait for Tommo.

There is an awkward silence. I look around and take in the scene, the running and fighting and screaming. The women sitting on the grass, or on plastic chairs under the trees out of the surprisingly hot sun. I put my shades on so I can study the corner where all the nannies sit to see if there are any especially attractive ones today without them knowing I'm doing it. There seem to be a great many Eastern European au pairs these days. Slavic house slaves, I think. Beauties, some of them, especially the Czechs. They speak good English too. You can have a conversation with them, which is more than I can with Tim, who has jumped into the silence with both feet and is rabbiting on about his kid, unaware that I'm not paying any attention. I'm just examining a tall blonde I haven't seen on any of my previous visits when the gate behind her opens.

I don't know if I'm actually salivating but there must

be something in my expression that causes Tim to stop right in the middle of a blow-by-blow description of the water birth of his son to follow my gaze.

'Hey, great,' he says. 'Another guy.'

An understatement. We're looking at six feet five and 250 pounds of solid muscle. He is so big the buggy he pushes looks like a toy. He stands at the gate, one massive paw shielding his eyes from the sun as he surveys the scene.

Then he spots me.

He lumbers over, pushing the buggy so effortlessly you somehow have the impression he's only using one finger. He halts right in front of me, blotting out the sun.

'Michael, how goes it?' He extends a hand, palm upward. I give it the merest touch. Tommo's warped sense of humour makes him liable to grab your hand and crush a few bones just for the fun of it.

'Tommo. Where did you get the kid? Yours?' I'm looking at the little girl of around two Tommo is just releasing from the buggy. Tim looks at me as if I'm mad. It is high unlikely, with her ebony skin, that she can have any genetic connection with Tommo who has the graveyard pallor of someone who spends his whole life working out in gyms (which is where I met him, of course) and only ventures out after dark.

'Ha, good one, Michael. No, she belongs to my friend Wendy.' He lifts the child out of the buggy with one paw. 'Run along and play now, kid.' He gives her a little nudge and she toddles off. Tommo turns to me. 'I borrowed her.'

Tim is offering Tommo a low five. Tommo brings his hand down on it as if swatting a fly. The impact sounds like the crack of a whip. 'I'm Tommo.'

Tim smiles bravely. 'Tim,' he croaks.

'Still reading them books, I see, Michael,' says

Tommo, picking up my biography of Donne from the empty chair and sitting down. He flicks the book open and stares at the first page in a not bad imitation of someone who can read. He closes the book and tosses it back to me.

He raises his eyebrows and inclines his head backwards to indicate something over his right shoulder. I follow the direction of his movement and see a car parked fifty yards away, the other side of the park fence. A fairly anonymous blue Vectra. There are two men in it. They look as if they might be workmen. The driver is reading a newspaper. His passenger sits smoking and looking casually out of the window at us. When he sees me looking at him, he shifts his gaze to the nannies and pretends to be interested in the big blonde.

'Surveillance,' whispers Tommo, bending towards me so Tim can't hear. He straightens up. 'I could do with a drink,' he says.

'You're out of luck,' says Tim helpfully. 'They've just finished serving tea.'

Tommo turns and looks at him for a long minute as though he's just discovered a new, inferior life form and is wondering whether to crush it. 'I said a drink.'

'Surprisingly, Tommo, they don't have a bar here,' I say. 'Something to do with the licensing laws perhaps, or more likely because this place is first and foremost for small children, in case you haven't noticed.'

Tommo smiles at me indulgently. He'd flatten some people for less than that – but he owes me. 'Just because they don't have a bar doesn't mean we can't have a drink. Some of us have come equipped.'

He bends and opens a bag in the carrying basket underneath his little girl's buggy. Tim and I peer at the contents. Several six-packs of beer.

'I've just done my weekly shop,' says Tommo. 'Now, who's for a bevy?'

I glance up and see Jennifer standing in the doorway of the play centre, looking at us. Is her expression a touch suspicious, I ask myself, or is it just my guilty nature? I smile and she gives me a little wave. 'You can't, Tommo, not here. You'll get us thrown out.'

'Can't have a drink? In this heat? It's inhuman, expecting people to roast out here, isn't it, Tim?'

'I'll say,' agrees Tim. 'A bar would be wonderful. TV too. All us guys here, they should get satellite TV. We could watch the cricket then.'

Tommo gives an exaggerated laugh and digs me in the ribs. 'Hear that, Michael? Tim's got the right idea. Listen, I'm having a drink. You're very welcome to partake of my beverages – providing you've got the right equipment.' He reaches into a nappy-changing bag on the handles of his buggy and fumbles around. He takes out his hand and opens it to reveal a child's plastic drinking beaker. It's lurid pink and has a picture of Minnie Mouse on it. He unscrews the top and tips out some orange juice. 'You happen to have one of these about your persons, gentlemen?' he says.

'Right on!' says Tim. He gets up, goes over to his buggy and strolls back nonchalantly, one hand dangling by his side, the back facing forwards, concealing something behind it, the way we'd hide fags behind our hands when teachers were looking at us in the school playground. As he sits down again he reveals a yellow plastic beaker with a picture of Winnie-the-Pooh on it. He exchanges a conspiratorial smirk with Tommo.

The subversive quality of the idea appeals to me. I reach into the carrier-bag on the back of my buggy and pull out Edward's red beaker. It bears a picture of a little character and the words Tommee Tippee.

'Red Stripe or Samuel Smith's?' asks Tommo.

'Lager for me,' I say.

'I'll have Sam Smith's,' says Tim. 'Good stuff that.'

Tommo bends over the back of his buggy, his enormous bulk concealing for a moment what he is doing. When he stands up I can see an extra bulge inside his zipper jacket, around his well-toned stomach. A six-pack on his six-pack. We hand him our beakers.

'Now, where's the bog?' he asks. I point him in the right direction and he walks slowly and carefully off, clinking slightly as he goes.

A few minutes later Tommo emerges from the adults' toilet holding the three plastic beakers in his hands. As he crosses the concrete apron in front of the building he nearly bumps into Jennifer. She smiles at him and points to the beakers. I can't catch what she is saying. Tommo smiles back, bending obsequiously and raises them to indicate the hot sun. Jennifer laughs.

Tommo lumbers across to us. 'Now let's see,' he says. 'What is it for you, Tim?'

'Sam Sm—'

'Ah-ah, careful now,' says Tommo. His eyebrows indicate a couple of mothers sitting nearby who are staring at us. 'Now, as I was saying, is yours Winnie-the-Pooh or Tommee Tippee, Tim?'

'Er, Winnie,' says Tim.

Tommo hands it over. 'And there's a nice Tommee for Michael.' I stretch out to take it from him, but Tommo swerves out of my reach. 'If you wouldn't mind handing that to Michael, please, Tim . . .' As Tim takes it and passes it to me, Tommo nods towards the car over the fence and whispers to me, 'Best if I'm not seen handing you anything, Michael. Know what I mean?'

He sits down and we all open the spouts in the lids of our beakers and sip our beer. I find myself wondering if taking it through the small hole in the spout has the same effect as drinking beer through a straw is supposed to have, not that I've ever tried it. I hope not. I still have two children here somewhere. Although it's warm, the beer tastes good, despite the faint hint of Ribena. I close my eyes. If time could only stop, I think. The May sun warming my face. The sound of kids screaming and laughing. A nice nanny or two to watch and dream about. And my sons, like this, with me, for always. Could I ask for anything more? But life is not arranged that way. It goes on and then it stops.

'Same again?' I open my eyes to find Tim standing over me, holding his and Tommo's beakers. I hand over Tommee Tippee, and off Tim lopes to the lavatory. As he passes Jennifer he holds up the beakers and I hear him shout to her, 'Thirsty work, this.' She smiles back, but looks slightly puzzled.

Oh, fuck, I think, he'll blow it if we're not careful.

While he's gone, I turn to Tommo. 'You have something for me, then?'

'Now, now, don't be so impatient, Michael. The last thing we want is those cops switching their attentions to you. Listen, in a minute I'm going to go and pick up little whatshername and take her into that room next to the bog, the one that says "Babychange" on the door.'

'You – change a nappy?'

'I didn't say that, Michael. Just shut it a minute and listen, will you? I'm going to be in there for a few minutes and then when I come out, you're going to duck in after me. You'll find a little present in there.'

Before I can answer, Tim looms above us, holding out the beakers. We each take our own and knock back the contents. I find myself chewing the plastic spout of mine as I anticipate the coke.

Tommo fetches us all another drink, then wanders off to find the little girl he arrived with. This proves a bit tricky as he has no idea what she looks like, and there is something of a fracas when he picks up someone else's child, but fortunately Tim remembers the right one and points her out to him. Tommo scoops her up in one paw, takes his nappy-changing bag off the buggy with the other and disappears into the babychange.

I get up and walk over to the sandpit.

'Look, Daddy,' says Edward, 'we've builded a castle.'

It's a heap of sand they've smoothed and rounded and poked holes into to make windows and doors. Jake's busy excavating a moat, but somehow he keeps getting his foot caught in the bit he's already done and making it collapse. I squat down and take his plastic spade from him. With swift chops, I dig all round the moat, marking out the line of it for him. I hand him back the spade. 'There you are. All you have to do now is empty out the loose sand.'

I return to our seats, using the opportunity to take a look at the policemen. They're talking to one another now. They aren't even bothering to watch the door of the babychange. The beer has made me bold, but underneath the heady feeling I'm aware of my heart palpitating. This could cost me my job, if I'm caught.

I walk over to the babychange and wait outside the door, as instructed. I suspect that having dumped whatever he's brought me, Tommo's sneaking a cigarette, there being large No Smoking signs all over the play area. The door has a frosted-glass panel and the word 'Babychange' is etched into it; if you look closely you can just see through the glass in the letters. I press my eyes right up to the B, trying to see what Tommo is up to. It's all a bit blurred, but I'm just getting it to sharpen up into Tommo's hulk when something pokes me in my right kidney and my head nearly shoots through the glass. 'What do you think you're up to now, then?'

I rub my bruised nose and turn to find Swamp Woman standing there, holding a large baby. It's crying, and no wonder – there's a strong smell coming off it. I'd cry too if I'd smelt like that.

'I saw you. You were trying to look through that glass. You're sick, you are. Fancy wanting to see a little baby having its nappy changed. You need treatment, you do.'

'I was doing no such thing. I was just trying to see if the person in front has finished. I want to go in there next, all right?'

'Oh, yeah?' Her face is screwed up in fury. 'That's a likely story. I suppose you expect me to believe that, do you?'

'Don't see why not. It happens to be the truth.'

'Yeah? Well, in that case, why haven't you got a baby?'

'Ah . . .'

'Well?'

'You know, I had a feeling I'd forgotten something. Hang on.'

I dash over to the sandpit, and grab Edward, sweeping him out of the sand so fast he's still holding his plastic spade.

'Put me down!' he yells. 'PUT ME DOWN, FUCK YOU!'

The hubbub around the sandpit ceases. Children and mums stop what they're doing and stare at us. I smile to show all the mums there's no problem. Edward lifts the plastic spade and hits me over the head with it.

'PUT ME DOWN, MOTHERFUCKER!'

I grab the spade, holding my smile tight to mask my anger – I probably resemble a ventriloquist doing an especially tricky speech – and wrench it from Edward's unyielding grasp. I toss it into the sandpit where it lands next to the toddler I took it from earlier. He flings himself upon it and lifts it aloft, flaunting it at me with a show of triumph.

I rush back to the babychange, praying Tommo hasn't come out yet. I don't want to think about what will happen if Swamp Woman finds whatever he's left in there for me. Edward kicks and screams in protest.

We arrive at the babychange to find the door still shut and Swamp Woman still standing outside.

'Where are we going?' screams Edward. 'I DON'T WANT TO BE HERE!'

'Just going to make you comfortable,' I say, smiling at Swamp Woman as I push past her to stand in front of the door. I don't want to mention the word 'nappy' because Edward doesn't wear them and hasn't for three or four months.

'That kid's never wearing a nappy,' says Swamp Woman.

'He is.'

'No, he's not. I know he's not.'

'How do you know?'

'I can see by looking at him. His bum isn't nappy-shaped. There's nothing but bottom under there.'

I push my face right into hers. 'Who's a pervert now?' I hiss. 'I'm warning you, madam, keep your eyes off my son's bottom or you'll be in big trouble.'

She's so stunned that for a second or so she's lost for words, which is all it takes for Tommo to open the door and come out and for me to duck inside.

The room reeks of an unusual combination of poo, nappy sacks and puff. Tommo has obviously been enjoying an inhaled chaser in here. I stick Edward on the floor and slip him a Jammie Dodger I secreted in my jacket pocket earlier to keep him quiet while I take a look round. There isn't much in here. A bare concrete floor. A little wooden table, and on it a plastic changing mat, on which in turn loiters a well-filled nappy sack. A roll of paper to put on the mat when you change your baby. A dispenser of nappy sacks on the wall. A sealed bin you stuff dirty nappies in. I can't see that Tommo has left anything. The door rattles. 'Come on, hurry up! What're you doing in there?' I wonder what the hell Tommo is playing at as I scan the whole room again.

Then my eyes light once more upon the mat and the used nappy sack. Whatever is in it looks too small to be a used nappy, although you never know. I untie the knot at the top of the bag very carefully and take a peek. Inside is an envelope, which proves to contain the magic white powder. Beside it is a joint and a box of matches.

'Come on! If you're not out of there in one minute, I'm reporting you!'

I hardly notice Swamp Woman rattling the door. I take a quick sniff of the coke and it feels good, but, responsible parent that I am, decide a taster will have to do for now. I stick the joint between my lips and light it. I extract another biscuit from my pocket and hand it to Edward. 'Don't tell Mummy,' I whisper. I help myself to a good lungful of puff.

The door rattles again. I'm about to tell her to bloody well wait, when Edward does it for me. 'GO AWAY!' he screams. 'WE DON'T WANT YOU AND YOUR SMELLY BABY IN HERE!'

'Right, that's it!' snaps Swamp Woman. The door stops rattling and it all goes quiet outside. I take another toke on the joint, and watch Edward eating the biscuit. I never grow tired of watching him eat. His movements are so delicate, the concentration on what he is doing total. Another toke. Suddenly I feel like laughing at the ridiculousness of my situation. What am I doing standing in a nappy-changing room at a kiddies' playgroup smoking a joint? What kind of life is this for a soon-to-be-fifty-year-old man? I ask myself.

Bang! Bang! Bang!

'Hello, hurry up, can't you? Other people are waiting.'

Jennifer's plummy tones. I nip out the joint, open the top of the window and flick it out. I pick up the plastic changing mat and wave it up and down a couple of times, fanning the smoke out of the window as best I can. The place stinks of cannabis, but then so does Swamp Woman so she probably won't notice.

'Why are you playing with that changing mat, Daddy?' asks Edward.

I pick him up without answering and open the door. Swamp Woman pushes roughly past me. 'I've reported you, mate,' she spits. 'You're in deep shit now.'

She slams the door behind her.

'You *were* a long time,' says Jennifer, who is waiting outside. 'What were you doing in there?'

'Difficult nappy,' I say. 'You don't want to know.'

'Oh, I see. Well, try to be a bit quicker in future. That lady was getting quite upset.'

I lean my head close to Jennifer's and say confidentially, 'Ah, well, she would, wouldn't she?'

'What do you mean?'

'It's the drugs. Desperate to get in there for a smoke of some illegal substance.'

'Surely not? What makes you think that?'

'I know the type. But don't take my word for it. You nip in there when she's finished. I bet you ten to one the place reeks of cannabis.'

I pop Edward back into the sandpit where Jake is having a bit of a strop because he's accidentally sat on the castle. It takes me two minutes to put it back to how it was and another two to calm Jake down.

When I rejoin Tim and Tommo, it's obvious Winnie-the-Pooh and Minnie Mouse have taken a bit of a hammering because Tim is looking the worse for wear and Tommo quite mellow, as if you could maybe bump into him and he wouldn't stomp you to pieces.

'It's your round,' says Tim, slurring his words enough to show me I've missed quite a few, and holding up his beaker. I load up my pockets from the diminishing stash in the bottom of Tommo's buggy and trot off to the loo with the beakers. Inside I decant booze into them. For a moment I wonder what to do with the empties, then I see a glint of metal from inside the plastic swing-bin which is so full that the top hasn't closed properly. I lift it up and find it's up to the brim with crushed beer cans. I put in my fresh empties and push the whole lot down, rip a few paper towels from the dispenser on the wall, crumple them and cover the evidence. I make sure the top is swinging nice and free, collect the beakers and open the door.

The first thing I see when I step outside is Swamp Woman's back. I start creeping past but then I realize she has too much on her plate to bother about me. Jennifer is beside her, talking earnestly.

'You can deny it all you like, but I'm not totally naïve. I know cannabis when I smell it and that changing room reeks of it. I'm afraid I'll have to ask you not to come here any more.'

'But – but it's not fair, I—'

'I'm sorry,' says Jennifer, 'but it's more than my life's worth. One whiff of drugs and the local authority will close us down.' She turns on her heel and stalks off.

Swamp Woman turns round and, even though it's me, says, 'But I didn't do anything. It's just not fair.'

'I know,' I reply. 'But sometimes life's like that.'

We have another couple of rounds and then Edward comes running up. He sees me with his beaker. 'Why are you drinking my Ribena?'

'I'm not, it's water. Daddy's thirsty.'

'Please may I have a drink?'

'It's empty now, I'll get you some more.'

In the toilet, I wash out the beaker in the sink, and fill it with water from the drinking tap. When I open the door, Jennifer is standing there, arms folded, the fingers of one hand beating restlessly on her arm. She's obviously been waiting for me.

'I want a word with you,' she says. She sounds quite tough. 'I've been watching you and your friends and I know what you're up to.'

'Up to?' I say. 'What – me?'

'Yes, you. I've reason to believe you've been consuming alcohol on the premises which, as I'm sure you know, is strictly forbidden.'

'Well, I didn't know, but I haven't anyway.'

'In that case,' she says, with a triumphant smile, holding out her hand, 'you won't mind me having a look at what's in that beaker?'

'It's only water.'

'If you say so, but I think I'll take a look for myself.' She's really enjoying this.

'I don't think you can.'

'Oh, yes, I can.'

'You've no right to search an innocent member of the public.'

'No, but I've the right to refuse you admission in future. And don't think I won't. I've already excluded one person today.' She sounds rather pleased with herself.

'Oh, well, if you put it like that . . .' I hand over the beaker. Jennifer unscrews the top, smiling at me as she does so, but her smile vanishes as she takes off the top and examines the contents. She sniffs it.

'Could be vodka,' I say. 'Best be sure. Go on, have a taste.'

Gingerly, she puts the beaker to her lips. She takes a sip. She frowns. 'All right,' she says, 'water. It seems I owe you an ap—'

She never makes it. In fact, it's all she can do to hold on to the beaker as the verbal assault hits her: 'WHY ARE YOU STEALING MY WATER, YOU BITCH? I TOLD YOU TO FUCK OFF! I DON'T WANT YOU HERE! YOU GO AWAY!'

I take the beaker and top from her, give her a smug smile, screw the top back on and hand it to Edward. He glowers at Jennifer, boiling over with self-rightousness. I take his hand and lead him back towards the others.

It's getting near to closing time. I find Jake and we all go and sit under the tree with one of the playleaders and the rest of the children and their mothers for the closing singsong. Tommo and Tim and their kids join us, and we all lay into 'Three Little Men In A Flying Saucer', 'Old MacDonald' and, Edward's personal favourite, 'Wheels On The Bus'. The way Tim goes at it you'd think he was at his rugger club's annual booze-up, though that isn't surprising since he's probably drunk as much as if he were. He even shouts out the names of animals for 'Old MacDonald'.

Jennifer's holding the gate open as Tim, Tommo and I push our buggies through. She's all contrite smiles and eager now to make up after her earlier mistake. 'Bye-bye, see you all again, I hope,' she trills. 'It's nice to have a few dads. I don't think I've ever heard "Wheels On The Bus" sung with quite such gusto.'

Outside I have Jake stand on the back bar of Edward's buggy, and Tim, Tommo and I push the children along side by side. We walk past the Vectra, Tommo and I studiously ignoring it. It's a quiet road beside the park, so we spread out across it and Tommo starts to run. Tim and I follow suit and soon we're all tearing along, racing our buggies against one another, weaving across each other's paths, children all laughing wildly, back and forth across the road, like some drunken, crazed ballet. For a moment I think Tim is so pissed he isn't going to stop at the intersection with the main road, but he does. My car is parked near the corner and as I unlock the boot, fold the buggy and put it in, I glance back at the Vectra, which has stopped some fifty yards behind us. The man in the passenger seat appears to be writing something and I wonder if it might be the registration number of my car.

Tim and Tommo are both on foot but going different ways so it's time for us all to say goodbye. While I put my boys in the car, Tommo turns to Tim and proffers his hand to shake. Tim folds his own hands safely in his armpits as though he hasn't noticed. 'Great meeting you, Tim,' says Tommo.

'Likewise,' says Tim. 'And thanks for all the Winnies.'

'Think nothing of it,' says Tommo. 'Tell you what, why don't you take a couple of tins with you?'

He bends and pulls a Tesco carrier from under his buggy, glancing under his arm at the Vectra behind him at the same time. He holds the bag out ostentatiously to Tim.

'Oh, I couldn't.'

'Course you could, go on.' Tommo sneaks another look at the Vectra.

As I get into my car I glance into the rear-view mirror and see the two policemen watching and talking intently.

'Thanks.' Tim takes the bag and swings off to the left, while Tommo turns to the right.

In the mirror I see the man in the passenger seat of the Vectra get out of the car and begin to walk rapidly towards the junction. The car starts up, crawls past me and pulls out of the end of the road, turning right and slowly following Tommo. The policeman on foot turns in the opposite direction after Tim.

Tim bounces along the road, happily pushing his kid. I can tell by the way his head keeps swinging up and down that he is singing. Must be some kind of record, I think. Comes to his first playgroup and goes home pissed and with a police tail.

SIX

Yet I found something like a heart,
But colours it, and corners had,
It was not good, it was not bad,
It was entire to none, and few had part.

The Legacy

The black furry caterpillars of Branko's eyebrows arch their backs in amazement as he examines what at first I take to be a length of supermarket till roll and for a fraction of a second I think he's alarmed at having overspent in Tesco. Then I realize he's looking at the computer printout from the blood-pressure monitor.

My heart is doing strange experiments with counterpoint, hammering away in an accelerating rhythm, its syncopated roar crashing in my ears. White-coat hypertension, I tell myself, although I know it's more likely white-powder rush from the couple of lines of chop I've just done in the waiting-room lavatory.

Branko removes his spectacles and wipes them with a tissue from a box on his desk. He puts them back on. He feeds the roll of paper through his hands, working his way through a range of expressions as he pays out my typical day. His brow furrows in puzzlement. His eyes widen in wonder. At one point his face splits into a wide laugh like a slashed melon and he glances up at me with what seems like admiration; at another he whistles with astonishment. Finally his fingers run out of roll and he sits staring at me with something like awe and shaking his head.

At last he speaks. 'What is it you *do*, my friend?'

'What do you mean, what do I do?'

'How do you earn your living?'

'I'm a—'

'No, wait, don't tell me!' He holds up his hand like a policeman stopping traffic. 'Let me guess.'

He stares at me, screwing up his eyes in concentration. 'Stuntman. You know, for the movies.'

I shake my head.

'Ah, then you work in the emergency room at a hospital, like those fellows on the TV? No? OK – fireman? Racing driver? Mountaineer? Bodyguard?'

To each increasingly bizarre guess, I shake my head. At last, he shrugs his acceptance of defeat. 'OK, I give up. Tell me.'

'I'm a professor of English literature up at the university.'

He breaks into a laugh and slaps the desk. 'Very funny, my friend. Now tell me the truth.'

'It's the truth.'

'In that case I would like to enrol in your classes.' He picks up the printout and waves it in front of me. 'Because, according to this, you lead a very exciting life.'

'I wouldn't say that.'

He rolls his eyes in disbelief and dangles the paper before my eyes. 'This was a typical day?'

'I wouldn't say that either.'

'I should hope not, my friend, because many more days like this and you will be dead.' He stretches the paper out in front of him on his desk. 'Here . . . and here . . . and here . . . your blood pressure was so high

I'm amazed you didn't collapse. You didn't collapse, did you?'

Once more I shake my head.

'And here, your heart appears to have stopped beating altogether. No wonder they can't find any teachers in this country if this is what they have to go through.'

'Listen, it should have been a normal day but – ah – things happened. Extraordinary things. Stressful things. Extraordinarily stressful things. And some of the stress was caused by the monitor itself. It kept going off at – uh – inappropriate moments.'

'Then why didn't you just turn it off, my friend? The nurse showed you the button to press if it was inconvenient for it to operate at any particular moment, didn't she?'

I think back to the nurse droning on and my not listening. If only my mind had stayed on track, how different things might have been!

'Besides, my friend, when I look at the readings for the night time, I see they are not so good either. Your BP is dangerously high even when you are sleeping. You must be a man who has very stressful dreams.'

I shrug.

'You have to face facts. Your blood pressure is unacceptably high, my friend. Now what are we going to do about this?'

'I told you before, I don't want to be on drugs. Maybe I could make some lifestyle changes.'

'That may help, yes. Lose a little weight, get some exercise. Cut out the booze. All good for the long-term, but for now you need medication.'

'I'm not sure—'

'What's to be sure about? I would not be doing my duty if I let you walk out of here with no treatment. My friend, let me spell it out to you. With these figures,' he holds up the roll again, 'you could be dead before you even reach the door. You are at serious risk of a heart-attack or stroke. You don't have time for lifestyle changes.'

He scribbles something on a little pad and tears off what he's written. A prescription form. He proffers it in his fat fingers. 'Take this to the chemist and get one down you straight away.'

'What are they?' I ask, taking the paper and trying to read the spidery scrawl.

'Beta-blockers.'

I push the paper back across the desk. 'I don't think so. They have side-effects.'

He lets out a sigh like someone sitting on a plastic cushion. 'All medication has side-effects. But these have nothing compared to the side-effect of your condition. They won't kill you. It will. How old are you, my friend?'

'Fifty. Well, nearly.'

'At fifty the guarantee runs out. From now on, things can happen to you, if you don't have help.'

Gingerly, I pick up the paper again. 'Look, just tell me exactly what the side-effects are.'

He swivels round in his chair and reaches a heavy tome from his bookshelf. He thumbs through it with the practised speed of a parson leafing through a Bible for the passage he wants. 'Sweating, nausea, faintness, dizziness, palpitations, insomnia, headache, involuntary twitching, indigestion, fatigue.'

'Hey, no kidding. That's some drug.' I pick up the prescription form again and look at it with new respect. 'Anything else?'

'Well, not really.' He avoids my eye by swivelling again to replace the book on the shelf.

'Tell me.'

'You have to realize it's only a possibility.'

'What?'

'Impotence.'

I flick the paper away and stand up. 'Oh, no, Branko, not that one. I was getting pretty interested for a moment there, it sounded like some heavy shit. But not impotence. I don't *do* impotence.'

He picks up the paper, takes my hand and pushes it into my palm. He folds my fingers over it, like a kindly aunt pressing money on a child.

'It's a *possible* side-effect. It only occurs in a minority of cases. But think about the alternative. A hundred per cent of people who are dead are impotent. Look, my friend, take the prescription and don't even think about it unless it happens. If it does, come back and we'll try something else. But this is the best drug for you right now. It's the most effective and it works fast.'

SEVEN

I am a little world made cunningly
Of elements, and an angelic sprite,
But black sin hath betrayed to endless night
My world's best parts, and, oh, both parts must die.

Holy Sonnets

On the desk in my study I find a book obviously left there by Alison, who is frustrated by my refusal to discuss my medical condition. I tell her talking about it won't do any good (and think, quite the reverse, it will just make it real, thereby increase my terror and stress and send my BP soaring), whereas she considers talking the first step towards *doing* something about it. (My idea of the first step towards doing something about it is more relaxed: cashing in my prescription for beta-blockers from Branko. The second step would be taking them, but I don't do that.) The book is called *The Silent Killer* with the sub-title *High Blood Pressure: all you need to know to get it down*. The blurb on the back identifies the author as one Dr Alfred Baretta (why do authors of self-help medical books always sound like members of the Mafia?) and claims he is one of America's leading experts on hypertension. I flick open the back cover of the book: 254 pages. Assuming my usual rate of reading, fifty pages an hour, we're talking a five-hour read here. As if I have the time for that!

I pull open the bottom drawer of my desk with my foot, bend and take out the bottle of Scotch and the glass I keep in there. I tip an inch of Scotch into the glass, put the bottle back in the drawer, kick it shut and thumb through the book. There are lots of charts and well-separated sections to nearly every page, each with a large heading, usually posing a question, such as 'WHAT ABOUT ALCOHOL?'. It's immediately evident that the acres of white space here mean I can up my normal rate and finish it in four hours or less. I flick to the beginning. 'WHO HAS IT?' demands the first heading. Well, I think, no need to send to know about that. I do. It's bloody ringing in the ears for me right now. But reading on I am gratified to learn that about a quarter of Westerners suffer too. Not alone, then.

Dr Baretta goes on to explain why hypertension goes under the soubriquet of the silent killer. Often the condition is symptomless and does not come to light until a routine check by a doctor reveals it or, more worryingly, the sufferer is felled by a heart-attack or stroke. 'Hypertension kills by stealth,' warns Dr Baretta. 'Rather like a Native American creeping up on the campfire of a group of sleeping cowboys, it advances slowly. First thing the victim knows is when it lets out a war cry, pulls out a tomahawk and goes for the scalp.' I find myself shivering and have to take another sip of Scotch, needing to feel its warm progress through my chest. Used as I am to extracting my information from dry and dusty academic books and ancient texts, I am not prepared for Dr Baretta's colourful way of putting things, but nevertheless, since it's probably too late to work now anyway, I read on.

In spite of the sneakiness (his word, not mine) of hypertension, it does, Dr Baretta explains (and I can

103

almost see him, a stocky, middle-aged man, rinsing a colander of freshly cooked pasta under the tap as he turns and speaks to me), have recognizable symptoms. He thoughtfully provides a check list and I take up my pencil and dutifully begin to tick.

Frequent headaches, especially in the morning
Well, yes. But I've always put them down to hangovers from either alcohol or drugs. Instantly I feel better. These headaches have, until now, always involved a tinge of guilt, being self-inflicted.

Dizziness
Ditto, previously put down to drink or drugs.

Blurred vision
Ditto, previously put down to drink or drugs. But, come to think of it, things often seem bleary when I haven't been imbibing.

Ringing in the ears
Check.

Nosebleeds
And to think I'd assumed these were caused by coke!

Depression
Check. Could my rampant morbidity have a physical cause?

Tension for no obvious reason
How would I know? With my life there is always a bloody obvious reason.

Facial flushes
Check. Well, there isn't always a mirror handy but
I've noticed my face getting hot when I'm yelling at
the boys.

Fainting
Possible. I often feel myself going weak at the
knees, especially in the presence of Harriet Bright,
but I haven't actually keeled over except under the
influence of drink or drugs.

I turn to the next section. 'HOW HIGH IS HIGH?'
features a little table showing different systolic and
diastolic pressures. I can't remember what these two
terms mean. They are the stalagmites and stalactites of
the hypertension world as far as I'm concerned and I
don't have time to look them up right now, but I know
from listening to Branko that it's the lower figure, the
diastolic, that matters most. The chart for it looks like
this:

Below 85	Normal
85 to 89	High Normal
90 to 104	Mild Hypertension
105 to 114	Moderate Hypertension
115 or above	Severe Hypertension

Underneath, a note says that in Dr Baretta's view a
figure of 85 or over requires immediate intervention. I
pull open my bottom desk drawer, the one I keep
the Scotch in, and take out my home blood-pressure
monitor. I also take out the bottle, thinking I might
as well since I'm in there anyway, and pour myself
another slug. I pull up my right shirt sleeve, slide the
cuff of the monitor over my upper arm and secure
it with the Velcro tab. I rest my elbow on the desk

and pump the rubber bulb with my left hand, keeping going until my arm hurts and the monitor reads 225. I release the bulb and shut my eyes, trying to relax, trying not to count the beeps as the cuff deflates. Finally the monitor lets out a long agonized beep and I look at the reading on the digital display: 165/120. That can't be right. I wait a couple of minutes then repeat the process. While the thing is beeping, I try to empty my mind. To not access any of the myriad marvels stored therein, to wipe the screen blank. This, I think, is how it will be when I'm dead. The long beep: 170/122.

OK, I say. Best of three.

After the seventh reading, all of them much the same, I decide it's time to quit. OK, so it's high. But, then, I have a great deal of stress in my life at the moment. Look at all the things I have to worry about. My promotion and the sinister fact that Tait is also doing the Kappelheim. The incident with Tamsin Graves and its possible repercussions. My debts, which are steadily mounting – especially with two boys and a coke habit both growing fast. Last but not least, and possibly connected with the latter, the hallucination (assuming that's what it was) of Agnes Ada. And I am under extra stress at this moment, just reading this book. I need to relax! I pour myself another slug of Scotch. I check my watch. I've skimmed sixty pages in half an hour. At this rate I will finish the remaining 194 in an hour and thirty-seven minutes.

'WHY IS MY BLOOD PRESSURE HIGH?' asks the next section. I have no idea, but fortunately Dr Baretta is on hand to answer. Hypertension does not usually have a single cause, he says. There are a number of risk factors, any or all of which may afflict an individual patient. I go through the check list.

OVERWEIGHT

This, apparently is a common cause. And the good news, says Dr Baretta, is that as soon as you start to get the excess pounds off, the BP begins to come down. I realize the book is resting on a layer of stomach that spills out over the waistband of my Levi's. I could maybe lose a stone and a half, get back to what I was in my college days. It might put me inside the safety zone. Well, that isn't a problem. I'll join a gym. Then I remember I already have. I enrolled a year or so back when the BP problem first came up, meaning to lose some weight. Instead I met Tommo and acquired a few more bad habits.

ALCOHOL

For some people alcohol is a trigger. Here, Dr Baretta gives the example of Erik, who did all the right things: he lost weight, took to jogging five miles a day, switched to a low-fat diet, gave up his favourite Havana cigars, took a less-demanding job and yet his BP remained stubbornly high. Further questioning by the intrepid Dr Baretta elicited the information that Erik was putting away three-quarters of a bottle of bourbon a day. The idiot! What did he expect? Didn't he know (as a footnote obligingly informs me) that the relationship between alcohol and hypertension had been established as far back as 1967? No wonder he wasn't improving! Erik went on the wagon and his BP returned to normal. As soon as he took up drinking again, it went up. 'I guess I can do without the bourbon,' Erik is quoted as telling Dr Baretta. 'After all, I'd sure as hell have to give it up if I was dead.' I sip my whisky. OK, I like an occasional drink, but I've never been a heavy drinker like Erik. No way have I ever drunk that much. Well, at parties, maybe, but on a daily basis, no.

I speed-read the section entitled 'SMOKING – STUB IT OUT *NOW*!' feeling smugly superior as Dr Baretta warns there is no single thing worse for your blood pressure than smoking:

Think about it. When you apply for life assurance, it's the first question they ask. Do you smoke? And if the answer is yes, they'll ask you to pay higher premiums. Because they're more likely to have to pay out on you! Statistics show smokers are three times as likely to die before age 60. And when you retire your pension provider will pay you a bigger pension if you smoke. But hey, don't get too excited about that. It's because they don't expect to be paying it very long!

Reading all this I am just so glad I don't smoke. Then I remember that's not strictly true. I do smoke a little. But I'm not a smoker. I smoke marijuana and, naturally, I have to have some tobacco to smoke it with. But, of course, that's not really smoking. There couldn't be enough tobacco to harm me, could there? Besides, dope relaxes you and anything that does that has to be good for your blood pressure. In fact, I think I could do with something to relax me right now.

I toe open the bottom drawer again and lift Professor Bald's biography of Donne to reveal underneath my bag of coke and my stash of dope. I'm tempted by the coke but remind myself that this is probably not the best time as I'm trying to relax here. I go for the weed, unfasten the bag, take out the packet of cigarette papers, and a packet of Marlboro Lights. I break open two cigarettes and roll myself a double-length monster spliff, congratulating myself on its expert tightness. I light up and take a long draw. The hot, harsh air causes my lungs to splutter, but I fight back the cough, so I can hold in the smoke. Moments later I can feel the delicious lightness in my limbs.

I slip Act One of *Die Walküre* – Goodall's recording in English – on to the CD player next to my desk and put on the headphones. I skip the opening music as too enervating and soon it's washing over me. 'Take this drink that I brought you,' sings Sieglinde. 'Cool water.' The way she sings it, you can almost feel your tongue hanging out for it. Except I haven't any handy now so I pour myself another slug of Scotch. I take a sip, then another hit of the spliff. This Alfred Baretta is certainly some writer! His style may not be the stuff of great literature, but it's simple and direct. And effective! I am now totally relaxed. I should probably take my blood pressure again now, but what the hell? I can't be bothered.

The book's next chapter is all about stress and its role in raising BP. Dr Baretta uses as an example a patient of his named Phil. He describes how Phil behaves at lunch, wolfing down his food before the good doctor has had time to unfold his napkin. I consider how fortunate Phil is to have Dr Baretta for his physician. It's a fight for me to get a five-minute appointment with mine while Dr Baretta makes time to have lunch with his patients. I find myself wondering who pays. His generosity is even more astonishing when you discover what it's like to have lunch with Phil. He talks all the time, spitting out his words (and probably bits of food) like machine-gun fire, shouts at the waiter, and counts up everything on the bill. Phil, it turns out, is something called a Type A person. These are the people, according to Dr Baretta, whose very personality creates stress and who are most likely to suffer from high blood pressure.

There's a check list and I obediently pick up my pencil again.

TYPE A PEOPLE

Talk fast and finish other people's sentences for them

Well maybe.

Are always impatient

Who cares? Let's get on to something more important.

Do more than one thing at once

Well, OK, I am switching on my PC as I read this, but I only want to check my e-mails.

Do not notice their surroundings

Guilty, but that would make Donne Type A too. Hmm, make a note, possible new angle on Donne. Donne the Metaphysical Hypertensive? Maybe not such a good title . . .

Are always working, yet always behind. They take longer and longer to do less and less

This is definitely the problem with my Donne book. I used to calculate a rate of five hundred words per working day, a working day consisting of perhaps four hours on the book, maybe four days a week, totalling therefore two thousand words a week, but I now seem to have slowed to some two or three hundred words per day some three days a week even though I am now working six hours a day on those days. That is a total of only eighteen hours to produce perhaps as little as 10 per cent of what I used to achieve in sixteen.

Are obsessed by numbers

I don't think so.

Are overly competitive to the point of compulsion

If that means hating Brady Tait, then I'm guilty.

Suffer from free-floating anxiety, guilt or hostility . . .

Well, yes, that's me: even though I am now stoned and relaxed from the joint, and mellow from the alcohol, something is still gnawing at my soul. I lean back in my chair, alternating whisky and joint, and gaze out of the window at the moon, a gibbous moon, a little bite missing from one edge, which somehow unsettles me. Dark clouds scud ominously across its surface, deepening the gloom in the back garden. Then, suddenly, light floods everywhere. I realize something has triggered the security light and am momentarily alarmed before I tell myself it's probably only a fox or next door's cat. I lean forward over the desk to see better and notice that the swing slung from the old apple tree is creaking back and forth. A dark shape occupies it. For a second I think it's a man but then it lifts its head to stare at me and I realize it's a chimpanzee. It bares its teeth in a horrific parody of a smile. As it swings towards me it lifts its right hand from the rope and waves at me.

I'm a statue of myself, too stunned to move. And then hot ash from the joint cascades on to my hand. The burn snaps me out of my reverie. I shut my eyes tight, telling myself this is not really happening. I look down at the garden again and see nothing. Nothing but the empty swing, creaking back and forth in the melancholy breeze.

EIGHT

But he who loveliness within
Hath found, all outward loathes,
For he who colour loves, and skin,
Loves but their oldest clothes.
The Undertaking

For a village of barely five hundred souls to have three churches – C of E, Methodist and Baptist – you might have thought we were heavy on religion. Nothing could have been further from the truth. In our daily lives we sought to demonstrate this by a meanness of spirit, and an unrelenting pursuit of our own ends which we learned by observing the elders of the various churches, wealthy farmers all, who made up for singing loudly on Sundays by spending the remainder of the week doing the rest of us down. Besides, we also had two pubs where the men of the village spent much of the week at their devotions, singing more lustily than ever they did in church.

Agnes Ada's religious position has perhaps been gleaned already from her attitude to respectability. She judged divine matters on a single-issue basis and her stance was often ambivalent. On the whole she didn't take much to the idea of a being more powerful than herself, but she was prepared to turn off the sound of her defiance, just in case. On some matters, though, she was not besieged by doubt. She had no time for clergymen, of whatever hue, and was not afraid to let them know it. At such times I always felt that taking on Agnes Ada must be like coming up against an Old Testament prophet.

His first week as vicar of St Peter's, Mr Harper had the temerity to knock on Agnes Ada's back door and rattle a collection box at her.

'What might that be for?' she demanded.

'For the waifs and strays, Mrs Cole,' he replied.

'Pshaw! exploded Agnes Ada. 'There wouldn't be so many waifs and strays if you parsons turned yer trousers round the way you do yer collars! Until then, I'm not paying for the consequences!' And she slammed the door in his face.

Don't mistake this for a lack of charity in my grandmother, though. Mr Harper aside, few were turned away from her door and over the years dozens of waifs and strays of various kinds beat a path there. Chiefly there were the cats, though I never saw Agnes Ada exhibit anything like kindness to a cat. Indeed, if one ever came within range she delighted in giving it a hefty kick. When this became impossible because of her arthritic hip, she'd take a swipe at them with her aluminium crutch instead. There was often a cat or two sailing through the air when you walked into Agnes Ada's. But somehow word got round among the local cat population that scraps and milk were to be had at her house and every so often a down-at-heel moggy would arrive at the back door. Often it would be a mangled old tom – scarred face, one ear bitten off, eye patch – who would sit on the back-garden fence and mew piteously. Agnes Ada would open the window and throw things at him – boots, saucepans, maybe even a hot flat iron, if she happened to have one about her at the time, and tell him to bugger off, or worse. But after a couple of days I'd call round and find the interloper outside the back door, tucking into a plate of scraps and purring loudly. A few days later you'd have to move the same cat from a chair before you could sit down in the house. The cat population was elastic: it expanded with new arrivals in the cold winters, then shrank at harvest time when the bolder animals disappeared into the wheatfield next to the estate, to hunt rats and mice fleeing the roaring advance of the combine harvester and themselves ending up prey to its insatiable blades.

The way cats came to Agnes Ada must have been somewhat akin to the manner in which she acquired Aunt Clara. Clara had been married to my grand-mother's older brother, Harry, who had died in an accident bearing some similarity to my father's when the horse pulling his farm cart slipped down a bank. On this occasion there was no water involved and the cause of death was an unambiguous broken neck. This had happened back in the twenties and, although Aunt Clara was not a blood relation, Agnes Ada had taken her in.

I remember once asking my mother. 'What's the point of Auntie Clara?'

'What do you mean?' said Mum. 'What do you mean, "What's the point of her?"'

'Well, why did God make her? What does she *do*?'

'Well . . .' Mum thought for rather a long time. 'She's company for your Grandma. And she does her sewing. Now, run along and stop asking silly questions.'

Before her marriage Aunt Clara had been a seam-stress and was apparently (I had never heard her say so but, then, I'd never heard her say anything much, but we'll get to that) appalled at the decline in quality of manufactured clothing. So she sat and sewed all day, going over the seams and hems and buttonholes and buttons of every garment any of us possessed, bringing them up to her own high standards.

A conversation with Aunt Clara might consist of two or three words, which never varied much. For example, if she asked me how I was she'd say, 'All right, Michael?' If I asked how she was, she'd reply, 'All right, Michael.' But she was far from silent. Every few seconds she made a small clicking noise, which came out as 'Tut' and sounded as though she was amazed or appalled by whatever was happening or being said although, contextually, it was often evident that neither attitude was intended. Put the tip of your tongue against the very front of your palate, just behind your front teeth, then release it, not silently, but wetly, and you have exactly the noise Aunt Clara made. Concentrating on her sewing, tutting away, Aunt Clara seemed to me to have something uncannily in common with Agnes Ada's oldest cat, a long-haired Persian hybrid called Fluff, who sat for most of the day on the dresser with her tongue protruding from her mouth.

In the way of people who have lived long together, there was a special understanding between Agnes Ada and Aunt Clara so that, for example, my grandmother would sometimes ask Aunt Clara if she fancied a bit of broccoli and, with nothing more than a 'Tut' to go on, proceed to boil a head of it to death. Sometimes Aunt Clara's opinion would be sought, perhaps of a new dress my mother was thinking of buying from a mail-order catalogue. 'Tut' would come the reply. 'Yes, I tend to agree with you,' Agnes Ada would say, leaving my mother none the wiser.

Still, even allowing for Agnes Ada's ability to translate (freely, I suspected) Aunt Clara's monosyllabic utterances, it was a surprise when one day my grandmother announced that Aunt Clara wished to be baptized. 'I've tried to talk her out of it,' said Agnes Ada, 'till I'm blue in the face, but she says Harry was baptized and she's worried they won't be together after she's gone if she don't embrace the same religion. I never heard nothing so daft in all me life.'

'Tut,' said Aunt Clara.

'Is she going to hev it done up the chapel?' asked my mother, as if they were discussing hairdressers.

'No,' said my grandmother. 'She wants it done just the same as Harry, in the river.'

This was exciting news. We Baptists practised a pretty plain religion. While our chapel wasn't quite as stark as the Methodists', we didn't go in for any of the fol-de-rols Mr Harper, who was said to be 'very High Church', was introducing into St Peter's, where the odd statue or two had been installed. Our services (apart from Harvest Festival, when the place looked like an overstocked greengrocer's) took place in an atmosphere of austerity. For an eight-year-old boy there was a distinct lack of visual distraction. The one spectacular detail our church offered was, for ninety-nine per cent of the time, hidden from view. I would be hard pressed now to say what special creed distinguished our kind of Baptists from other Christians, other than our belief in the importance of total immersion. Not for us the namby-pamby sprinkling of water on a baby's forehead. Our initiation involved being ducked right under. Of course, my own baptism had taken place when I was a baby so I had no recollection of being plunged into the water, but I imagined the occasion as being something like the immersion of the baby Achilles by his mother Thetis in the waters of the Styx. It was comforting to believe that this brief dip had rendered me invulnerable to the forces of darkness. The baptisms of most of our congregation had been the same. But every so often an adult convert came along, usually someone like Aunt Clara who married into the Church. Then the boards in the floor of the chapel were lifted to reveal a large water tank and it was there that the ceremony would take place, always with a full house, people even thronging the first-floor gallery to gawp. It had only happened once in my lifetime, and although my mother swore I'd witnessed the event, I remembered nothing of it.

Of course, until the comparatively recent innovation of the tank, total immersion of adults could only be performed in the river and apparently that was how Harry had been baptized. He had missed out as a child because his own parents had converted some time between his birth and Agnes Ada's, and although she had been dipped, as were all babies, in a font in the chapel, Harry was already too big for that and somehow they never got round to him. So when he was grown-up, he'd had it done in the river.

You could say what you liked about Agnes Ada (and people often did, though never to her face) but you could never criticize her generosity. Although she argued vehemently against Aunt Clara's plan, once she saw that her sister-in-law was set on it she threw herself into the project to make it happen.

She put on her best coat and an old broad-brimmed black hat with a feather that she normally reserved for funerals, or rare trips to Ely, and marched up to the minister's house. At first he was insistent that river immersions had been consigned to history and that he would not be resurrecting the custom. But Mr Hale was a timid little man, barely more than five and a half feet tall, and it didn't take much for Agnes Ada, who had seen off far loftier clergymen in her time, to beat him down. In the end he even became quite enthusiastic when he realized the publicity angle the occasion afforded. There hadn't been a total immersion locally for years and the *Ely Standard* would certainly send a reporter and maybe even a photographer. Mr Hale probably envisaged hordes of new recruits beating a path to his door, swimming costumes at the ready.

A swimsuit was something Aunt Clara didn't possess. None of us did. We were nearly fifty miles from the sea but in those days it might as well have been a million and none of us had ever been there. So Agnes Ada organized a shopping expedition and on a half-term Thursday morning, market day in Ely, the whole family – my grandmother, Aunt Clara, Mum and I – embarked on the early bus to Ely. This was such a rare treat for me that I almost didn't mind being dressed up in my smart trousers and best home-knitted jerkin, although I was peeved at being forbidden my balaclava, which I currently wore everywhere because it made me look like Roger Moore in *Ivanhoe*, on the grounds that it was a hot day. I didn't argue because I didn't wish to be left behind especially as the only place in Ely where you could buy a swimsuit was the Co-op and that was only four doors along Market Street from Wilkes's toy shop.

So the mood on the bus was a fever of excitment. My mother occasionally went to Ely while I was at school, but Agnes Ada and Aunt Clara rarely ventured there. Local produce, the butcher's and baker's vans, the weekly delivery from the International store in Ely and mail-order catalogues supplied them with pretty well all their needs. Why would they want to waste the bus fare?

'Ely?' Agnes Ada used to fume, if you got her on the subject. 'You can keep it. All the traffic roaring about and them old farmers drinking more than they should, and the hustle and bustle, people pushing and shoving, they int got no manners, town folk.' You would have thought she was talking about London. 'Ely, my arse!'

'Tut!' Aunt Clara would echo.

There was a great deal of this during the half-hour or so it took to get to the metropolis. It was only four miles from the village to Ely and the bus took the most direct route, with no deviations, but the journey could take anything from fifteen minutes to an hour, depending on what we called the Gates. It was a source of great pride and misery to us that this stretch of road contained the largest concentration of level crossings anywhere in the country – three sets in under a mile, all of them on main lines. People joked that if you made the whole journey without getting caught once then that was the day to do your pools coupon or ask the girl out, because it was your lucky day. If it wasn't, and it rarely was, you might have to wait ten minutes or more at one, two, or sometimes even all three sets of gates. Each pair held within their territory a little wooden hut where the gate-keeper spent his day. When the bell rang to signal a train approaching, he would amble out and close the gates, one after the other. Then the long wait began, until eventually the rails would sing in a metallic whining voice, then rumble and roar until finally an express or an interminable goods train trundled past. Afterwards came the agonizing wait for the gate-keeper to emerge from his hut. They were elderly men, whose reward for a lifetime spent in more taxing work upon the railway was the right to see out their working days in this soft sinecure, and they didn't move fast. The tension now came from the fear that, as sometimes happened, another train might be due, probably from the opposite direction, and the gates would remain closed for as long again. And that was not all. The first crossing on the way to Ely was separated from the other two by the hump-backed bridge over the river Ouse, which hid them from view. But if you were caught at the second set there was the additional suspense, as you watched the old fart amble languidly from his hut to open the first gate, pausing perhaps to extinguish a roll-up beneath his foot, that you might see his colleague from the third set appear and stroll across to *close* his gates. And there was always the possibility, rare but not unknown, that you might have a two-train wait at each set of gates.

On this particular day we were caught only at the third set.

'Tut!' said Aunt Clara, as the bus shuddered to a halt.

'Now then, Clara, stop panicking,' snapped Agnes Ada, who was sitting next to her. 'I don't anticipate there'll be a run on bathing-suits at the Ely Co-op. I don't imagine they'll be stampeding into the place and clearing them out of swimwear.'

'Tut!' said Aunt Clara.

'Exactly,' said my grandmother. 'Your worry is more whether they've got any bathing-suits in the first place. How many people round here want to buy a bathing-suit, do you think?' She looked around the bus, which was packed with women whose uniform of cardigans over floral cotton dresses and headscarves or turbans made it difficult to imagine them glamorously half naked, as I was to find only a few years later when I spent so much of my time trying desperately to do so. 'Why would anybody in their right mind stock bathing-suits for this lot?'

'Tut!' said Aunt Clara, and there was, for once, a note of wistful anxiety in it.

'Don't go on so, woman!' snapped back Agnes Ada. 'If there's a bathing suit to be had in the place, you shall hev it, so stop fretting.'

Eventually the train came, the bus went, and we disembarked in Market Street. Agnes Ada hustled us across the road and towards the Co-op. At the Rex cinema I paused to look at the stills from films displayed in glass cases on either side of the entrance arch. As luck would have it, these included photographs advertising Sunday's double bill of Steve Reeves films, both featuring the former Mr World as Hercules. And, in the few seconds before my mother yanked me away, I tried to construct a narrative from the half-dozen or so pictures there, much as, years later, I would do the same with the pictures on the walls of Tamsin's room. It was a great frustration that I could never get to see a Sunday double bill because I had no money, and even if I had had, there were no buses on a Sunday. It was one of the big disappointments of my life when, years later, I saw the muscle-bound American Reeves in one of his films and discovered it to be an epic only of poor acting and unlikely dubbing from the Italian in which it had been made.

As we reached the Co-op door I made a bold, insouciant bid to walk straight past and thus in the direction of Wilkes's, but again Mum's hand grabbed the collar of my jerkin and she hauled me into the Co-op.

Inside we followed a sign that said 'Lingerie' and trooped upstairs. This in itself was a touch of glamour and excitement in our lives. The Co-op was the nearest thing Ely possessed to a department store, mainly because it was the only shop with an upstairs. Agnes Ada marched us to the centre of the room and coughed loudly. Immediately a young assistant appeared. She eyed us suspiciously as we stood, obviously uncomfortable, in our best clothes. Agnes Ada sported a long floral dress over her support stockings, a short blue cardigan and her black hat with the feather. Aunt Clara was sweating away in her green iridescent raincoat. There was no possibility of rain on this baking hot day, but it was lined and Aunt Clara always felt the cold. I, well, I was a boy and as such automatically to be treated with suspicion. Only Mum, who I remember was so pretty that day – slight frame shown to advantage in a close-fitting red frock and her blonde curls falling about her face – looked as though she hadn't just emerged from the swamp. But the young woman got her face into a smile and treated us courteously. You couldn't be too careful if you were a shop assistant in Ely: while most of the locals were as impecunious as they looked, some of the farmers, in today's terms, were millionaires, although their wives appeared no different from the rest of us. It was only when they spent their money that you found out.

'Yes?' said the woman.

'We want to see some bathing-suits,' said Agnes Ada.

'Is it for yourself?' asked the woman.

Agnes Ada gave her a look that would have fried a cat. 'Me? Display myself in a little bit of cloth no bigger than a dishrag?' she barked. 'You better watch what you're saying, gal.'

The poor woman was so flustered by this that she practically kowtowed.

Fortunately Mum intervened. 'It's for my mother-in-law's sister-in-law,' she said.

The woman looked mystified.

'Her!' roared Agnes Ada, pointing at Aunt Clara and grabbing her sleeve to wheel her back as she tried to creep out of the door.

'Colour?' asked the woman.

'The colour don't matter, int nobody going to see the colour,' said Agnes Ada. 'She int only going to wear it the once and she'll have summat over the top on it, so it don't much matter what it's like. It's what it covers that counts.'

The assistant sought elucidation from my mother with a look that said, 'You're obviously the warder, you sort it out.'

'Something plain, perhaps,' said Mum.

'What size?' asked the assistant.

This caused our three women to go into a huddle of muttering, which reminded me of the scrums in American football that I'd seen on telly in the Marx brothers' *Horse Feathers*. I almost expected Harpo to suddenly emerge.

Eventually Agnes Ada broke ranks and said, 'Well, she's got a thirty-four double C bust.'

'Agnes Ada!' Aunt Clara whimpered in protest.

'Perhaps we'd better measure you,' said the assistant, producing a tape measure from her skirt pocket. 'Now, if you could just slip your coat off . . .'

Aunt Clara let out a shrill giggle and clutched her raincoat tight around her. 'Tut!' she protested. 'Tut! Tut!' Agnes Ada grabbed the lapels of the coat and tried to pull them apart, but Aunt Clara hung on to her coat for dear life so it didn't open an inch. Agnes Ada was tugging so hard I was amazed that the lapels didn't just rip off, until I remembered that Aunt Clara would, of course, have been over them so many times that wild elephants having a tug-of-war with it couldn't have torn a single one of the coat's seams.

'Clara, give over, will you?' hissed Agnes Ada. 'Let her measure you.'

The woman gave a discreet cough. 'It's all right, dear, if you want to keep the coat on. I can measure you underneath it.'

Reluctantly Aunt Clara relaxed the edges of the coat and the woman slipped her arms around her inside it, while Clara held the coat around her, so that someone walking in on the scene might perhaps have thought Clara was changing into the bathing costume there and then, as children are sometimes changed at the seaside by prudish parents – although of course, any interloper, like me at that time, would probably have had no knowledge of such seaside happenings.

She pulled out the tape-measure, examined it and made a mental note. Then she plunged back in and repeated the exercise with waist and hips. 'You want a twelve,' she said. 'Just take a seat while I see what we've got.'

She trotted off. Agnes Ada took advantage of the interlude to berate Aunt Clara. 'Keeping your coat on, you daft 'ap'orth, what were you thinking of? As if people haven't seen a woman with her coat off before. Come to that, you're the only bugger daft enough to wear a coat on a day like this. I'm scorching!'

'Tut,' said Aunt Clara, miserably.

The woman returned with a single garment. She held it up. It was plain black with a flap designed to conceal the crotch area. The collar was high and there was no fear of the 34 double C bust being visible. It even had long sleeves. Everyone stared at it. Even Agnes Ada looked crestfallen.

'Well, Clara, it's not as though you'll be wearing it in the South of France,' she said eventually.

'Tut,' agreed Aunt Clara.

'We'll take it,' said Agnes Ada.

'Is that all you've got?' interposed Mum, earning herself a shocked look from Agnes Ada.

'Well, it is, really. I mean there is another one, but . . .' she looked at Aunt Clara . . . 'I don't think . . .'

'Let's hev a look at it anyway,' said Mum. 'We int in a hurry.'

'Speak for yourself,' snapped Aunt Ada. 'The White Hart will be open by now.'

Mum smiled at the assistant. 'Would you mind just fetching it, please?'

The woman rolled her eyes but trotted off again. A moment later she was back, bearing a scrap of bright red

124

material. She held it up by the shoulder straps. It was in two shades of red. The background was a faded scarlet, on which bloomed roses in a deeper red. It had ruching all down the body, and at the bottom a little skirt in several layers of flounces. Even as an eight-year-old boy who knew nothing of fashion or the world beyond the Fens, I could tell it was a thing of great beauty.

Nobody spoke. Even Agnes Ada would have been unable to deny the exquisite nature of what she was looking at. Aunt Clara gazed at it with her mouth open, reminding me so much of Fluff that I almost expected to see her tongue poking out. Her normally dim and watery eyes seemed to sparkle in the artificial light.

'Tut!' It came out like I'd never heard it before: a sigh you might expect from someone who has been given a glimpse of paradise. Slowly she lifted herself from her chair and advanced towards it, heedless that her coat fell open as she moved. She stretched a tentative hand towards it and touched the material, which had a satiny sheen, rubbing it between thumb and forefinger.

The assistant smiled. 'Go on,' she said, thrusting it gently towards Aunt Clara. 'Hold it. It's so soft, isn't it?'

Gingerly as though the flowers were real and might shed their petals with too much rough handling, Aunt Clara allowed the bathing-suit to drift into her hands. Holding one strap in each hand she peered inside and I knew she was examining the seams, inspecting the workmanship.

'It's all treble-stitched,' said the assistant.

Aunt Clara held it to what I now knew to be her 34 double C bosom and turned to face Agnes Ada.

'Clara, it's not practical. When your smock gets wet that'll show through it and you'll look like a scarlet woman for all the world to see. How can a woman who won't show herself without a coat stand up in front of the whole village half naked in something like that?

How can you put a delicate thing like that in a muddy old river? Clara, it's just not practical.'

'Tut.' This time a soft moan.

Sniffing in annoyance, Agnes Ada stood up and drew herself to her full height. She marched over to Aunt Clara. 'You silly old fool,' she hissed, taking hold of the costume. Aunt Clara released it immediately, the fear of its being damaged greater than the fear of its loss. Agnes Ada hurled the costume at the shocked assistant, who fielded it deftly.

'Wrap it up!' snorted my grandmother. 'We'll take it.'

We marched along Market Street to the White Hart, my grandmother almost goose-stepping (Uncle Frank had often demonstrated what he called 'the Nazi way of marching' to me) with a mixture of fury at Aunt Clara and pride in her own beneficence. On the way I attempted to stop and peer at the plastic toy soldiers in Wilkes's window, but was yanked away once again by my mother. 'You're not having any toys today,' she said. 'You can wait till your birthday. It's only another week.'

We passed through the arch and into the courtyard, which both dated from the time when the White Hart had been a coaching inn, and Agnes Ada opened the side door into the snug. The three women went inside while I waited, leaning idly against the open door. The air inside was thick with tobacco smoke and the fumes of beer breathed out by ruddy-cheeked farmers, in town for the market. Agnes Ada pushed through them and returned a moment later with a bottle of Vimto and a packet of Smith's crisps, which she handed to me. 'Go and hev a look round the cattle market, Michael, and make sure you're back here for twelve o'clock sharp.' I could hardly hear her for a sudden gust of laughter from inside the bar, the kind of laughter that comes from drinking too much. On market day the White Hart was open all afternoon and the men inside were not even half-way into a heavy day's drinking.

It was just as noisy in the cattle market, although a different kind of noise. The harsh squealing of pigs, strangely human as if small children were being tortured somewhere. The crowing of a cockerel. The low moan of cattle. I liked to look at the animals, for there were few in the village. One man kept pigs, most people had chickens, but the black peat soil was too valuable to waste as pasture. One field in the village was given over to a couple of horses, but the rest of it was under wheat, barley and sugar beet.

The novelty soon wore off and I grew bored with the gabble of the auctioneer and the animals, morose and immobile in their pens and, although it was strictly forbidden, wandered back to the White Hart yard and then through the arch into Market Street. A few more steps and I was outside Wilkes's shop. I looked at the plastic figures in the window, mainly cowboys and Indians with the odd kilted Scots Guard and a couple of Second World War stretcher-bearers carrying a wounded man. I could see the bald pate of Mr Wilkes bent over a Tri-ang tractor, whose bright red tin seemed dull in comparison to Aunt Clara's new bathing-suit, while a couple with a toddler watched him manipulate the steering-wheel to demonstrate the movement of the front wheels. Without thinking what I was doing, I found myself pushing open the glass door and walking in. Mr Wilkes glanced up at the sound of the doorbell, surprised no doubt – as I was myself – at a child coming into the shop alone. Then the man in the couple he was serving asked him something, and he was forced to turn his attention back to him.

I wandered slowly, as if with no particular aim, to the rear of the shop, which was darker, the bright sunlight not penetrating there. The place had a distinctive smell, perhaps of metal or brand new plastic or polish, or a mixture of all three, that I couldn't quite get hold of.

From the front of the shop I could hear the drone of the couple talking. Wilkes was a good salesman and knew when not to speak. At one point he lifted his head towards me and called, 'Are you all right over there, young man?'

'Yes, thank you,' I replied. 'I'm just looking.' It was what I'd heard Mum say in the dress department at the Co-op where she often browsed but rarely bought. The politeness of my tone seemed to reassure Wilkes and he returned to selling the tractor. It was quite a large toy and its sale wasn't to be lost for the sake of someone like me who might spend ninepence or a shilling at most.

And then I saw them, on the glass display stand where the Britains soldiers always stood and my mouth must have dropped open in awe. Half a dozen members of what seemed to me a new, undreamed-of super-race. Had I but known the words I might have exclaimed, 'Oh, brave new world, to have such people in it.' Three cowboys and around the neck of each was attached a piece of cardboard the shape of a speech balloon in a comic strip. On the balloon was written, 'I'm a Swoppet!'

The one that caught my eye most was a gun-fighter. He held his six-guns in his black-gloved hands, blazing away at an enemy only he could see. What struck me straightaway was that the pistols were not moulded into his hands as with normal plastic figures, but were separate. Around his waist he wore a gun-belt of flimsier plastic than the rest of him and the two holsters were empty. I was about to reach out and touch him when a hand came from behind me and took hold of him.

'That's a new line, just in today.' I followed the

movement of the little gun-fighter and found Wilkes standing behind me. He smiled. 'Swoppets. Something special these are.' Deftly he removed the guns from the man's hands and placed them in the holsters. He grabbed the man's head and snapped it back so that it came off in his hand, causing a small gasp to escape me at such wanton destruction. Then I saw the ball of plastic below the man's neck and understood. 'Head can be removed, and transferred to another figure. Neckerchief removable.' He snapped the man's waist. 'Body and legs detachable and transferable. Buy two of these and what you actually have are six different figures. What will they think of next, eh? And all for one and threepence.'

He reassembled the figure and placed it back with its two fellows. 'We're waiting on some Indians, should be in next week. Mounted figures on the way too. No more of this being on foot or on horseback, a figure can be either. You choose. I think, young man, you're looking at the future of plastic figures. I can't see anyone going back to the old kind once they've had a Swoppet.'

At that moment the man called from the front of the shop. Wilkes gave me an apologetic smile and hurried back to him. I turned and gazed at the Swoppets.

One and threepence. It might as well have been a pound. Or a hundred. It was unthinkable Mum would give me such a sum. And even if she did, she'd count it as the height of decadence to spend so much on a single figure.

I looked towards the front of the shop. Wilkes was deep in conversation. Suddenly, without my telling it to, my hand reached out towards the gun-fighter. I glanced back up the shop and Wilkes lifted his head to look at me. My hand shot back as if I had just touched something red hot. Wilkes looked away again. My heart was racing in my chest. My mouth had gone dry. I could taste the salt from the crisps. My hand shot out, grabbed the gunman and was back in my trouser pocket before I knew it.

I stepped back from the display, and sauntered slowly across the shop where I pretended to look at some cricket bats. I heard footsteps approaching. My face was burning. If I was quick maybe I could get across the shop and put the figure back.

'Like to hold one? That's a Don Bradman, that is. Look, signed by the great man himself. Like cricket, do you?'

I dared not look up. I knew Wilkes would see my guilt written all over my face.

'Want to try it out, get the feel of it?' I shook my head.

'Go on, no harm in trying it.'

'I haven't any money,' I whispered.

'I know that. Doesn't matter. Hold it a minute, play a couple of strokes with it. It's a magnificent bat, is that. Not every day a boy like you gets to hold a bat like that. Come on.' He had hold of my arms, tugging my hands from my pockets. The gun-fighter was clenched in my right hand. I could feel him hot and sticky with my sweat. As Wilkes pulled my arms I released him, praying he wouldn't slip from my pocket and that his shape wouldn't show there if he stayed put. My hands came free and Wilkes slid his down on to them and placed them on the handle of the bat. I could feel the corrugations of the wound-string grip.

'Not like that,' said Wilkes, 'like this,' and he positioned them. 'Now, edge down here on the crease, like so. Look up. There. Just so. Doesn't matter who's bowling you. Could be Freddie Trueman. That's a bat to wallop anyone all over the field, that is. Don't you agree?' I nodded and stood rigid, staring, as far as he knew, at some imaginary bowler, but in fact, over his shoulder at what was surely an unnatural space between the two remaining Swoppets on the glass stand.

The shop bell rang. 'All right, young man, come back on your birthday. Got one coming up soon, have you?' I nodded. 'Come back then and get yourself a bat.'

He took it from me and stood holding it, watching me as I walked off towards the door. While I'd been standing there I couldn't feel the plastic figure in my pocket, it was too light to register. But as I moved I felt his bony shape dig into my thigh with every step, pricking into me, so hard it seemed I wouldn't make it to the door without crying out. You never heard the word shop-lifting in those days. It wasn't known either as a crime or something children did for a laugh or a dare. We just had stealing and this was the first time I'd ever done it.

I made it to the door at a limp, feeling Wilkes's kindly blue eyes boring into my back, expecting any moment to hear him shout, 'Wait!' But suddenly my fingers were on the door handle and the door was opening and the noise cascaded in from the street and I was running, the little man in my pocket stabbing my leg furiously with the barrels of his guns.

On the way back from the White Hart to the bus stop Agnes Ada was in a mellow mood. When we reached Wilkes's she stopped, undid the clasp of her old leather bag, put in her hand and pulled out her purse. I hung my head, praying that Wilkes would not be looking out, or if he were that he had not yet discovered the theft of the Swoppet. Though how could he not have?

Grandma's long bony fingers dug into the purse and emerged with a florin. 'Here,' she said, holding it out to me. 'You bin a good boy today, Michael. Here's two bob, you go into Mr Wilkes's and get yourself whatever you want. Go on.'

I shook my head.

'Go on, take it. Hev it towards your birthday. Go on. We got ten minutes before the bus, hurry now.'

I fought back tears of regret that time could not unravel itself and be remade differently. I turned and ran off up the street.

'Damn and blast the boy!' I heard her curse behind me. 'What the heck's got into him now?'

At home I got out my bike and pedalled down the Soham road for about a mile. I stopped, left my bike on the verge and sat on a little bridge over the drain, dangling my legs above the murky brown water. It was so deep here even a man could drown, my mother had often warned me. Somewhere far off I could hear the lonely pee-wit pee-wit of a lapwing. I looked around and there wasn't another soul in any direction as far as the eye could see. I took the gun-fighter from my pocket and examined him. If anything he seemed even more magnificent now. I took the guns from his hands and put them in the holsters. I took them out and put them in his hands again. I snapped off his head and removed his kerchief and the Swoppet label. I replaced the head without them, then removed it and put them back on. I pulled him apart at the middle and put him back together again. I held him six inches from my face and examined the perfection of the detail of his own, the painted features, the moulded cheekbones. Then I dropped him between my legs and into the drain. For a moment or two he bobbed on the surface and then he sank. And for a split second, in the topmost part of the water, I could see him as he sank and I wished I could swim so I could dive in and pull him out.

I walked back to my bike telling myself it was only a plastic figure and not understanding what I was so worked up about. A light breeze had got up and the smell of silage burned my nostrils, like the scent of regret, and I knew that nothing in my life could ever make me feel this bad again.

NINE

Death be not proud, though some have called thee
Mighty and dreadful, for, thou art not so,
For, those, whom thou think'st, thou dost overthrow,
Die not, poor death, nor yet canst thou kill me;

Holy Sonnets

I wake in my normal way. That is to say, I drift into consciousness with an awareness of a free-floating anxiety, hovering like the invisible cloud of some accidentally released noxious gas in the room around me. I drag myself from the duvet whose twisted confusion on my side of the bed – as opposed to the neatly untroubled linen on Alison's half – bears testimony to another night of angst-ridden dreams, all now lost to memory but leaving behind this residue of fear. What is the significance of the chimpanzee? For a moment I flirt with the idea of a simple explanation. An escapee from a wildlife park, perhaps? Unlikely, as there isn't one near here, and even if there were, why would it wave at me? It occurs to me that the poet Rochester kept a pet monkey. Perhaps he would make a more fitting subject for me than Donne?

Alison is already up, having risen no doubt to the reveille of Edward's early-morning wails. I stretch, pad to the bathroom, try not to look at the ageing wreck in the mirror and splash cold water on my face. I trudge to my study and switch on the computer. It, too, groans at the prospect of starting another day, then clicks arthritically and gradually whirs itself awake. Some time ago I found myself so overburdened with work, trying to juggle so many different things at once, that I became paralysed by fear and could do nothing at all. Finding me, head in hands, slumped sobbing over my desk, an eighteen-year-old temporary secretary, named, I think, Tracy, gave me a piece of advice for which I was so grateful that I later rewarded her by taking her out for a drink and, later still, fucking her. Her advice was this: when it all gets too much, make a list, the theory being that once you see what you're up against you'll find it's not so bad. As you work your way through the list, point by point, the reasons for your fear will diminish even as you cross them off.

So I begin to type, giving names, as it were, to my fears:

1. The incident with Tamsin. What if she blabs? I have never parted on bad terms with any of my student dalliances before. Could this have repercussions? I resolve to avoid all future infidelities, at least with students. A secondary worry here is, what if Tamsin somehow works out what the blood-pressure monitor was? What will that do for my young-at-heart (or, worse, at-cock) romantic reputation? Will I ever be able to get another student into bed? (Not that I'm planning to, of course, having just resolved never to again, but I would at least like this to be a matter of choice and not something enforced upon me by having a name for bodily decrepitude.)
2. The Kappelheim. There can be no doubt that Tait's inclusion on this makes him a serious

contender for head of faculty. And what of the sinister involvement of the Dean? Is she finally about to take her revenge for being dumped all those years ago? Resolve never again to indulge in sexual liaisons with colleagues. (Unless, of course, possibility of affair with Harriet Bright comes up.)

3. The hallucination/ghost of Agnes Ada. Am fearful/excited by the idea of a supernatural manifestation as indicated by the movement of *John Donne – Poetical Works* from chair to floor, although accept possibility of being mistaken about its original position. Could it, for example, have fallen to the floor after landing on the chair? After all, this often happens with inanimate objects. They slip and slip imperceptibly down a slight incline until they make us jump when they land with a thump on the floor. Except that I don't remember any thump. Although, of course, I had other concerns, the auburn-pubed Ms Graves, the hiding of the BP monitor. And there is also the matter of the chimpanzee. Although there is something familiar about the animal, I have never actually known one of his species, beyond a nodding-through-bars acquaintance, that is. So we're talking about hallucination here. Inspired by drugs (see below).

4. My consumption of drugs, especially cocaine, is spiralling out of control. This is definitely not good for my work and possibly not good for my health (although not necessarily since I always feel better after taking them) and definitely not good for my bank balance. I am currently in debt to the tune of several thousand pounds with little hope of restoring my position unless I achieve promotion, something on which I was (ha ha!) banking,

although which now seems not the dead certainty I previously thought it (see 2 above).

5. Those policemen at the playgroup. Did they take my registration number? If so, why? What might they do with it?

6. My children. I have a terrible sense of missing their childhood as they are growing up so fast (see below 8) but don't know what to do about this as I am always so busy and when I'm not I often avoid their company because I never know how to amuse them. Resolve to take more photographs.

7. My BP: 160/115 when I took it just now on my home BP monitor but, then, this is perhaps not the time to take it when I'm so full of anxiety. Still, it has to be said it is high, dangerously so, according to Branko, who says I am risking an early death (see below 8). And yet I cannot bring myself to take the beta-blockers, which even now reside in my desk drawer along with all my other dangerous drugs.

8. Death. I am another day nearer the cemetery. Even if I have a wonderful day (unlikely given 1–5) tomorrow is another day and so on, petty pace until last syllable, etc., leading inevitably to physical decay (no fucking, nursing home, catheters *et al*) and inevitable demise. What is the point in living? Well, certainly, none at all. And definitely in that case no point in worrying about points 1–7.

Feeling thus more positive, I head downstairs to join my family.

Breakfast presents me with an unwelcome opportunity to observe my children growing up. Alison has partially absented herself to make the numerous phone calls necessary to organize our sons' social life, which requires planning of a military precision not otherwise seen outside the Pentagon. 'Can Alfie come over for a playdate?' I hear her asking some mother or nanny. Playdate! The word suggests to me a tryst with a nubile young woman wearing a teddy rather than a small child wielding one as a weapon with which to beat the child inflicted on him by his carer today. This is how our children will grow up: shunted from one house to another in people-movers to play with this or that kid they may or may not like, bonded by their mothers' choice of other-mother friends, imprisoned by our fears of paedophiles who wait to pluck solitary un-shepherded children from the streets and star them in live Internet sex shows for their sicko friends to watch, and by the terror imposed upon us by the traffic whose whump-whump over the speed bumps outside our home serves not to reassure us but to remind us of its ever-present threat.

'Why is nobody getting me any breakfast?' screams Edward, in a tone that a stranger would interpret as, 'WHERE THE FUCK'S MY FOOD?'

I shoot an inquisitorial glance at Alison as I pick up the newspaper and take my reading-glasses out of their case. She mouths, 'I'm talking. You get him something.'

'COME ON, WHERE THE FUCK IS IT?' – Neighbours' probable version to Social Services, should Edward ever have an accident involving, say, a broken limb.

'Now, now, Edward,' I say calmly. I'm temporarily relaxed in my appreciation of the pointlessness of everything. 'That isn't the way to ask, is it?'

'I tried saying please and nobody did anything,' he fumes back.

'All right, all right, what do you want?'

'What do we have?'

'You know what we have.'

'Please could you remind me?'

I walk over to the double cupboard required to hold all our breakfast foods. I pop a bowl off the shelf above and stick four Weetabix into it for myself. I'd dearly love the egg and bacon fry-up I always used to have but Alison, a vegetarian, has brought up the boys in her faith, and were I to indulge myself the air would be rent with screams of protest ('YOU KILLED A PIG FOR THAT!' 'THAT COULD HAVE BEEN A FUCKING CHICKEN!') so these days I make do with cereal. Though I do wonder whether I'm getting enough cholesterol.

'Weetabix. How about a nice Weetabix like Daddy's having?'

'I want toast,' says Jake.

'Please,' I say.

'Please.'

I take a loaf from the bread bin, extract four slices, and bung them in the toaster.

'WHAT ABOUT ME, FOR FUCK'S SAKE? WHAT ABOUT MY BREAKFAST? I ASKED FIRST!'

'Yes, but I knew what I wanted.'

'I DON'T CARE, I ASKED FIRST!'

'But why should I wait for you to decide when I know what I want?'

'BECAUSE I ASKED FIRST!'

'Daddy, Edward just pinched me.'

'Go to the other end of the table, then, where he can't reach you.'

'YOU'RE STILL NOT GETTING ME MY BREAK-FAST!'

'I don't see why I should be the one to move when he's the one doing the pinching.'

'It's just easier, Jake. Come on, one awkward child is enough.'

'I'M NOT AWKWARD, I'M HUNGRY!'

'Well, what do you want? We have ordinary cornflakes, maple-syrup-flavour cornflakes, Weetabix, Rice Krispies, Frosties, Oatso. How about some nice Oatso?'

'Yes, Oatso.'

'Please.'

'Please.'

I take out the packet of porridge oats. I open it, pull out a sachet, and open it with one hand and my teeth while taking a Pyrex bowl from the cupboard. I pour oats into the bowl, take milk from the fridge, kicking the fridge door shut as I pour milk into the bowl en route to the microwave. I put the bowl in, set the timer to two minutes and press the start button.

'Actually, not Oatso. I want maple-syrup corn-flakes.'

'Edward.'

'Please.'

'But I'm already making the Oatso.'

'I DON'T WANT OATSO. I CHANGED MY MIND. YOU MADE ME RUSH TOO MUCH! IT'S NOT FAIR! I WANT MAPLE-SYRUP CORNFLAKES!'

The toast pops up. 'We could do Jungle Gym on Tuesday . . .' says Alison.

'Daddy, my toast has popped up.'

'I know.'

The microwave pings. I take out the Oatso.

'I'M NOT EATING OATSO. IF YOU GIVE ME OATSO I WON'T EAT IT AND THEN I'LL DIE.'

'You won't die. You might burst if you get any redder with rage. Come on, eat the Oatso.' I tip it from the Pyrex bowl into a breakfast bowl. I put the bowl on the table. Edward pushes it away.

'Daddy, you need to butter my toast now. I don't like it if it's left too long because it goes all hard and hurts my teeth.'

'In a moment, Jake.'

'I'M NOT EATING FUCKING OATSO!'

'Well, it's just that it's nearly had as long as it can have without getting too hard.'

I take the toast out of the toaster, slap it on to a plate and butter it fiercely. I finish one slice, cut all the crusts off, bisect it diagonally to make two similar triangles – and I mean 'similar' according to the strict geometrical definition, for they must be exactly equal – take a plate from the plate rack, pop the toast on to it and slide it across the table to Jake.

'I WANT MAPLE-SYRUP CORNFLAKES, FUCK YOU, DADDY!'

Normally I would scream back, but today I feel the afterglow of my list. My angle on all this, at least temporarily, is that none of this matters anyway so why get worked up over it? The *Independent* offers me a silent siren call from where it lies, virgin and untouched, on the table. I open the cupboard door, take out the maple-syrup cornflakes, grab a bowl, pour flakes into it until it's full, and plump it down in front of Edward.

'THAT'S NO GOOD, THERE ISN'T ANY MILK!'

'Daddy, where's the rest of my toast?'

I go back to the fridge, take out the milk and pour some on to Edward's cornflakes.

'STOP! STOP!' he screams. 'YOU'RE DROWNING THEM!'

I pick up the bowl and drain some of the milk into my own breakfast bowl. Then I speed-butter the other three slices of toast, chop off the crusts with a precision born of long cocaine use, divide them into similar triangles again and stick them on Jake's plate.

'They do enjoy Mini Maestros, but it's awfully expensive . . .' drones Alison.

I pour more milk over my Weetabix, put on my glasses, chuck away the main section of the paper, and open the review to page six, Obituaries.

The first thing I see is that Joey Ramone, the punk-rock star has died. I'm alarmed to find that he was, as I am, forty-nine, but am somewhat heartened that he's taking up one of today's obit places and not someone nearer to home, someone more like me. My reasoning is that the Ramones were notorious for their rock lifestyle *par excellence* – drugs, booze, women, fast living, etc., and although, of course, this is, to some extent, my own lifestyle, I cannot claim to practise it with quite the élan of such infamous hellraisers. Besides, I tell myself confidently with the heady assurance of my list, I'm in the process of changing that lifestyle. Unlike poor Joey Ramone, I can quit before it's too late. Then I read further and discover the cause of his death: lymphatic cancer. I look up to ask Alison if she thinks too much sex, drugs and booze can cause this, but she's saying, 'Well, it's a nice idea, but they've had pizza once already this week . . .' I don't know what to think. On the one hand, if Ramone's excessive lifestyle caused the cancer, does that let me off the hook? Or is my sub-Ramones decadence enough to do it? Does just a little bit of what you fancy do you harm? On the other hand, if it was nothing to do with his lifestyle it raises the terrifying prospect that even if the heart-attack your lifestyle deserves doesn't get you, there are still weird things lurking around out there to finish you off out of the blue. Things you cannot do anything about by cutting down on the worst excesses of your vices.

Seeking comfort against this disturbing thought, I glance down the page to the next obit. Giuseppe Sinopoli has died at the age of fifty-four after suffering a heart-attack while conducting a performance of *Aida*. This is especially worrying as I've always considered conductors healthy coves who live and remain compos mentis – even working, for Christ's sake! – into their nineties. A gratifying example of what vigorous exercise and an enjoyment of great art can accomplish for longevity. Something I might take up at some future date. My heart is pounding rather hard now.

'Daddy, are these maple cornflakes organic?'

'Yes, probably.'

In the obit's accompanying photo, Sinopoli looks gratifyingly overweight. A short, fat Italian. No doubt stuffed with creamy-sauced pasta and pizzas loaded with so much mozzarella as to render them rubbery enough to serve as car tyres. Reading on I discover that he had a reputation for being 'difficult' and at various times fell out with every major opera house in the world. I breathe a sigh of relief. Well, that's it, then. It's obvious. A Type A personality.

'I'm not eating these if they're not organic! I could swallow lots of chemicals and they might kill me!'

'Edward, I'm reading, be quiet.'

'I WILL NOT BE QUIET. YOU SHUT UP. YOU'RE NOT A NICE DADDY. DO YOU WANT ME TO DIE?'

'Yes,' says Jake.

'YOU'RE TRYING TO POISON ME!' Edward screams.

'SHUT UP!' I scream back.

'He's right, Daddy, they're not organic,' says Jake. 'They haven't got the organic symbol on the box.'

'Thank you for that, Jake!' I snap.

'DADDY, I'VE SWALLOWED SOME OF THESE CHEMICALLY CORNFLAKES. I'M GOING TO DIE!'

'EDWARD, SHUT UP. JUST SHUT UP, DO YOU HEAR?'

'But, Daddy, he's just upset because—'

'And you shut up too!'

Ignoring Edward's loud sobs and Jake's disgruntled toast-crunching, I stare back at the picture of Sinopoli. Now I think about it, he does look an uppity little bastard. Definitely Type A. Of course, so am I. But then I won't always be this way. I can do relaxation exercises, meditation, that sort of thing. Just as soon as I get the time . . .

Both boys are screaming now. Edward has left his seat and is punching and pinching Jake, who is thumping him back. I skip most of Sinopoli's life's work and reach the small summary at the end. Suddenly I am no longer at all surprised by his demise: it says he leaves a widow and two sons.

In my pigeonhole at work is a note from the Dean, asking me to drop in on her at two o'clock. I find myself somewhat cheered. No doubt she feels bad about having sprung the change to the Kappelheim upon me and wishes to make amends by explaining in person. Perhaps my feeling that she is vengeful has been mistaken. After all, Jane and I go back a long way and despite the – perhaps – abruptness of its ending, our affair was conducted with great affection as well as healthy lust. Do not our shared fumblings, the intermingling of our bodily fluids, as with blood brothers, confer for ever on our relationship an intimacy that puts us on the same side?

In the morning I have my class on Jacobean poets. I am relieved to find Tamsin absent, but then this very relief gives way to anxiety. Why is she absent? Is she embarrassed by what happened (or rather didn't)? I am distracted and, let me be the first to admit, not at my usual swaggering front-of-class best. Like a wild animal sensing some weakness in its prey, a boy called Bennet, a tyke from Tyneside, who at best is irritating in my classes, is particularly disruptive this morning. He lets none of my points pass unnoticed and argues with everything I say. As usual he criticizes Donne to needle me. He even has the temerity to suggest that Donne was a plagiarist.

'And Shakespeare wasn't, I suppose?' I fire back at him, finally exasperated beyond endurance. 'All great writers pilfer from others. It's what they do with their haul that counts, wouldn't you say?'

Bennet has restored my sense of unease, polluted the atmosphere around me with unnamed fear, so that I walk around as if under a cloud of it, like some character in a cartoon. It is with some trepidation that I knock on the Dean's door, the confidence of the early morning having disappeared like . . . well, like powder from a sheet of glass.

'Enter!' Jane's voice is imperious. She's standing, talking on the phone, and motions me into one of the two armchairs on the customer side of her desk, which is massive, teak or mahogany or some such. I was never much good on woods or furniture, having little interest in either. It's topped by that green leather important people like to have on their desks, presumably as a symbol of opulence, since it has always struck me as highly impractical. I can imagine, were it on any desk of mine, it being all too easily ripped, the kind of use it would get. The rest of the room is equally luxurious. The pile of the carpet is deep and soft. As I consider Jane's heavy thighs, outlined by the skirt of her black suit, and her ample bosom, which strains for freedom against the single button fastening her jacket, I find myself thinking what a womanly figure she has. How those breasts would be like comfortable and comforting pillows for me in this time of trial. How, in contrast, all my conquests of late have been anorexic girls, with no restorative, maternal powers in their bony bodies.

The Old Soldier stirs restlessly on my leg as Jane looks knowingly into my eyes from her telephone call, sharing with me her boredom and frustration with her correspondent on the other end of the line, and thereby conferring on us an echo of the intimacy we once enjoyed. I wonder could I not just lay her down, sink into that soft beige pile and make mature and easy love to her? A shag upon the shag, as it were. But then her eyes flick away and the moment passes. I am left with only the carpet to contemplate.

Jane's office is sumptuous, especially considering the university's dire financial straits. So much has been spent on appearances since the last Conservative government waved its magic wand and transformed an unprepossessing polytechnic into a university. Now we have our own logo, which is some kind of fish although I can't remember why: the town is nowhere near the sea nor has any connection with fish. We used to have security men guarding the front door. Now they are called porters and have swopped their paramilitary uniforms for something that makes them look as if they work in a rather good hotel. But at the coal-face, at least in the Department of English and Drama, things remain the same. The ancient tables and chairs, graffitied by generations of disgruntled graffiti experts who never made it to a proper university. The books with their own *pentimento*, the ink-stamped word 'polytechnic' inadequately obscured by layers of fish logos. Still, the transformation is not without its advantages for teachers. We are now part of the university system. In the same league. Third division, even Nationwide Conference, we may be, but it's possible to work one's way up. Especially for someone who has been a dynamic head of department, for example. Someone who has displaced a drunken old fool and brought in radical new ideas. New teaching methods. A new curriculum. Someone go-ahead and – I stop myself because I realize I'm describing not myself but Tait. A click as the phone is replaced in its cradle.

Jane walks around the desk and perches her bottom on the front, half leaning, half sitting on its teak/mahogany edge. Her skirt rides up an inch or two and she watches me watching it for a moment or so, in the manner of someone who knows me well enough to know this little distraction will have to be got through before we can get down to business.

'Well, Michael,' she says, when my eyes lift at last and look into hers, 'how are you?'

'I'm well. Fine. Absolutely fine. Never been – uh – fitter. And yourself?'

'Michael, we're not here to talk about me. I'm a little concerned about you. One hears things.'

'Ah, then perhaps one shouldn't listen—'

'One hears things that suggest someone is struggling with . . . How can I put it? Some personal demons.'

'Me? Demons? No, not me, Jane. Not me at all. I don't do demons.'

She fixes me with a stony stare and, instinctively, I look away and find myself looking straight into the mad gleam of Uncle Frank's eyes. My initial shock is not so much at seeing him there, sitting large as life in the partner chair to my own – the apparition of Agnes Ada has prepared me somewhat for dead relatives – but at the way he looks. It's not Uncle Frank as he was in the late sixties when he died, paunchy and jowly, a few thin strands of hair stretched across his zippered pate, (the scar proudly displayed as a medal of his wartime service), mouth sunken, false teeth loose. No, this is the Uncle Frank of nearly a decade earlier, in his prime, his pomp, as he was that day when he almost killed me, slim, his chest well toned under his T-shirt whose sleeves bulge with biceps and the rectangular outline of his cigarette packet. He smiles at me, raising his eyebrows at the Dean in what I take to be a gesture of enquiry.

It's a moment or two before I can catch my breath. 'What's happening?' I gasp.

'I'm about to tell you, Michael, if I can have your full attention for a moment. Michael?' It's the Dean's voice. I'd forgotten she was here.

I tear my eyes, with some difficulty, from Uncle Frank, and turn back to her. 'I'm sorry, I didn't ask him to come, I – I—' And then, of course, I see it's me she's looking at, brows knitted in puzzlement, and not my uncle's ghost.

'Michael? Are you with us?' That 'us' throws me and I start thinking all over again that she can see him then realize it's just a figure of speech, a habit academics have from teaching classes, the 'academic we', as it were.

'Yes. Yes, of course. I – uh —'

'You want to know what's going on?'

'Do I?'

'That's what you just said.'

'Right. Yes. Uh – why you wanted to see me.'

She lifts herself off the edge of the desk and strides businesslike around it.

'You fucked this woman, right?' I look at him and see he's appraising the swing of her buttocks, accentuated by her rather too-high heels. 'Well, I can see why. She's built for fucking.' He turns to me. 'Oh, and don't mention I said the F-word if we see your grandmother.'

'Will I see her?'

'See whom?' Jane is behind her desk now, shuffling papers. She has her spectacles on and is looking over them at me, her expression confused. 'You mean Ms Graves?'

'What? What was that? Who did you say?'

'You asked if you would be seeing Ms Graves again.'

'Tamsin? What's she got to do with it?'

147

'She's the one you fucked the other day, right, boy? Or didn't. I remember now, you were interrupted.'

'Ms Graves has made a formal complaint against you.'

'Jane I didn't fuck her.'

'That's right, he didn't fuck her. My mother was there and she could tell you.'

I turn to him again and hiss, 'Keep quiet,' but he pretends not to hear and gives Jane a grin, which, of course, she doesn't see. He pulls the pack of Player's Navy Cut from his sleeve, stretches out his leg so he can reach down into his jeans pocket, and pulls out his flip-top lighter. He taps a cigarette on the pack, sticks it between his lips and torches it up. With his first exhalation he blows a smoke ring; a wreath of blue smoke drifts across the room.

'I must say I find that hard to believe, Michael, given your reputation. And what I know about you. Michael . . . ?'

Uncle Frank is extending the pack to me now and I wonder what would happen if I took one, but then he withdraws it and makes a dismissive gesture with his hand. 'Nah, you've got enough health problems already, Michael.'

'Michael? Michael?'

'What?'

'Why should I believe you? You can't even look me in the eye.'

I turn away from Uncle Frank and face her now. 'I didn't do it, Jane.'

'Yes, well, that's as maybe. Certainly it seems to me that the intent was there. Anyway, fucking is not the issue here.'

'I hate to hear a woman use the F-word. No way would I let her meet my mother.'

'Shut up!'

'I beg your pardon?'

148

'Sorry, I was . . . er . . . talking to myself, as it were.'

She gives me a look which is half genuine concern and half fear that she may be closeted with the mad axeman. Which, of course, she is, except that he's been dead for thirty-odd years and probably can't hurt her.

'Michael, I don't know what's happening to you. You had so much promise. Such a bright future ahead of you.'

'We none of us have that, Jane, if we did but know it.'

'Don't get all philosophical on me, Michael, I'm a bit old for the world-weary poet bit. I've done Donne, remember?'

'As if I could forget.'

There's a pause during which I smile at her, I hope seductively but more likely just lecherously. She pulls herself out of her momentary trance and picks up the papers in front of her again. 'As I was saying, what you did or did not do with the Old Soldier is not the main issue here. Ms Graves alleges that you attempted to tape-record her having sex with you.'

'No, I didn't do it.'

'She says she found the machine.'

'She's mistaken.'

'Oh, come on, a twenty-year-old woman should know what a cassette recorder looks like.'

'You'd think.'

'Hey, Michael, you don't have to take a beating on this, tell her what really happened. Tell her about the blood-pressure thing.' Uncle Frank is leaning forward now, as if he's about to do it himself. The thought fills me with panic, the idea of any of my colleagues meeting any of my swamp-people family and especially this one and I begin to reach out my arm to stop him, and then I think, Wait a minute, he's a ghost, for Christ's sake, if he makes contact with Jane, caste won't be an issue.

Jane is about to say something else when she pauses and sniffs the air. A mist of cigarette smoke hangs around her.

'Michael, can you smell smoke?'

'Smoke? Er, I don't think so. What kind of smoke? You think something's burning?'

'I don't know. Cigarette smoke, perhaps? Never mind, forget it.'

Uncle Frank takes a long haul on his cigarette, holds it in his lungs until it looks like he's going to burst and lets it out in a steady stream straight at Jane.

'Michael, if you come clean with me, I may be able to help you.'

For a brief moment I consider it. Telling her about the BP monitor will get me off the hook with Tamsin. But it means confessing my physical frailty: she's hardly likely to appoint another potential stroke victim to succeed Stan. What's more (and, if I'm honest, more important to me), it means admitting that her one-time lusty lover is over – and well on his way down the other side of – the hill. I can't bring myself to do it.

'Jane, there's nothing to come clean about. I didn't fuck the girl – my word on it as a serial adulterer. And I definitely didn't tape or try to tape her. That's all I have to say. Now, unless there's anything else . . .' I rise from my chair and turn as if about to make for the door. But the dramatic effect of my gesture is lost as Jane is sniffing again.

'It *is* smoke. I can definitely smell it. It's very strong.' She, too, has risen and is walking around the room now, sampling the air from different parts of it. 'Yes, there's no doubt about it. Surely you can smell it too, Michael?'

A cloud of Uncle Frank's fumes hits me, making me cough. But I don't mind. It's as though half a century of fear has dropped off me in an instant.

I grab Jane by the arms, pull her towards me and kiss her hard on the lips. 'You can smell the smoke! You can smell the smoke!' I cry. I put my arms around her and hug her tight, ignoring her muffled protests as I squeeze her to me. She struggles, breaks free and pushes me away.

'Michael, have you gone mad?' she says.

Uncle Frank is sitting smoking with a calm smile on his face, tapping the ash off the end of his cigarette into the palm of his hand. I grab him under the elbow and he rises out of his chair.

'This is my Uncle Frank!' I shout. 'You can't see him, but I'm very pleased to say you can smell him. Or his smoke, at least.'

Uncle Frank stands appraising her, perhaps contemplating some unholy coupling, then nips out the end of his cigarette between finger and thumb and places butt and ash in his T-shirt pocket.

Jane looks right through him at me. 'Michael, I had hoped we could smooth this thing over today, here between us. But I see it's quite hopeless. I don't know what's happening to you, but you're obviously too far gone for me to help. I have no alternative but to convene an ethics committee preliminary hearing to investigate the allegations against you. You can expect a meeting next week.'

'I will, Jane, I will. Thank you, Jane, thank you!' I try to kiss her again but she retreats behind her desk. I don't mind: exhilaration courses through my veins and I'm wired without any help from Charlie. As soon as I'm out of the room I'm running down the corridor. I want to leap for joy.

'Uncle Frank, I could kiss you too,' I shout, causing a couple of passing students to move out of my way warily, but when I turn round, he's no longer there.

*   *   *

For the first time in months I do not have a burden of depression. I'm fired up with enthusiasm for living. I am filled by a strong sense of purpose. Jane smelt Uncle Frank's smoke! He exists somewhere. I'm not going crazy. And if this life is not all there is then I no longer need to debate whether this or that is worth my precious time. I can just get on with, well, living. In this mood I stride manfully into the library, eager to kick-start my stalled Donne project. And am immediately stopped in my tracks by an overalled maintenance man pushing a wheelbarrow. It's loaded with books. Close by are piles of tea-chests from which another man is extracting piles of books and placing them in another wheelbarrow.

I stop the first wheelbarrow and pull out a few books. Vaughan, Spenser, Rochester. 'What's going on? What are you doing?' I ask the man, who's impatient to be gone.

'Taking these to be disposed of,' he says, setting down the wheelbarrow handle to straighten his back. 'Bloody heavy they are too.'

At this moment the inner door to the reading room opens and out steps the librarian, Sarah Gault. 'What's happening? Where are all these books going?' I ask. 'They're surely not being destroyed.'

'What else do you suggest we do with them? Nobody wants them, they're not worth anything.'

'Not worth anything? Look at this – Vaughan. And this, Rochester. Ben Jonson. Spenser. Some of the greatest poets in the English language and you're just dumping them. It's cultural vandalism.'

'Well, hardly, Michael, we're merely removing them to make way for something else. There will be as many books as before, they'll just be different books, that's all. We're trying to update the stock.'

'Update the stock. You speak as if these are old

horses being sent to the knackers because they can't get it up any more.'

'Michael, there are huge numbers of modern novels issued every year. Those are what people are studying. We have to keep up with demand. Many of these books languished in the store room because no one requested them.'

'Modern novels? They'd have to be bloody good to displace these, if you ask me. But of course no one did ask me.'

'Now now, that's not fair. A consultative paper went out to all departments. Dr Tait replied on behalf of the English and Drama department. He made the selection of deletions.'

'Tait! I might have known.'

'Well, he did respond . . .'

I bend over the barrow and take out another handful of books. 'Euripides, Epicurus, Socrates . . . You're getting rid of all these?'

She nods. 'There's no point in having books people don't read.'

'Carlisle, Newman, Hume . . . what will this mean for Theology?'

'We don't have a Department of Theology any more. There just weren't the number of applicants to support it, even though application virtually guaranteed acceptance and a pretty automatic degree.'

'You're telling me people aren't interested in religion any more?'

'Of course, but they want to examine it from a more contemporary viewpoint. We have to make space for all the works being published on New Age religions.'

I raise my arms and let them fall in a gesture of exasperation.

'Can I take this load now, Dr Gault?' The maintenance man lifts the handles of his wheelbarrow.

'Yes, please do.'

I scoop a handful of poetry books from his load and wrap my arms protectively around them. Forgetting my new-found thirst for life I follow him out of the door and watch him trek across the campus. 'What are you going to do with them?' I call after him.

'Burn them!' he shouts back.

I stand and watch as he wends his way around the main administration block, from behind which, right about where the Dean's office is, rises a column of black smoke.

TEN

When thou wilt swim in that live bath,
Each fish, which every channel hath,
Will amorously to thee swim,
Gladder to catch thee, than thou him.

The Bait

I never got to see Aunt Clara in the red bathing-suit, of course. It was put on upstairs at Agnes Ada's and then concealed beneath a long white cotton shift while Mum and I waited anxiously down below. We could hear my grandmother chiding her: 'Come on, woman, git a move on. You'll be late for your own baptism. You've got enough stitches in that thing to last till kingdom come, now come on.'

'She's going over the baptism robe one last time,' Mum whispered to me. 'In case of accidents.'

I wondered what accidents might occur to rip apart a cotton shift but before I could think of any the two women came down the stairs. Agnes Ada was clad in her best black dress ('Weddings, funerals, baptisms, they're all the same to me. I've got one good dress and it'll have to do for the lot!') and already wearing her feathered hat. 'I've had this thing on my head for more than an hour,' she complained. 'That's how long I bin going up and down them stairs chivvying her along.'

Normally Aunt Clara would have flinched at such harsh words, but today she had an aura of great calm. She was not a pretty woman but there was always something a little other-worldly about her, and today she seemed positively angelic, standing there in her long white cotton robe through which, by moving around her and getting the window behind her, I could make out just a shadow of the red bathing-suit. That I could see it was important to me as several of the village boys were choosing to ignore what I told them and insisting she would be naked underneath and that you'd be able to see her breasts and perhaps even pubic hair once the shift was wet. Although she had put on no makeup, as befitted the solemn occasion, she wore a beatific smile that caused my mother to say, 'Clara, you look radiant!'

The effect was marred somewhat when she donned her iridescent green mac, which looked especially odd with the shift hanging below it and, further down, her feet in rubber sandals, but she was shy about appearing in just the shift and, besides, she always felt the cold. Not that she'd gain much benefit from the mac: we lived a mile from the river and Mr Hale was driving us there in his Morris Oxford. We all crammed in with me between Mum and Agnes Ada in the back. It was the first time I'd ever been in a motor-car (I didn't count Uncle Frank's beaten-up old pick-up truck as a car) and it was a particularly gratifying initiation as the village's single street (called, somewhat superfluously, Main Street) was lined with people who'd come to witness the event. As we drove past many waved and Aunt Clara responded by lifting her hand and waving regally back.

'Silly old bugger,' snapped Agnes Ada, 'thinks she's Queen Shit.'

'Ahem, if you please . . .' said Mr Hale, from the front. 'May I remind you it's Sunday, Mrs Cole?'

156

'I know which bloody day it is, parson,' she snapped back. 'I swear seven days a week. There's no rest for the wicked.' And she chuckled to herself for the rest of the journey.

The river Lark is a minor and insignificant tributary of the Great Ouse. In those days it brimmed with bream and carp, and fishermen came from as far afield as Sheffield and Manchester. But there its fame ended. It was not, as many rivers are, celebrated in legend or song. In the village post office only one picture post-card featured it. Even in those days the photo must have been ancient: it depicted a couple in what looked like clothes from an earlier era. She wore a white dress with red polka dots and her curled blonde hair was flying out behind her as she held his hand – he was in a blazer and Oxford bags – and they ran together down the riverbank, laughing so deliriously you couldn't help but wonder what they'd been up to, especially when you turned the card over and read the caption, which said '*River Lark*', with only that capital L on the second word to indicate that this was not soft porn.

Such liveliness on the river's bank was rare. It was a lazy old river, not getting up much speed, flowing as it did across the flat plain of the Fens, and its sluggish appearance didn't quite gel with the picture Mr Hale had painted when he'd expressed doubts over the wisdom of taking a frail old lady into it. You would have thought he'd been talking about a raging moun-tain torrent. But, then, the man was short and had a right to be cautious about getting into deep water. Perhaps this was why it had been decided that, rather than risk the river proper, the baptism would take place in a thin arm of it, an artificial bay, dug to connect the river to the pump-house, where, during times of heavy rainfall, water was pumped into the river from the lower-level drains that were fed by the system of field dykes.

That summer was exceptionally dry and the pistons of the steam pump had been silent, so the water in the small bay must have been there for weeks and was stagnant. Large beds of reeds had sprung up and we boys would tug them up to catch the eels that wriggled out and take them home for supper.

It seemed like the whole village had turned out for the spectacle of a woman getting wet. The throng crowding the riverbank was supplemented by people who had driven or cycled out from Ely and the surrounding villages. There was even a coach party of Baptists from Soham.

'Tut!' said Aunt Clara nervously, as Mr Hale helped her from the car. Every eye was on her as the crowd parted to allow them up the riverbank and down the other side. Once they were through, though, the crowd immediately re-formed, so intent upon the star performer that they ignored the rest of her party.

'Out of the way, *if you please*!' bellowed Agnes Ada, making free with her elbows to clear a passage for us. 'I'm her sister-in-law.'

At the foot of the bank Aunt Clara shrugged off her mac and handed it to Agnes Ada, looking up at her with a pleading expression. Surprisingly, Agnes Ada smiled. 'Don't worry about all them buggers watching. Think about your Harry. That's who you're doing it for.'

Mr Hale was already in the water, his white cassock floating out around him from his waist. He reached up and helped Aunt Clara as two of the chapel wardens took her by the elbows and lowered her into the river. She took a moment to steady herself and then stood calmly beside him, her robe floating too so that she and the minister looked like two gigantic water-lilies.

A soft breeze wrinkled the surface of the water as Mr

Hale reached into the chest area of his cassock and took out a Bible.

'Here we go!' sighed Agnes Ada, and pulled a resigned look on to her face.

'A voice of one crying in the wilderness . . .' began Mr Hale, and I drifted off, lost in contemplation of the water, which was covered with a thin film of bright green algae. I heard a scurrying in the reeds by my feet and saw what looked like a short piece of rope slither off the bank as a rat slid into the water.

Mr Hale was determined to enjoy his ten minutes of fame, in fact so determined that he stretched them into twenty, setting some kind of record for the time taken to read through Matthew three. When he reached the final verse, 'And lo a voice from heaven, saying, This is my beloved Son, in whom I am well pleased,' he looked up into the sky with such a fixed stare that some of the spectators shoved one another and craned their necks, trying to catch a glimpse of the implied heavenly dove.

Eventually Mr Hale got his gaze back down on to Aunt Clara. He put one arm around her, made the sign of the cross with the other, and said, 'I baptize you in the name of Jesus Christ Our Lord.' He whispered something to her, which must have been on the lines of 'Relax', because her whole body went limp and she allowed herself to fall back in his arms. In a flash she disappeared below the water to an audible gasp from the crowd and almost immediately reappeared as Mr Hale, surprisingly strong for such a little fellow, hauled her out and upright again.

There was a loud cheer from the riverbank and Mr Hale broke into a smile then gave a dismissive wave, as though he had just scored the winning goal in a football match but was too modest to have it acknowledged. As Aunt Clara was lifted from the water

I saw the cotton shift had turned transparent and the red bathing costume shone brightly through it, which, with the green algae that clung to her hair and the shift, gave her a Christmassy look.

This was to be the only glimpse of the red bathing-suit any of us was afforded, for she was soon swathed in several towels, with the green iridescent mac as the final layer, whipped into the Morris Oxford and back home to Agnes Ada's. That even this was indeed a very small glimpse was confirmed when a boy in my class named Malcolm Chambers approached me and said, 'See? I told you: You could see all her titties.'

It was a week or so later that Aunt Clara became ill. When I went round for my tea one night while Mum was at her job cleaning the village school, she was lying on the settee, her normally pale cheeks flushed and sweat on her brow.

'She's got the flu,' said Agnes Ada. 'She's done nothing but complain about her aches and pains all day. Well, woman, you've only yourself to blame. If you will go jumping in the river on a cold day, what can you expect?' There was a bucket beside the settee and I turned away as Aunt Clara leaned up and vomited thick orange bile into it. Amazingly, as she retched, the noise she made sounded like a long, agonized 'Tu-u-u-u-u-u-t!'

The next day she was no better. The area around her eyes looked bruised, as though someone had given her two black eyes. Her skin was yellow.

'Wouldn't have the doctor,' said Agnes Ada.

'Tut,' protested Aunt Clara.

'It's not making a fuss. And it's free now. The bugger can just drive over from Ely. That's his job. Anyhow, fuss or not, I'm gitting him here tomorrow if you're no better in the morning.'

The doctor was duly summoned and diagnosed flu. He advised bed rest, keeping the patient warm and feeding her plenty of wholesome broth. But Aunt Clara had no appetite. She pushed away the bowls Agnes Ada proffered, and was so listless that no amount of bullying could provoke a reaction. After another two or three days there was no improvement and she suffered several nosebleeds. Leaving Mum to tend her, Agnes Ada marched through the village to the public phone box and again summoned the doctor.

I was there when he came downstairs. 'Is she a farm worker?' he enquired.

'Pshaw!' scoffed Agnes Ada. 'She int never worked since the day she was married. I kept her the whole of her life. She's been in mourning the best part of forty years.'

'Well, could she have come into contact with any sewage?' he asked.

Agnes Ada gave him a look that would have melted stone. 'Just what are you implying, you old goat?'

'I'll consider that a no,' said the doctor. 'Anyway, I've taken a blood sample. I'm going to get it over to the laboratory in Cambridge today. Meanwhile, here's some penicillin. I want you to give her these tablets every four hours.'

Next day when Mum met me out of school she didn't go inside to begin work as usual, but grabbed my hand. 'Come on, Michael, it's your Auntie Clara. She's very ill. Grandma thinks she's going fast.'

We stopped only at the phone box where Mum again called the doctor. Her face was creased with worry as she put down the receiver. 'He's on his way,' was all she said.

At Agnes Ada's I was ushered up into Aunt Clara's bedroom. The first thing I thought was how peaceful she looked. I had never seen her hair down before and was astonished by how long it was: it lay all around her, like a fine grey shawl spread out on the pillow. Her skin was horribly yellow now, and inside her blackened eye sockets the whites of her eyes were suffused with blood. 'She kept rubbing at them because they were so sore,' Agnes Ada whispered, 'but they don't seem to bother her no more.'

Aunt Clara looked up at me and smiled. I bent and kissed her cheek, which was like kissing a hot kettle. I noticed a crust of dried blood inside her nostrils.

She whispered something, and Agnes Ada bent low over her to hear. 'Don't be so daft, woman, what do you want to look at that for now?' But then Aunt Clara became agitated, so my grandmother put down the cloth with which she'd been mopping her brow. 'All right, if you must.'

She went over to the chest of drawers in the corner of the room, on which I noticed – the first time I'd ever seen it, for I'd never been inside this room before – a framed sepia photograph of Aunt Clara at her wedding. Uncle Harry stood beside her, tall and rough, every inch the uncouth farm lad, and you could tell, even on the monochrome picture, that his hair was fair and his cheeks ruddy. Aunt Clara looked no different from now – well, from how she was before her illness anyway – and I realized then what a girlish old lady she'd been. Something youthful always hung about her, in spite of her seeming melancholy.

Agnes Ada pulled open the bottom drawer of the chest and took something out. I caught sight of a flash of red. She turned and held it up by the shoulder straps. No one spoke. Aunt Clara raised herself up on her elbows and gazed at it for a long moment. Finally she let out what we all knew instinctively was her last 'Tut!' It was barely audible, yet indisputably an expression of awe. The effort was too much for her and she sank back on to the bed, death rattling in her throat. Agnes Ada, still holding the bathing-suit, now bunched in one hand, rushed to the bedside and shook her, but Aunt Clara was limp as a doll. My grandmother slapped her cheeks, at first gently, but then, as her desperation increased, more robustly. Then she put her ear to her chest and listened. Half a minute later she lifted her head and shook it at my mother, who let out a loud sob. Agnes Ada angrily tossed the red bathing-suit into a corner of the room.

Just then there were steps on the stairs and a tap on the door. The doctor came in. I expected Agnes Ada to say something like 'About bloody time too!' but when the doctor looked at her she just shrugged and turned away. He went over to the bed, sat down, took Aunt Clara's wrist and held it. After a moment or two he sighed and laid it down. 'I'm sorry,' he murmured. 'It wasn't flu, after all. It was as I suspected, though not soon enough, I'm afraid. Weil's disease. It's carried by rats. They pass it into water in their urine. She must have been in some infected water.'

Nobody said anything. There was still no rebuke from Agnes Ada and even the doctor looked surprised at this. Then I noticed her eyes were moist and her lips had folded in on themselves to keep from trembling. Mum went over to her and put an arm around her. 'Don't get upset, she'll be all right,' she said. 'She's in a better place, just like she wanted. She's with her Harry now.'

'Yes,' said Agnes Ada, spitting the words out. 'Lucky she got herself baptized.'

ELEVEN

Then since I may know,
As liberally as to a midwife show
Thyself;

To his Mistress Going to Bed

This morning Tamsin is sitting in the front row of my class. I'm surprised to see she's talking to Bennett: I hadn't known they were friends. She isn't the sort to tolerate nerds. He's leaning right across her, his cheek almost familiarly close to her breast, that same breast whose nipple was clamped to my teeth only a matter of days ago. When they see me, they pause in their conversation to look up at me, then Tamsin whispers something and Bennet laughs, then looks up at me again, his habitual sneer larger than ever.

I've hardly started today's topic, Donne's attitude to death, which I've chosen so I can try out a few ideas as preparation for the Kappelheim, when I'm interrupted.

'Bit of a dinosaur, really.'

I look up from my notes with a sigh. Bennet has a challenging expression. His arms are folded defensively as though he expects trouble.

'I . . . er . . . I . . . beg your pardon?' The pause is for Tamsin, who is looking exceptionally attractive. Her hennaed hair shines against a black polo-neck sweater.

Below it she wears a tartan skirt so short I wonder momentarily if there's even enough of it to show all the tartan of whatever clan it is or if it has had to be chopped off in the middle. Her legs are bare and crossed and, as I look at her, she uncrosses them and recrosses them the opposite way. It all happens in a flash, an apposite word for me to choose because in that fragment of a second I am afforded a glimpse of something russet. My mind leaps back to the moment when I was lying on her bed and she divested herself of her underwear. Can it possibly be she isn't wearing any now? She's smirking at me, deriding my confusion.

'I said he was a bit of a dinosaur.'

The leg uncrosses and recrosses. Did I see it, or didn't I? Can it be she's wearing underwear the colour of her pubic hair? Is russet the kind of colour anyone would wear? Can you even get knickers in such a colour? A moment's reflection tells me you can. I've often prowled the underwear sections of department stores, usually while waiting as Alison tried on dresses. I've spent hours scanning displays of scanty garments and, when I consider the matter now, I recall I have seen lingerie in not only the most popular black, white and red, but also pastel shades of every colour, pink, dark green and, yes, autumnal gold, crimson and russet too.

'Er . . . sorry . . . who? Who are you talking about?'

'It's not who I'm talking about, it's who you're talking about. Donne, of course. Your main man.'

Uncross, cross.

I open a drawer of my desk, take out a tissue and wipe my clammy brow. I can feel blood suffusing my cheeks. They aren't the only place it's rushing to, either. There are signs of the Old Soldier getting into battle order too. What is it with me? Surely not all men my age are so obsessed with women's bodies? As an

165

adolescent I told myself this was a phase. Am I condemned to it into my dotage? Why, only the other week when my car was in the garage, I was sitting on the bus and an attractive young woman got on. The bus was full and I was about to offer her my seat when I noticed her pudenda, visibly split in two by her too-tight trousers, a matter of inches from my face. I could not resist looking at it. I confess I was ungentlemanly in two different ways: I did not offer her my seat and for the rest of the journey I stared at her crotch. An eye-level thrill, as it were.

'In what way, a – uh – dinosaur?'

'Well, it's obvious, man, isn't it? I mean, even in his own day he wasn't exactly at the forefront of thinking, was he? I mean, this was a time of terrific expansion in knowledge. Think of the scientific discoveries that occupied other writers like Francis Bacon. Think of the advances in astronomy, medicine and so on. Donne scarcely mentions them.'

'Well, I . . . er, I don't see what exactly that has to do with today's topic, which is Donne and Death.'

Uncross, cross. I let out a little whimper and pray it's inaudible. Tamsin's eyes twinkle maliciously at mine.

'That's just my point, man. He doesn't challenge the Christian view of death, does he? Look at what Shakespeare was saying in *Measure For Measure* – "Aye, but to go we know not where and lie in cold abstraction." All that stuff about being blown about in the viewless winds. I mean, that's atheism, man, that is! It's what people were thinking at the time, but Donne, he goes right on toeing the party line, doesn't he? Even to the extent of taking holy orders.'

'Listen, this is all very interesting, I'm sure, Mr Bennett, but I don't think it's terribly relevant to what we're talking about now. I can't really think—'

'No, you can't think about it, can you? And you know why you can't think about it?'

Uncross, cross.

'What? I mean why?'

Uncross, cross. I'm sure I see it this time.

'Because you're too busy looking up her skirt!'

There's a stunned silence. Tamsin uncrosses her legs and sits with them slightly apart. I am caught still staring at them but I can't shift my gaze for fear that doing so will be an admission of guilt. Slowly I raise my eyes to stare straight into Bennet's. Out of the corner of my eye I notice Tamsin now has a smirk to match his, as though he's lent her one of his old ones for the occasion.

Too late I realize they've set a trap for me, one I've just sprung.

'That's a pretty serious accusation, young man, and one that I entirely refute.'

'You saying you didn't have your face half-way up her muff, then, are you?'

'I most certainly am.'

Bennett screws himself round in his seat to face the rest of the class. 'OK, hands up! Who else thinks the Professor here was looking up Tamsin's skirt?'

Immediately two young women in the row behind him thrust up their arms. For a momment I'm staggered. Laura and Gabrielle. Both of whom I've had dalliances with in the previous term. Both of whom I've nurtured tender thoughts for, even after the passage of time decreed it was time to end our transitory affairs. I assumed they felt the same way towards me, the same affection, and am rendered speechless by the aggressive looks of triumph they display now. So stunned am I, I hardly notice the other arms going up among the dozen or so students here, until only one boy, who sits alone in the back row,

Toby Fraser, my star pupil, my protégé almost, bless him, has his down.

'What, Toby, you don't think he was peering up her snatch?' sneers Bennet. 'What are you? Teacher's pet or something?'

'I – I couldn't really see anything from back here,' Toby falters. 'I couldn't see where he was looking.' He pauses, and the rest of the class regard him expectantly. 'I 'spect he was, though,' he says at last, and slowly his arm rises.

Bennet turns around. 'That's why you like Donne so much, isn't it? Because he liked to put it around, didn't he? Another dirty old man like you. 'Cept Donne wasn't that. He was a dirty young man, but he grew out of it, didn't he? You never will, unless you're stopped. Well, now you have been.'

My blood is pumping in my temples. I'm probably up to suicide bomber on Branko's blood-pressure job scale now. The floor's coming up to meet me. I cling to the edge of my desk for support. I look at the faces before me and their raised arms, but they're starting to spin. I stagger to my chair and slump into it.

Bennett stands and faces the class. 'Right, I think that's it. Class dismissed. It's *done* for today.' He turns to me. 'But we aren't *done* with you, matey.' He's leaning right over, his face pressed up against mine. 'Oh, no, we haven't *done* with you by a long chalk!'

I sit, hands pyramided before my face, forefingers pressing my eyes shut, and listen to the sounds of the room emptying: a chair leg screeches insolently against the floor, books are slammed shut boisterously enough to wake not only the dead but the ashamed. There is whispered laughter. At last everything is silent and I assume I'm alone, hearing only the roaring waves in my ears telling me my diastolic and systolic are in the danger zone. It's several minutes before I grow easier with myself. The breakers calm and I become aware of the breathing of another soul, just in front of me. I spread my hands across my face fearful to face her.

'Tamsin,' I say, 'if you've stayed to gloat I—'

'Tut!' It's said mournfully, as if burdened with all my regret. 'Michael,' this single syllable counsels, 'you've brought all this upon yourself . . .'

Tentatively I splay my fingers and peep through their latticework, like a child cheating at hide and seek. She's wearing the red bathing-suit and nothing else, sitting in the seat newly vacated by Tamsin, her watery eyes staring at me.

'Tut,' she says again, but differently this time, an expression of sympathy.

I get up so suddenly I knock my chair over, and hurry to pick it up. I shrug an apology. A small smile creases her lips. The humble little smile I remember.

'Aunt Clara,' I say, 'I'm so glad to see you. So very glad.' I walk over to her and bend to kiss her forehead. It's cold and soft. I remember how she always felt the cold. 'You must be freezing, let me get you something. I have a sweater in my desk drawer.'

I turn back to the desk, go round it and open the deep lower drawer. I rummage around and find the sweater at the bottom, under a pile of books, take hold of it and, with some difficulty, tug it free.

'Here you are, put this on.' But it's too late, she's gone, and if anybody glances in right now they will see me, to add to all my other woes, offering a sweater to an empty chair.

The cafeteria. Lunchtime. I'm here to brazen it out, as Agnes Ada would have said. To show I'm not afraid of them or of what they can do to me. Even so, it takes all my nerve. As I enter a hush descends, leaving only the ghostly clattering of plates from the servery at the far end. I walk the whole length of the room with every eye upon me. Conversation springs up again in my wake and out of the corners of my eyes I see people whispering behind their hands and smiling. Worse, after I've collected my lunch and stand holding my tray looking for a space to sit, I spot Tamsin and Bennet. Not only that but they're with Brady Tait. What's this all about? Was he a conspirator in my humiliation this morning or is he merely savouring its recounting over lunch?

I sit alone and make a good show of eating my meal, pretending to be interested in Gardner's biography of Donne, which I prop up in front of me. Truth to tell, I'm making a sorry job of reading the same page over and over and I'm relieved when Harriet and Karen march up, like two bodyguards sent to look after a star witness, and plump themselves down at either side of the table.

'We've come to show support for you,' says Harriet.

'Yeah,' says Karen, 'and also to find out. Was she or wasn't she?'

'Was she or wasn't she what?'

'Was Ms Graves wearing any panties?'

'I don't know because I didn't look.'

'Wasn't how I heard it.'

'And anyway, Karen, this is England. You are English. Harriet and I are English. Panties is an American word. The English word is knickers.'

'Aw, Michael, spare me your pedanticism at a time like this.'

'Pedantry,' I mutter.

'You can joke, Michael, but you're in big trouble.'

'Can they get me for it?'

Harriet studies her hands and screws up her mouth. 'Not for looking up her skirt. The other stuff that's going around, maybe. They can dismiss you for gross moral turpitude.'

'What's that?'

'It means they don't like you to fuck the students.'

'Oh, come on. Like they couldn't have said no. Like it was all down to me. It takes two, you know.'

Karen immediately begins rocking from side to side in her seat and singing the old Tamla song 'It Takes Two'.

'Yes, well,' says Harriet, watching her disdainfully, 'I don't think the university council will have the Marvin Gaye take on the situation. They're more likely to think it only takes one dirty old professor.'

I turn to face her and our eyes meet.

'*Dirty old professor?*'

She lays both her hands on one of mine with a rueful smile. 'OK, not so old, then.'

'I still think it's crazy. What's so wrong with fucking people? They're adults. They can vote, join the army. Surely they're entitled to screw whomsoever they want to?'

Harriet shakes her head like a parent frustrated with a child who doesn't understand what it's being told. 'They're your students, Michael. Going to bed with them is an abuse of your position of authority.'

I lean back and push the idea away with my hands. 'Hey, now, hold on a minute here. I did not abuse my position. I did not compromise my integrity. I have fucked those two girls in my class, it's true, but I have also given them consistently low grades.'

'Oh, no!' Harriet buries her head in her hands.

'What?' I say.

She looks up shaking her head. 'Michael, you're hopeless. You fucked them and then you gave them low grades?'

171

TWELVE

Tired, now I leave this place, and but pleased so
As men which from gaols to execution go

Satire 4

The Ad Hoc Preliminary Investigation Sub-Committee
of the Ethics Committee consists of five people, four of
them well known to me. Jane, as Dean, is head of the
main committee and responsible for nominating
the members of the sub-committee. Interestingly, she
has nominated herself. She is also, by the rules,
required to nominate someone from my faculty and,
again interestingly, has chosen Brady Tait, who, it is all
too obvious, means me no good. It is my right, in the
interests of fair play, to request two other members of
the committee and I've asked for Stanley Horgan and
Karen. The chairman of the sub-committee is Daniel
Grace, a member of the law faculty, selected for his
knowledge of college rules and, where necessary, the
laws of the land. The meeting takes place in an ante-
room of the University Council Chamber.

I enter to find the members of the committee already
seated on one side of a long table, with a solitary chair
ranged opposite them on the other side. It's like facing
a sedentary firing squad.

'Ah, hello, Michael,' says Grace, shuffling papers and

smiling up at me. He has the kind of bald head that looks like it's never had hair on it, a soft, wrinkly baby's head. 'Good of you to come.'

'I wasn't aware I had any choice in the matter.'

He clears his throat and raises his eyebrows. 'There's always a choice, in everything we do,' he says. 'Now—'

'Wait a minute, I have something to say,' I interrupt.

Grace is surprised. 'Yes?'

'I do not recognize the right of this committee to try me.'

'I don't know what you mean, Michael. This isn't a trial. It's merely a first-stage investigation into allegations that have been made concerning you. If these prove groundless then the matter can end here. It's what we all hope for, I'm sure.'

There's a mutter of 'Of course,' from the Dean, echoed weakly by Tait.

'It's kinda like a grand jury,' says Karen.

'Very well, but I dispute the right of this committee even to do that, when one of it's members – ' I nod towards Tait ' – has a conflict of interest.'

'How so?'

'Tait and I are in line for the same job. It's in his interests for me to be found guilty. He's not neutral. He's hostile.'

'I refute imputations to my objectivity,' says Tait. 'Michael, I'm on your side. It does the faculty as a whole no good to have these kinds of allegations kicking around. As for the job, I'm confident I can win it on academic merit without recourse to dirty tricks.'

'Besides,' says Grace, 'this is just a preliminary investigation. Should it move forward to an actual inquiry then you would, of course, have the right to legal representation and to challenge the choice of judges. Now, can we get on?'

'Very well.'

173

Grace puts on a pair of spectacles and peers at the papers before him. He takes a pen from his inside breast pocket and scribbles a note on the top page. He clears his throat again. He's not enjoying this. 'Michael, I have to ask you some very personal questions, and I hope you'll understand this is as painful and difficult for me as it is for you.'

'I doubt it. It's far harder to answer personal questions than to ask them.'

'Michael, I had hoped we could get through this in a reasonable and civilized manner.'

'I regard the whole business as unreasonable and uncivilized.'

'Very well. Let's begin. Michael, have you ever, while on the faculty here, slept with one of your students?'

'Yes.'

There is immediate consternation. Grace looks to his right to Tait and Jane, who both mutter something to him. Karen puts a hand over her eyes and shakes her head. Stanley gazes at me with something like admiration. Eventually the muttering subsides.

'I'm grateful for your frank admission,' says Grace. 'It wasn't quite what I was . . . er . . . expecting.'

'You didn't expect me to lie, did you?'

'Well, I had hoped, Michael, you might have been able to deny the allegations we have to put to you. With such a response, I'm at something of a loss to know how to proceed.'

Tait leans across Jane. 'May I suggest that rather than grilling Michael like some errant schoolboy we merely ask him to elaborate on that last reply? It could save everyone a great deal of distress.'

'I don't know why anyone else should be getting distressed, but I'm happy to do so.'

'Very well,' says Grace, 'go ahead.'

174

I notice Stanley leaning back and rubbing his hands together. His prurience is such it's suddenly possible to believe this decrepit old man really wrote two or three what were then called racy novels in the Seventies.

'I slept with Alison Saunders when she was my student. But it was several years ago and, besides, the woman is married now, to me.'

'Ah!' says Grace, and his sigh carries a heavy burden of disappointment. For me, I am sure, rather more than for the long haul of work he now sees unfurling before him.

'I was a very junior member of the faculty when this occurred. The fact has been public knowledge for a number of years, and I would have thought that, though technically a trespass, it ought to be covered by some statute of limitations by now.'

More hubbub. Karen sneaks me a smile at the committee's obvious disarray. Grace looks more than a little put out. His bottom lip curls out in his determination to plod on.

'I think you're being disingenuous with us, Michael, but if you want to play that game, we can go the long way round. Very well. Other than your wife, have you ever had sex with any of your students?'

'I refuse to answer that question.'

'That's it, Michael,' says Karen. 'Take the Fifth.'

'The Fifth Amendment has no application in this country,' hisses Tait.

'On what grounds do you refuse?' asks Grace.

'On the grounds he may incriminate himself, of course.'

'Thank you, Karen. With friends like you I hardly need look for enemies. That's not my reason at all.'

'Well, what reason can you possibly have?'

'On the grounds of teacher-student confidentiality. If I had slept with one of my students, it would be a breach of that to make it public. A teacher has a responsibility to his students – '

'I'm glad you see that, Michael.'

' – and that means he cannot publish details of their sex lives revealed in private. In my view it's the same as doctor-patient confidentiality.'

'I thought it was doctors and nurses they were accusing you of,' chuckles Stanley.

'But you surely can't be serious? This is refusing to defend yourself. Are you saying you haven't slept with one of your students?'

'No, I am refusing to answer the question on the grounds that to do so might be a breach of confidentiality.'

'But, Michael, surely it then follows that if the answer were "No" there would be no confidentiality to breach?'

'That may be so, but it's also true that by giving any answer at all I would be establishing a precedent by which one of my colleagues might in future be judged. Therefore I refuse to answer the question.'

Grace shakes his head. 'Michael, you are doing yourself no favours.'

I smile back. If the sub-committee is stalled I may be able to buy time to talk to Tamsin. I begin to rise from my chair.

'Hold on, Michael, we're not finished with you yet,' says Jane.

'No, I'm afraid not,' says Grace. He shuffles the papers like a deck of oversize, flimsy cards, putting them this way and that, getting the edges straight. Suddenly he looks up at me. 'Very well. Forget sex. Did you or did you not attempt to make a clandestine tape-recording of one of your students? I'm not asking about the situation. Just answer the question. Did you or didn't you?'

'Categorically not. I can swear absolutely that I have never done anything like that.'

'Michael, I have to say I've received a submission from a witness who's making this claim. Now, the committee has not interviewed her as yet, but we have an extensively detailed statement from her. Are you sure you don't want to reconsider what you've just told me?'

They're all staring at me. I can see from the expression on Karen's face that this allegation bothers her. She was expecting some kind of explanation. She takes off her heavy specs, blows on them, and rubs them on her jumper. There is something like distaste on her face, as though I have just released an unpleasant smell and am refusing to own up to it. But how can I tell the truth? It means my promotion going down the pan, not to mention my reputation between the sheets. And why should I? Why, because of some silly girl, should I humiliate myself before their self-righteous gaze?

'Well?'

'No. All I will say is that the allegation may have been made in good faith but that it's the result of mistaken observation. Now, if you're quite done with me . . .'

'For now,' says Grace. 'We're done for now.'

I start to rise from my chair.

'Wait a moment, please, Michael.'

I let myself back down again.

'We won't keep you much longer. You will understand, of course, that while you are under the – uh – cloud of these allegations and while our investigation is taking place it would be inappropriate for you to remain an active member of the teaching staff.'

'Now, wait a minute – I'm still capable of doing my job.'

'That's as may be, but we have a duty of care to our

students and until such time as you're cleared of any suspicion we would be neglecting that duty if we allowed you to teach them.'

'You make me sound like some kind of pervert.'

'I didn't say that, Michael. Your suspension is effective as from this moment. You will remove yourself from campus and stay away. You will not communicate with students except on urgent matters that relate to outstanding work and then only by post.'

'This is madness! You talk as if I might damage them in some way.'

'Above all, you will make no attempt to contact either in person, by telephone, post or e-mail or via an intermediary, Ms Tamsin Graves.'

'What about strangling her? Is that allowed?'

'Another remark like that, Michael,' snaps Grace, 'and it goes on the record.'

'Fuck the record!' I stand up a bit too fast and my chair tips over behind me. But it's not like with Aunt Clara the other day. This time the gesture is intended. 'You've taken away my job. What am I supposed to do now?'

'Why not look on it as a golden opportunity,' says Tait, his shark's smile finally breaking cover, 'to get your Donne done?'

I find my office door open and two maintenance men waiting for me. They have a stack of plastic crates. 'Can I help you?' My manner is brusque: I don't like the look of this.

'We've come to help you clear your office,' says one. I recognize him as the man with the wheelbarrow the other day. 'If you stick everything in the crates, we'll carry it to your car.'

'What makes you think I'm clearing my office?'

'Dean's orders, Professor.'

178

I phone Jane. 'Are you throwing me out of my office? I thought this suspension was temporary, pending the investigation.'

'Of course it is, Michael,' she purrs, 'but you know how desperate for space we are. We can't afford to leave your office empty for however long it takes. You'll get it back in the event of the committee exonerating you.'

'What if I don't clear it?'

'Then the janitors will crate up your things and put them in store.'

I put the phone down.

'Well, Professor?' says the man who spoke before. Suddenly the picture of him pushing the wheelbarrow of books to his bonfire leaps into my mind.

'Forget it, I'll do it myself.'

In traffic on the way home, I check my mobile phone and find a text message: **It doesn't have to be like this. Meet Thai Tavern 9pm tonite. Tamsin. Be there.**

THIRTEEN

Th' earth's face is but thy table; there are set
Plants, cattle, men, dishes for Death to eat.
In a rude hunger now he millions draws
Into his bloody, or plaguey, or starved jaws.
                    Elegy on Mistress Bulstrode

I emerge from the lavatories at the Thai Tavern and
walk stright into Uncle Frank. It's a good job I've just
done a couple of lines or I might be more fazed by this
than I am. 'What are you doing here?' I hiss. I don't
want the waiters at the far end of the restaurant to hear
me.

'What would we be doing here? Eating, of course. It's
a restaurant, isn't it?'

'We?' Then I look past him and see them in the booth
behind him. Agnes Ada and Aunt Clara. But no chimp.
Thank God for small mercies, as Agnes Ada might say.

'Won't you join us?' says Uncle Frank, gesturing to
the place next to Aunt Clara on one side of the table.

'I can't, I'm meeting someone.'

'We know that,' he says, putting a hand on my
shoulder and pushing me down into the seat, 'but
you're early. And we sort of need you to order.'

As Uncle Frank sits down beside Agnes Ada I lean
towards her. 'What are you doing here? You got me into

enough trouble showing up like that the other day. All this mess I'm in wouldn't have happened but for you.'

'It wouldn't hev happened if you hadn't been there in the first place!' she bites back.

Uncle Frank lays a hand on her arm. 'Mum, can we forget all that for now and just get ordered?'

It takes a while for Agnes Ada to find her glasses and put them on to study the menu. As she examines it I examine her. She looks how I remember her best. Her skin is soft and unlined, her hair a silvery grey. I notice she's not wearing the apron and dress she had on the other day, but a different floral cotton frock. Smarter. Aunt Clara's similarly attired.

'Why did you get dressed up?' I ask her.

'What do you mean? Why wouldn't I get dressed up? I'm not going out for dinner wearing my old rags.'

'Why not?'

'Well, I want to look smart, of course.'

'For Christ's sake! No one can see you! Or can they?'

'That's got nothing to do with anything,' she snaps, ducking my question. 'I wouldn't never go to no restaurant looking like you do. Jeans, my arse!'

I realize even Uncle Frank is wearing proper trousers tonight.

I look at my watch. Ten to nine. Four college jocks, big guys, rowers or rugby players, slide into the next booth, behind Agnes Ada and Frank.

'Well, you'd better tell me what you want,' I whisper. 'Tamsin will be here soon.'

'Humpf!' snorts Agnes Ada, at the mention of Tamsin's name, and applies herself to the menu. 'Where's the roast beef? I should like a nice piece of roast beef. And gravy. It seems such a long time since I've had gravy.'

'Tut!' agrees Aunt Clara.

'Mum,' says Uncle Frank, 'they don't have no gravy. Look around, it's not English, this place.'

She and Aunt Clara turn their heads and run their eyes over the gold twisted pillars, the murals of Thai temples painted on the walls, the silk hangings, the huge red china dragons.

'Tut!' says Aunt Clara.

Agnes Ada doesn't comment, but manages a kind of disparaging shrug with her mouth and returns to the menu.

'Well, it says they hev gravy here. "Stir-fried chicken in coconut gravy". Humph. Coconut gravy. What will they think of next?'

'Would you like me to explain the food?' I ask.

'We don't need any explaining, Michael,' says Uncle Frank. 'I used to eat hundreds of takeaways from the Chinky place in Broad Street.'

'Uncle Frank, it's not Ch—'

He holds a hand up. 'I know, I know. I mustn't say that word. Chinese. There, satisfied?'

'So what do you want?'

'I'll have what I always had from the Chink – the Chinese.'

'Which is?'

'Number twenty-five.'

I look at the menu. Red prawn curry in coconut milk with sliced bamboo shoots mixed with sweet basil.

I look back at Uncle Frank, as he tosses the menu aside.

'You're sure?'

'Of course I'm sure. I always have the same numbers. Twenty-five, forty-two and a portion of sixty-seven.'

'But the numbers here aren't the . . .' I begin, but then I think, Oh what the hell, let's just get on with it.

'What about you, Grandma?'

'I'll have the coconut gravy. Number forty-eight. And a nice bit of fried chicken. I don't know what they mean by stir-fried but I suppose it's like Chicken

182

Maryland. Thirty-seven, the one with the pineapple. Oh, and some veg to go with it. Number sixty.'

'And you, Aunt Clara?'

'Tut.'

'Forty-seven,' translates Agnes Ada.

'Tut.'

'Thirty-three.'

'Tut.'

'Thirteen.'

I look at my watch. Nine o'clock. Tamsin's late. A diminutive waitress in black silk tunic and trousers approaches.

'Are you ready to order, sir?' Like her stature her features are on a miniature scale. With her careful makeup, she looks like a porcelain doll.

'Yes, please. Could I have numbers twenty-five, forty-two, sixty-seven, forty-eight, thirty-seven, sixty, forty-seven, thirty-three and thirteen, please?'

She blinks. 'You're expecting a large party, sir?'

'Er, no, just me.'

She smiles. 'Is too much food.'

'Too much? I'm – uh – very hungry.'

'You won't be able to eat so much, sir. Besides, some of these things require rice. You haven't ordered any rice.'

'Oh, bring some rice, then. Enough for three.'

The girl glances anxiously towards the front of the restaurant, as though making sure none of her colleagues is watching, then ducks down and slides into the seat opposite me, causing Uncle Frank to shuffle hurriedly up against Agnes Ada to get out of the way.

The girl leans over the table and whispers earnestly at me, 'Is too much food for one person. Is obscene amount of food! People in my country are starving. All over third world people are starving.'

Her irises are so dark, I notice, they are almost black. I think of asking for her phone number so we can discuss third-world politics later, but decide it's probably not a good idea with my family here.

'I – um – I haven't eaten anything today,' I say. 'I missed breakfast and lunch.'

'You order more than family in Thailand eat in one week.'

I can't believe my luck. Of all the waitresses in all the Thai restaurants in this country I have to get the one with a social conscience. Hardly anyone anywhere of any nationality has one any more. But she has. There isn't any reply I can give her that will make sense. But, fortunately, I don't have to because there's a shout from the front of the restaurant and she rises from her seat.

'At least think about what I say,' she hisses, and runs off.

As she hurries away, I call after her, 'Thanks, and could you bring three plates and three sets of cutlery, please?'

Ten minutes later there's still no sign of Tamsin, but the girl and two male waiters arrive at our table with a trolley groaning with food. They unload dish after dish on to the table.

One of the waiters, a tall boy with his hair in a ponytail, places the last on the table and says, 'You eat all this?'

I nod.

He walks away shaking his head.

'Gravy? I don't call this gravy?' says Agnes Ada. 'Don't look nothing like gravy.'

There's an explosion from Uncle Frank as he sprays prawns over the table. 'Bloody hell! This isn't a twenty-five! It's not meant to be hot like this, my mouth's on fire! Here, taste it.'

I'm just forking a prawn into my mouth when one of

184

the jocks next door sticks his head over the carved wood screen separating the two booths and says, in an Australian accent, 'Strewth, you must be one greedy bastard!' He disappears and reappears with another boy beside him. They both stare at me so I feel obliged to carry on eating. It's simpler than trying to explain.

'Amazing he's not fat, really,' says the new jock. Eventually they grow tired of watching me and disappear again. I put my fork down.

'Tut,' says Aunt Clara.

'Thank God for that,' says Agnes Ada. 'At least someone's happy.'

I'm just wondering how much more I can take of this when I look to the front of the restaurant and see Tamsin enter. It's nine thirty.

'I have to go!' I tell my relatives and jump out of my seat. I sit down in a booth across the aisle just as Tamsin arrives.

'Sorry I'm late,' she smiles, though I can tell she isn't.

'You sit this table now?' It's the little waitress.

'Yes,' I say.

'You want I should move food from other table over here?' she asks.

Over her shoulder I can see the Cole family still tucking in.

'Er, could you just leave it where it is?'

'Other food?' asks Tamsin.

'It's too complicated to explain.'

'You go back to other food?'

'No. I mean, yes. Maybe.'

'Could we have a selection of starters, please?' Tamsin says to the waitress. 'And a bottle of the house white?'

The waitress doesn't move. She looks at me. 'You want *more* food?' she says.

'Is there a problem?' says Tamsin.

'No, no problem!' says the little waitress, flapping her arms in frustration. 'Half the world starving, but you just go on eating. Not to worry.'

Tamsin does a double-take at me and looks back at the waitress. 'Oh, and could I have a red prawn curry, please?'

'Red prawn curry? You want *another* red prawn curry? I suppose next you want more rice?'

'Yes, please. Plain boiled, please.'

The waitress stalks off. '*More* rice. As if the three he have already is not enough!'

Tamsin looks as ravishing as I've ever seen her. Her dark hair contrasts with her white T-shirt through which the contours of her small breasts are clearly visible, the dark shadows of her nipples declaring her bra-less. For a moment I wonder if it might be possible to settle all this by simply getting her into the sack but part of me has enough sense to know this is just the white devil newly inside me talking.

'You're looking . . . well.' I'm determined to be charming. If I can keep calm I may be able to end my problems tonight.

'It's a shame it's so hot tonight,' she smiles, teasingly, 'or I'd have put my Arran on, knowing how you feel about knitwear.'

'Ouch!'

The waitress returns with the wine and wine-glasses. She slams the glasses down on the table, a sound echoed by the four jocks across the aisle who are on tequila slammers now.

The waitress pours a taster of wine into my glass.

'It's OK, just pour,' I say.

She tips the bottle angrily and wine gurgles into my glass, some of it slopping on to the tablecloth. She repeats the process for Tamsin.

'Food come in a minute, if you can wait that long!' she snaps, and stomps off.

I take a sip of the wine. It's icy cool. 'Well?'

'Well what?'

'Why did you get me here?'

'I thought the situation was getting out of hand. I wasn't sure I wanted to wreck your career and I thought that if you'd do me a favour . . .'

'I won't give you better grades.'

She laughs. 'My grades are OK, I don't need you for that.'

'Well, what do you need me for?'

'Do you remember that day, in my room?'

'How could I ever forget?'

'Do you remember I said everyone knew about you and the drugs?'

'I – um – I think so.'

'Well, it's true.'

The waitress returns with the trolley, pushed by the ponytailed boy. The girl unloads dishes from it, thumping them down on the table. The boy raises an eyebrow at me but says nothing.

'Enjoy your meal! Don't think about anyone else while you eating it!' The waitress shoves the trolley off up the aisle, banging into carved pillars and dragons en route.

There's a guffaw from across the aisle and I see the jocks are now drinking pints of lager and tequila. They're all very drunk. The Australian sees me looking at them. He stares at the food on our table. 'Shit, man!' he says. 'Let me know when you're going to barf – I'd like to see that.'

Tamsin picks up her chopsticks and expertly lifts a piece from a plate of vegetable tempura. She dips it in chilli sauce and places it in her mouth. She chews delicately and with great concentration, not unlike the way Edward chews, I find myself thinking. This is followed by the uncomfortable thought that she's much nearer in age to my infant son than she is to me and I wonder what on earth I was doing fucking her. Or, rather, not. She begins poking at a minuscule fish cake, then looks up and says, 'Come on, dig in. You may as well, you're paying.'

I pick up a prawn in my chopsticks and dip it into the sauce. I'm not hungry. There's more noise from across the aisle. The jocks are having some kind of drinking contest. One counts, 'One! Two! Three!' and slaps the table, whereupon they all lift mugs of beer to their lips and drink them down in one. One guy, a six-foot-sixer with the overdeveloped laterals of a rower, slaps his mug down on the table and shouts, 'Mine again!'

I look back at Tamsin.

'OK, here it is, then,' she says. 'I have some friends who would like to get hold of some Charlie. They're having difficulty. I need someone to get it for me.'

More noise from the jocks. I turn to look again. Behind them Agnes Ada's talking to Clara, while Uncle Frank keeps looking over his shoulder at the jocks. He has that mad glint in his eye that always used to alarm me when he was alive. When he was alive! What am I thinking about? What's happening here? My head spins. This is just another trick my brain is playing on me, I tell myself. My breathing is laboured, coming in short, unsatisfying gasps. I make myself take a deep breath, right down into the bottom of my lungs. I hold it in, the way you might a hit from a spliff, giving the oxygen time to get through to my brain. It's some strange effect of the coke, that's all it can be. The answer is to anchor myself in the normal world. I avert my gaze from the odd trio and concentrate on the food in front of me. I reach out for my wine-glass but my hand is trembling and in the short journey to my lips it shakes, spilling wine on my sleeve. I take a long draught of wine, all but finishing it. With exaggerated care, the way a drunk might, I set the glass back on the table.

'What?' says Tamsin. 'What's the matter with you? You've gone all funny again.'

'Nothing, I'm perfectly fine.' I struggle out a weak smile. 'Never been better.' I lift the chopsticks and attempt to pick up a piece of tempura. It slides from between them and the sticks cross hopelessly like some virgin's legs on her first date. I make another attempt, but my grip is too feeble and although I manage to grasp the tempura as soon as I raise the sticks it drops back on to the plate. I can feel my blood pumping, my face growing hot. I stick my fingers inside my collar and work them around to loosen it. I try again and this time press too hard. The tempura catapults from between the chopsticks and flies into my lap. My head's pounding. I taste blood where I'm biting my lip. I pick up the tempura with my fingers, place it between the ends of the chopsticks, make sure the grip is solid and transfer the thing to my mouth. I chew it with nervous rapidity and swallow it so fast I have no sensation of tasting anything.

'Perfectly fine,' I say, lifting my head to look at Tamsin, who is staring at me now. I lean forward confidentially. 'What do you think of those people there?' I nod vaguely across the aisle, but more in the direction of my family's table.

Tamsin helps herself to a mini pancake roll before glancing across, so as not to make the action obvious. She turns back to me and shrugs. 'Just four louts. Rowers. Rugby-players. Jocks getting pissed. I don't think anything of them at all. They're not the kind of people who interest me.'

'Tut!' It's so loud I think Tamsin must have heard it. But it's obvious she hasn't, just as it's clear she has seen no one but the four beer drinkers.

I look sideways again. Uncle Frank looks like he's about to leap from his seat and start a fight with them, but Agnes Ada places a restraining hand on his arm. She says something to him that I can't hear and the three of them get on with their meal, though in truth it's difficult to ignore the drinkers now as their volubility is increasing with every round the little waitress brings.

'Well?' says Tamsin.

'Well what?'

'The stuff. Can you get it?'

For a moment I'm carried away by the image of myself as someone who possesses something Tamsin wants and has access to a mysterious, dangerous and illegal trade. But I know this is just an inhaled swagger. My survival instinct takes over. None of this makes sense. I notice a plume of smoke rise up from the booth behind Tamsin and instinctively lower my voice. 'Tamsin, you can buy cocaine in practically any pub or club in this town. There are places you only have to run your hand over the lavatory cistern to get almost enough for a line. People deal in the halls of residence. Why would you need to ask me?'

She concentrates just a little too hard on picking up another tempura and dipping it in chilli sauce. She puts it into her mouth and chews it thoughtfully. There's a smear of red sauce on her lip, bright as arterial blood.

'It's the amount I need. A hundred grams.'

I whistle. 'That's a lot of coke. You're talking three grand.' I like the way it feels in my mouth. Three grand. In any other context – say, buying a car, or a house or discussing expenditure at work – I would talk in thousands of pounds. But already I'm adjusting my language to suit its unaccustomed lowlife métier.

'Yes, but can you get it?'

The boast is out before I can stop it. It's the coke talking. Talking about more coke. 'Of course I can get it. A hundred grams wouldn't be a problem to me.' Immediately I've said it I know I shouldn't have. I watch Tamsin chase the last tempura round the dish and snare it. She smiles at me as she places it between her lips.

Across the aisle they're having more tequila slammers, banging their glasses on the table. The little waitress is wringing her hands and looking anxiously at the equally small barman.

'I can get it, but I'm not saying I will.'

Tamsin fixes my eye. There's more uproar next door. I glance across. All three drinkers are focused on the fourth, who has a pint of lager in front of him. One of them holds a stopwatch. Uncle Frank is half out of his chair.

Tamsin puts her hand on my wrist. 'Well, if you don't, Professor Cole, you're going to be out of a job. I'm offering you a way out. Let me spell it out. The moment I get the coke I withdraw my evidence from the committee. We're both happy.'

'You want me to *give* you the coke? That's blackmail.'

She smiles. 'Don't be silly, of course not. Cash on delivery, isn't that how it usually works? Come on now, what do you say?'

'I don't seem to have much choice.'

'You're cheating, you bastard!' yells one of the jocks. 'You took a breath there. All in one go it's meant to be.'

I glance across and see Uncle Frank pick a prawn from his plate and flick it back over his head towards the booth behind him. I can't see where it ends up because one of the jocks is obscuring my view.

'Who did that?' screams the big jock. He looks across at the boy he was berating a moment earlier. 'I don't like people throwing food at me, you bastard.' He picks up the plate of milky yellow curry in front of him and pushes it, silent-screen custard-pie style into the face of the other man. The other guy struggles against the press of the plate, then manages to push it off. He stands up, his chair tipping over behind him.

'You're asking for it, cuntface!' He grabs the other by his sweatshirt and pulls him across the table. The Australian, who's next to him, tries to restrain him but he shakes him off, releases the first guy and punches the Aussie instead. In a moment a bottle is broken and fists are flying. Broken glass showers across our table.

'This is turning ugly,' I say, as sirens start screaming. 'Let's get out of here.' I'm desperate to be gone. If this should end up as an item in the local newspaper, I do not want to be mentioned as one of the witnesses, and especially not as the one having dinner with Tamsin Graves. I fling banknotes at the barman and steer Tamsin towards the door. Turning back I see two men rising from the booth behind ours. They move purposefully over to the drunks and one grabs the troublemaker in an arm lock. Suddenly I realize I've seen the duo before. The car outside the playground. The one that followed Tommo, Tim and me. They're policemen.

The little waitress holds the door open for us. 'Thank you, come again,' she says, with crisp formality, then tacks on, in a whisper, 'Capitalist pig!'

I guide Tamsin out of the door, my hand on her waist. She removes it. 'Please,' she says, shooting me a disparaging look.

We're no sooner outside than she hails a passing minicab and is in it before I can stop her. 'Remember, Michael,' she says, as she's about to close the door, 'I talk to the committee Thursday next week. Unless I have the goods the day before.'

The door slams and I'm left standing in the dark wondering what I'm doing here tonight, wondering what I'll do about Tamsin's request, but most of all wondering about that hard rectangular shape I felt in the small of her back which I know could not possibly have been a blood-pressure monitor.

I glance back through the restaurant window. As I expected, besides the waiters there are only the four boys, seated again at their table now, as one cop talks to them and the other speaks into a mobile phone. There is, of course, no trace of my family. As I start the car I try to remember what that boy said before he attacked the other. Did he mention something hitting him? And if so, could it have been something thrown by one of the other boys? Could it all come down to this, I ask myself, the existence of an afterlife dependent on a red hot prawn?

I head towards the gym, which isn't far away. I may as well drop in on the off-chance Tommo will be there. He often is at this time of night. I can sound him out about the drugs. I fear entrapment and yet, if there's the slightest chance that Tamsin's request is genuine, I want to seize it and recover my job.

It's been raining and the car glides between the pools of light around the street lamps with an eerie hiss.

The gym is in part of an old red-brick warehouse, an unprepossessing building, functional rather than attractive. Which is a pretty good description of the gym itself. It's not the sort of place anyone (me, for instance) would go to find young women in buttock-cleaving leotards. In fact, there are no women members. I discovered the place a year or so ago when my blood pressure first became a potential problem.

'Get some exercise, join a health club,' Branko told me. I called up several and this was the cheapest, so I ended up here. But just as it has no fashionably attired women members, it also has no flashy reception area, no salad-serving restaurant, no shop dispensing sweat-bands, leotards and squash racquets. In short, it's not a health club, it's a gym. The clientele are mainly boxers, a few office workers, slumming it by coming here to slug it out with the one or two professional boxers who frequent the place (mainly to relive their old fights with Ted the barman, ducking and weaving as they drink), and Big Boys, guys who have no interest in fitness but have become hooked on muscle-building to the extent that their bodies are now muscle-bound, thighs so swollen they can hardly walk, biceps so enormous they have to hold their arms out from their sides. Steve Reeves and then some. And then, of course, there's me.

My first time here I met Tommo. I was lying on my back attempting feebly to lift the weight from the rack above me. I suspected this wasn't what I was meant to be doing, that hypertensives should not be lifting heavy weights, but that was all the Big Boys were doing. Some were lying on their backs like me while others stood above them, taking the load of the weight until they were ready to hold it themselves, then slowly releasing it into their expert hands, accompanied by the sound of the supine fellows' sharp exhalations. Others stood hefting hand weights but with a practised ritual I knew was beyond me.

I felt like a young girl at her first dance, ignorant of the latest steps and afraid to take the floor. I had a strong desire not to stand out, to be accepted by this new knotty-sinewed clan, so I eschewed the conspicuousness of the bike and treadmill and lay down under a bar loaded with weights. I began to push up, allowing myself a couple of outward pants of breath.

The bar didn't move. I pushed up again. Still nothing. I closed my eyes, gritted my teeth and pushed once more. I could feel myself growing hot, my muscles tightening. And then, suddenly, the bar lifted. For a moment I was struck with wonder. I'd done it! What had seemed impossibly heavy a second or so earlier now felt as light as a feather! I'd only been a gym member a matter of minutes and already my strength had improved!

'I wouldn't do that if I were you, sunshine,' said a deep voice. At the same time I felt a tug on the bar and realized it was moving higher than I was lifting it. I opened my eyes and found Tommo's shaven head inverted above me. He smiled. 'I think,' he said, 'you could do with a little help.'

After that we had a nodding acquaintance. Occasionally, when I'd pinned myself to the floor with an over-ambitious barbell, he'd pluck it off with one finger and rescue me. But that was about it.

Until I left the club late one night and came upon shadowy figures in the car park. There were three young guys – one of whom was sitting astride a bulky shape on the ground – who, I'm sure, could I have seen them in daylight, would have had all the major risk factors: shaved heads, tattoos (probably facial) and multi-piercings. They certainly had the worst, because moonlight glinted from the knives in their hands. At the sound of my footsteps they looked up, startled, and I thought I was about to be mugged. Then my eyes grew accustomed to the dim light, and the shape on the ground was transformed into Tommo. I wondered how such slight youths – even three of them – could have got the better of him until I noticed the black pool beneath his head and realized they must have taken him by surprise and struck him on the back of the head.

I was relieved to see his eyes were open, and surprised, when they met mine, to see in them the appeal of a frightened animal. 'Help me!' he called, stranded on his back like a beetle.

I stood transfixed, mesmerized by the light flickering from the blades. The three thugs stared at me expectantly.

'Help me!' called Tommo again.

I was unable to move. I wanted to tell him, I don't do helping. I don't do altruism. I don't do risking serious injury.

'Help me!' This time his voice was reduced to a croak, the diminution in volume expressing his loss of hope in me.

I was about to turn and run when inspiration seized me. I plunged my hand into my pocket, took out my wallet, extracted my university library ID card, which bears my photograph, and flashed it at them.

'Police!' I shouted, striding boldly towards them. The one sitting on Tommo rose shakily to his feet. For a split second they looked at one another and then, without a word, scattered across the car park and melted into the night. I returned library card to wallet, wallet to pocket, and helped the still-dazed Tommo to his feet, reflecting, not for the first time in my life, on the many – and often surprising – uses of literacy.

About a week later Tommo came up to me in the gym bar and said, 'If you was wanting to build up your muscles, I can get you something that'd help. You'd look good in a matter of weeks.'

'No, thanks,' I said, 'I've decided to give up the weights. It's bad for my blood pressure. But I could do with something to give me a lift . . .'

Tommo is in the bar tonight. I tell him what I need. I promise him the money in a couple of days.

'What's all this, Michael?' he asks. 'Sounds like a bit more than personal use.'

'It's a work thing,' I tell him. 'I need it for work.'

As I drive home my head is swimming from the events of the day. I'm breathless and dizzy as I climb the stairs to my study. I sit in the dark for a long hour clutching the packet of beta-blockers I was given when I cashed in Branko's prescription. I'm frightened of taking them, but I'm even more frightened of not. I press the back of the foil sheet and ease out a pill. I take out my Scotch, pour myself a slug, and wash the tablet down.

FOURTEEN

Come, Madam, come, all rest my powers defy,
Until I labour, I in labour lie.
The foe oft-times, having the foe in sight,
Is tired with standing though they never fight.

To his Mistress Going to Bed

I wake next morning with a sense of something different about me. I know immediately it's more than the mist of free-floating anxiety that shrouds all my days. It's as though overnight I've morphed into something else and gingerly I touch my head, examining it as a blind man might, fearful I may feel a pair of Kafkaesque antennae or a proboscis or some other evidence of transformation. But all is normal. Gradually the sleep clears from my eyes and the feeling of unease begins to evaporate with it. From beside me comes the reassuringly irritating whistle of Alison's low-grade snore. Sunlight leaks in around the edges of the blinds. I steal from the bed, careful not to wake Alison and pad to the en suite. There it is again, something not quite right. For a moment I wonder if Branko's dire predictions have come true and I've suffered a stroke during the night. I examine myself in the mirror, half expecting to find one side of my face frozen. I mouth the first lines of 'Air and Angels',

'Twice or thrice had I loved thee, before I knew thy face or name . . .', to make sure I haven't lost the power of speech. The visage peering anxiously back at me from the mirror is at least mobile and symmetrical or, anyway, as symmetrical as it has ever been.

I turn, lift the lavatory seat and begin to pee, and then I realize. The Old Soldier in my hand is not as he has been at reveille for at least these last forty-five years, which is as long as I can remember. Instead of his swinging exuberance as I walked to the loo he was dangling listlessly. For the first time in my conscious life I've woken without an erection. Puzzled, I return to the bedroom and regard myself in the full-length mirror. The glass shows a tall white figure. Face lined with anxiety. Hair grey and retreating, revealing a domed forehead, which speaks of intelligence. The shoulders and upper torso not exactly fleshy, but definitely slack. The abundant chest hair grizzled. Further down a slight but growing paunch shades the object of my attention: a curled pink invertebrate bearing no resemblance to the Old Soldier's stiff-backed, ready-for-action military bearing.

I creep back to bed and as I lie there pondering the state of my penis I'm suddenly aware that my mouth is dry, my teeth furred; running the tip of my tongue over them gives me an image of standing stones coated with moss. For a moment I wonder why. I didn't drink much last night, or no more than usual, so it can't be that. And then my brain finishes its morning stretching and yawning and gets to work, I remember the tablet I took and know right away why my penis isn't working.

At first despair creeps over me as I contemplate the bleak choices offered by my condition and its treatment. On the one hand, according to Branko – and I have no reason to doubt him – certain death. On the other, another kind of demise, the ending of my life as

199

a man. I lift the covers. 'It's death or dishonour, old friend,' I whisper, to the spineless wretch lying at the fork of my legs. But then another thought strikes me. Waking without an erection, while not normal, is far from the same as being incapable of one at all. It may, may it not, be possible to have the best of both worlds? To take my medicine and still have a penis that functions, albeit not spontaneously.

I begin to caress the Old Soldier but after several minutes he remains resolutely irresolute, sliding evasively about inside his skin, giving me the distinct impression that could he but speak he would say, 'Leave me alone. I'm not interested in all that any more.' I switch hands, in an attempt to fool him that we've got lucky, but he doesn't buy it. Nothing happens.

So I decide to enlist the aid of fantasy, or rather history, since with my record I have no need to overtax my imagination; what I require is already in the files.

I select a favourite from my undergraduate days, an encounter with a beautiful Asian medical student whose overdeveloped bosom and bottom had earned her a part-time job as a croupier at the Playboy Club. Of course what I replay now is not so much the actual tryst as it occurred but the digitized perfection of it, remastered and edited for maximum effect. I've seen this version so many times it would be fair to say I've lost the original plot. I watch as Jodie (that was her exotically unlikely name) sits on my bed and struggles frantically to undo the laces of her over-the-knee black boots before pulling off her hot-pants (yes, it was that long ago!) and tearing off my clothes. There is a delicious moment when she frees the raw Young Recruit (as he was then) from my underpants – which takes two attempts because she has underestimated his bulk – and marvels at his size (remember, this is the director's cut) before straddling me and impaling herself upon his rigid pylon.

'Oh, oh,' she gasps, 'I can feel you right inside me,' a line that almost certainly wasn't in the original 1970 version of the script.

As Jodie humps my younger self, bleating in ecstasy (dubbed, of course), my older watching self becomes aware of a weightiness in his hand. Something is stirring down below. I pause the movie and lift the covers for a quick peep. Nothing very discernible yet, but still, a clear sign the wires are not all down, something is getting through.

I drop the covers, shut my eyes and, by a super-human suspension of disbelief, transmogrify my gnarled old fist into Jodie's silky young vulva. She's bouncing up and down on me now in time to the Stones' 'Brown Sugar', which seems to have kicked in on the soundtrack while I've been away, a sure sign of directorial duplicity since the record hadn't been released at the time of the events my memory is replaying here.

'You're so—' gasps Jodie on the upswing. 'Uhhhh!' she sinks down on me. 'Big! Just so – uhhhh . . . hard! You're just so—'

Her face freezes and then disappears as I shut off the film and open my eyes to peer under the sheets again. Sure enough the Old Soldier is bursting out of my fist, a stand-up guy, ready for action, and looking as though his temporary insubordination never happened.

I pad over to the full-length mirror for a critical examination. Has he always pointed quite so much towards the floor? Is there a slight flaccid quality about him? Is his tip perhaps a bit less bulbous than its norm?

I walk back to the bed and stand by Alison's side. I reach down and shake her shoulder. She mutters something and tries to brush off my hand. I grip her tighter and shake her again. 'Wake up, there's something I want to show you!' I hiss, not wishing to wake the boys along the corridor.

'Whassamatter?'

'Take a look at this!'

Her eyes open and she finds herself staring at my erect penis, its tip three inches from her face. 'Very nice.'

'Well, what do you think of it?'

'I've seen it before. Now let me go back to sleep.'

'You don't understand. What would you say about its hardness? Is it really hard, do you think?'

'Well hard. Now put it away and let me sleep.'

'You don't understand. Feel it.'

'Michael, the boys will be awake any minute, I'm not in the mood for this now. Maybe Saturday night.'

'I don't want to fuck you. I just want your opinion. Have a feel of it.'

Eyes closed she stretches out her hand and envelops the Old Soldier's shaft.

'Well?' I say.

'OK, OK.' And her hand begins moving back and forth in synchronicity with the whistle and snore of her incoming and outgoing breath.

'Oh, well,' I tell myself, my mood a mixture of celebration and relief, 'might as well make sure the rest of it's working too.'

FIFTEEN

O how feeble is man's power,
That if good fortune fall,
Cannot add another hour,
Nor a lost hour recall!

Song

Uncle Frank whistled as he tossed tools into the back of his old Ford pick-up. We were parked beside his house in Ely, the one he'd shared with Aunt Lois until she'd upped and left him. The pick-up was backed up to the open garage doors where he kept his tools. The inside of the garage looked like a junk heap to me, with tools and bits of wood strewn all over the floor, but Uncle Frank seemed to know where most things were.

'Now where the fuck did I put that saw?' he muttered to himself, toeing a plank out of his way. He caught me looking at him and paused to raise a finger at me. 'Listen, boy, don't you go telling your grandma I used the F-word. You didn't hear me say that, OK?'

I nodded.

He picked up the saw, lifted it and blew sawdust off it. It reminded me of gun-fighters on TV blowing their smoking guns after shooting someone. 'Better put this saw horse in too,' he said, hefting it over the tailboard.

He looked across at me. 'That can be your kin job, carrying it up the tower. I int carrying it up two hundred and sixteen feet, I can kin tell you. Shit! I done it again. Michael, don't mention the F-word!'

I hadn't actually registered that he had sworn again. Uncle Frank had swearing down to such a refined art that he'd honed the adjectival form of the F-word to a truncated last syllable – 'kin', rather like a bit of wood he'd planed down to almost nothing, taking the roughness off it. So half the time people never even realized he was cursing.

You could even have argued that technically he wasn't, but that didn't cut much ice with him. My father's younger brother was the apple of his mother's eye and he was paranoid about anything that might take the shine off her shimmering image of him. Actually, he was pretty well paranoid about everything, but that's something else. Right now he slammed the tailgate of the pick-up and snapped his braces with satisfaction. I slipped my thumbs under the bright red braces I'd put on specially today because I was working with him and imitated the gesture, although not the sound. I didn't have it off properly yet.

I climbed into the passenger side of the pick-up cab and sat back with my feet on the dashboard. Uncle Frank clambered in a minute later.

'Get your feet the fuck off the kin dash,' he barked, lifting his boot and kicking them sideways. He leaned over and flicked the dash with his fingertips. He spat on his fingers and rubbed at it, revealing the shiny imitation wood beneath. The dash was covered by an archaeological thickness of dust, empty cigarette packets, cigarette coupons, dead flies, a Swiss army knife, a pile of pocket-sized Commando war comic books, Wrigley's chewing-gum wrappers and, here and there, pink rocks of chewed-out gum, stuck so hard you couldn't pry them off with your fingers. I wondered if that was what the Swiss army knife was for, not that I'd have dared ask.

As the exhaust of my Golf would be so many years later, the pick-up's was holed and we set off with a sports-car roar. Uncle Frank turned and grinned at me. When he smiled you could see why women liked him – women who didn't know him, that was. He was handsome. He wore beaten-up old jeans and a tight white T-shirt that showed off his muscles. He liked to keep his cigarette packet tucked in the short sleeve of his T-shirt, something he'd seen Marlon Brando do in a film. He fancied he looked like Brando and some-times he'd be driving along when he'd suddenly start looking in the rear-view mirror, pulling faces at him-self, and say, 'What d'you reckon? Marlon Brando, right?'

Of course I'd agree. Why upset him when you could avoid it?

'You really think so? You're not just saying that?' He'd shoot me an anxious glance.

'Oh, yes!' I'd nod enthusiastically – anything to get his eyes back on the road.

But he'd just look in the mirror again and push his lips out in what he imagined was a Brandoesque smile. 'I guess you're right. Yeah, I can see what you're talking about now.'

In truth, of course, he looked nothing like Brando. When I think about it now, if he resembled any film actor it would be Jack Nicholson, in his edgy, nervy *One Flew Over the Cuckoo's Nest* days. Of course, we didn't know about Nicholson then. He became a star long after Uncle Frank drove his Mini Cooper S into a tree at sixty miles an hour, a difficult feat to achieve in the Fens where you really had to go looking to find a tree. Anyway, Uncle Frank was almost as good-looking as the young Nicholson, assuming you ignored the livid red zip across the top of his skull where his hair was thinning and the scar showed through.

Right now he put the radio on: Max Bygraves singing 'I'm A Blue Toothbrush', one of my favourites. Uncle Frank switched it off with an angry twist of the dial. 'Kin Jew boy!' The gears seemed to snarl as he crashed them. 'That's all you get on the radio or the telly. Hitler had the right idea about them.'

I didn't say anything. I'd read *The Diary of Anne Frank*, but I wasn't up to taking on Uncle Frank on behalf of persecuted peoples.

He stuck out his left hand so fast I flinched. I thought he was going to hit me, but it turned out he was just reaching for one of the war comics.

'Talking about the war,' we hadn't been but that didn't matter to Uncle Frank, 'you should read this. Wolf Troop. It's about an élite corps of the Waffen SS. They dress up like Americans to infiltrate Allied lines. Crack troops. Incredible courage. You have to hand it to those men. They should've won the war. If the kin yellow-bellied Japs hadn't attacked the Yanks and brought them in, they kin would've too.'

Given his history, Uncle Frank's admiration for Hitler and all things Nazi should have been surprising, except, of course, he was a lunatic. Surprising because, indirectly, Hitler was responsible for his lunacy. Uncle Frank had been blown up during basic training by a faulty grenade. At least, that was the official version, the way Agnes Ada told it. Rumour in the village, substantiated by a number of people in the same unit, including a couple who claimed to have witnessed the incident, insisted Frank Cole had always been a mad bugger and a typical bit of craziness, him trying to hit a live grenade with a piece of wood, pretending he was playing cricket, had led to his injury. Whatever, he came out of the war after only three weeks in it with a metal plate in his head and a disability pension.

'You said the F-word.'

His left hand dropped the comic book and flew at me so fast I didn't see it coming. It beat me around the head and face in such a flurry of blows it was like being attacked by a demented bird.

When it had finished it started pointing at me. 'Don't let me ever hear you say anything to anybody about what I might or might not have said, got it?'

I didn't answer and the hand took off and hit me again. 'Got it?'

'Got it.' I sniffed.

We parked alongside the Dean's meadow and went into the cathedral through the south door. As we strode along the nave, we passed a cleric in a long grey cassock who spotted Uncle Frank's tool-bag and said, 'Hello, come to do some work?'

'Carpenter,' Uncle Frank replied. 'They asked me to have a look at the flagpole.'

'Ah, yes, I remember now.' He smiled at me. 'See you've brought your assistant. Hello, young man. Going up the west tower, are you?'

I didn't say anything. Uncle Frank had his hand on my shoulder. The bird he'd been slapping me with a few minutes ago was now a claw, and it squeezed my shoulder hard, pinching up the flesh behind. 'Say hello, Michael,' said Uncle Frank.

'Hello,' I muttered to the marbled floor.

Another squeeze. 'Ow!' I said, under my breath.

'The gentleman asked you a question, Michael.'

'Yes,' I said. Uncle Frank released me and suddenly, without thinking, I took off down the nave, heading for the west door.

'Hey, come back!' called Uncle Frank. I stopped

just inside the entrance and turned back to see him shrugging and saying something to the clergyman. They walked towards me.

'Children don't understand about churches, they just want to have fun, don't they?' said the cleric. 'How old are you, young man?'

I didn't answer. 'Nine,' growled Uncle Frank.

I finished the labyrinth and dodged past Uncle Frank again.

'Michael, come back here!' he called, but even he couldn't yell his head off in a cathedral so it came out as a whispered shout, which echoed eerily off the limestone Norman arches.

I heard the clink of metal as he set down his tool-bag and the strident ring of his feet on the stone floor as he came after me. He caught up with me in the Lady Chapel. He strode in like he was going to kill me, but then caught sight of the middle-aged woman, a tourist by the look of her, sitting in one of the wall niches. Somehow, even without her, I would have felt safe here. There was too much light coming in from the windows on all four sides. Uncle Frank would have felt too exposed to hurt me here.

'Come *on*!' he hissed.

'I want to find the one with the head,' I said.

Suddenly he was all smiles. 'All right, why not? Let's see if we can find the one old Cromwell missed.'

There were statues all around the walls of the chapel but nearly all of them had been decapitated and otherwise despoiled during the Reformation. It was a popular local misconception to blame this vandalism on Oliver Cromwell, whose former house stood on the other side of the cathedral green.

'There!' I said, and we both looked up to see the head of the Green Man, peering out between stone tendrils in the frieze above the main statuary. His pagan face contemplated us with a malevolent grin that when I eventually turned to look up at Uncle Frank's face, was not unlike the smile I saw there.

He marched me swiftly back to the west tower, where he bundled me through a small archway and we began climbing stone steps.

'I should tan your hide for what you just did,' he whispered behind me, and I scampered up the damp-smelling twisting spiral staircase as if I had a terrier at my heels. We came to a small landing. I was out of breath. I turned to face him.

'Nobody here to help you now, Michael. Not so cheeky now, huh?' His hand flicked out at me, quick as a lizard's tongue, and I ducked before I realized he had never intended to hit me.

He laughed at my cowardly reflex and it was that, the humiliation of being so tricked, that made me suddenly bold. Our positions were those of Jim Hawkins and Israel Hands in my favourite colour plate in the mobile library's copy of *Treasure Island*. Hands is pursuing Jim up the mast of the *Hispaniola* and Jim has turned to face him, pointing the pistol down at him, and the caption reads. 'One more step, Mr Hands, and I'll blow your brains out.'

Of course I couldn't say that. I had no pistol. So I clutched the only weapon I had. 'Hit me again,' I said, my voice so throaty with fear that for a second I wondered if any sound was coming out, 'hit me again and I'll tell Grandma you used the F-word.'

He started towards me. 'I mean it! I mean it!' I screamed. 'You hurt me again, and I'll tell her about every time I've heard you say it!'

He stood staring at me. His eyes were black holes in the dim light. We must have been like that for a good half-minute. It seemed hours.

Suddenly he shrugged and broke into a smile. 'OK,

Michael, I guess I just got a bit carried away. Didn't mean to hurt you. Sorry. Now, can we get up here and get the job done?'

We climbed the rest of the way to the top of the west tower and I stood looking out for miles in every direction, thinking that since the cathedral was often called the Ship of the Fens I was right up in the crow's nest, just like Jim Hawkins. Occasionally Uncle Frank would have me pass him something as he worked at repairing the struts supporting the flagpole. At one point he left me alone to go back down for some timber. After he'd been gone ten minutes or so I suddenly had the feeling he wasn't coming back. What if he locked the door at the bottom on me? Would I be able to make anyone hear? And if not, how would I get down? I tried to peer over the crenellated walls, to see if it was possible to climb down, but I wasn't tall enough to see anything. I started to panic. What if he'd left? What if I were up here all night? Would there be ghosts? I could see the cemetery stones down below. What if those people came out at night? What about all the monks who had lived and died here? What of Hereward's men, slain resisting the Normans?

Then Uncle Frank was back. He'd not only brought the timber but our dockey bags too, and we sat at the highest point we could, at the foot of the flagpole, and ate our sandwiches while he pointed out and named all the villages we could see.

It was three or four hours after we'd gone up that the job was finished and I'd had a good day. The early discord had been forgotten and Uncle Frank had been funny, telling me jokes and singing. It would be something to tell Owen and my friends about, going right to the top of the cathedral and helping mend the flagpole.

On the way down, Uncle Frank, who was ahead,

stopped by a wooden door. 'Let's take a look through here for a minute,' he said.

He opened it and I followed him out into what must have been the upper gallery. On one side was the outer wall of the building, on the other a single metal rail where the floor ended. The area between was full of rubbish. A tarpaulin. Some loose timbers. A pile of rubble.

'Take a look,' said Uncle Frank. 'You can see right down into the cathedral.'

I wasn't sure. The single metal rail didn't seem a lot to have between me and what must have been at least a sixty-foot drop.

'Go on,' he urged. 'It's your last chance. It might be years before I get another job to do here. This bit's not open to the public. Something to tell your friends.'

Cautiously, almost sliding my feet, I made my way over to the edge. The rail was high, obviously put there for adults. I could practically have walked under it. I clutched it tightly with both hands. It was cold and clammy with that damp that goes with old buildings. I bent my head and looked down. Far, far below I could see people. They seemed not much bigger than ants. I looked across and saw the opposite wall and suddenly had a horrifying sense of the nothingness between. I looked down again, my eyes shinning down the facing wall. My head started to go a little dizzy, almost as if I were moving it round and round. I needed to stop looking at this before I was compelled to jump and then there was a hand on my back, propelling me forward into empty space and I realized I'd relaxed my hold on the metal pole and now, under the force of the push, my hands just let go and I went under it. I was falling, falling forward.

And then all at once I was bouncing back. My feet were still on the edge of the precipice and the rest of me was being tugged back to the vertical. But I'd no sooner got upright again than I was off once more, tipping forward again, and this time I didn't spring back, I just hung there. There was a sharp biting pain in my shoulders and I realized what was going on. Uncle Frank was holding me by my braces.

'Ha, Michael! That fooled you!' He laughed. 'Had you going there, boy!'

'Help!' I screamed. 'Help!' Down below people continued walking around, no one could hear. There was a flash of movement before me and I watched as a swallow flew the length of the nave. I had the giddy sensation of looking down on the bird's back as it passed.

But I wasn't thinking about the bird. I wasn't thinking about the people down below, who I knew would not be able to reach me in time should I fall. I was thinking abut Aunt Clara, who had died the year before. More precisely, what I was thinking was, How long have I had these jeans? When did Mum buy me these braces? I was trying and trying to think, was it before or after Aunt Clara died?

I hung like that for what seemed like hours, but was probably no longer than it took the swallow to fly the length of the nave, 248 feet. Years later I would come across Bede's likening of the brevity of a human life to the flight of a sparrow through a mead hall. I knew nothing of that then. All I knew at that moment – for the very first time – was that death was something that could happen to me and one day would.

Having given me this gift, Uncle Frank jerked the braces and hauled me upright. Shaking, I flung my arms around him, clinging on for dear life. Seizing a handful of my hair in his fist, he pulled up my head to look at him.

'Michael, you had them same jeans on the day Clara

died. Don't you remember you wore them with the cuffs turned up because they were too long? And I sat and watched her going over those braces myself. So what were you worried about?'

'I won't mention it! Uncle Frank, I won't mention the F-word to anyone ever again!' I whimpered.

He ruffled my hair. 'No,' he said. 'I don't think you will, Michael. I don't think you will.'

SIXTEEN

But since that I
Must die at last, 'tis best,
To use myself in jest
Thus by feigned deaths to die.

Song

Beta-blocked and consequently calm, especially now that the Old Soldier has been tested in the line of fire, as it were, and not found wanting, and is – justifiably – at ease after his exertions, I'm ready to face the day. But what sort of day will it be? I have no job to go to, but I cannot stay at home: I have not confessed my suspension to Alison. This is not, of course, because of the questions about my employment prospects and our consequent financial future it would throw up, but chiefly that were I to do so I would have to disclose the reasons for it. How can I admit seducing (no, worse, failing to!) a student and *thereby* jeopardizing all our futures? It's this thoughtless recklessness for which Alison will berate me rather than the infidelity itself – although we will both know it's the latter that matters to her most.

So I say my morning goodbyes as usual. I get into the car, which yesterday I parked around the corner out of sight, and instantly the boxes of books on the back seat are a weighty reminder of my new status. Perhaps I could be a new kind of visiting academic? One who just drops in on different educational establishments, complete with mobile library, delivers a lecture or two and departs. I'm relieved to find that in spite of the car having been parked on the street all night in what is, according to signs on the lampposts, a High Crime Area, nothing has been stolen. Not that I expected it to be. Why would people who can't read steal books?

In the absence of any direction from me, the car sets off on its usual route towards campus. I realize this is the last place I want to be. I'm not *allowed* to be there, for a start. And then it hits me: I have literally nowhere to go. Cole's occupation's gone. His willy won't work unaided any more and his occupation's gone! For the first time in thirty years, I don't know what to do with myself. I drive around aimlessly or, rather, sit aimlessly in morning rush-hour traffic jams, in beta-blocked mode, feeling superior to the poor wretches in the cars beside me, biting their nails and desperately watching their clocks. I enjoy the look of surprise on their faces when I let them out of side roads, smiling beatifically all the while. You can see them thinking, Who is this nut, this innocent abroad, who doesn't know to cut people up?

Eventually the traffic thins. Everyone else has gone to work, leaving me, and a few school-run mums who lingered too long chatting at the school gates after dropping off, the only people on the road.

I head out to the ring road and drive around it a couple of times, which kills another forty minutes. The irony of me, who fears each tick of the clock, being so profligate with time!

Eventually I wear out most of the morning in this weary way and then, in a fit of generosity, partly born of guilt and partly from affection for the selfless and uncomplaining way she (albeit unconsciously) manipulated my member earlier on, I phone Alison, make up an excuse about my tutorials being cancelled and offer to take her shopping.

I park my bookmobile around the corner and use the excuse of Alison's car already having the child seats in it to take hers. But if I expected to escape my sense of doom, I was wrong. The conversation in the back of the car during the short journey is enough to remind me how early the dread arrives. How our awareness of self has barely registered before there emerges a conplementary understanding of our eventual demise. It goes like this:

Jake: 'I'm four and a half now, I'm a big boy.'

Edward: 'Well, what am I, Yake?' (In spite of Edward's phenomenal speaking abilities he has occasional difficulties as though someone put them there just to remind you how young he is. The chiefest being he cannot pronounce the letter J and it comes out as a Y, rendering one of his most uttered words as 'Yake').

Jake: 'Well, you're not a baby. That's obvious.'

Edward: 'Why am I not a baby?'

Jake: 'Well, because you don't lie about screaming waagh! waagh! waagh! all the time and you can talk.'

Edward: 'Am I a toddler, then, Yake?'

Jake: 'No, you're not a toddler because you don't toddle.'

Edward: 'What is toddle?'

Jake: 'It's when you're really little and you've only been walking a little while and you wobble all over the place and fall over a lot. Anyway, you're not a toddler because you can talk properly and you don't wear nappies.'

Edward: 'So what am I, then, Yake?'

216

Jake: 'Well, you're not a baby and you're not a toddler and you're not a big boy so you're not anything. I'm a big boy, but you're nothing. That's what you are, you're just nothing.'

In the rear-view mirror I see Edward's lower lip begin to tremble. Jake starts talking about other things. We're stuck in traffic. I put a tape on. Eventually the tape reaches the end of the side and there's silence until a small voice from behind croaks, 'I *am* something. I'm Edward.'

Alison turns to me and mouths, 'Oh!' at me, a gesture I automatically mirror, the parental bond for a moment overcoming our continuing marital strife.

Jake must sense something of the pathos of Edward's statement, too, and in his customary good-hearted way seeks to make amends, by playing up the compensatory advantages of Edward's less significant place in the family.

'Anyway, I'm two years older than you and I'll always be two years older than you.'

'But, Yake, what about when I'm four too?'

'When you're four, I'll be six and when you're six I'll be eight and when you're eight I'll be ten . . .' It goes on and on like this.

'. . . and when you're a hundred and four I'll be a hundred and six and I'll probably die then but you'll still have two more years left. We'll never be the same age and I'll die two years before you do.'

A long silence. In the rear-view mirror I see Edward's brow creased in concentration until finally he speaks.

'I don't want you to die, Yake.'

If shopping is the new religion, then the mall is its cathedral. It's here we come when we need solace and comfort. We find it not in silence and dark contemplative corners but in harsh lighting and brash

217

noise. Ely Cathedral took more than a century to build. The men who began it knew they would never see its completion. An act of faith. The builders of our modern-day church threw it up in a couple of years. They need a quick return on their cash. They don't have centuries to spare. And in a decade or two when its shape and décor begin to date they'll tear it down and build anew. *Sic transit gloria*.

The present architects are practical men. They have dispensed with transepts and the concept of the cross. They don't want corners that are difficult for security cameras to scan. It's all nave here.

We emerge from the basement car park on to the floor of the nave where, for contemplative souls, the architects have thoughtfully provided a fountain so that, should you wish, you may sit down by its waters and rest. And it is much used! Every space on the wall around the water is occupied by a teenager, each contemplating the text message on his or her mobile phone. Or yelling invocations into it to whoever is out there: 'I'm at the mall!' 'I'm at the mall!' 'I'm at the mall!' they shout. We take the long escalator, the one that travels from bottom to top with no stops en route. Up we go. Past galleries of shops. Past Gap and Next and Racing Green! Past Warner Brothers and Boots and Body Shop! Above us is the Plexiglas roof in which is set a circle of coloured plastic, mimicking stained glass, depicting not God or a prophet or an angel but something that looks curiously like the head of a cockerel. An unexplained, mystic symbol to give us food for thought.

But it's tangible food we're after, for the escalator stops short of the stars and deposits us on the top floor, where a large sign tells us this is where to take the sacrament. It manages this without words: a picture of a plate, flanked by knife and fork, conveys the message.

The Peterborough stone masons who cut the blocks for Ely Cathedral could not read or write. Each put his own mark upon the blocks he shaped to assure correct payment. A thousand years later we have delved thousands of years back into the past to communicate with those who do not read and write – save for text messages – and returned to pictograms. Other pictures tell us where to make a phone call, where to pee and where to change our babies. All without words. It makes me look again at the stained-plastic cockerel and wonder what the message I'm not getting is.

The Food Court, as the mall guide says it's called, features a number of 'outlets', each offering different fare. Chinese, Mexican, Italian, Fish 'n' Chips, Burgers, Deli. I opt for cholesterol-enriched fish and chips, the boys both want pizza and Alison salad, which means I have to queue three times while she sits and watches the children.

Twenty minutes later I return with fish and chips (cold), pizza (cold) and salad (warm and limp). Edward eyes his pizza suspiciously when I plonk it in front of him. 'Is this pizza vegetarian?' he asks.

'Yes, of course it's vegetarian,' I tell him.

'Are you sure it's vegetarian?' he says.

'Of course, now eat up.'

'But can I trust you, Daddy? How do I know you're not trying to smuggle meat into me?'

'Daddy wouldn't do that, darling,' says Alison, with what strikes me as totally misplaced confidence in someone who is already contemplating smuggling an office-worth of books into the marital home.

Edward picks up a piece of pizza and has just started to nibble it when he notices my meal. 'WHAT'S THAT YOU'VE GOT THERE?' he yells.

'It's fish,' says Jake. 'I can smell it.'

'Yes, it's fish,' I sigh.

'I DON'T WANT TO SIT NEXT TO SOMEONE WHO'S EATING FISH!' screams Edward. 'I WON'T FUCKING DO IT!'

He slides off his chair, carefully takes hold of his plate and carries it slowly across the eating area, stopping a couple of tables away. He places his plate on the table and sits down. Jake makes to follow him but Alison lays a restraining hand on him. 'Not you, Jake, you're old enough to know better.' Poor Jake, always the one who has to behave.

Our heads are bowed as we eat our food, but not in prayer. We're avoiding eye contact with Edward, hoping other diners will think he's nothing to do with us.

'IT COULD BE WORSE! HE MIGHT BE EATING A HAMSTER!' we hear.

Alison gives me a look that says I have only my carnivorous self to blame. Jake can hardly eat for laughing.

'AT LEAST IT'S NOT A GERBIL!'

As I chew rubbery fish I am filled with longing to phone someone up and yell, 'I'm at the mall! I'm at the mall! Come and get me out!'

The mall has been cleverly built on to the carcass of an old department store, which is attached to the east end of the nave. It's here that we repair after lunch. The purpose of the trip is for Alison to find a dress for the Kappelheim, which – since the lecture falls on my fiftieth birthday – will serve too for the triumphant party she's planning afterwards, an admirable piece of economy on her part, she says.

On the second floor of the store Alison looks at frocks, flicking through racks of them at an astonishing rate as though she has taken the clothes-buying equivalent of the speed-reading correspondence courses advertised in newspapers. My role is to keep the boys amused while at the same time remaining close enough to a fitting room to pass judgement on her selections. I regard this as an act of selflessness likely to reduce the amount of suffering I'll have to endure in purgatory, if not the real thing then its earthly version, my life with Alison.

To entertain the children I initiate a game where they hide behind racks of clothes while I push Edward's buggy up and down, whistling and looking nonchalant until they leap out at me, shouting, 'Boo!' whereupon I gasp and clutch my chest, playfully enacting the very heart-attack I fear.

After ten minutes my mind has taken on a kind of numbness, almost as though I have been genuinely shocked, enough perhaps to tip my blood pressure off the scale and precipitate the long-awaited stroke, one so severe it deadens all my brain. I think how I've never been so bored as I sometimes am in the company of small children. I remember a moment of sad insight: I must have been nine or ten, when I was playing with my toy soldiers and suddenly thought, I hope I never grow too old to love playing with these, while at the same time knowing somehow that inevitably I would.

And then I see it. Right in front of me, on one of those mannequins that has no head or limbs, as though it has been modelled on the victim of a torso murder. It isn't the same, I realize that almost straight away, but it's sufficiently alike to take me back. The shoulder straps are a tad too narrow, and the high-cut legs would have been considered indecent in the 1950s. And it is only one colour with no pattern, and that one colour is a touch too bright. But it's a red bathing-suit none the less and, however inaccurate to the memory I carry inside me, it's enough to pluck that particular chord.

I wonder now at the pictures of Aunt Clara playing through my mind. I think of the day we bought the bathing-suit and my theft of the Swoppet. I realize how this connects with my earlier thoughts about playing with soldiers. I begin to marvel at all the things my brain holds, like a saturated sponge, dripping experiences and bits of arcane knowledge all the time, it sometimes seems, letting them leak away for ever, but then again, perhaps not, perhaps still the sophisticated computer children's science books purport it to be. I think of the multifarious items stored in the particular collection of molecules that I regard as me and marvel at the idiosyncrasy of the collection. I can pull out video clips of, say, the duel between Ronald Colman and Douglas Fairbanks Jnr at the end of *The Prisoner of Zenda*, the fourth English goal in the 1966 soccer World Cup final, a moment when a Playboy Bunny slid up and down the memory-enhanced length of my young cock, filmed from the viewpoint of a third person although no one else was present at the time. There are audio files containing all the Beatles songs (sung by the original artists), complete Christmas carols, the plaintive stuttering start of the Vienna Philharmonic's recording of Mahler's last completed symphony, poignant because it is meant to represent the composer's erratic heartbeat, a symptom of the illness he knew was going to kill him, and because the recording was made when the Nazis were at the gates of Vienna and life was about to change irrevocably for the Austrians, not least for Bruno Walter, the Jewish conductor. I can summon up the crown of Jake's head putting in its first appearance between Alison's legs, a goal I once scored for the school second eleven from what still seems an impossible angle. These same molecules contain the mirror sequence from *Duck Soup*, the major poems of John Donne (1572–1631) *verbatim*, huge selections of Shakespeare, plus numerous other poems and excerpts from prose works, including the plots and instantly available critiques of hundreds of novels, bleeding chunks of Wagner, especially *Die Walküre* (sung in English); hundreds of jokes (although these latter are encrypted so as not to be retrievable, especially when the memory bank is addressed with the command, 'Know any good jokes?' but can be accessed only to register ennui when I hear them again). The feelings I experienced reading *Anna Karenina* for the first time; the feel of Patsy Clarke's pubic hair, the first girl's private parts I ever touched. The list goes on and on. A whole lifetime in the assembling, it would take years to unravel it all. I stand and gaze at the red bathing-suit awed for a moment by my own mind. How my particular arrangement of molecules can hold this individual collection of images, feelings, memories such as have never before been or will ever again be assembled in the entire history of the universe. Not that it is better or worse than anyone else's collection, but because of its uniqueness. I am stupefied by the sudden knowledge that all this will, one day, be broken up and the components lost as the molecules return once more to water, dust and gas, retaining no memory of what they have been, melting anonymously into the heedless universe. An idea that horrified Donne, I'm thinking, when suddenly there's an urgent tug on my sleeve. Jake.

'Daddy, Daddy, come quick, Edward's gone!'

'Oh, yes, as if I'm going to fall for that one.'

'No, Daddy, it's not a game, it's true. He's disappeared.'

For the briefest of moments I see the floor coming up at me. I grasp a clothing rail beside me for support. But the expected physical trauma doesn't come. Beta-blocked, it's as if I'm observing it happening to someone else. I'm seeing my panic as I once saw the red swim-suit, through a veil. Simultaneously my miraculous mind puts on a video of a notorious piece of CCTV footage showing a young child, about Edward's age, being led from a shopping mall not unlike the one we're in now by two older boys. While I'm watching this I recall a newspaper description of a bundle found on a railway line, which turned out to be the child's despoiled body.

I scan the shop around me, finding it hard to breathe. 'Please, God, not now,' I pray, to a being in whom I have no faith at all (what I really need is Agnes Ada, but in her absence He'll have to do), 'not now. I'll have the stroke or heart-attack tomorrow, but let me keep going now.'

'What do you mean, disappeared?'

'He ran into the lift and the doors closed and he was gone.'

'Show me!'

I follow him round the escalator well to the lift in the far wall. There's no sign of Alison. I press the button to summon the lift. Nothing.

I bend and seize Jake by the shoulders. 'The arrow on the top of the lift, was it pointing up or down?'

'I don't know.'

I shake him, harder perhaps than is necessary, even supposing one espoused a belief in shaking as an effective mental stimulant, shifting my anger at my own negligence on to him. 'Think. You have to think. Was there anybody in the lift with him?'

'I don't know. I don't think so. I didn't see. He ran in and the doors shut behind him. It wasn't my fault.'

'OK, OK.' I look around again and still can't see Alison. Perhaps she is in a fitting room, but I've lost my bearings now and can't remember where they are. I grab Jake's wrist and half drag him to a sales desk. A young assistant is carefully folding a cardigan.

'Listen, I need you to—'

'Won't keep you a moment, sir,' she says, without looking up.

'Put that down and listen, this is urgent!' I snap, seizing the cardigan from her, a small part of my multi-tasking brain finding time even in my panic to enjoy rumpling it up again. 'Look after this child, I've lost his brother.'

'I can't do that, sir. If you just wait while I call Security—'

'There's no time for that. He's two years old and he's gone off in a lift on his own. He could be kidnapped or go down to the ground floor and walk out on to the street. Call your guards and get them looking for him. Jake, you stay here.'

All this time I have my eye on the lift, and at the moment I finish speaking, see the arrow above it light up. The down arrow. I let go Jake's hand and tear across to it. A gaggle of old ladies, three or four of them, are standing in front of it. I push through as the lift jerks to a halt.

'Hey, I beg your pardon!' snaps one.

'Young people today,' mutters another.

I ignore them and stand before the lift doors. They hiss open and reveal . . . nothing.

'Come on, come on, either get in or get out of the way,' says an elderly lady in a camel coat. 'There's others want to use it even if you don't.'

'It's all right for you youngsters,' protests another. 'You can use the escalators, some of us can't. I come over all funny on escalators.'

'That's just like me, dear,' a third woman puts in. 'I was all right on them till I got to the Change and then I could never go on them again.'

At this moment the lift doors begin to close. The first old lady, who's built like a running back, barges me out of the way as she makes a rush for them. She tries to grasp the edge of one of the doors, but it shakes off her hand with mechanical glee and closes. The light above the lift goes out, signalling its departure.

'Now see what you've done,' the woman in the camel coat spits at me. 'We've gone and missed it now. It could be ages till the next one.'

'It'll be the same one, dear,' says the first woman. 'There's only the one. We'll have to wait here till it comes back for us.'

'One lift isn't enough for four floors,' moans another.

I'm trying to keep calm. I'm trying to keep out all thoughts of where Edward might be, of who might have taken him by the hand . . .

'What floor's this?' I ask one of the women.

'Second, of course,' she replies. 'Don't even know what floor you're on. Typical!' She doesn't say of what.

If there are four floors, and the lift has come down it means Edward must have got out at one of the two floors above us.

I push through the crowd of oldsters. I run to the till where Jake is now sitting on the assistant's chair.

'Where's the escalator?' I ask.

'I spoke to Security, sir. They said for you to wait here.'

'Where's the fucking escalator?'

'Over there.' She points to the centre of the floor. I run over to it, colliding with another old woman on the way. It's hit-and-run, really. I haven't even breath to say sorry.

'Bastard!' she yells after me. The escalator turns out to be going down. I run round the escalator well and find the companion stairway going up. I start up it two steps at a time. Half-way up a huge black guy in a leather jacket blocks my way. It isn't like being on the London underground where you can overtake easily. This is a narrow store escalator, not much wider than one person's width. The guy in front of me is built like the side of a barn.

'Excuse me!' I say, trying to ease him out of the way. Pointless. It would take a bulldozer.

He turns and gives me a look that would freeze water. 'What's your hurry, man?' he says, in an accent that might be American or West Indian. 'You just have to have them new threads, huh? You can't wait a single moment, that it?'

'Listen, I lost my kid. He's up there somewhere. He got in the lift on his own.'

'Well, why the heck didn't you say so? Come on, man, I'll help you look.'

He steps off the escalator on to the third floor with me running into his back.

'Listen, you take this floor, man, I'll check out the one above. What age of kid am I looking for?'

'He's two!' I run over to the lift. No sign of Edward. In fact, this being Tuesday afternoon, the whole place is quiet. I tear around, barging into racks of suits and sweaters. My own jacket gets caught in another on a clothes carousel and for a minute I'm twirled around it. I stop and try to free my jacket, tugging at it so the whole carousel wobbles. I take a deep breath and examine the jacket. The one it's attached to is a drab olive moleskin thing I wouldn't be seen dead in. I look up and see an attractive, youngish woman watching me, probably the only customer under seventy in the store, apart from the black guy and me. Even in this moment of dire emergency I find myself horrified she'll think I'm interested in this awful jacket. 'Listen, I'm just hooked up on it,' I want to shout. 'I wouldn't dream of wearing anything like this!' And then I wonder whether being so incompetent as to be caught on the jacket might be worse than liking it, and then I remember the situation I'm in.

My jacket button is caught in the plastic thread attaching the price tag to the other jacket. Slowly I disentangle it. Free at last I look around. No Edward.

I run back around the other side of the escalator. No sign of him. I suddenly think, Why did I trust the safety of my child to a complete stranger? What if I've just alerted an opportunist paedophile to the presence of an unattended infant? But then I reassure myself. The black guy seemed OK and genuinely kind-hearted.

I take the escalator up to the fourth, in three bounds. I meet the black guy coming from the lift area. He gestures to the lift. 'He just got in the lift again. The doors closed 'fore I could get there.'

A hiss of relief escapes my lungs. Though Edward may not be safe, at least I know what I'm dealing with here. But I still need to find him.

'Which direction was the lift going in?'

'Hell man, we's on the top, ain't only one way it can go.'

'Thanks!' I start for the escalator.

'I'll come with you,' he says. 'Help you check them lower floors.'

We hit the third and arrive at the lift just in time to see the doors close again.

We run back to the escalator.

'Hey, man, you have some serious childcare issues you need to address,' pants my new friend, as we pound down it, like a couple of TV cops, even down to our racial mix.

'I only took my eye off him for a minute, for fuck's sake!'

'That here's just what I'm referring to, man. I ain't never heard no kid talk like that one. Stood there in that lift yelling at me to go fuck myself!'

We do our buddy-cop routine down the escalator again, my new friend elbowing out of the way an oldster couple at the top who are just about to mount it. We hit the second floor just in time to see the lift doors close again. The minute we hit the first floor, I hear raised voices coming from the direction of the lift. We race over and push our way through the small geriatric crowd gathered there.

In front of the lift stands Edward, flanked by two burly men in the blue paramilitary livery of the store's security force. Each has hold of one of his arms, and he is twisting his small body this way and that, trying to tug himself free.

'LET ME GO!' he screams. 'LET ME GO!'

People in the crowd turn to one another.

'Did you hear that?' says one old lady to her neighbour. 'Did you ever hear language like that from such a small child?'

'Well, no,' says the other, 'but what can you expect? I mean, a child that age shoplifting.'

I push through the crowd and retrieve my son. The security men insist on accompanying me back upstairs to verify with the sales assistant there that I am indeed the person to whom the child belongs. Reluctantly, disappointed that the sensation is over, the crowd disperses. I wave to my erstwhile friend. He walks over to me. 'Thanks for your help,' I say. 'I'd still be chasing around upstairs but for you.'

'Friend,' he says, 'you need more help than I can give you. Have you ever heard of family therapy?'

'You don't understand. It's just his manner. He doesn't really say—'

The guy shrugs and turns to go. He glances back

over his shoulder at me. 'Family therapy,' he mouths silently. 'Try it.'

The lift comes and the security men usher Edward and me into it.

'Am I under arrest?' he asks.

'No, of course not. These nice men just helped Daddy find you.' I pick him up and hug him. The security men smile. They walk me over to the pay desk and the assistant says, 'Oh, you found him OK, then? This one's been as good as gold.'

I thank the security men again and, having ascertained where the fitting rooms are, pop Edward in his buggy, where he puts his head on one side as though exhausted and ready for sleep, and place Jake's hand firmly on the buggy handle, then wheel them over there.

We've just arrived when a curtain swishes angrily to one side and Alison emerges, looking icily beautiful in a pale blue dress.

'I've been waiting hours to show you this,' she hisses. 'You were supposed to stay here.'

SEVENTEEN

I have already lost half a child
                    Letter to Sir Henry Goodyer

Why am I so fearful for Edward? I think, Maybe he looks so like an angel because that's what he's meant to be, that he was stolen from Death. Although, of course, you know enough by now, as I do, to grasp that that's impossible. Borrowed, yes. Stolen, permanently saved from, no.

Three years ago. Ten o'clock on a balmy summer Saturday night. We were on the city ring road where dusk had just fallen and the traffic was dying out as people found their way to pubs, restaurants and clubs. We were on our way home. We'd been to Ely to tell Mum the good news: there was to be a new, fourth member of our little family. Alison had just come through the final test. He or she (I didn't know which, I didn't want to, Alison did but was strong enough not to tell me) was cooking nicely.

The traffic was moving fast. I was listening to some speedy music too. It might have been the opening movement of Beethoven's seventh or the third movement of the Pathétique, I don't remember, except it was one of those pieces that make you think of horses galloping and I was weaving from lane to lane, shoving the gearstick down to third to accelerate past another car, slipping between it and the one in front like a grateful bridegroom between the sheets, when Alison spoke from the back seat. It was a wail of annoyance and I presumed it to be rhetorical. I didn't want to get involved in this. I had my music and my game with the traffic.

Alison was in the back seat because Jake, who was eighteen months old at the time, had been fretful and unable to drop off. I'd pulled in at the motorway services and Alison had clambered into the back beside him, where she could stroke his hand and hum him to sleep.

He'd been off for about half an hour when we hit the ring road and I began my little mechanized dance.

'Didn't you hear me, Michael? I'm soaked!'

'What do you mean, soaked? How come?' I braked to avoid the rear of the car in front, looked in the mirror, saw the outside was blocked and switched to the inner lane. 'How come?'

'It's Jake's bloody water bottle. The Tommee Tippee thing. It must have leaked. It's all over my dress.' I turned my head and could see her rifling through the pram bag she carried his stuff in. She pulled out the drinking cup. 'That's funny.'

'What?'

'It's full. But it can't be. We haven't got any other liquid with us. Oh – oh, Michael. Oh, no!'

I took the pressure off the accelerator. She was sobbing now.

'What, Ali, what is it?'

'Michael, it's me! It's me that's leaking. My waters have broken.'

I reached my hand back and squeezed her knee. 'Hold on, it's OK. Don't panic. I'll get you to the hospital. It will be all right.'

'Michael, it can't be all right. I'm only sixteen weeks. If my waters have broken it means I'm in labour and if the baby's born now it will die.'

'Listen, stop worrying. Let's get you to the hospital, find out what's happening. We must only be four or five miles away. We can be there in no time.'

And now my little dancing dodging game with the other cars began in earnest. I switched off the music as the sound seemed to stop me thinking. I moved into the fast lane, slotting in just in front of a BMW roaring up on the outside, making him brake hard. I ignored the angry strobing of his lights in my rear-view mirror. Moments later I braked again, slid into a slot inside, went down to third, revved the engine and shot past the two cars on the outside then sneaked in front of them. I remember wishing I had one of those flashing sirens TV cops sling on to the roofs of their cars. I drove like I *did* have one of those little flashing lights. Other drivers, though, just didn't get it and a new symphony played now, in and around the car, the blast of car horns and the squeal of tyres harmonizing with my crashing of the gears to synthesize blind panic.

When we arrived at our exit roundabout the traffic was jammed up in front of me for a couple of hundred yards. I was in the outside lane but by keeping my hand on the horn I managed to squeeze through the middle and slip into the inner. The pavement here was broad and empty. I drove the car up the kerb and roared along the pavement to the astonishment of the trapped drivers. God, I found myself thinking, what if the police stop me? Then I thought, Wait a minute, I *want* the police to stop me! Eventually I reached the roundabout, and hand stuck on horn, shot off the pavement on to it. A few minutes later we pulled up outside the hospital.

My heart, which had been in my mouth while I was driving, seemed to drop like a stone into my stomach. The hospital was dark and deserted. The main foyer wasn't showing a light. Only a glimmer was visible in the little glass cubicle off to the side of it.

'What's happening?' I gasped to Alison, lifting my hands, which were still trembling from gripping the steering-wheel too hard. 'Where is everybody? It can't be closed, can it?'

'Oh, shit!' she sobbed. 'I never thought. It's a maternity hospital. They don't have an A and E department. They won't take me as an emergency.'

'Yes, they will. Come on, let's get out of the car, they'll have to see us.'

I helped her out and lifted Jake from his car seat. I shucked him against my shoulder and hugged him to me, hoping he'd stay asleep, although he was already starting to stir. I pushed open the main entrance door and we walked over to the porter's cubicle. Alison was finding it difficult to walk because of the stuff running down her legs.

The cubicle was empty. I banged on the glass with the flat of my hand. Nothing. I tried the door. It was locked. 'Ssh, ssh!' I hissed to Jake, who was stirring because of the noise. Holding him on one arm against my shoulder I walked around the foyer trying the various doors off it. All locked. I went back to the porter's cubicle and banged on the glass again.

'Stop!' shrieked Alison. 'You're going to break it.' Jake was waking now, letting out a feeble cry. I stopped banging. The silence was so sepulchral you could hear the vibration of the glass as it slowed to nothing again. And then, suddenly, another noise. The distant flushing of a toilet. It came from behind a wooden door next to the porter's cubicle. I peered through the slot of glass in the door and saw an elderly man in uniform coming along the corridor beyond, casually adjusting his trousers as he walked. I banged on the door but he didn't approach it. Instead he turned off sideways through another door and into his porter's cubicle.

I moved to the glass window in the centre of his glass wall. There was a speaking hole in it, like the ones in banks.

'What's up?' he asked.

'My wife's a patient here. She's having her baby here. Her waters have just broken,' I said truthfully, omitting the technicality that the event was five months ahead of schedule.

'All right, sir, don't worry,' he said. 'I'll get your wife up to the labour ward.'

'I'm not in—' Alison started to say, but I turned and mouthed to her to keep quiet. Fortunately the man was on the phone and hadn't heard what she'd said.

'Listen,' I hissed to Alison, 'let's just get in here and find a doctor. If we're sent to another hospital it could take hours.' The porter put the phone down and there was the sound of him unlocking the wooden door. He emerged with a wheelchair. 'Come on, love, have a seat and we'll get you upstairs now.'

Jake was crying fitfully as I followed the man pushing Alison along the corridor to the lifts. As we waited for the lift to descend to us, the porter bent over Alison and gave her a warm smile. 'At least it's not your first, love,' he said. 'You'll know the ropes this time.'

Alison let out a sob. 'There, there, don't worry, love. It'll be all right in a minute.' Over her head he mouthed to me, 'A bit emotional.'

In the lift the man attempted to chat to us. 'How old's this one?' he asked.

'Eighteen months,' I replied.

'Haven't left it very long between them, have you?'

Another sob escaped Alison. Jake let out a whimper of sympathy. I didn't make any reply.

The porter unlocked the door of the ward and wheeled us along a corridor to a desk where a couple of midwives sat writing.

'Here's Mrs Cole, the one I just phoned up about. Her waters have just broken.'

One of the midwives, a large black woman, opened a book and began writing in it without looking up. 'We'll just take your details, love, then we'll get you sorted out.'

I waited until the porter was outside and had locked the door safely behind him.

'You don't understand,' I said. 'My wife's not in labour.'

The woman was clearly puzzled. 'But your waters have broken?'

'I'm not due yet.'

'When is your due date?'

'November the twenty-fifth.'

'So you are . . . ?'

'Sixteen weeks.' Alison burst into tears again. The woman rose from her seat, walked around the desk, bent over the wheelchair and enfolded Alison in her large arms. I thought how comforting it would be to be pillowed against those matronly breasts. As she held my wife, the woman patted her back with one hand. I thought, We pat animals, but never people, except when we can't think what to say.

'You poor thing,' was all the woman could come up with now. 'You poor thing.'

Releasing Alison, she said to the other midwife, 'Lucy, get Dr French right away.' She turned back to Alison. 'Let's get you into the exam room.' She started to wheel away the chair, then stopped and turned back to me. 'You can come as well, sir. It's your baby too.'

A drama such as the death of an unborn baby should have a grand setting, a whole theatre full of people all frantically trying to do something. Or perhaps a cathedral of mourners keening to mark the significance of the event. But the room we were shown to resembled a cross between a utility room and a cupboard and I found myself thinking how ordinary an event death is, just another of the many in our lives, played out in ordinary rooms like the rest of them. In such an inauspicious place I, too, would probably have my final moments.

Alison was helped on to a metal gurney, upon whose vinyl top was laid a single sheet. At the end was a butler sink. There was room enough to stand beside the bed, but only just: the opposite wall was taken up by a floor-to-ceiling cupboard. The door was beside this cupboard, facing the butler sink.

'Now, try not to worry,' said the midwife, bustling a couple of pillows behind Alison. 'It may not be as bad as you think. Doctor will be here soon.'

At that instant the door opened and a young doctor came in, stethoscope over his shoulder. For a moment he and the midwife were unwilling partners in an awkward dance as she tried to leave and he to get in via the same limited space. Finally they rotated and she was able to go.

The doctor perched himself on the end of the bed with a clipboard and began to ask questions. Name. Date of birth. Number of children. Alison croaked out the answers while I found myself teetering forward on tiptoe, wanting to say, 'Listen, can't we save the baby first and fill in the forms later?' Finally I could stand it no longer. 'Look, is this really necessary? Her waters have broken, she's only sixteen weeks.'

He shot me a kindly smile and it was then that I saw how young he was, not much more than a boy. Alison's long fingers tendrilled around my own and gripped them hard.

'I understand, but this won't take long and it has to be done,' he said. 'Do you know the sex of your baby?'

'Boy.' It came out as not much more than a whisper. Alison shot me a wan smile by way of apology, one that said, 'A hell of a way to find out but, then, what does it matter now?'

Eventually the form was completed and the doctor conducted a cursory examination.

'Well, I'm afraid it looks like your waters have broken, all right,' he said.

'What does that mean?' I asked. 'Has the baby died?'

'I can't tell you that. I'll have to get a foetal heart monitor down here. But, um, I think you ought to take care of that first.'

He seemed to be nodding at my arm, the one I had underneath Jake. I shifted Jake to the other shoulder and took a look. A thick sludge of shit was running down my arm, from the hand, which was underneath Jake's bottom, to the elbow below.

I looked at the disposable nappy, which was all Jake had been wearing in the hot car. The adhesive wings on either side had come unstuck, loosening the nappy and allowing the poo out. I remembered the same thing had happened with all the nappies we'd taken to Mum's. They'd obviously all come from the same defective pack so we'd had to keep discarding them, one after another, all day. We weren't worried about putting our last one on Jake for the journey back because we had others at home. Except now we weren't at home.

'I haven't any more nappies,' I told the doctor.

'I see. That's a problem.'

'But surely you must have some here. I mean, a maternity hospital . . .'

'Yes, of course, but all ours are for newborns. We haven't anything anywhere near his size. Wait a minute, I'll just pop upstairs and get you something to clean him up.'

He squeezed past me and out of the door. I stood there thinking that this was a strange priority, worrying about one child's faeces when another was dying a few inches away, but somehow I had to remove this mess from my arm. After a couple of minutes the doctor reappeared with a packet of baby wipes. I set Jake down on the edge of Alison's gurney and washed my arm at the sink. I stripped off the dirty nappy and cleaned him with the wipes.

'Back in a minute,' said the young doctor, and disappeared again.

Jake was half asleep and Alison stroked his blond curls to soothe him. It hit me that what we might be losing was another such child, another Jake and all the Jakes to come, the ones we didn't even know yet.

The doctor returned with the midwife. 'We haven't any nappies big enough so we're going to try to rig something up with this.' He waved a large sanitary towel, which I realized must be an extra-absorbent one for after labour. He had scissors and some gauze bandage. He fixed the towel under Jake's crotch and pulled the bandage over it then used surgical tape to hold it in place.

'A bit Heath Robinson,' he smiled proudly, 'but it should do the trick.'

The door opened behind him and the midwife pushed in a small trolley bearing the foetal heart monitor. She plugged it in and checked it. The doctor took a lead and placed the monitor on Alison's stomach. I held my breath. At first there was a loud screeching noise, like feedback at a rock concert, and the doctor reached hurriedly for a dial and adjusted it.

Then the room was filled by the cavernous KER-CHUKKA-KER-CHUKKA-KER-CHUKKA of the baby's heartbeat, like a war drum played fast and loud. For a moment my own heart began to speed up and I was filled with panic: it didn't seem possible anyone's heart could go on beating that fast without bursting but then I saw the doctor wasn't concerned and I remembered that the heartbeats of unborn babies are always fast. The doctor pressed a button on the machine. A coil of paper spewed out. He tore it off and studied it. Then he looked up at us. 'Well, as you can hear, the baby's still alive,' he said. 'The heartbeat is perfectly normal.'

I smiled. He didn't smile back. Neither did Alison.

'What?' I said. 'That's good, isn't it?'

He bit his lip. Alison squeezed my hand harder.

'I wish I could give you a positive answer to that,' he said, 'but I'm afraid I can't. You see, the waters have broken and, from what Mrs Cole has said, she's lost a substantial amount of fluid. It's not really likely the baby can survive in there without fluid.'

'But it is possible?'

'Well . . . look, first things first. There's a hole in the foetal sac. Now, assuming you don't go into labour, and I would expect you to, the open hole means there's a high risk of infection, which may itself either kill the baby or trigger labour.'

'What do you expect to happen?'

'To be brutally honest, I'd expect your wife to go into labour within the next forty-eight hours. Certainly within the next fortnight. As you know, a baby can't be viable until around twenty-three or twenty-four weeks. Or he may just die of infection.'

'What can you do?'

'I'm very sorry, but there isn't anything anyone can do.'

'Isn't there any way to repair the hole?'

'There have been attempts at that sort of thing but none has been successful.'

My mind flailed around, searching for straws. 'Have you ever heard of this happening and the baby remaining alive until full term?'

'Well, we did have a case here where someone's waters broke after twenty weeks and the baby remained alive until the twenty-ninth week when she went into labour.'

'And?'

'The baby was born but it was unable to breathe. That's only one case. All the others have ended as I just told you. I'm very, very sorry.'

'You mean we just have to wait for the baby – him – to die?'

'I'm sorry, but if you want the truth, yes.'

'But – but supposing he didn't? Could he survive in there without amniotic fluid?'

'Theoretically, yes. But the problem is the baby needs the fluid for his development. He floats around in it. Without the fluid he wouldn't be able to move. His limbs might be deformed. They might fail to grow properly. They could end up stiff and unmovable. A child could be horridly crippled, unable to walk or move its arms. You have to ask yourself, would you want that for your baby?'

'B-but he could survive?'

'Theoretically, yes. But the main problem would be the lungs. You see the baby breathes the amniotic fluid in and out and that develops the lungs. Without it the lungs wouldn't develop. This is what happened to the child I told you about earlier. It was born but it couldn't breathe. We put it on a ventilator, but it wasn't able to breathe for itself. As soon as the ventilator was switched off, it died.'

There didn't seem to be anything else I could ask.

'It's no use,' Alison said, gripping my hand. 'You just have to accept it, Michael. That's all we can do.'

But I was unwilling to accept it. It had taken Alison years to conceive Jake, which is how I ended up such an old father. It had taken a lot of treatment to conceive this second child. The one who only needed to stay put for a few more miserable weeks to become a person. I was struggling to find another avenue of hope but before I could speak the doctor said, 'Uh-oh!'

A wet, warm patch was spreading out on my T-shirt as the makeshift nappy failed to dam the flow of Jake's urine.

I laid him beside Alison and removed the pad. He moved in close to her and fell asleep. I took paper towels from the sink and dried him.

'Hold on to him a minute, can you?' I said to Alison. 'I can't think until I've sorted this out.' I remembered there was an all-night petrol station opposite the hospital entrance. 'Maybe they sell nappies,' I said.

'Don't leave me,' Alison pleaded.

'I have to get something on him,' I said. I had a sudden urge for action, a need to do something. This was something I could sort out.

I bounded down the stairs, went past the porter, who gave me a cheery wave, and across to the petrol station. In the little shop attached to it was a queue of ten people. I looked all around the shelves but I couldn't see any nappies.

I walked to the front of the queue. 'Excuse me,' I said to the Asian boy on the till.

'What do you think you're doing?' It was a little guy at the back of the line. Dirty jeans, sweaty white singlet. Earring. Nose-ring. Head not shaved, but dangerously short hair. 'There's a queue.'

'I just want to ask a question,' I said.

'Yeah? Well, tough. Get in the queue, mate.'

'Listen, I'm not pushing in, I just want to ask if they've got something. There's no point my queuing if they don't have it.'

'Get in the fucking queue!'

A very fat woman a couple of places ahead of him turned round. 'He doesn't have to queue to ask a question. That would be quite ridiculous.'

'No, it wouldn't. Suppose he asks if they've got something and the guy goes out the back to check? Or has to look on his computer? Or make a phone call? It'll hold us all up.'

I couldn't think of an opposing argument. All I could think about was the pressing need to get a nappy on Jake. The one thing I could do for Alison. Get back, be there beside her, get her born-and-living son nappied up.

'He's right,' said a middle-aged man at the front of the queue. His accent sounded Greek. 'It's those things that take up all the time. Someone like me, I just come in and buy a packet of cigarettes. I'm in, I'm out, it's so quick you don't hardly see me. But when they start asking questions . . .'

'You see? It's what I'm saying,' said Singlet.

'Oh, for goodness' sake!' said the fat woman. 'What is it you want, dear?'

'Nappies.'

She lifted her chin and yelled over the heads of the people in front. 'Hey, boy, do you have any nappies?'

The boy carried on punching keys on his till. 'Nappies?' he shouted.

'That's right. Nappies for little babies.'

'Top shelf on the right!'

I looked up and saw a solitary pack of nappies. The chances of it being the right size were pretty remote. I lifted it down. The nappies were for a boy and they were Jake's size.

I turned back to the queue and waited my turn. It moved agonizingly slowly. The big woman got served. 'Remember to get plenty of nappies in next time you go shopping,' she said, as she passed me going out.

Eventually my turn came and a moment later I was running across the road, clutching my precious purchase. In the side room I held it triumphantly aloft to show Alison.

'They had some, then,' she said.

'One packet left, boy's and Jake's size,' I said. 'Can you believe our luck?'

EIGHTEEN

It quickened next a toyful ape
                    The Progress of the Soul

Fortunately the aimlessness of my first day of suspension proves untypical over the next few days, as I find myself not only gainfully unemployed (I have been suspended on full pay as is only right since the allegations against me are unproved) but also fully occupied. It's a full-time job preventing Alison knowing I no longer have one. For a start there are all the phone calls I have to make to her to ensure she doesn't make any to me. And if she doesn't answer and the answerphone kicks in I'm unable to leave a message in case that merely provokes her into phoning me. So I have to call again. Eventually this becomes so tiresome (especially when I'm so busy!) that I make up an unlikely story that we are having new phones put in at work and that it will be best for the foreseeable future if she calls me only on my mobile number.

Then there are the plastic crates of books on the back seat of my car. Those in the boot are a lesser problem since there's no reason for Alison to look in there and in the past she's so frequently expressed disgust at the messy state I keep it in it's unlikely she'll do so. My car is usually parked on the street outside the house –

Alison's occupying the drive – where there is more than a fair chance she may pass it and notice its new resemblance to a mobile library. So I continue parking around the corner. It's not likely Alison will notice my car's absence from the front of the house and, since parking is always a problem in our neighbourhood, it's feasible I might occasionally have to park elsewhere. I reinforce this idea by walking around the house muttering to myself, 'Some bastard with a new BMW pinched my parking place again. I've had to put it round the corner.' Even though this seems to work and my car's low profile is not remarked upon, I know it's only a temporary solution. There's still a chance of her seeing it. Although few people in our neighbourhood use their legs for anything other than operating the foot controls of their cars Alison occasionally strolls round to one of the neighbourhood convenience stores. Should she do so she might easily come across my car and all the books.

Then there's the risk she may ask me to take the children somewhere. To run them to nursery, for example. It's not too difficult to imagine the scenario: Edward looks inside the car and screams, 'WHERE AM I SUPPOSED TO SIT WITH ALL THOSE FUCKING BOOKS IN MY PLACE? IT'S NOT FAIR, IT'S JUST NOT FAIR.'

No, I have to get the books into the house as quickly as possible and today I have a plan. I cruise past the house. It's mid-norning. Jake goes to nursery every morning and Edward just two mornings a week. But I know this is one of Edward's days, which means Alison will more than likely have taken the opportunity to do some unencumbered shopping. My precision planning has also taken into account that it's also not the cleaning lady Mrs Thursby's day, although there is still the remote possibility that her carpenter husband, who is supposed to be putting up some shelves in the boys' room, may have turned up. But luck is with me. The driveway is empty: no Alison car, no Bill Thursby van. I pull into it. I open the front door, intending to switch off the burglar alarm before going back for a crate of books, but when the door opens, the alarm doesn't bleep.

I'm just registering the implications of this when the door between hall and kitchen opens and Alison emerges. 'Oh, hello,' she says. 'What are you doing back at this time?'

'Er, umpf, books,' I splutter.

'Books?'

'Yes, I – uh – forgot a couple of books.'

'Oh.'

I shut the front door behind me to deter her from wandering outside where she might glance into my car. I scamper up the stairs to my study, grab the first two books I see and scamper back down again. She's not in the hall so I wander into the kitchen. She's washing a shirt in the kitchen sink.

'Didn't think you were in,' I say, putting my arms around her from behind. She shrugs me off. 'Your car wasn't in the driveway.'

'No, it's out front, on the street. Didn't you see it as you came in? There was a space so I thought I'd park there and leave the drive free for you. You're always moaning about having to park round the corner lately.'

I give her an uxoriously light kiss and make my way of the front door, knowing I can open it with no risk to her coming out because she's up to her elbows in washing. All I can think is, How can I park in the drive when I come home tonight without her seeing the books? Decide I'll have to continue not working even later than usual, get home after dark and leave very early in the morning to avoid any chance of this.

My hand's on the front door when she calls me back.

'What is it?' I ask, returning to the kitchen. She nods at the two books on the table. 'You almost forgot what you came for.'

'Thanks,' I say, trying to squeeze anything like irony out of my tone. I pick them up and a moment later I'm backing out of the drive, the crate in the back seat two books heavier than when I arrived.

The rest of my day is aimless and frustrating, apart from a brief trip into town to the bank where I persuade them to increase my overdraft by three thousand pounds. But after I've dropped the money off to Tommo, I have nothing left to do. The two extra books on the back seat are a constant reminder that I'm not getting anywhere. And Alison's having left the drive free for me means it's going to be a very long not-working day. In desperation I visit the town's only cinema and see the films at both screens.

Even this involves a certain amount of subterfuge: I have to remember to dispose of car-park tickets and cinema stubs. I must not return home smelling of popcorn, which, outside the context of the cinema, would be a hard thing to explain having eaten. Of course, while all this cloak-and-dagger stuff would tax an ordinary person, it's meat and drink to a practised adulterer like me. I relish the ingenuity of my deceit, the lengths to which I go to avoid detection. But I am not without regret. I just wish I had fucked someone to do all this for.

Even the cosy anonymous dark of the cinema is not without hazard, though. Half-way through the second film my mobile rings. I can't not answer it in case it's Alison. It's Alison.

'Ssh!' hisses everyone around, as I say hello while pushing past them for the exit.

'Who are all those people telling you to be quiet?' Alison asks.

'I was in – uh – a meeting.'

'A meeting? This late? It sounded like a big one. God, academics really earn their money, don't they?'

'You can say that again.' I'm in the foyer now. There's no one around.

'Anyway, I was just phoning to tell you that Mr Thursby finally came and measured up for the shelves.'

'Does that mean he's actually going to do them?'

'Well, he's left his tool-box here.'

'That's a start. Listen, Alison, I have to go, I don't want to miss the end.'

'The end?'

'The . . . er . . . end of the meeting.'

'Bloody hell! Keen or what? It's only a job, you know, Michael.'

An hour later I arrive home exhausted. Watching a thriller on beta-blockers has been a curiously un-involving experience. I really didn't mind whether the hero was killed or not. Wondering if it's simply the drug or if I've ever really cared what happens to anybody, I open my study door and am alarmed to find the room illuminated by the ghostly light from the computer screen, although I'm sure it wasn't on when I went out. I close the door behind me, suddenly worried that Alison may have visited the room during my absence. I move towards the desk to check the computer. Then I see the silhouette of a man's head and shoulders behind the desk and stop dead. We've been burgled! I am alone in the room with a potentially dangerous stranger! Maybe someone high on drugs and crazed! Higher and more crazed than me even! Then I realize the figure is not a burglar at all, but Uncle Frank. He's sitting in my office chair, working the computer keys. He glances up at me then resumes what he's doing. I let out a sigh of relief. But immediately I start to panic again: maybe a burglar would be better. As it is, I have to confront either the ghost of a dead relative or the very real prospect that I'm going mad. I think about running away, escaping my demons whatever they may be, but just then Uncle Frank leans back in the chair and grins up at me. 'This is fun,' he says.

'What's fun?' I'm wary. There are huge caches of my work on that machine, including most of my book on Donne, such as it is. Of course, Luddite that I am, much of it is not backed up, or if it is, on disks whose whereabouts are unknown.

'I'm chatting to this bird in Oklahoma,' he says. 'I've been telling her to stay away from you. Did she tell you she always sits at her computer totally nude? She likes going into chat rooms, mingling with all those strangers, while she's naked. It turns her on.'

I walk round the desk and switch off the modem. Uncle Frank doesn't blink.

'Virtual nudity, she calls it.'

'What do you think you're doing? Who said you could touch my computer? There's information on there I can't afford to lose.' I realize that in this incarnation Uncle Frank is actually younger than me and that I'm talking to him the way an angry parent might.

He raises his eyebrows. 'Yeah, I know, I found some of it. You sure love looking at titty, don't you? And then your friend from Oklahoma came on—'

'What are you doing here?'

'Well, I thought I'd like to try some of this marijuana.' He hooks the toe of his workboot under the handle of the bottom desk drawer and pulls it open. I stride round the desk and kick it shut. He looks up at me, fierce and mean, the way he'd sometimes look when I was a child and he was thinking about hitting me. Then he turns the chair away from me, bends and opens the drawer with his hand. I reach down and slam it shut. He's up and out of the chair so fast I hardly know it's happening. He seizes me by the lapels of my jacket and thrusts his face into mine. His breath is cold and stinks of mould.

'Don't you ever do any kin thing like that to me again, understand?'

'No, I don't understand. What's happening around here? What are you? Are you just an hallucination? Where do you come from?'

He pulls me tighter to him. I can't help flinching from his breath, the stench of decay and rotten meat.

'Maybe I'm your fucking conscience, Michael. Maybe I've come hotfoot from hell to sit on your shoulder and set you right about a thing or two. Where are the dead, Michael? Where are the dead? Are they in heaven or hell? Or are they all around you here in this room? Or do they just exist in your head? Well, Michael, let me tell you this: nobody gets to know before they go.' He shoves me away from him, letting me go. He flicks imaginary dust from his T-shirt with his fingertips. 'Now, how about that joint?'

Dazed, I walk round the desk, sit in the chair, open the drawer, take out all the dope paraphernalia and try to roll a joint. Thank God he didn't find the coke! The idea of Uncle Frank on coke doesn't bear thinking about. My hands are trembling so much I keep spilling tobacco and resin, but eventually I manage to produce a reasonable-looking, if somewhat loosely packed, spliff. I've made it two papers long and Uncle Frank is suitably impressed.

'Wow, that looks like it could do some damage! I never had this stuff before. It wasn't around a lot before I cashed my chips in.'

I light it, take a hit and feel the warmth radiate through me. I hadn't known how cold I was. I pass it to Uncle Frank. He holds it for a second or two, examining it as though he's wondering whether or not to go ahead, then shrugs and takes a pull. Immediately he's coughing. He bends double, alternately coughing and wheezing. He stretches out his arm, waving the joint, asking me to take it and I do. Then he stumbles round the room, banging into things. I'm alarmed at the amount of noise he's making. I'm worried he may wake the boys or that Alison will hear. Then I think, What if she does? What if she comes in here and sees Uncle Frank? Wouldn't that change my whole life?

The coughing subsides and he sinks into my chair, striking his chest with his fist. 'Fuck, that was hot! You never told me it burned like that.'

He coughs again. 'OK, give me another drag.'

'Go easy on it. Draw it in slowly.'

He's a little nervous of it now as he puts it gingerly between his lips. He takes a cautious puff then closes his lips, holding it in. He winks at me. 'Whoa! This is more like it.' He takes another hit.

'Actually you're supposed to share it,' I say, unable to stop myself smiling.

He takes another hit. 'Share it? Isn't that a bit unhygienic? I don't want to be nasty, Michael, but with this Aids thing you have now . . .'

'You can't get Aids from a cigarette. Besides, you're already dead.'

'Oh, yeah, there is that.' He passes me the joint. The turmoil inside me is calming. I can handle this. Whatever else, he's not going to harm me, at least not at this moment. He's leaning back in my chair now, his boots on the desk. Suddenly I feel resentful at the impudence with which he has imposed himself on my life.

'What were you doing in the restaurant the other night?'

'We came to give you moral support.'

'Moral support!'

'Wasn't my idea, it was your grandmother's.'

'Did you throw a prawn at that guy?'

He shrugs. 'Fucking food was inedible. Anybody would want to throw it. Foreign muck. I never had any time for the Japs.'

'They weren't—'

'Listen, lots of the boys in the East Anglian Regiment were killed by those slitty-eyed little fuckers. I probably would have been, too, if it hadn't been for my accident. I hate the little bastards.'

'They weren't Japs, they were Thais.'

'Same thing. They're all the same.'

'Don't you have any where you are?'

He smiles up at me. 'You never give up, do you, Michael?' Suddenly there's the sound of footsteps on the stairs. 'Uh-oh, time for me to be going. Besides, I have to meet your grandmother. Oh, which reminds me, when you see her next – and yes, you will be seeing her again—'

'Don't mention the F word?'

He snaps his fingers. 'Hey, that's right. Never mention that.'

'Just one thing before you go, Uncle Frank. The chimpanzee. What's all that about? Why the monkey?'

'The chimp? The monkey, as you call him, Michael, is your grandfather.'

I'm almost too stunned to speak. The footsteps are on the second flight of stairs getting closer. 'My grandfather? Listen, I understand Darwin, but I thought the whole process took a few million years. My grandfather wasn't a monkey.'

'Of course he wasn't a monkey, Michael. But maybe

he's like that now because that's how you remember him.'

I'm looking right at him and he's smiling back at me and then he isn't. Suddenly he just isn't there.

My mind's racing, trying to make sense of what he just said. It's true, my memories of Granddad are indistinct. I always think of him as small and hunched, with hair parted in the centre of his skull, very hairy and with a projecting jaw and his face mainly teeth. A chimpanzee, in fact. But does this mean I've somehow summoned him back in that form? Or does it mean I hallucinate him as I recall him, just as I conjure up Uncle Frank as the young man who's most vivid to me?

I'm interrupted by a knock at the door. Alison is always respectful of my privacy. She would never allow herself to stoop to sneaking as a means to unearth my crimes and misdemeanours. Well, respect is the reason she'd give, to me and herself. But perhaps, too, she's fearful of what she may find.

'Come in.'

She sticks her head round the door. 'Oh, I thought you had someone here.'

'Nope.'

'But I heard you talking. I know I heard you. Oh, Michael, talking to yourself. This is getting really bad. You need help.' She sniffs. 'This place stinks. And it's not just that joint you've been smoking. It smells, well, fusty, like something died in here. It needs a good clean. You'll have to put your books away so I can get Mrs Thursby to do it.'

I do not want Alison to see whatever it is Frank has up on the computer screen. She does not, of course, know that on the evenings when I am up here supposedly working on Donne, I am sometimes miles away, living a virtual life, wandering Internet chat rooms. Nor does she know about Abby from Oklahoma, or any of

254

the other women I've met there. So I slide into the chair behind the desk so newly vacated by Frank. I note the seat is not at all warm. Alison plumps herself down on the battered old sofa I sometimes lie on while waiting for inspiration to strike (i.e. sleep). She shoots me a woeful smile.

'Well,' she says, 'what about another spliff?'

I roll one eagerly, light it and carry it over to the sofa. I pass it to her and sit beside her. And there we are for some time, in the dark save for the glimmer of the computer screen and the glowing orange jewel of the tip of our hemp cigarette, just an old married couple sharing a spliff.

Eventually it burns down. Alison stubs it out in the ashtray. She places a hand on mine and pats it gently. She brushes a tear from her eye as she rises from the sofa. 'See you in the morning,' she says.

I'm left in the dark, listening to the soft retreat of her footsteps down the stairs to our bedroom. I find myself wishing it could all be different. But that's impossible: it would require me to be different first. And that, I know, can never be. Fifty is too late for an old dog like me to be learning new tricks.

Still, there's a book to be written and, as a journey starts with one step, or a life with one breath that leads in the end to the final wheeze, so a book starts with a word or two. I shift myself and sit down at the computer. But before I can even begin to think about Donne my hand has moved the mouse and connected the modem. Words begin appearing on the screen.

Frank
Where did you go? I was so enjoying our talk. I so agreed with what you were saying. You seem to know what I'm thinking. How do you do that?
Abby

Abby [I type]
Frank isn't here any more. He had to go away. In fact, to be completely honest, Frank is dead. Sorry to be the one to tell you.
Michael

NINETEEN

Some man unworthy to be a possessor
Of old or new love, himself being false or weak,
  Thought his pain and shame would be lesser
If on womankind he might his anger wreak

Confined Love

I roll up Cherry's long skirt, which seems to take for ever as the material bunches, making it cumbersome in my hands so that it keeps slipping down.

'You should have worn a short skirt,' I say.

'Ah, but then I would have had to wear knickers.' She's working on my belt buckle. Eventually I have the skirt up to her waist and my hands are at last able to clasp her grateful buttocks. In pornographic literature hands are always said to 'clasp' buttocks rather than any other word. 'Clasp' is the verb for buttock-holding. And pornographic this certainly is, according to the legal definition, intended to inflame and corrupt – well, perhaps not the latter so much, since he is already about as corrupted as it's possible for a penis to be, but certainly the former, in order to get the Old Soldier up and about because once again he has slept in past reveille.

Cherry tugs down my trousers and underpants and my oldest ally leaps out.

'Ooh, these tiles are cold!' She shivers, as I press her buttocks against the wall. 'Come on, hurry up, the bloody pasta will be *al dente* by now.'

She is referring to the pasta that is cooking downstairs. We're in Cherry's house, where she and her husband are hosting a dinner party at which I'm a guest. She has detailed her husband, a colleague of mine, to watch the pasta. It has a cooking time of twelve minutes – which, allowing a minute for us to sneak upstairs and another to sneak back down, affords us ten minutes in which to have a fuck.

I am fumbling, trying to force an entry. 'Thank God I'm using dried not fresh,' gasps Cherry, wrenching my member from my grasp and attempting to insert it. 'It's no good, your penis is just so fantastically, enormously, *unbelievably* long. You'll have to lift me higher.'

I try but she keeps sliding down the tiles, which are slippery with condensation as the hot air generated by our passion meets their cold surface. So clasping (that word again!) her buttocks even more tightly I move her away from the wall and carry her, shuffling because my ankles are hobbled by my trousers and underpants, over to the large reproduction Victorian wash-basin.

I have her suspended over it when there's a rattling at the door.

'Sorry!' pleads the voice of another colleague's wife. 'But could you hurry up? I'm desperate for a pee.'

'What do we do now?' I hiss into Cherry's ear.

'Well, like the woman says, bloody get on with it!' She reaches down for the Old Soldier ('Bloody hell! It's as big as a baguette!') and thrusts him towards his destination, but then the door rattles once more and he begins to go flaccid again.

'Oh, no, what's up? Or, rather, why isn't it?' Cherry pants.

'It's the woman outside. It's too much pressure when

he's under pressure already. We'll have to do without her.'

'Pity,' says Cherry. 'I found that rather exciting.'

I press stop and rewind.

I lift Cherry away from the wall, shuffle over to the repro Victorian sink and perch her on the edge. She seizes the Old Soldier, who has now recovered. All is silent apart from our respective pants and groans. No rattle from the door. No woman outside. Colleague and his wife not even invited to the party. Amazed line about baguette from Cherry again. She inserts Old Soldier.

'God, this is good. It's so big,' she moans, 'so stiff . . .'

I glance down and, sure enough, the Old Soldier is, if not quite the creature of Cherry's remastered imagination, at least no longer the flaccid apology for a penis he seemed ten minutes ago. I step from the shower, brush myself cursorily with a towel and walk into the bedroom where I examine myself or, rather, him, in the mirror. He certainly looks angrily erect and ready for action, perhaps disappointed to find no one perched on the sink or slipping down the tiles and that my dalliance with Cherry is something from the files, a dinner party from the mid-nineties, heavily edited and glossed up for his benefit.

Although I am pleased to see the Old Soldier at attention, as it were, I cannot help worrying whether he is not looking a little downcast. That is, rigid he may be, but ought he to be pointing so listlessly towards the floor? Should he not be sticking straight out, like a lancer's weapon at the charge? I turn sideways and detect an almost 45-degree angle of decline. (Decline may be an unfortunate choice of word, given the circumstances!) Used he not to be horizontal? How I wish I could remember! How I wish I'd made a note before I began taking the bloody tablets – after all, I knew the risks. But, then, the deviation of your erection from the horizontal is not necessarily the sort of thing you anticipate at such times.

Perhaps it's all right and he's always sloped around like this. Perhaps he's not actually doing it that much and it's simply my anxiety exaggerating the tilt. If only there were some way of checking; it would bring me great peace of mind.

Suddenly I remember Bill Thursby's tools in the boys' room and instantly a solution pops into my head like the first shaft of morning sunlight illuminating a room. I open the bedroom door. There are vague noises from downstairs, but Alison will be giving the boys their breakfast and is unlikely to come up here for hours yet. I creep along the corridor to Jake and Edward's room and find the tool-box where Bill has conveniently left it. How wonderful Fate can sometimes be, when she is on our side, I tell myself. No sooner does she present us with a problem than she offers us the solution. I open the box and trawl through hammers, drill bits and bevels, all of which I recognize from my time as Uncle Frank's gofer. Memory calls me to linger over them, to renew acquaintance with the touch of them and recall their individual names, but I know I cannot. I must get on before Alison comes upstairs or, even worse perhaps, I lose my reason for being here. At last I find exactly what I'm searching for.

By now, of course, the Old Soldier has gone off duty so I press play on my Cherry video again. 'I just can't get it in, I'd need a bloody ladder to be tall enough for that thing,' she moans, in an out-take from the early part of the scene where I was still trying to screw her up against the wall. 'Hurry up, the pasta will be ruined . . .'

She's such a good actress (at least in this new cut) that the Old Soldier responds accordingly. I shrug off my dressing-gown and examine him in the boys' full-length mirror. Hmm, he still has that downcast look about him, but perhaps forty-five degrees was a bit of an exaggeration, or perhaps this time my fantasy was better. I take Bill's spirit level and lay it along his length, attempting to balance it there. Fortunately it's a lightweight plastic one and the Old Soldier is able to bear it quite easily upon his broad back. The trouble is, every time I let go of it, to get an unassisted reading, as it were, it slips off him and tumbles to the floor. I walk over to the boys' chest of drawers, rifle through and find an elastic band. I return to the mirror and stretch it over the spirit level and the Old Soldier, thereby attaching it to him. A tool upon a tool, as it were. I let go. The Old Soldier bobs up and down. Inside the spirit level's glass capsule, the bubble of air sways back and forth.

'Keep still!' I order. 'You're on parade now, for Christ's sake!'

The bubble is definitely off centre and up towards me, indicating the Old Soldier is pointing down, although not much, and then, of course, one has to remember to take into account the weight of the spirit level. I lean back a bit to help lift my penis and the bubble creeps slightly the other way.

'Pretty good, for a man of fifty!' I'm telling myself, when I hear the creak of a floorboard. Before I can move the door is flung open.

'Oh, my good God!' gasps a female voice. 'Whatever next?'

I raise my eyes to look at the doorway. Just in time to see Mrs Thursby's retreating back.

TWENTY

Licence my roving hands, and let them go
Behind, before, above, between, below.
O my America, my new found land,
My kingdom, safeliest when with one man manned
                                    To his Mistress Going to Bed

I'm dressed and out of the house very quickly, off to not
work without any breakfast inside me. I can hear Mrs
Thursby and Alison talking in the kitchen and have no
wish to face the resulting interrogation, should Mrs
Thursby have spilled the beans. My only hope is that
she will dismiss it as one of those silly little sexual
things men get up to and not mention it to my wife. If
she tells Alison, the repercussions of the latter finding
out about my suspension will be so much worse. While
I might have fudged the facts of the Tamsin incident
and got away with it, to be twice caught naked with an
inappropriate piece of equipment – a blood-pressure
monitor, a spirit level – and claim innocence might be
thought to be stretching things a bit.

All this is going through my mind as I drive around.
I scarcely notice where I'm going, for in truth the
answer is nowhere. Eventually I find myself on
the street that leads to the university sports ground and
the woodland beyond. I park the car, experiencing a

frisson of unease as I'm locking the door and catch sight again of all my books in the back. This is partly guilt, because I know I should be heeding Tait's advice and working on my Donne, and partly anxiety that my books might be more at risk in this technically safer but more academic part of town. I dismiss this latter worry almost as soon as it rears its head: although students can read, few choose to. Jesus! Why read a book when you can pull out your mobile phone and share shouted inanities with some airhead friend a couple of blocks away?

I walk across the sports fields, brogues squelching in the waterlogged turf. I take the modern aluminium footbridge over the river and enter the woods the other side. I experience an involuntary, brief cheerfulness at the blossom everywhere, but this dissipates as I think it's almost summer again. How many more do I have ahead of me? Will it be next year that the blossom is here without me to see it? It will be one year, and not so far from now, perhaps.

There are many footpaths through the woods and any number of routes you can take. I find my feet following the one Alison and I always took. This was where we used to come when we were first seeing each other. Away from prying eyes although, even in those days, it was no big deal for a lecturer to be sleeping with a student. Any rule against such relationships was mostly observed in the breach.

There are minor differences in the footpath now that irritate me. A certain Toytown appearance has been introduced: the way they have edged it neatly with strips of wood, the little *faux*-rustic signs pointing to the sports field, the bluebell glade, the weir. Again, I am aware of the passage of time, and how Alison and I have erected little barriers to contain our relationship neatly within certain boundaries. The little signals we give each other that are not signposts to follow but rather prohibitions, keep-off-the-grass notices, saying 'Don't go there.' It's the places we could go if only we dared that make our relationship such a trial. Alison knows what I am seeing when I lie with my eyes wide open at three o'clock in the morning. When she read that sign in the fossil museum over my shoulder all she could do was shoot me a look of sympathy and say, 'Scary, eh?' If I ever allowed myself to open up to her about my fears, we both know it's confirmation, not comfort, I'd find.

I stand on the footpath across the weir and look down at the seething water below. If only I had the courage to throw myself in! To end all the worry and speculation! I could almost stand being dead now, rather than spend the next twenty or thirty years (if I'm lucky, or unlucky, depending how you look at it) worrying about it. But, of course, I have my lifelong horror of water, so I cannot do it. If only I were able to swim, I tell myself, maybe I could drown myself.

I walk for hours round and round the woods, out again across the sports fields, through the streets. Of course, my mood brings on the rain, but I turn up the collar of my jacket and trudge on. I've nowhere to go. Eventually it gets past the time when I could legitimately finish work and return home. But I have used working late as an excuse for my adulterous comings and goings so regularly that were I to go home on time for once Alison would smell a rat. Not to mention the books in the car. Not to mention what Mrs Thursby might have mentioned.

Suddenly I feel damp and cold. My feet trace a familiar route through the deserted wet streets. I climb a set of steps and ring the bell. The intercom crackles unintelligibly.

'It's me, Michael. I'm cold and wet and have nowhere to go.'

The door is buzzed open. I climb a couple of flights of stairs. A door opens. 'Come in,' she says. 'I'll give you shelter from the storm.'

I stand in her vestibule, making a small puddle on the parquet floor. I feel like a small child who has just wet himself.

'Hey, lookatcha! Don't you have enough sense to come in outa the rain? Well, get out of those wet things, why dontcha? I can't believe this – Michael Cole in a woman's apartment and he has to be told to take his clothes off?'

'Very witty I'm sure, Karen. Do you have a – uh – dressing-gown?'

'A robe? Sure.' She disappears and returns bearing a long pink velvet wrap. 'Sorry, I'm all out of boys' robes at the moment. You can take your things off in the bathroom. Put them on the radiator in there, they'll soon dry.'

Moments later we're sitting side by side on the sofa, sipping hot chocolate.

'So,' says Karen, 'how have you been? It must be so weird not having a job to go to.'

'Especially if you have a family to go to it from.'

'You didn't tell Alison?'

'I didn't tell Alison.'

She shakes her head. 'Michael, what are we going to do with you? Your whole life is falling apart and you're just stumbling through it while it happens.'

'Isn't that what we all do anyway?'

'Nope. Some of us get on with it. We work hard and gain satisfaction from that. We keep our minds alert so they don't become morbid. We enjoy literature, theatre, music. We have friends who make us feel good. We carry umbrellas when it rains.'

She turns to me and smiles. Her eyes are teasing me. 'We make ourselves feel good by offering succour to the poor in spirit.' She picks up the towel I have dropped on the floor and rubs my hair with it, hard at first, but then her fingers slow and I feel her great affection for me.

She leans towards me and places her lips on mine. She kisses me gently and for a long time. Her tongue slides between my lips and my own rushes gratefully to meet it. She puts her hand inside the dressing-gown and strokes the hair on my back.

'What's happening?' I croak. 'What's this all about?'

'I guess you just look pretty in pink.'

She stands and takes my hand, gesturing to me to rise. She leads me into the bedroom. She undresses quickly, in a businesslike fashion. I notice her thighs are thick and her bottom sags, although she's still quite young. I feel sorry for the way her pale flesh dimples. Around her waist is a belt of superfluous flesh that jiggles as she moves. Naked, she walks over to me and pulls off the robe. 'Pity, you were cute in it but it has to go.' She tugs off my underpants and pushes me on to the bed. She leans across me, rubbing her face in my chest hair. She growls, comically. She kisses me again. Her breasts are heavy but not pendulous. She lifts my head and presses it against them, but offering comfort, not sex. She touches and strokes me with such tenderness that, to my surprise, I find myself replying in kind. Normally I don't do tender.

Eventually she takes the Old Soldier in her hand and I see her glance at him.

'What do you think?' I'm anxious not to miss an objective opinion of the state he's in.

'What do you mean, what do I think? It's a willy, isn't it? I mean, willies are willies.'

I can see the Old Soldier cringe at this disparagement of his individual attributes.

'No, I mean, how stiff does he – uh – it – how stiff does it feel?'

She stares at the Old Soldier and then at my face, puzzled. 'Well, I hadn't really thought there were degrees of stiffness. I kinda reckoned willies were two-speed, if you know what I mean. Either on or off. Floppy or not.'

She leans over to a bedside drawer, pulls out a condom and expertly wraps the Old Soldier. She stretches one leg over me and lowers herself on to him.

'So it's stiff enough?'

'Oh, yeah. Mmmm. It's stiff enough.'

Afterwards – and it's quite a long time until afterwards – we're lying on our backs sharing a spliff and I'm thinking, That may quite possibly have been the best fuck I've ever had, and starting to scroll through a few classics from the past when Karen exhales a long stream of marijuana smoke and says, 'That was a pity-fuck.'

'Hey, no, hang on, I did it because I wanted to, not out of pity.'

She sits up. 'That's so typical of you, Michael Cole! I wasn't asking, I was telling. I pity-fucked you, not the other way round.'

'You pity-fucked me? But why should you pity me enough to – to—'

'Oh, listen, Michael, don't get me wrong. I enjoyed it. I've wanted you in my bed for a long, long time.'

'So you fancy me. How can it be pity?'

'Unlike you, I don't sleep with everyone I fancy. Even if I do feel a bit miffed when they sleep with everyone *but* me. But today I felt sorry for you. You were dripping your misery all over the parquet and I figured I liked you enough to take away the pain for a moment or two.'

'More than a moment!'

'OK. But that's it. It wouldn't have happened without the rain or your situation. Listen, Michael, it's all any of us can do in this life. Forget about the misery for a while. And offer that to other people.'

She watches me, leaning on one elbow while I lie back and take another hit on the spliff.

'Michael Cole,' she says at last. 'MC.'

'So?'

'MC. Male Chauvinist.'

'You think I'm a male chauvinist?'

'Nope. I think your initials stand for Me Chauvinist.'

'What's that?'

'Well, chauvinist means violently patriotic.'

'I do know that. It is sort of my job to know what words mean.'

'Yeah, so a male chauvinist is someone who's violently patriotic in favour of his sex or, to put it another way, anti-women.' Naturally she pronounces it 'ant-eye', the American way. 'Ant-eye women.'

'You think I'm anti-women?'

'Oh, no, Michael, I think you're anti-everyone. That's what I mean, Me Chauvinist. You belong to a nation of one. You don't care whether other people are men or women. If they're not you, then they don't matter. Your great hero Donne said no man was an island. But he got it wrong, Michael. Because you are. An island, floating all alone in the middle of a hostile sea.'

The spliff has burned almost to the roach and it's getting hot. I take another drag, which brings tears to my eyes and makes me cough. Spluttering, I hand it to Karen and pull myself to my feet. I stagger to the kitchen, pour myself some water and gulp it down.

Back in the bedroom, I begin to pull on my clothes. Karen nods at the Old Soldier, who I realize – a moment of joy – is erect.

'Hey, it's in top gear. Wanna go round the block again?'

'No, thanks, I think I've had all the pity I can stand for one day.' And it's not just the spliff that's making my eyes water.

TWENTY-ONE

Methinks all cities, now, but anthills be,
Where, when the several labourers I see,
For children, houses, provision, taking pain,
They're all but ants, carrying eggs, straw, and grain;
Obsequies to the Lord Harrington, brother to the
Countess of Bedford

'You realize you'll have to buy Mrs Thursby's husband a new spirit level?' Alison doesn't look up from the kitchen worktop where she has a couple of onions on the chopping-board. She's holding a large Sabatier and picks up one of the onions to peel it.

'Why? There's nothing wrong with the old one.' Thank God for beta-blockers, I tell myself. My heart scarcely skips a beat. This is the first time Alison has mentioned yesterday's incident.

'Apparently he says he doesn't fancy it after where it's been.' She's peeling the other onion now, tongue between her lips in intense concentration.

'Oh, no, you mean she told him about it?'

'Well, of course she told her husband about it. She had to explain why she'd handed her notice in. It's a real pisser, she's the best cleaner we've ever had.'

'Handed her notice in? That's a bit over the top, isn't it?'

'After what you did? Some people might consider it sexual harassment, you know.'

'That's crazy!'

She slices the onion in two, the blade making a hard noise against the board. She turns and waves the knife at me. I take a step back.

'You try to involve the poor woman in some per-verted bondage sex game—'

'Bondage? That's ludicrous!'

'Is it? You had her husband's spirit level lashed to your prick—'

'It wasn't lashed, it was an elastic band.'

'Oh, well, that's all right, then, isn't it?' She has two hands on the knife now, ready to start chopping. 'Mrs Thursby said it was the most horrible thing she'd ever seen.'

'God, that's a bit rich. She's probably only seen Mr Thursby's. I feel quite offended.'

She starts chopping the onions now, with what seems to me unnecessary cruelty. Chop chop chop chop chop.

'Well, aren't you at least going to attempt to explain?' she says. There are tears in her eyes now, but of course that could just be from the onions.

'Listen, I've been having some – um – erection problems lately. That's how come I had the spirit level—'

'Using it as a splint, were you? Bit big to have strapped to your willy, wasn't it? What were you planning to do with it?'

'Oh, what's the use of trying to explain anything to you?' Feigning annoyance to terminate the interrog-ation, I turn and leave the room. There's a much easier way to ease my troubles. All that chopping has made my nose water.

*   *   *

271

I'm determined not to let the Mrs Thursby incident or the Karen pity-fuck depress me and prevent me having a productive day. This is the day I will get all of those books into the house. In the early afternoon I cruise past and see, to my joy, that Alison's car is not there. I park along the road and stroll back to the house, intending to make sure, and have just turned into the driveway when I hear the sound of a car coming. I peep between the shrubs at the front gate and scan the road. Sure enough, it's Alison. I duck behind the pyracantha just as she pulls into the driveway.

The bush isn't very tall and I have to squat on my haunches to make sure I'm out of sight. The sound of the car door opening and shutting. Another door opens. Joyful sounds of children fighting. Car door shuts.

'Mummy, Mummy, look, I've found an ants' nest!' Jake's voice. The child is obsessed with insects.

'How lovely, darling!' Completely unconvincing response from Alison who is terrified of any creature smaller than a cat in inverse proportion to its size. Gets hysterical, for example, about nits in children's hair.

'Can I play with the ants, Mummy?'

'Well, yes, of course, darling, just don't hurt them, that's all.' (This because she once read a newspaper article that claimed all serial killers begin by torturing and killing small animals. If Jake squashes an ant he may turn into the Yorkshire Ripper. If he then puts it into his mouth he'll grow up to be Jeffrey Dahmer.) 'And keep away from the road and don't bring any of them into the house.'

I peep through the bush, parting leaves like some Monty Python parody of a Victorian explorer in darkest Africa. Jake's squatting on the footpath to the front door, which Alison has left open, presumably to keep an eye on him. I contemplate the chances of whipping from behind the bush and out of the driveway without

Jake seeing. He *is* preoccupied with the ants. And if he does catch me, I can pretend I've just arrived home on some pretext or other. On the other hand, if Alison happens to come or look outside as I emerge from the bush (as, given my luck recently, is bound to happen) I'll find myself with a great deal of explaining to do. The curious thing is I find I have no anxiety about any of this. I can feel the beat of tension in my brain but it's in that other room, at one remove from me. I think how aptly named are beta-blockers, for it's as though a barrier has been erected between me and my emotions. Not that there was ever much traffic between the two, anyway.

I hear Jake talking. Edward must have come back out. I peep again. No, he's on his own. He's talking to the ants! I have a child who talks to ants! 'Do you want to come over here?' he's saying, and I watch as he lifts an ant delicately on one finger and moves it to another part of the path, smiling and chattering away all the while. 'I could build you a house out of Lego, you know. It would be cleaner than all that dirt.'

I decide I may as well stay put. After all, I have nothing better to do with the afternoon, and I'm being paid to do it; the bush is reasonably comfortable and the entertainment's good. Why not? Of course, the downside is that ants are one of the things that set off my morbidity. The idea that an ant has a life just as I have a life. Why should I imagine mine is any more significant than its? When I'm dead I'll be just as dead as it will be. Our intelligence will then be the same. Ants and dinosaurs, they have the same effect. It's best to avoid extremes of size in my state of mind.

Suddenly I hear the patter of tiny feet and Edward appears. He watches as Jake carefully places the ant he's holding on the footpath, then lifts his foot and stamps on it. Jake lets out a wail of despair you could

273

hear a mile away. Edward smiles smugly. I think of road-traffic accidents, cancer, hypertension, strokes and wanton boys playing with us. They kill us for their sport and we don't even know they're doing it.

The ensuing fight brings out Alison, and my two sons are dragged inside, the front door slamming behind them.

I wait a moment or two, allowing them time to make their way to the kitchen at the back of the house, where the boys usually sit fighting over drawing or Lego while Alison carries out the continuous task of fixing food for them.

'Hey, you, what do you think you're doing?'

I glance behind me and realize that, although I'm hidden from my own house and pathway by the bush, I am clearly visible over the front hedge of our garden, especially from the upstairs windows of the houses opposite. It's from the one directly facing ours that an old lady is now striding towards me.

'What do you think you're doing, lurking about like that? Get out of here before I have the police on you!'

'Er, it's OK,' I say, 'it's me, Professor Cole. I'm allowed to lurk. I live here, remember?'

'Oh,' she says, nonplussed. 'But what are you doing creeping about like that?'

'I was, er, just doing some gardening,' I stammer.

'Gardening? In those clothes?' We both examine my jacket, my too-clean Levi's and my polished brogues, now smeared with mud.

'Well, not so much the practical stuff. More sort of design, really. I'm, uh, planning to make a few changes.'

She stares at me, mouth puckered up like a cat's arse. 'Oh, yes?' she says, in a tone that means, 'Oh, no, you're not.' 'Well you just mind what you get up to. I've got my eye on you.'

'I beg your pardon!' I'm quite affronted now.

'I know all about you, Professor,' she says, managing skilfully to make the last word sound simultaneously like a recognized term of abuse *and* an august title to which I'm not entitled.

'I don't know what you mean,' I say, pushing past her and making my retreat, walking swiftly along the pavement towards my car.

'I mean I know what you've been up to,' she shouts after me. 'Mrs Thursby does for me too.'

TWENTY-TWO

I ask not dispensation now,
To falsify a tear, or sigh, or vow
Love's Exchange

Having been foiled in my attempts to get all my books and papers into the house in one fell swoop, I'm forced to smuggle them in piecemeal. Each evening when I return, I load my briefcase with as many books as it will hold. I stuff papers down my shirt so I rustle as I walk and have to remember not to give my children a crackly hug.

After a couple of days I know exactly how those men must feel who smuggle pornographic magazines into their homes. (Actually I know already – I'm one of them!) After only a few more non-working days I have nearly all the stuff from the car distributed around my study. I've been careful not to dump it in one conspicuous pile in case Alison looks in. I don't want her to notice there are more books in here, an increase in the volume of volumes, as it were. So I've spread them out rather like those POWs in a film who distributed the earth from their escape tunnel, via their trouser legs, all over the prison camp yard.

Having achieved all this without arousing Alison's suspicion I feel a sense of accomplishment that I realize has been lacking for a long time in my real work. I find myself beginning to think, I rather like this. I can do this!

Tonight is the night I aim to take in the last books from the back seat of the car. I open the front door carefully, slip inside and close it slowly so it won't slam. I have a dozen books secreted about my person and the last thing I want is to bump into Alison.

'Michael!' I'm half-way up the first flight of stairs. 'Michael, wait a minute . . .'

I'm up the rest and the next flight at a gallop. In less than five seconds I'm inside my study, leaning back against the door, breathing heavily. It's then that I notice the dark shadow of someone behind the desk, illuminated only by the computer screen's glow. 'Not again, Uncle Frank,' I say. 'I thought I told you to keep off the Internet.'

The silhouette of a hand reaches out and tugs the cord of the desk lamp. It's not Uncle Frank. I can hear Alison's feet pounding up the stairs.

'How the hell did you get in here?' I ask. 'What are you doing at my desk?'

He slips a hand inside his jacket and flashes a piece of plastic at me. 'DS Hammond from the local CID, Professor Cole. Your wife—'

'Michael?' It's Alison from outside. 'Are you all right? I said he could wait in your study. I didn't want the boys seeing him.'

'It's OK,' I call back. 'Nothing to worry about. Go back to the boys, I'll take care of this.' There's a pause and then I hear her footsteps retreating down the stairs. I turn back to the policeman.

'I'm sorry, I didn't realize who you were,' I mutter. 'What's this all about?' He has a small head and slicked-back hair, like a ferret or a weasel. He looks vaguely familiar. Then I remember where I've seen him before: the Thai Tavern, the playground.

'I'm with the Drugs Squad, Professor Cole.'

My heart skips a beat – has he searched my desk and found my stash? But then I always keep it locked. My hand finds my keys in my jeans pocket and clenches itself protectively around them. 'What do you want with me?'

'You look a little concerned, Professor. You wouldn't have anything to hide, now, would you?'

'No, of course not!' I snap.

He smiles. 'If you don't mind my saying so, sir, you seem to have something concealed up your jumper.'

'What? Oh!' I slip out Frank Kermode's *Shakespeare's Language*. 'Er, just something I didn't want my wife to see.'

He extends a hand. 'Mind if I take a look, sir?'

I hand it to him. He studies the front cover, turns it over and reads the blurb. Then he thumbs through it, pausing to read a line or two here and there before handing it back to me. 'Can't see any harm in it. Likes to keep an eye on what you're reading does she, then, your wife?'

'Er, no, look, it's rather complicated. Can we move on to the purpose of your visit? I have work to do.'

'Really, sir? Not what I heard, sir. I heard you'd been sus-pen-ded, sir.' He draws it out like that, as three separate syllables. 'Take a seat, sir.' He indicates the old sofa, as though this were his room, not the other way round. I sit down carefully on it, fearful of suddenly crumpling and giving everything away. 'Do you know a Gary Thomson, Professor?'

'No, I don't think so. Is he a student?'

'No, Professor, and I think it's rather disingenuous of you to suggest you don't know him. My colleague and I observed you together on – let me see . . .' he dips his hand into the side pocket of his jacket, pulls out a notebook and flips it open . . . the fifth of this month at a children's playground.'

'Tommo.'

'You may know him by that name, sir.'

My brain flounders, but thank heavens for beta-blockers because I remain calm. 'Yes, it's true I saw him there. I know him from the gym I use.'

'That would be Walker's Gym, in the Lower Grange Road?'

'Yes.'

'Go on.'

'Well, that's it, really. Just bump into him there sometimes. Pass a word or two.'

'You pass a word or two. Not drugs?'

'No.'

'He's not a friend, then?'

'No. Oh, no. Definitely not a friend. Definitely.'

'So this meeting at the playground—'

'Was entirely accidental. I was there with my children. He was there with a – a – a friend's child.'

'And he hasn't sold you any drugs, sir? Supplied you with illegal steroids or Class A drugs?'

'Class A?'

'The ones that get you into trouble, sir. Cocaine. Heroin. That sort of thing.'

'No.'

'Do you know a Mr Timothy Royce, sir?'

'Never heard of him.' A little sigh of relief escapes me here. We're on to safe ground. The truth.

'You were with him on that day, sir. You spent a long time in his company and left with him and Thomson.'

'Oh, Tim!'

'Ah, so you do know him?'

'Not really. I just met him that day, that's all. Never seen him before or since. He was just another parent as far as I was concerned.'

279

'And you didn't see Thomson pass him anything?'

'No, not that I can remember. Such as what?'

'A carrier-bag?'

'No, I don't think so.'

'And he didn't pass you anything?'

I can't help pausing for a moment before I reply, just enough to gauge the literal truth of my answer, one that will fool a lie detector because it is, *strictly* speaking, the truth. But the moment's hesitation is enough for Hammond to note. He looks at me expectantly. 'No nothing at all.'

He sits and stares at me until I feel uncomfortable. As though he has X-ray vision like Superman and can see into my soul. It's probably something they teach them in police college, I tell myself, and sit staring back, beta-blocked calm equal to his training.

Suddenly he breaks eye-contact, shuts the notebook and stands. 'Well, thank you very much, Professor. That's all for now. You've been a big help. Sorry to have troubled you.'

'That's all right.' I get up and rush, a little too eagerly I tell myself even as I'm doing it, to open the door for him.

He walks through it, and then suddenly he turns. 'Oh, just one more thing, sir.'

'Yes?' It comes out as a croak.

He taps his nose in a confidential manner. 'I won't say a word to the wife about the Shakespeare.'

After Alison has let Hammond out she runs up the stairs and bursts into my room. 'What was that all about?' she says. 'Have you been up to something in the park?'

'In the park? What on earth do you mean?'

'You know,' she says, tears pricking her eyes, 'with your willy.'

TWENTY-THREE

Busy old fool, unruly sun,
Why dost thou thus,
Through windows, and through curtains call
   on us?
Must to thy motions lovers' seasons run?

The Sun Rising

I didn't answer Alison last night, shaken as I was after the interview with Hammond and by her question's revelation of how low her opinion of me has sunk. That the first suspicion she leaps to is that I'm a flasher. 'I haven't anything to flash!' I want to yell at her. 'It's too floppy!'

But I might as well have told her the truth, because this morning everything is blown apart anyway the moment I sit down to breakfast and find a copy of the *Sun* by my cereal bowl.

'What's up? The newsagent out of the *Independent*?' I quip.

Alison looks up from pouring milk for the boys and I see her face is red and that she's been crying.

'Page four,' she says. 'If you can get past the tits.'

It's the main splash on the page.

Donne don done for porno taping student

A UNIVERSITY LECTURER was sacked last week after being caught red-handed making a steamy secret porno video tape of one of his students. Randy prof Michael Cole, who is an expert on John Donne,* was also believed to be high on illicit drugs at the time.

'He duped me into going to bed with him,' dusky beauty Tamsin Graves, 20, told the *Sun*. 'He tricked his way into my flat by saying he'd help me with my essay on Donne and then before I knew it he had my clothes off and was trying to tape me. Luckily he started having some kind of bad drug trip and I spotted the taping device and threw him out before things went too far.'

Cole, who is in his late fifties, was unavailable for comment but a spokesman for the university said, 'The matter is under investigation. Naturally we abhor the idea of anyone taping a student without his or her knowledge and would bring the full weight of disciplinary procedures down on anyone who did so.'

*John Donne was leader of the metaphysical group of poets in the eighteenth century and notorious for using poetry to lure young women back to his flea-infested lodgings for sex. He later reformed and became a priest.

I find myself thinking that the average *Sun* reader or, indeed, every *Sun* reader, will read the headline as 'don don done' rather than 'done don done' and am just deciding it doesn't matter when my reverie is broken by Alison.

'Well?'

'Well what?'

'Is it true?'

I try to explode with righteous indignation but find myself strangely calm. I know I'm upset but it's as though my heart's throbbing in some other poor sod's chest and is nothing to do with me. My beta-blocked eruption falls rather flat.

'Of course it's not true. It's full of inaccuracies for a start. I mean, eighteenth century! Donne was born in the sixteenth and died in the seventeenth. He didn't, so far as anyone knows, live in flea-infested—'

'That's not what I'm talking about. Did you—' She stops and looks at Jake and Edward who are eating breakfast. 'Boys, come here, special treat before Jake goes to nursery. You can watch a video.'

She takes them into the sitting room whence come the happy sounds of them fighting over which tape to watch. Eventually she returns.

She leans against the worktop, arms folded. 'Did you video yourself having sex with this girl?'

'No. I did not have sex with her. I did not video her.'

'Then why have you been sacked?'

'I haven't been sacked, I'm suspended. Also, I'm not in my late fifties. Although I probably will be if I have another couple of weeks of this.'

'So she made the whole thing up?'

'No. It's all quite innocent. Well, fairly. I gave her a lift home—'

'Huh!'

'And we were talking about Donne, she'd missed some classes. She invited me in, and she, er, misread some signals and took her clothes off, then I dropped the blood-pressure monitor and she thought it was a cassette-recorder and got hysterical.' *Shit!* I think to myself. *These beta-blockers are good!*

Alison stares at me. She has no makeup on and her face is blotchy from all the crying. I feel sorry for her for looking so unattractive and pathetic when she wants to look angry.

'You expect me to believe that?'

'Of course. As a child I was taught that if I told the truth I would be believed.'

There's a long silence. Alison bites her top lip with her lower teeth and stares out of the window. A female blackbird is tugging at a worm on the lawn. We watch the unequal struggle until the bird wrenches the worm free and takes wing with it wriggling in its beak.

'What are you thinking?' I ask.

She swallows as if with effort. She continues to stare out of the window. 'If you must know, I'm thinking the D-word,' she says at last, almost in a whisper.

'Donne? What's he got to do with it? I mean, I can see that if it hadn't been for Donne I wouldn't have been anywhere near—'

'Not Donne, you fool,' she snaps, firing me a Gorgon glance. She rolls her eyes sideways in the direction of the sitting room and then mouths something silently to me.

'*Divorce*,' her lips shape. 'And this time the boys may not be enough to stop me.'

I've been calling Tommo ever since Hammond's visit last night but each time the same message comes back. His phone is switched off. I try again in the car, but with the same result. I'm just putting my phone down when it rings.

'Hello, Professor, you haven't forgotten, have you?' Tamsin.

'How could I, you bitch, when you've plastered me all over the *Sun*?'

'Would have thought you'd like that. Being in there. You know, among all the tits. Seem to remember that was your thing.'

'It's not a bloody joke. My wife's talking about divorce.'

'And, of course, you've done nothing to deserve that, have you, Michael?'

A beat or two's pause before I can speak. 'But, Tamsin, the *Sun* . . .'

'It wasn't me. Honestly. I just answered their questions when they phoned me up. I didn't tip them off.' Suddenly she sounds like what she is, a young girl, nineteen or twenty, a student making excuses for not having her essay in on time. For a moment it's as if I'm the one giving her a hard time and not the other way round. I like it this way round.

'Well, somebody did. Your friend Bennet, I suppose. He hates me enough.'

The briefest of silences. I hear her deep intake of breath before she speaks. 'I really couldn't say.'

Ah, she's got herself back together again. The tough persona she probably picked up from some TV show or other. Cool. In control.

'Anyway, that's not why I phoned you. Do you have the goods?'

'Well, not exactly, but I'm, well, expecting them.'

'You'd better have them, Michael. We had an understanding.'

'Ah, but I'm just wondering if we do have one any more. Haven't you already broken it? What about the *Sun*?'

'I can't do anything about the *Sun*, it's already happened. Besides, that's not what matters to you, is it? You get me what I asked for and I don't speak to the committee. That was our understanding.'

I'm forced to bite back the bitter bile of fury rising in my throat. I know she's right. Even if she were to go to the newspaper and say it was all a mistake, even if they printed a retraction, it would be in small print on page thirty-five. The damage to my dignity before the wider world is already done. I have to let that go. But without her evidence, where it most matters to me, in the orbit of the university, I'll be exonerated. Alison may believe my version of events – after all it's not all lies, and she's swallowed more unlikely stories before. What's certain is, I'll save my job. If Tamsin withdraws her allegations I may even emerge with my career prospects intact. Against all odds, Cole triumphs again!

As if reading my thoughts, Tamsin breaks in on them: 'Michael, you can still save your job. Doesn't that matter to you?'

'Of course.' I'm thinking on my feet here (as it were – I'm actually on the ring road in the car), tap-dancing. If I can't get hold of Tommo there won't be anything to give Tamsin. But better not to tell her that on the phone. Better to see her tomorrow, explain in person and hope she'll show mercy.

'OK. Then meet me at the weir. One o'clock. And don't come empty-handed.'

At the gym Ted is just opening up the bar. 'Looking for someone, Prof?' he asks. Before I can answer he ducks behind the bar and I think this must be some reflex from his fighting days. But when I peer over I see he's simply putting on another barrel of bitter.

'Yes, is Tommo around?'

'Tommo?' His eyes widen. 'You haven't heard, then?'

'Heard what?'

'The Old Bill came and arrested him last night. Took him right out of the weights room. Wouldn't even let him have a shower.'

TWENTY-FOUR

Little think'st thou, poor flower,
Whom I have watched six or seven days,
And seen thy birth, and seen what every hour
Gave to thy growth, thee to this height to raise,
And now dost laugh and triumph on this bough,
Little think'st thou
That it will freeze anon, and that I shall
Tomorrow find thee fall'n, or not at all.

The Blossom

'Hmm, baby's stopped growing. Weight hasn't changed for two weeks.' Mr Deaver, the consultant, looked up from the papers in front of him. 'We can't risk leaving him in there. We could try inducing you but, frankly, with the history of this pregnancy, I wouldn't advise it.'

'You mean you'll do a Caesarean?'

'I mean the little fellow isn't growing so I'm going in there to get him out.'

'When?' asked Alison.

Deaver picked up the phone and punched buttons with military brusqueness. 'I have to go in after a baby ASAP,' he barked. 'When's the next theatre opportunity?' A brief pause. 'OK, book it.'

He looked up at us. 'Fifteen hundred hours today, that's when we'll be going in. OK?'

I hefted Jake into my arms. 'It's nearly twelve now. I have to get him home, find someone to look after him and get back here.'

'Well,' said Deaver, 'what are you hanging about for?'

A minute later as Jake and I waited for the lift, I reflected on the irony of everything happening in such a rush now. The last five months had passed agonizingly slowly. Contrary to all predictions and any medical history we'd been able to come across, Alison had clung on to our baby. Or he had clung on to her. After a week in hospital, during which all the doctors' predictions that she'd go into labour failed to come true, she was allowed home. She was to remain in the house, to keep as still as possible and to avoid all possible sources of infection. She was not allowed to lift anything remotely heavy and certainly not her boisterous eighteen-month-old son.

We sloughed off our old routine and grew into a new one. I took a six-month sabbatical, which I'd been storing up to work on the Donne book, and became Jake's full-time carer. It seemed fairer than employing a nanny, since Jake would have to cope with having only half a mother for however long the baby survived. We bricked up our minds against the inevitable. When the doctors told Alison she'd go into labour at any moment, or that infection and miscarriage were inevitable, we bunkered down with the only fact that mattered: the baby was alive.

Every week I'd drive the three of us to the hospital. It was Alison's one outing. There she'd be scanned and an attempt would be made to measure how much fluid remained in the baby's sac. This was an uncertain science and we learned to recognize which ultrasound technicians were most proficient in their art. How can you measure the volume of something seen only on a screen in two dimensions? Especially when the picture constantly changes as the baby turns and squirms. Although we were happy when he turned because that meant he had enough fluid to do so, and so help develop his growing limbs. The measurements came in square centimetres and we soon learned what was good and what was bad. Twenty was where he should have been. After the night in the car he went down to five. But the next week we discovered that the amount of fluid could go up as well as down. As the baby fed off the placenta he peed, adding precious liquid to his diminished pool. Of course, there was still a hole in the sac through which fluid constantly leaked. On a bad day Alison would change pad after pad and on those days, lie as still as she might, we both felt our son's life ebbing away.

Time moved differently from how it had moved all my life. Instead of rushing towards life's inevitable conclusion, it slowed so one day struggled to limp into the next. But move it did, measured out in the weekly scans, when we might be momentarily buoyant on a higher volume – or, rather, area – of liquid, only to realize it might already be leaking away. Then there was no hope, only the long wait until the next scan.

At the same time Jake began to say his first words and as his vocabulary snowballed, we could only sit wishing away this precious time. Milestones were reached. At twenty-two weeks a viable baby was possible. All right, the odds were it would be brain-damaged and physically handicapped, but it had a chance of living. At twenty-eight weeks most premature babies would survive. At thirty-two most would survive with few after-effects.

En route Alison was given antibiotics to enable her to resist infection and premature labour. For a time there were two steroid injections, once a week. I'd drive her to the hospital in the morning for the first, and twelve hours later a friend would take her for the other. Without the injections, if the baby was born early, his lungs would be stuck together and he'd be unable to breathe. On steroids Alison puffed up like a toad trying to scare off a predator. Her skin was covered in red blotches. She was unable to sleep. She saw herself as a hatching tank, undergoing all manner of indignity for this baby who, when he kicked without the cushion of water, bruised her insides in return.

The funny thing is that during those five months I was the nearest I've ever been to happy. Well, if not happy then not under my usual depression. Sure I'd lie there every night beside Alison feeling a desperate helplessness that my son might be dying inside her and there was nothing I could do to stop it. But I never thought, Oh, well, what's it matter? In another hundred years he'll be dead anyway. I never thought that. I couldn't think further than the next few months. I was too caught up in the here and now, doing what I could to help Alison in her stoical devotion to the unborn child, and for the rest busy watching the other child grow and run at life head on.

And now here I was, in the lift, with my nearly-two-year-old all-walking, all-talking son, wondering if the doctors would have the last laugh after all. Had there been enough fluid at the right time? Had the baby been able to suck in enough of his own urine to stretch and develop those lungs? Would he just not breathe when the moment came?

I glanced at my watch. It had taken five minutes to get downstairs. I pushed Jake towards the car park, but then an unmistakable smell hit my nostrils. It was at least a forty-five-minute drive back home. I had to change his nappy. I doubled back on myself and found the babychange room. The red marker on the lock told me it was occupied. I waited. I tried the handle to hurry the person inside up. 'All right!' yelled a voice. 'I got twins, this is going to take some time.'

I wheeled Jake to the men's toilet where there was no babychange facility. There wasn't room to change him in a cubicle and the whole lavatory was small and cramped. I laid him on the floor in front of the urinals.

'Floor cold, Daddy!' he protested and struggled to get up.

I pushed him back. The door opened. A maintenance man came in, ignored us and stepped over Jake to the urinal. Jake looked at the huge legs passing over him in alarm.

'Mummy!' he screamed. 'Mummy!'

'Mummy's with the doctor. Come on, Jake, it'll only be a minute.'

'No!' he screamed.

I decided that by now the babychange was probably free, so I picked him up, stuffed him back into the buggy and wheeled it out of the loo and along the corridor. I was three steps from the babychange when a woman carrying a baby appeared from nowhere and swung in through the door.

I wheeled Jake back to the men's. I peeled off my sweater and put it on the cold tiles and laid him on it. 'Look, Jake, we're probably going to get poo on Daddy's sweater,' I told him.

'Poo on Daddy's sweater!' he chortled, and carried on laughing all the time I was changing him. Afterwards, rolling up my shit-stained jumper to pop into the changing bag, I glanced at my watch. The whole thing had cost me twenty minutes. With the two journeys taking maybe an hour and a half, I had an hour to find someone to look after Jake.

In the car I floored the accelerator. It was lunchtime and the traffic was thin. I did my dance around the ring road again. Once off it, I avoided traffic black spots with a couple of back doubles and, cornering screechily as a Hollywood cop, was home inside forty minutes.

Indoors I began to collect everything Jake would need at someone else's house. His Tommee Tippee cups, yellow for water, blue for milk; nappies; change of clothes; Little, his special teddy bear, and a couple of familiar books as I might not be back by bedtime. As I moved around I had the phone crooked between shoulder and chin, trying to get hold of someone I could leave him with. Two of Alison's best friends were heavily pregnant and it didn't seem fair to lumber them with an additional child. Anyway, either might go into labour, which would give them the problem of what to do with Jake as well as their own children. I tried another friend. No reply. I left a message on her machine. Ditto two more. Why was everybody out? It was November, for Christ's sake! But then I tried Fiona and her phone was engaged. At least she was at home! I busied myself with more preparations, packing Jake's favourite food and a jigsaw he always liked doing. I tried Fiona again. My last hope. Still engaged. Finally I had everything ready. Still engaged. Rather than wait for her to finish the call I decided it would be quicker just to drive there. I put Jake and his things in the car and set off. Fiona lived about four miles away, which wasn't really a problem except that it was four miles in the wrong direction. I'd be that much further from the hospital. I got to the end of the road and realized I'd forgotten the camera.

I reversed up the one-way street, jumped out of the car and dashed into the house. I was all fingers and thumbs over the burglar alarm, which went into intruder mode. Waagh, waagh, waagh, it screamed, like a new-born baby. I soothed it, then searched the drawer where the camera lived. No camera. It had to be in there. I tugged the drawer right out and tipped the contents on to the kitchen table. No camera. I tried the next drawer. No camera. I tried another three before I found it, by which time the mess on the kitchen table made it look like the house had already been burgled so I didn't bother setting the alarm on the way out.

The clock in the car said one fifty. I screeched around suburban streets again to the incongruous soundtrack of *Postman Pat*. There were roadworks, and a huge traffic jam had built up. I tried calling Fiona on my mobile but I couldn't get a connection. Finally, I reached the end of her street. It was blocked by a removals van, which was obviously going to be there all day.

'Sorry, mate,' shouted one of the removal men, 'but there's nowhere else for us to put it. The road's sort of closed for the rest of the afternoon.'

Since the road was one way and I couldn't get in the other end, I drove the car up on to the pavement, put the flashers on, grabbed Jake and legged it along the street. Hot and breathless I arrived at Fiona's house and rang the bell. I looked at my watch. Nearly two. Fiona didn't appear. I rang the bell again and thumped on the door. Still no answer.

Then the neighbouring front door opened. An old lady stuck her head out. 'Looking for Fiona?' she said. I nodded. 'You've just missed her.' She managed to get a note of satisfaction into it that made me feel like spitting at her.

'Do you know where she's gone?' I asked.

'The park. I think that's what I heard her saying. I was on my way in as she was on her way out and—'

I didn't hear the rest as I was already scooting back to the car. The park! What kind of mother took her kids to the park in November? And should I be leaving my child with her?

I drove there, peering right and left all the time in the hope of spotting Fiona. Five past two, still no sign. At the park I screeched to a halt and hopped out with Jake and all his stuff, and tore across the grass to the playground. Fiona was there, just letting the twins out of their double buggy. Amber, a leggy blonde child of three, was climbing the steps to the slide.

'Fiona!' I gasped.

'Michael, what is it?'

'I need you to look after Jake. They're going in after the baby at three!'

'Going in? Where are they going in?'

'Into Alison. To get him out. Listen, I can't stop. Can I leave Jake with you?'

'That might be a bit tricky. We're supposed to be meeting my friend Maggie here. I'm looking after Charlotte. You know, she's in Amber's class at nursery? I'm happy to look after Jake as well, but I don't think I could manage five of them across the main road. That could be very tricky.'

At this point there was a shout and we looked up to see a woman a hundred yards or so across the park. She waved and a small girl, obviously Charlotte, began running eagerly towards us. The woman walked away.

'Maggie!' I called. 'Come back!'

'It's no good, she's due at work in five minutes. Even if she could hear you she couldn't help.'

'Listen,' I said, as Charlotte arrived and hurried into the playground, 'what if I take you back home now, and then shoot off?'

'Fine,' she said, 'if you've bought a people-mover since I last saw you.'

'It's the Golf.'

'Well, you can't get two adults and five children into a Golf. At least not in any way that I'd be happy for my children to travel.'

'OK, let me think.' I looked at my watch. Two twelve. 'Listen, why don't I take Jake and Amber and Charlotte and you follow as fast as you can with the buggy?'

'That's not a bad idea. OK.' She turned to the playground. 'Amber! Charlotte, come on now. We're going home.'

'But, Mummy, we only just got here,' said Amber, from the top of the slide.

'Yes, I know, darling, but there's been a change of plan. Come on.'

Amber slid down the slide.

'All right, you've had your slide, come on now, Amber.'

'No,' said Amber.

'Amber, this is really important. Michael has to get to the hospital to see Jake's baby brother being born.'

'I want another slide.' Amber mounted the steps again, closely followed by Charlotte who was giggling. Jake began laughing too.

Fiona pushed open the playground gate and strode into it.

'Amber, come down this minute!'

'No. We want a slide, don't we, Charlotte?'

'Yes,' said Charlotte.

'Get down this instant!' yelled Fiona. Two fourteen.

'No,' said Amber, and slid down the slide again. Fiona grabbed her by the arm but Amber wriggled free and ran up the steps to the slide.

'Five more minutes, Mummy, then we'll come.'

Fiona turned to me and held her hands up in a gesture of helplessness.

'Fiona, I don't have five more minutes.' Two fifteen.

Fiona turned to face her daughter again. '*Amber*, Michael hasn't got five minutes. Get down off there this instant!'

'No.' Two sixteen.

I walked over to the slide. 'Amber,' I said, 'if you come now and you're really quick I'll give you a big bar of chocolate.'

'How big?' she said.

'The biggest you've ever had.'

'And Charlotte?'

'The same for her.'

'OK.' Both girls were off the slide and half-way across the park in thirty seconds flat. Fiona gave me a dismayed look.

'Child psychology,' I said. I hefted Jake on to my shoulder again and ran after the girls.

Ten minutes later Fiona puffed round the corner of her street with the double buggy. I hugged and kissed Jake. All at once his future misery crashed over me like a huge breaker on the seashore. If all went well, this was my last moment with him as my only child. The final second of his specialness. And he didn't even know.

'Daddy will be back soon,' I said. 'Have a nice time with Amber and Charlotte. Be a good boy.'

'Mummy come back too?' he said.

'Mummy too.' I kissed him again and thrust him into Fiona's arms. I legged it to the car and as I drove it off the footpath and turned back the way I'd come, glanced at the clock. Twenty-eight minutes past two.

There I was again, doing that crazy dance around the ring road. In one lane, switch to the next, cutting people up, their horns blaring in competition with *Postman Pat*, which had come on again when I switched on the ignition and I hadn't thought to turn off. I broke speed limits and ran every red light and in the end I roared into the hospital car park at four minutes to three.

I jumped out of the car and felt in my pocket for change to buy a parking ticket. Empty. Oh, well, fuck it, they'd have to give me a ticket. Then I saw the sign. VEHICLES WITHOUT A TICKET WILL BE CLAMPED. The logistics of the situation took over. If I came out and the car was clamped I might have to wait hours before I could have it freed and go and fetch Jake.

I ran inside where there was a small shop selling flowers, sweets and books for visitors to take to patients. 'Do you have change for a twenty-pound note?' I asked the assistant, who was serving a woman with a magazine.

'Just wait your turn,' she said.

'I can't wait, they're going in after my baby any moment now, I have to be there.'

'Going in after your baby? Oh, one of Mr Deaver's patients. Well you better hurry. He won't wait, you know.' She opened the till, gave the woman her change and said, 'Sorry, I can't change that.'

I started to turn away. 'Wait,' she called after me. 'If your wife's in labour you don't need a parking ticket. Just leave your car number with the porter.'

I rushed over to the window of the porter's cubicle. It was the same elderly man who'd let us in all those months ago. 'I want to leave my car number with you. My wife's having a baby.'

He squinted at me. 'Really? It doesn't seem that long since she had the last one.'

'Listen, my car's number. It's—'

'Wait a minute, sir, I need something to write it down with. Now where did I put that pen . . .?'

He began searching around on the desk. 'Come on, you old fool!' I wanted to scream, but somehow, even in my panic-stricken state, I knew not to. The phone rang. His hand reached out to lift the receiver.

'It's a C-section,' yelled the woman from the shop. 'Mr Deaver's doing it!'

'Shit!' said the man, turning from the phone. 'Why

didn't you say so?' Magically he found the pen. 'Hurry up now. What's that number?'

I blurted it out.

'Sorry, sir, didn't get that last one, was that a B or a V?'

'B!' I shouted, and was off down the corridor beside his little cubby-hole and on to the stairs because I didn't trust the lift. Seconds later I emerged at the third floor and tore along to where I'd left Alison. She wasn't there. An Oriental woman was in her place, flicking through a magazine.

'My wife, the woman who was here, where is she?'

'What?' said the woman.

'My wife. Alison, Mrs Cole. Blonde. Long legs – you won't have been able to see them, of course. Where have they taken her?'

She shook her head. 'Sorry, no speak English.'

I turned away and back into the corridor where I all but ran headlong into a uniformed figure. It was the big sister who'd admitted us that night all those months ago and had been there earlier today.

'Mr Cole!' she said. 'Where have you been? We've been looking everywhere for you. Your wife is in the theatre now. Come on, I'll show you the way.'

She led me along the corridor towards a sign saying 'Theatre'. A red light was on and a sign next to it said, 'When red light is on do not enter. Operation in progress.'

The sister pushed me through the door. Immediately I was confronted by Deaver, wearing green medical fatigues and a plastic shower cap. He was holding up his hands while a nurse put rubber gloves on them.

'Ah, at last,' he said. 'The father. It's always the same, get them pregnant then leave them to suffer alone.'

'I'm sorry, I—'

'Just a joke,' he said, without smiling. 'You'll find scrub-downs in that room there.' He nodded behind me. I entered a small box room lined with shelves.

'Put your clothes in here,' said a nurse. I removed my shoes, trousers and shirt. 'Take a set and put it on. Hurry up, we're nearly ready to start.'

I took out a set of the green fatigues. I pulled on the trousers but they were too short and I couldn't pull them up to my waist. The nurse reappeared.

'Those are obviously the wrong size,' she snapped. She gave me a withering look, studied the shelves and pulled out another set. 'Try these.'

'Hurry up, Dad,' shouted Deaver's voice. 'We're ready to go in.'

Fumbling and stumbling I tugged on the clothes, finally pulling on the plastic cap.

'Don't forget the slippers,' barked the nurse, and I found a pair of white canvas shoes. I was just putting them on when she said, 'No, no, no, socks off, please.'

Finally I was ready and she ushered me into the theatre where I saw Alison lying on the operating table. At least, I assumed it was Alison because all I could see was her body from the chest down. Across the chest was fixed a canvas screen.

I looked around the room and was staggered by the number of people. When Jake was born there had been only Alison, a midwife and myself in the room, and frankly we could have done with a few more, I'd thought at the time. But here were Deaver, another doctor, an anaesthetist, three or four nurses and two women, whom Deaver introduced as paediatricians. 'As the baby is almost certainly going to need special care, Dr Rowlands here will whisk him off as soon as we have him out.'

Dr Rowlands smiled. 'Don't worry, Mr Cole. Your baby will be well looked after.'

'OK, go and join your wife at the spectators' end,' said Deaver.

I walked to the other end of the table and Alison smiled angelically up at me.

'How are you feeling?' I asked.

'Wonderful, the epidural kicked in five minutes ago. If anything happens to you I'm going to marry the man who gave it to me.'

'How long will the operation take?' I asked the man adjusting dials on a machine nearby, obviously the object of Alison's affections.

'About forty-five minutes. Take a seat and relax.'

I sat down beside Alison and held her hand.

'OK everybody?' called Deaver's voice. 'Right, action stations. I'm going in.'

'I wish he wouldn't keep saying that,' said Alison. 'Makes me feel like a war zone.'

'I meant to bring my Donne,' I said. 'I thought you might like some poems, but it was such a rush.'

'Never mind,' she replied, 'we can talk instead.'

'What do you want to talk about?'

She gripped my hand hard. 'Oh, Michael, what if he can't breathe? What if we've been through all this and he can't breathe?'

Before I could answer there was a slurping noise from the other side of the screen. Then pieces of blood-soaked cloth were tossed on to the floor. Then, suddenly, total silence and 'Waaa-waaa,' the muted cry of a baby.

I looked up over the screen and saw Deaver holding the bloody form of an infant. It looked very small after Jake.

'Well, he's out! Here's your baby, you people. And well worth the wait. OK, I'm just handing him over to Dr Rowlands so's she can check him then take him to Special Care. You'll get a little look at him first, assuming there's nothing too urgent.'

'Oh, let me have him, let me have him!' cried Alison. 'I'm sorry but I just can't wait.'

'My dear,' said Deaver, 'you are the most patient woman I've ever met. Just hang on in there for a few more minutes. Now I'm going back in to repair the damage.'

I didn't know what to say. Time had speeded up again. It had all happened so fast.

'I – I thought it was supposed to take forty-five minutes?' I said to Deaver.

'That's right. This long to get in there and get him out. The rest to repair collateral damage. Now let me get back to work.'

I watched as Rowlands and a nurse sponged the baby and then placed him in the scales. Rowlands seemed to be examining every pore of his skin. She shone lights in his eyes. She opened his mouth and peered down his throat. Finally she picked him up and placed him on Alison's chest. 'Your baby doesn't need special care,' she said. 'He's absolutely fine. Why don't you just feed him?'

And as I watched Alison lying there, nursing Edward, I wanted to punch the air and yell, 'One–nil to the Coles. One–nil to the Coles. That's one you didn't get!' It was just the exhilaration of the moment, you understand. Of course, I already knew that nobody gets away for ever.

TWENTY-FIVE

Man is the world, and death the ocean,
   To which God gives the lower parts of man.
The sea environs all, and though as yet
   God hath set marks, and bounds, 'twixt us and it,
Yet it doth roar, and gnaw, and still pretend,
   And breaks our banks, when 'er it takes a friend.

                                       Elegy on the Lady Markham

The last but one day of my forties does not begin auspiciously. Once again the *Sun* awaits me at breakfast.

Randy Prof flashes Mrs Mopp

RANDY PROF MICHAEL COLE flashed at a cleaning lady in a bizarre attempt to engage her in kinky sex, it emerged yesterday. Cole, 72, sacked last week for making porno movies of his students without their knowledge, exposed himself to cleaner Deirdre Thursby, 57, when

she went into his sons' bedroom to clean. Not only that but the naked academic tied his tool to one of her carpenter husband's in the hope of luring her into his bondage games.

'It was totally disgusting,' the distraught Mrs Mopp told the *Sun*. 'I've been cleaning for forty years and I've never seen anything like it. He was standing there bold as brass with my husband's best spirit level tied to his thing.'

Deirdre, who has cleaned for Cole, his wife Alison and their two sons for seven years, immediately handed her notice in. Particularly upsetting was that she had always regarded herself as one of the family. Her husband Bill often did odd jobs for them.

'I wouldn't have minded so much if he hadn't touched Bill's things,' said Deirdre. 'God knows what he's been up to with his other tools. Bill's had to throw them all away because he doesn't know where they've been.'

Cole was in hiding last night but a neighbour said, 'He's a very strange man. He does weird things like parking in the next road when there's spaces right outside his house and he's always lurking behind bushes as though waiting to spring out on you.'

I read it without comment and toss it contemptuously aside.

'Where's the *Independent*?' I ask Alison.

'I think the *Sun*'s more relevant to our lives just now,' she replies, briskly. 'Perhaps it will review your book when it's done.'

The wind blowing off the river is cold for May but luckily Edward and I are wearing our padded jackets, his yellow, mine black, and we don't feel it as we stand at the rail and look down at the weir. Indeed, the water where the weir tumbles into the river below foams, and spray rises up like steam so you could almost think it's boiling.

'There's a very lot of water, Daddy,' says Edward. He has to shout above the roar of the water.

'Yes, a very lot of water.'

We stand and gaze at it for another five minutes or so without speaking. Mesmerized. Then, suddenly, I'm aware of a third person standing beside us.

' "I saw rain falling and the rainbow drawn on Lammermuir," ' she murmurs.

'What's that?' I ask.

'Stevenson. From "Weir of Hermiston". This place always brings it to mind. It's just word association. Every time I come here it makes me think of it.'

'You know Stevenson?'

'I'm doing my dissertation on him,' says Tamsin. 'There's no need to sound so surprised. I do read books, you know.'

'Really? I had you down as someone who reads the *Sun*.'

She ignores the jibe and the bitterness with which it is delivered. 'My father's a Scot and he used to read Stevenson to me when I was little. He's interesting, his fascination with the symbiosis between good and evil. It's in all his books. Not just Jekyll and Hyde, but Ballantrae as well. And there's Long John Silver, of course.'

She smiles, and I realize it's something she can't help doing without appearing flirtatious.

'Is that what attracted you to me?' I ask. 'You saw me as a Jekyll and Hyde?'

She laughs. 'You? No, I don't think so. You're no Jekyll and Hyde. More like Hyde and Hyde.'

'Daddy, Daddy, I want a slide,' says Edward, so we walk back along the towpath to the small playground beside it. I turn Edward loose and he's off and up the steps to the slide. We watch him a moment or two.

'Cute kid,' says Tamsin.

'Yeah.' I grin ruefully. Regret is in the air, like the spray from the weir, which is wafted towards us on the cool breeze. We turn away and contemplate the river.

'OK, let's not waste any more time,' says Tamsin. 'I'll take the – uh – delivery now and you can get back to your childish games.'

I look around, trying to see if it's a trap, if there are any police visible, but I can't spot anyone. The river-bank's deserted except for an elderly woman walking a Labrador. If she's a plain-clothes cop, she's pretty good at it. She's got the walk off perfectly. The fishing season hasn't started yet and it's too cool for casual walkers.

'Haven't got it,' I say at last.

'What do you mean, you haven't got it?' She's done a bit of a Jekyll and Hyde herself here. Her smile has disappeared and her mouth is tight and puckered, as though someone used too many stitches on it and pulled them too tight.

'Why not?'

'I had a problem with the supply line.'

'What's that supposed to mean?'

'My contact. He got himself arrested. Couple of days ago.'

'Did he have the stuff? Did they find it?'

'I don't know. I just know he was arrested.'

'I don't believe you. We had an agreement.'

'We had a threat and a possible response to that threat. I can't help you. You'll have to go ahead and do your worst. I'm tired, Tamsin. I'm tired of all the problems you've been giving me. It's wrecked what was left of a not very satisfactory life.'

'I didn't wreck it, you did. When will you face up to the fact your actions have consequences? You tried to seduce me.'

'That's true.'

'And you tried to tape me.'

'Not true, not that you'll believe—'

'Well, here's a surprise for you, Professor. I taped you. In the restaurant. I got the whole conversation on tape. If they caught your friend with the stuff then I should think it will be enough to get you for conspiracy to supply drugs.'

I don't say anything. I'm somewhat dismayed that anyone can hate me so much.

'I wouldn't be surprised if you end up in prison.'

'Now wait a minute—'

But it's no use. She turns and walks away and all I can do is enjoy the view of her elegant arse disappearing across the walkway over the weir and probably taking with it what's left of my life. For a moment I contemplate running after her, trying to reason with her, but there's no point. She doesn't want reason, she wants blood.

Suddenly I remember Edward. I turn back and walk towards the playground, looking for him as I go. But I can't see his bright yellow coat. The slide is empty. One of the swings is occupied now, by a girl of eight or nine, but the rest of the playground is deserted. Panic rises up like vomit in my throat. I break into a trot. Maybe he's lying down in the sandpit. Maybe he took the coat off. Maybe he's behind the slide, or the roundabout. Yes, that's it, that's big enough to hide him. He must be behind there.

He's not.

I run over to the girl. 'Did you see a little boy in a yellow coat?'

She doesn't answer. I wonder for a moment if she might be deaf.

'Did you see a little boy in a yellow coat?' I shout it this time. She carries on swinging, her face looming closer as the swing brings her towards me, then backing off as the swing retreats.

I grab the chains of the swing. 'Answer me, can't you? Why won't you answer me?'

'My mum told me not to talk to strangers,' she replies.

'But I'm not going to hurt you, for God's sake, I just want to find my son.'

'He went that way.' She points to a gate at the far end of the playground that I hadn't even known was there. It's wide open.

I run to it, feeling as if my brain is overheating. Thank God for the beta-blockers, or if not God then Branko. Without them I'd be dead now. Allied to my panic is a suffocating sense of guilt. If I hadn't been preoccupied with Tamsin when I was supposed to be watching my child. If I hadn't been too busy with the consequences of my sordid sex life. With drugs, for Christ's sake!

Outside the gate a small path leads to the towpath. 'Oh, God, please, no,' I mutter. 'Not the river, please!'

And then I see him. Or, rather, not him but a little blob of yellow, bobbing in the water. The current has pulled him into the centre. He's about fifty metres upriver of the weir and the rush of water is sucking him towards it. I run along the bank, keeping pace with him, but only just, since when he hits midstream he's in the faster water. I put everything I've got into it. My lungs feel like they're sticking together, the way his almost did before he was born. Thoughts flash through my head. How will I tell Alison? After all she went through to get him here safely. The irony! This child who almost never made it into the world through lack of water now leaving it swamped by this raging torrent.

I make it to the walkway over the weir and run along to the middle. Edward is about ten metres off, floating towards me. Our eyes lock. I can't hear him for the roar of the torrent cascading off the weir, but I can see his lips saying, 'Daddy! Daddy! Help me, Daddy!'

I climb over the railing and hang on to the lower rail with one hand and stretch the other towards the water as he floats under. I stretch as far as I can. 'Grab my hand, Edward! Grab my hand!' I yell.

His small arm comes up and his fingers strain towards mine. Their tips touch, his icy-cold as death, and I try to stretch another inch, it's all I need another inch, to curl my fingers around his and pull him out. But it's no good. There isn't another inch to be had. Our fingers part and he disappears under my feet.

I climb back on to the walkway, breathing heavily. I look down. All I can see is the boiling white cauldron of water, all I can hear is its hungry roar. No sound of a child, no cry of 'Daddy', no such cry ever again.

And then, suddenly, a flash of yellow, which immediately disappears under the rush of foam. And then, a little further on, there it is again, as he's vomited out by the power of the water tumbling down behind him, into the relative calm beyond.

Suddenly I remember the Swoppet, and how, after I'd dropped him into the drain, I longed to be able to dive in and fish him out. But it's impossible. The special terror water has always held for me means Edward has chosen the one way to die where I'm powerless to help him. I'm frozen to the spot, watching him bob up and down, still screaming silently for me to save him.

'What are you waiting for, bastard? Jump in!' I turn. Uncle Frank, Agnes Ada, Aunt Clara and Granddad are beside me.

'I can't! I can't swim! You know that!'

'Come on,' snaps Agnes Ada. 'You hev to hev a go. Believe me, it'll be easier than telling that child's mum what you've done.'

I look at their faces. 'Aunt Clara, you understand. You died because of the water. You surely understand.'

She stares accusingly back.

'Go on, damn you!' snarls Uncle Frank. 'You've only got seconds left!'

I look down at the foam below and hesitate again. And then I look further downriver at Edward, who has drifted from the centre now and is not moving quite so fast. And suddenly I know which of the two terrors is worst. I can sooner face the water than try to go on living without him. Without another thought, I grasp the top rail and vault over.

Of course I have no idea how to dive and I hit the water feet first, plunging into it with the velocity of a depth charge. Down, down I go, until the motion slows and stops and suddenly I'm moving upwards again. I can see bubbles of air escaping from my mouth and heading for the surface in clusters and suddenly I remember I have seen this before, this green water folding me in its murky embrace, the bubbling out of me. It's as though the moment has been foretold, perhaps in a dream that presaged my death. I wonder if I am drowning as significant parts of my life flit across my terror-stricken brain. Aunt Clara emerging from the water, the weeds clinging to her. The Swoppet sinking into the still water of the drain, a stream of bubbles issuing from my mouth . . .

Suddenly I'm shot to the surface of the water, breaching the glass ceiling above me, and into the air, which my lungs clutch at desperately. For a moment I don't know what's happening and then I'm aware that I'm floating. How can this be? All I know how to do is sink. Floating I don't do. Then it hits me. My jacket. Waterproof and packed to eight togs with the down of the wonderful eider duck, which traps air in its feathers to keep warm. It's a cushion of air all around me. I'm wearing an airbed! I raise my head and look around. To one side I can see the yellow blob in the slower part of the river. I start to paddle with my hands, but progress is hard as the jacket is so buoyant. Nevertheless I persist and gradually, after what seems like hours, just as my arms are about to give out, I can see Edward.

Like me he is being held afloat by his jacket, Unlike me, he is face down in the water, as motionless as flotsam. I summon up a last ounce of energy, renew my paddling and, swallowing water all the while, eventually I reach him. I get my arms around him and pull his head out of the water. His eyes are closed, his cheeks are frozen, there's no sign of life.

I can't hold him any longer and his face drops back into the water.

'No!' I cry. 'No! Don't let this happen! Please, somebody, please, don't let this happen!'

I'm aware of figures on the opposite bank. Help is at hand, if only I can keep him alive a moment or two longer, assuming he isn't already dead. I roll over on to my back and drag him out of the water again, so that his head is resting in the crook between my arm and my body. I paddle with my free arm, pushing the water as hard as I can. I even flip my feet up and down, the way I've seen people do in films. Somehow, in this fashion, I move closer to the bank. Closer and closer we go. I try to look at him to see if he's breathing, but raising my head even an inch almost makes our frail vessel capsize. I renew my efforts with the paddling until something hits my head. I look up and see the arching branch of a willow tree. I grasp it and pull myself up. The water is shallow here. Edward topples off me, and it takes a superhuman effort to lift him out of the water. He's so heavy from all the water in his clothes, but I manage it, and stumbling and splashing I'm able to get to the bank. A man, is sliding down it towards me. 'Here,' he says, 'grab my hand,' and takes hold of me. I look up and find myself staring into the eyes of DS Hammond. 'What are you—'

'Just happened to be passing,' he says. 'Now, come on, let's get the kid out of there.'

Seconds later, his partner arrives and the two of them bundle Edward up the bank then pull me up. We lay Edward on the ground. Hammond's partner has already called for an ambulance.

Edward lies still as a mannequin. His face is white with cold, his lips blue. His hair is streaked across his face, the way river weed stuck to Aunt Clara's a lifetime ago.

'Do you know how to resuscitate?' I ask.

'Christ, no, we're coppers. I mean, some policemen do, but we've never done the training.'

Fortunately I have. And, strangely, it was always meant to be for Edward. When he was on his perilous voyage into this life, it was felt he might be a sickly child so I took an infant-resuscitation class. I flail around in my mind and recall a plump nurse counting and saying, 'Breathe for the baby, breathe for the baby,' over and over again. But that's all.

Think, I tell myself, think.

'He's not breathing,' says Hammond, who has pulled Edward's jacket open and laid his head on his chest. 'Shouldn't we open the airway, or something?'

'Yes, you're right.' I pull Edward's head back and his lower jaw open. I stick my fingers down his throat to check for any obstructions. Then I put my first two fingers on his neck and feel for a pulse.

There isn't one.

The resuscitation. I can't remember how it goes. I know I should press his chest to get the heart working and I know I should give him the kiss of life to get him breathing. And I know I should do one several times for every one time I do the other. But I can't remember which. Is it four breaths to every compression? Or five? Or the other way round? If I do the wrong thing will that make matters worse? Or is doing anything better than doing nothing and watching his life just slip away?

'Come on, think, Michael,' says a voice at my elbow: I look round. It's Uncle Frank. 'You can do this shit, you just have to think. OK, now, I'm going to help you. Place the heel of your hand over the middle of his chest, right where the ribs meet. Now press. Count one elephant two elephant, remember, that's how the nurse told you to count seconds, then press again. Do it five times. OK, now hold his nose closed, put your mouth over his and breathe into him. Just once.'

It's awkward trying to get my mouth over his. I remember we were practising for newborn babies using rubber dolls and their faces were so small you had to put your mouth over both mouth and nose, but Edward's face is bigger than that now: I can't cover both with my mouth. And yet, when I'm holding his nose with my fingers, there's hardly enough room to get my mouth over his. Still, at last I manage it and breathe into him. 'OK,' says Uncle Frank, 'now the compressions again. Remember one elephant, two elephant, five for every breath. Keep it going now.' I'm worried I might break Edward's small ribs as they spring up and down under the pressure of my hand, but I keep going anyway. Press and breathe, press and breathe.

'Professor, I – I'm sorry,' says Hammond, 'but it's not working. 'Professor, listen—' He puts his hand on my arm, but I shrug him off like a troublesome fly. Press, press, press, press, press breathe. Press, press, press, press, press breathe. Nothing. Nothing. And then . . . and then, suddenly, a low moan from somewhere deep in Edward's chest. Oh, God, is that the death rattle? Is that what it sounds like? I saw Aunt Clara die and yet I don't remember.

A small cough and a mix of brown bile and river water escape his lifeless blue lips. I wipe it away with my sleeve. Is he breathing or was the water merely expelled by the compressions? I can't see his chest moving. Another cough. More bile and a copious amount of water. Then he's still, perfectly still.

'Edward, wake up, please wake up!'

His eyes flip open, like those of a child's doll when you sit it up. They stare straight into mine. 'Daddy,' he says, 'was I swimming?'

TWENTY-SIX

Death I recant, and say, unsaid by me
Whate'er hath slipped, that might diminish thee.
                              Elegy on Mistress Bulstrode

'I still don't understand how he came to fall into the river,' says Alison. We sit at either side of the hospital bed, connected by the child upon it, sleeping now after his ordeal, apparently none the worse for it but kept in overnight for observation. The moment I arrived at the hospital, I called Alison, who dumped Jake with a neighbour for the night and rushed to my side, bringing a change of dry clothes for me with her. On the face of it, now, we're two relieved parents keeping vigil by their reprieved child, devoting our full attention to him. But not I. My mind is anywhere but in this room. I'm wondering what Hammond and his mate were doing in that isolated spot. What sinister plot had they hatched with Tamsin Graves that took them there? I had no chance to ask Hammond before Edward and I were bundled into the ambulance and driven here. And that's not all. Another anxiety floats around this more immediate one. A powerful remembrance of the water wrapped all around me and my lips uttering air bubbles, like speech balloons in a child's comic, only empty, wordless, giving no hint to the image's true meaning. Had I really had some premonition of this moment in a long-ago dream? The truth lurks tantalizingly out of reach, like the shadow of someone perceived through a curtain, a red bathing-suit through a cotton shift, a dark shape I can't quite touch.

'I just don't know,' I reply. 'You know how it is. I only took my eye off him for a moment. You wouldn't have thought it possible for him to end up in the river in that short time.'

'But—'

She gets no further. There's a tap on the door and Hammond's slick head appears around the edge. 'Excuse me, Professor,' he says.

'Yes, of course, come in.'

'All right, is he, the little one?'

'Apparently, yes, no harm done.'

'Good, very good.'

'You may remember Detective Sergeant Hammond, Alison. Sergeant Hammond was at the river.'

'Oh, thank you for what you did,' says Alison.

'Didn't do anything, really. It was your husband who was the hero.'

Alison beams at me and, of course, for a second I enjoy bathing in the warmth of her gaze until I think how undeserved it all is. Without my villainy there could have been no heroism.

'Er, I was wondering, Professor, if you'd mind accompanying us to the station?'

'The station?'

'Yes, just to answer a few questions.'

'Oh, all right. Of course.'

'But surely that isn't necessary?' says Alison, as I get to my feet. 'I mean, it's fairly straightforward what happened, isn't it? Edward just fell into the river and Michael jumped in and pulled him out.'

Hammond looks somewhat flustered. 'You'd think

315

so, madam, but you know how it is. There's always paperwork these days.'

'Are you up to this?' she says, her eyes examining me as if for signs of wear and tear. She turns to Hammond. 'He's not been well lately,' she tells him. 'He should be in bed resting after a shock like this.'

'I'll go straight home afterwards. Promise.' I squeeze her shoulder. The feel of her flesh gives me a strange sort of comfort, as though I were the sleeping child and she my mother. There's nothing like a near death for bringing a couple together.

Hammond's mate, who's introduced as Detective Constable Rogers, escorts us to the car. There's someone in the back. At first I think it's a policewoman, but when Hammond opens the door for me I see, with a shock, that it's Tamsin Graves.

'What's going on? What's she doing here?' I demand.

Hammond presses my shoulder gently down. 'If you'll just get in, sir, we can sort all this out at the station. I'd advise you to come, sir. Believe me, it's in your best interests.'

The journey to the police station is conducted in complete silence. Tamsin stares straight ahead, ignoring me, and I fight back the urge to say, 'Bitch', to her, at least out loud.

The police station isn't at all how I expected. There's no cheery Dixon of Dock Green type behind one of those counters with a lift-up barman's flap. Instead we're confronted by a glass wall and a locked door. Hammond punches numbers into a combination pad beside the door, which buzzes open. He ushers us through and leads us down a corridor. He stops at a door marked 'Interview Room 1', raps on it smartly and opens it. 'Oh, sorry,' he says, and closes it again. We all troop further down the corridor where he repeats the operation with a door marked 'Interview Room 2'. This time it's empty and we march inside. There's a desk with one chair on one side and two on the other. Hammond takes the single chair and indicates the two opposite for Tamsin and me.

We sit down. Hammond glances up at Rogers. 'Kieron, get some coffee for us, will you, please?'

Rogers gives him a strange smile and says, 'Right-ho, guv.' It's like they're cops in some creaky stage play – *The Mousetrap*, perhaps. Rogers disappears. Hammond puts his hand in his jacket pocket and pulls out a plastic bag. I can see there's a cassette tape in it.

'Wait a minute,' I say, 'isn't this a little unusual? I thought you had to caution someone before you interrogated them? And what's she doing here? If I'm being accused of something, shouldn't I be seen in private? Or with a solicitor, not with my accuser?'

Tamsin looks at him as though she hasn't thought of this, but as if she, too, would like to know the answer.

Hammond purses his lips, and shrugs. 'That's how things are done at a, uh, more formal stage, sir. For the moment, Ms Graves has made certain allegations and produced certain evidence to back them up. We thought it might be useful to put those allegations to you in an informal setting, in her presence, so she knows everything's above board, then see if things need to be taken further.'

He opens the seal on the plastic bag and takes out the cassette. There's a large tape machine on the desk, into which he inserts it.

'Now,' he says, 'this is a tape-recording Ms Graves made of your conversation by the river today. I haven't had time to review it myself, not with the accident and everything.'

He presses play. There's a roar like static on a television. I find myself almost straining to hear Errol

Flynn's voice. Or is it Tyrone Power's? But there's nothing, only the roaring noise. After ten minutes of this Hammond switches off the machine and removes the cassette, dropping it carefully back into the plastic bag. He shrugs. 'Sounds to me like all we got there was a nice recording of the weir, miss,' he says. 'I can let the technical boys have a look at it, see if they can enhance it but, I have to say, I think it's unlikely.'

He leaves the bag on the desk, slips his hand into his other jacket pocket and pulls out another plastic bag. He takes out another tape. Before he can say anything the door opens and Rogers comes in with a tray, upon which are four mugs of coffee, steaming hot. He puts it down and places a mug before each of us. He pours milk for all of us except Hammond, who evidently likes his coffee black. Then he stands leaning against the wall as Hammond continues: 'This is a tape Ms Graves made of your conversation at the Thai Tavern last week.' He inserts it in the machine and presses play.

Immediately it's like the start of *Siegfried*, Mime hammering away at the hero's sword. Hammond mouths the word, 'Chopsticks.' Then the conversation between Tamsin and me begins. It's not very clear because of the noise of the four jocks at the next table, but the word 'coke' is plainly discernible, as is my boast, 'Of course I can get it.' I'm about to tell Hammond to switch it off when I hear something else, a voice I recognize, saying, 'Frank.'

'Stop,' I say.

'What?'

'Stop the tape.'

Hammond presses pause. 'Play it back a few seconds.' He presses rewind and then play. There's a great deal of noise through which the single word is audible, at least to me: 'Frank.' It's Agnes Ada's voice, I'm sure of it. Caught on tape. The decisive, objective

318

proof of her existence after death and outside my own head. 'Did you hear that?' I ask.

'Hear what?' says Hammond.

'Someone say "Frank"?'

'Can't say as I did. Anyway, what's it got to do with anything?'

'It has everything to do with everything,' I reply. 'Play it again, would you?'

'Well, really, Professor, I—'

'Please.'

'All right.'

He rewinds and presses play again. This time I know what to listen for and it seems clearer than ever. 'Did you hear it?' I ask Hammond.

'Well, maybe,' he replies. I can see he just doesn't care.

'What about you?' I ask Rogers. He shrugs. In desperation I turn to Tamsin. It's the first time I've spoken to her since the weir. 'What about you? Please, it's important. Forget everything else. Just tell me if you heard someone say, "Frank." '

She, too, shrugs. 'Perhaps,' she says. 'It's difficult to tell.'

'Can we get on now, please, sir?' says Hammond, and switches the tape on again. We run through the whole conversation between me and Tamsin, but what we are saying becomes less and less distinct as the noise from the next table increases. Eventually the fight breaks out and Hammond switches the tape off. 'Well, it's all a bit unclear,' he mutters, removing it from the machine.

'I don't think so,' says Tamsin. 'I think there's enough there to prove what I've told you about this bastard.'

Hammond pulls a face. 'Perhaps. I'm not sure if it's enough for a court, miss. Maybe the technical boys can do something with this one. They can work wonders bringing voices up. Here, Kieron, take this down to

Forensics, would you?' And he tosses the tape towards his confederate. As though taken by surprise, Rogers springs forward from his leaning-back pose, almost spilling the coffee he's holding, and flaps at the tape with his free hand. It bounces off his palm in a perfect parabola and lands straight in Hammond's mug.

Both men contemplate it.

'Bloody hell, Kieron, look what you've done now,' says Hammond at last.

'Sorry, guv,' says Rogers. 'You took me by surprise.'

'Quick!' Tamsin shrieks, 'Get it out!'

'Right, miss,' says Hammond, suddenly transformed from efficient Drugs Squad officer to bumbling plod. He puts two fingers into the coffee and immediately pulls them straight out. 'Bloody hell, that's hot!' he gasps. He opens a drawer in the desk, pulls out a pencil and dips it into the coffee. He joggles it about for what seems like ages and finally lifts out the cassette with the pencil through one of its holes. He holds it in a pathetic parody of the way detectives on TV always hold guns by the trigger guards when they find them at the scene of a crime.

We all look at the cassette. There's a strong smell of plastic. Tape is hanging from the housing, limp, as though stretched by the heat.

'Bugger, that's not done it much good,' says Hammond.

'You idiot,' says Tamsin, turning to Rogers. 'How could you?'

'Sorry, miss. Nothing like it's ever happened before.'

He takes the tape from Hammond's pencil, withdraws a tissue from his trouser pocket and makes a big display of drying off the cassette.

'Don't worry, miss, I'll get it down to Forensics,' he says. 'They can work miracles these days, you'll be surprised.'

Tamsin looks at him as though about to spit fire, but

then her face crumples, and she jumps up and dashes from the room.

I catch up with her on the station steps. I grab her arm.

'Leave me alone, you bastard!' She means it as a snarl, but there's a catch in her voice that spoils the effect. I should just let her go. It would be safer for lots of different reasons. But I can't. It's the look her face had a moment ago. The same look Jake has when I blame him for something Edward's done. The child's naïve belief in justice.

'Let me go!' She almost yells it.

'Listen. Please. Just for one moment.'

'What for? More of your lies?'

'The truth. Use it how you will. Tell your friend Bennet if you like, let him plaster it all over the tabloids.' She looks down and studies her shoes, as if in the hope of finding an appropriate response there. Finally she brings her gaze up again and her doe eyes stare into mine.

'Tamsin,' I say, 'I'd like you to keep my confidence, but there's nothing I can do to make you.'

I let go her arm. And I tell her about the BP monitor. I tell her about my silly vanity and my fear of losing my job. At first she tries to interject protests, but gradually she quietens and listens until I'm done.

'Oh, Michael, why didn't you tell me this before?' she says. 'You could have ended up in jail but for that silly accident. Why did you let it all go so far?'

It's the most difficult confession of all. The one I can only just force from my reluctant lips.

'I'm fifty the day after tomorrow. I was trying hard not to be.'

Hammond takes me home.

'Do you think they will be able to restore the tape?'

He laughs. 'Nah, no chance. Take it from me, it's kaput. You're in the clear.'

We drive on a minute or two in silence. He gives me a puzzled glance. 'What's up, Prof? You look almost disappointed.'

How can I tell him that his bumbling assistant has destroyed not only the case against me but also what might possibly have been the empirical evidence of an afterlife? How can I explain that, like a bank robber who hides his loot before being captured, I would happily have endured a jail sentence with my pay-off to look forward to?

The car pulls up outside my house. As I open the car door, Hammond says, 'Wait a moment, Prof. You've been lucky this time. That was a freak accident today, the tape getting destroyed like that. But it won't happen a second time, believe me. Next time you'll get your just deserts.'

I sit and nod soberly.

'Listen, sir. I deal with scum all the time. The people who get involved with drugs don't usually have a lot going for them. Drugs is their only escape from not being able to handle their lives. You got too much going for you to be like that. Take my advice. Keep away from your friend Thomson. Stay away from drugs. Stick to your nice wife and your little boys. Or next time you'll end up in big trouble.'

'Thanks,' I mumble, as I get out of the door. 'Be seeing you.'

'I hope not, Prof,' he says, as I close the door. 'I sincerely hope not.'

In the middle of the night I awake from an obscure and troubling dream, and remember where I was once under water watching my life bubbling away from me.

TWENTY-SEVEN

Turn thou ghost that way, and let me turn this
                                        The Expiration

It has long been one of Alison's many complaints that,
unlike most of her wealthier friends (i.e. the ones not
married to academics), we cannot afford a people-
mover. My excuse for not buying one, besides poverty,
has been that we don't really need a minibus for us and
two small children. But now I'm not so sure. It's
definitely cramped in my battered Golf as I take the
exit off the ring road that will lead me back to Ely.
Uncle Frank is beside me, drumming out some unsung
rock 'n' roll song on the dash. Behind him, in the back
seat is Aunt Clara. Next to her, as the smallest member
of the party, is Granddad, who is eating a banana. And
squeezed behind me is Agnes Ada, her long legs so out
of scale with this vehicle that her bony knees stick
through my seat's flimsy back, pressing into my spine.
It's no use, I tell myself. If I'm going to keep ferrying my
dead relatives around, I'll have to get an MPV.

Right now the engine is groaning in protest at the
extra weight and rattling with old age and general
exhaustion, belying the punctured exhaust's Ferrari
roar.

'Is this thing safe?' says Uncle Frank.

323

'Of course it's safe. Do you think I'd take my kids out in something that wasn't?' After what happened yesterday, the question hangs in the air.

'Well, what's that banging coming from the front, then? That don't sound too good to me.'

'It's the front bumper. It's a bit wobbly. I was attacked by a concrete post in a car park. It sort of ripped one side of the bumper loose. But it's OK, the other side is tight enough to hold the whole thing on.'

'Let me get this straight,' he says. 'You're driving this kin—'

'Language!' shrieks Agnes Ada, from the back. 'I don't want to hear no F-word.'

'Sorry, Mum. But let me get this. You're driving around with the bumper hanging off and you think it's safe?' His voice is going up in volume all the time and he's waving his arms about. 'What if another car hits us? The kin – sorry, Mum – bumper drops off and we end up with someone else's engine block in our lap. You call that safe?' He flicks me with his fingers. 'Do you? Do you, huh? You call that safe?'

He does this for at least a couple of minutes and I sit there taking it until I remember I'm bigger than he is now, grab his arm and push it away from me.

'Yes, I bloody well do.' I carry on driving. 'Besides,' I say, 'what's it matter to you if we crash? You're dead already, remember?'

'Oh, yeah,' he concedes. 'There is that.'

There is that. My mind worries at the phrase in the ensuing silence. What is it about it that jars? Then I realize it's not just the one phrase; it's all Uncle Frank's speech since his reappearance. Everything has this fake American flavour. The words, the phrases, the intonations. He could be Karen's brother. I try to remember if he always talked like that and feel sure he didn't. OK, so he probably saw a lot of American

324

movies. He was always taking his many girlfriends to the Rex cinema, though I'd never thought they got much film-watching done in there. It was more the double seats, the love seats in the back row that they went for. And for a while he drove a taxi cab at the American base at Mildenhall, ferrying US airmen around – but he always struck me as a real old Fen boy, a Fen Tiger as he proudly called himself. So why does he now have this transatlantic drawl? And why is his slang so up-to-date?

Of course! Why didn't I use my academic expertise before and save myself all the angst? This is the answer; through textual analysis, through a study of the language itself, I have reached it. It's obvious that 'Uncle Frank' isn't a dead relative from the east of England of thirty-five years ago. Everything about the way he talks indicates that he's from now, and where else could he have acquired such speech patterns except from my own mind? I created him. He's my hallucination. After all, nobody else heard anything on that tape yesterday. I'm bouncing along the dual carriageway now with an exuberance born of my relief. These are hallucinations. Drug- and alcohol-induced manifestations of my overheated imagination. I am their God! I can vanish them just as I created them!

So occupied is my creator's mind with its new-found power I don't notice a white van cut in on me from the outside lane until it's too late. I brake sharply and just manage to avoid testing Uncle Frank's doubts about the front bumper on the back of the van by about half an inch. Instantly his fist reaches across me and he's maniacally punching the horn, then holding his hand on it for a long ear-splitting blast, the horn being the only thing that works properly in this old heap of a car. Finally he lets go.

'Tut!' from the back seat.

Uncle Frank turns round. 'Listen, Aunt Clara, I know that might seem like overreacting to you but, believe me, when you've been killed in one car crash, you don't want to be in another.'

'Tut,' she says placatingly.

I'm hardly listening. I'm thinking about Uncle Frank's hand punching that horn. Could it have been my hand? Was I doing that? Am I turning into one of those people like the Yorkshire Ripper who hear voices or blame imaginary people for their actions? I can't believe this. I saw the hand upon the horn. I heard its blast. But, then, suppose my passengers are real after all. How to explain those speech patterns? Unless, perhaps, they've been observing the world since the different dates of their demises. Maybe Uncle Frank has spent thirty odd years watching American TV. Maybe purgatory is some kind of waiting room where the deceased are condemned to an eternity of watching reruns of *Friends* and *Ally McBeal*? 'I'll be good from now on, God!' I promise silently as I pull up behind the white van at a red light.

The driver's door of the van opens and a bulky man steps out. He lumbers towards us. Shaved head. Earrings. *More than one in both ears!* Hunt-the-skin tattooed arms. I try to wind the window closed, but the stiff mechanism jams so I rest my arm nonchalantly on the open sill. I have to move it when he thrusts his large head through the window space so that he's framed like someone on television.

'What the fuck do you think you were hooting at me for, mate?'

'I wasn't hooting at you.'

'Don't give me that. I could fucking hear it. My mate in there could hear it too. Are you calling us liars?'

'No, I didn't say there wasn't any hooting. There most certainly was. It's just that I wasn't doing it.'

'You weren't, eh? Then who was?'

'My Uncle Frank.'

'Your Uncle Frank?'

'That's right.'

'And where, pray, might this Uncle Frank be?'

I give him what I hope is a mad stare. An old photograph of Charles Manson pops into my mind and I try hard to think it into my expression. 'Right beside me,' I say.

'Fuck off!'

'Here, watch your language. Not in front of the ladies.'

'Ladies?' He's looking worried now.

'My grandmother and her sister-in-law.'

'In the back seat, are they?' His head pulls back from the window.

'That's right. And let me warn you, my uncle Frank can get very upset with people who swear in front of his mother.'

He looks at me with a slightly alarmed expression. 'OK, mate, no offence meant. Listen, just don't . . . er . . . Tell your uncle not to be so trigger happy with the horn, all right?'

I don't reply. I just carry on with my best *Helter Skelter* stare until he turns and trots back to his vehicle because the lights have changed to green.

We've been rattling along the motorway for about ten miles when there's a sighed 'Tut' from the back.

'What's the matter, Aunt Clara?' I ask.

'She's asking are we nearly there yet?' interprets Agnes Ada.

'Nearly there? We've only just started. It's another couple of hours.'

'Well, she's saying she's not comfy and she's bored. There's nothing to look at on this here road 'cept cars and we seen enough of them to last a life-time.'

'Well, no one asked you to come,' I say.

'We wanted to come, Michael. We thought you'd need a bit of support. And we'd like to see Ely again.'

'Well, you didn't have to come *with* me,' I protest. 'Couldn't you have just gone on your own? Flown or appeared, or whatever it is you do.'

'Er, it's not that simple,' interposes Uncle Frank. 'We're kinda attached to you.'

'But I thought you were going to Oklahoma on your own?'

'I never said that. I said that *you* couldn't. I didn't say I was.'

'What's this about Oklahoma? Int that in America?'

'Nothing, Mom. Nothing for you to be a-frettin' about.'

'Tut!'

'Well, it still don't solve the problem. Clara's bored. And your Granddad don't help none with all that itching. Stop it, Bert! Stop that scratching now! You're making me itch. You've a lot to answer for, Michael, making your granddad like this.'

'What's these here things?' asks Uncle Frank, picking up a cassette from the shelf under the dashboard.

'Cassettes. They're small tapes. They play music and stories.'

'I remember them,' says Agnes Ada. 'They had them before I went.'

'After my time,' says Uncle Frank wistfully. 'What's on 'em? Got any Beach Boys?'

I rifle through the pile of tapes. 'Nope, sorry, they're all story tapes we have in the car to keep the boys amused.'

'I like a nice story,' says Agnes Ada. 'Put one of them on.'

I select one at random and slot it into the player. We sail on down the motorway, a voice saying, 'One day, Pooh Bear . . .'

Nearly two hours later, from many miles away, we sight Ely Cathedral riding like a ship at anchor on the flat, featureless sea of the Fens.

'There's the cathedral,' says Agnes Ada.

'Tut!' enthuses Aunt Clara.

'Don't it just look grand?' says Uncle Frank.

Our route takes us through the old village, but I refuse to turn off to look at our street. It's enough to pass the vicarage and see the three or four new steps up to the front door to know how much time has passed.

As we hit the outskirts of the city – if a place as small as Ely can be said to have outskirts – Agnes Ada says, 'I don't remember this road. It weren't like this.' And 'What's happened to the Black Horse? What hev they done with that?'

I give them a brief tour around the one-way system.

'Look at that Tesco's, Clara, that weren't there before. Thass one of them big ones, that is. They hev dresses and things in there.'

'Tut?'

'Yes, and bathing-suits too, I dare say.'

I point out the site of the recent Anglo-Saxon excavations.

'Excavatin'? Diggin' up dead people?' snaps Agnes Ada, with a shiver in her voice. 'I don't hold with that. They should leave the dead to rest in peace.'

Can this really be coming from my mind? If I had lain beneath the earth for a thousand years, I would long for someone to come along and dig up my old bones and expose them to the sun.

*   *   *

I pull into the car park of Mum's sheltered housing unit, jerk on the handbrake and switch off the engine. Nobody moves. 'Well,' I say, opening my door, 'shall we go in and see Mum?'

'I don't think we'll do that, Michael,' says Agnes Ada, opening her own door and getting out. 'I expect she's only got a small place. And we think it's best you talk to her about . . . well, what you come to talk to her about . . . on your own.'

'If you're sure . . .'

She nibbles at her lips. 'I'd like to see your mum, but this int the time. Besides, it's market day and we'd like to have a look at them new shops.' She eases Aunt Clara out of the car and takes her by the arm. The two of them wander off up the hill towards the market-place, arm in arm, eager to see the changes wrought during their absences of a quarter and nearly half a century respectively.

I turn to the others.

'Uncle Frank?' He's helping Granddad out of the car. Granddad immediately begins a high-pitched chattering and lopes off towards a clump of trees.

'Nah, your mother and I, well, we never did get on.' He clasps my hand tight and pulls me to him. 'Take care of yourself, Michael,' he says, and hugs me for what seems like an age.

'You'll be coming back with me?'

He drags a hand through his thinning hair. 'Nah, I don't think so, we might like to stay here for . . . well, this is where we belong. Don't you go forgetting us now.' He lets go my hand and runs after Granddad, who is swinging from the lower branches of a sycamore tree.

Mum is surprised to see me. 'You didn't phone,' she complains. 'You always phone.'

'I came in a bit of a hurry, I didn't get chance. Besides, I thought you'd be pleased to see me.'

'Well, I am pleased. But it's market day.' I notice she has on one of her best floral dresses and has rouged her cheeks. Over-rouged them actually, as usual, giving her an over-ripe appearance, an apple ready to fall. Not a good impression for an eighty-year-old to make.

'Well, I won't be staying long. An hour or so at the most, I should think.'

'Not staying long? An hour? Is that all you can spare your poor old mother?'

I recognize the whining tone, the same passive-aggressive technique honed over years of practice at subverting Agnes Ada's iron will. 'No, but I thought you wanted to go to the market.'

'Market? I'm not bothered about no market. I've seen enough of Ely market to last me a lifetime. Besides, it's all I can do to drag myself along there. It's no fun when you're on your own, day after day, just looking at the same four walls.'

I know this isn't true as the housing unit has a thriving community room where Mum plays a leading role, doing everything from making tea to calling out the bingo numbers. I wait for it to run its course.

'Well,' she says finally, 'sit yourself down a minute. You'll be stopping long enough for a cup of tea, at least?'

I sit down and while she busies herself next door in the small kitchen, appraise the room. It's modern and functional, unlike Mum's old furniture – the heavy oak sideboard, the mahogany chairs – which looks so out of place against the cream-painted walls and grey carpet it gives the feel of a museum. In the centre of the room stands what would now be a collector's item: the Formica-topped gateleg table, which will be too flimsy to bear even Mum's frail little body when the time comes to lay her out. Not that that will happen here: she'll be in some undertaker's sterile funeral home.

Mum returns with a tray bearing teapot, cups, saucers and milk, which she sets down on the table. We sit and wait for the tea to brew.

'Nice of you to come and see me for your birthday,' she says. 'I must remember to give you your card before you go. Save me posting it. Pity you couldn't have let me know you were coming, though. I've already put a first-class stamp on it.'

The tea is ready and she pours it and hands me a cup. We sit and sip it for a moment or two without words.

'Nice cup of tea,' I say. 'Nothing like a cup of tea for refreshing you.'

'Yes, that's true, except I'll be weeing all morning now. My bladder's not what it was. It'll be murder at the market having to go up and down those steps in the ladies'.' She takes another sip. 'It's hard to enjoy this cuppa now when I know I'm going to suffer for it later.'

'Listen, Mum, I didn't come because it's my birthday tomorrow. I came to ask you something.'

'Oh,' she says, putting her cup down on a small side table and shifting herself in her chair as though trying to get comfortable for an interrogation. 'You'd better ask away then, hadn't you?'

'Mum, it's about Dad.'

'Your dad? Well, I'm sure I've told you all I could about him over the years. You don't want to hear all that again, do you? Only I can't do a lot of talking these days, it gets to my throat. And then I hev to start drinking tea to ease it, and before long I won't be fit to be at no market.'

'Mum, it's something I need to know about.'

She sighs. 'All right, then, if you must. I'll hev missed the best bargains soon anyway.'

'Well, something happened to me yesterday. I fell into some water. I could see bubbles coming out of my mouth and going up. The water was in my mouth. I can still taste it. My lungs felt like they were going to burst.'

She picks up her tea and stirs it, although she stirred it a moment ago. She concentrates on the spoon trawling through the brown liquid. She doesn't look at me.

'In the night I had a dream. I was soaking wet and crying. It was as if I was the only person in the world. When I woke, I suddenly realized what it was all about.'

She lays the spoon in the saucer, carefully, as if afraid of making a sound. She lifts her gaze and her lower lip trembles as she looks at me, but she draws herself erect and stares me straight in the eye. 'All right, Michael, what's your question?'

'That day Dad died, I was with him, wasn't I?'

She doesn't reply, but looks down at the floor as though the answer might be hidden among the swirling flowers on the rug beside her if she could only find it.

'Wasn't I?'

'Michael, that were a long time ago, you was only a small child, why not leave things as they are? You'll only go upsetting yourself.'

I set down my cup on the floor beside me, and go across to her. I kneel before her and take her upper arms in my two hands. She's beginning to weep.

'Now look what you've gone and done,' she says. 'You've gone and upset me.'

'Mum, you'll just have to be upset. I need to know the truth. I need to know what happened.'

Tears flow down her cheeks making silver trails through the rouge. 'All right, if you must, but you won't thank me for telling you.'

I let go her arms and she pulls a handkerchief from her cardigan sleeve and dabs her eyes.

'Yes, you were with him. I'd gone to Ely with Agnes Ada to get some new curtain material. He was ploughing the three-acre, so he took you with him. At first you rode on the tractor, but after a while you became restless so he set you down—'

'Wait a minute, how do you know all this?'

'Some women were working in the next field. Ivy Gudgeon and a couple of others. They'd stopped for dockey and they sat and watched it all. Anyway, your dad set you down at one end of the field and left you to play while he kept ploughing. There was no harm you could come to where he left you. The dyke that side was pretty dry. And you was just sitting playing tractors in the dirt. Anyway, you probably don't remember but the three-acre was a long narrow field so it took him some time to do a whole furrow. When he reached the far end and made the turn, he looked up for you, but you weren't where he left you. Then he see the women running across the other field and waving and shouting. Course, they was miles away, weren't nothing they could do. Then he saw what they was shouting about. You'd wandered right across the field to t'other side, which was the drain side. Now, that drain was more than twenty feet across and at least ten feet deep. You was standing on the edge with a great clod of earth held in both hands over your head, fixing to throw it. Your dad's heart must've been up in his mouth as he put his foot down on the accelerator and hammered that tractor down and across the field towards you. You heard the roar of the tractor just as you threw the clod. You turned your head to look at the tractor and you forgot to let go of the clod. And into the drain you sailed after it. Well, it took your dad a good minute or so to get over there and he drove the tractor right to the edge, swerving just as he reached it. He jumped out of the seat and was down the bank of the drain in seconds and probably all he could see of you by that time was a few bubbles, showing where you'd gone under. The drain was pretty still and covered with weed. Your dad didn't hesitate. He hadn't an ounce of fear in him, that man. He heaved off his wellingtons and his coat and jumped straight in. He was a good swimmer, your dad. He dived down and he had hold of you right away. By this time the women had reached the edge of the drain and were trying to get down the bank, but it was as steep as a cliff and they was heving trouble. Just then, up comes your dad, holding you in one arm and somehow he manages to make his way over to the bank. There was nothing he could get a grip on, so he stuck you on to the bank, and told you to hold on to the grass. He tried to get himself up, but he slipped back off the muddy side and went under the water again.' Her voice chokes up. She pauses to wipe her eyes and take another sip of tea. 'I don't know, I shall be weeing all day,' she says.

'Well, what happened then? Did he just drown? Couldn't they get him out?'

'No, he didn't just drown. What happened then was that the tractor, which he'd left sideways on to the edge of the drain with the engine still running, gave a little shudder, the way a tractor engine will from time to time, and tipped itself over and fell right into the drain on top of him. Missed you, fell right on to your dad.' She's at the hanky again now, dabbing angrily at her eyes. The rouge is smeared all over her face, like war-paint.

'And that's how he come to die. He was badly crushed and drowned too. That much you heard before is true.'

We sit in silence for a while, with only the ticking of the ship's-wheel clock on the old sideboard measuring the silence.

'Why did you never tell me the truth?' I say at last.

'It was Agnes Ada who said we shouldn't. She said you'd grow up blaming yourself, thinking you killed your father. You never talked about it, and after a couple of years you just seemed to accept our version of things. You seemed to hev wiped it from your memory.'

'But I hadn't. It was in there somewhere. And yesterday it just came back. It left its mark.'

'Oh, yes, it left its mark. You was always scared of water after that. You wouldn't go near it. They gave up trying to teach you to swim at the grammar school because you were so frightened.'

'Was that all?'

'Well, only that when I tried to show you pictures of your dad, you'd get upset. You'd throw a tantrum and try to tear them, so I put them all away and never tried to show you them again. When you were older you asked once or twice why there were no pictures of your dad and I made an excuse and said they'd got destroyed by a leaking pipe in the attic and that seemed to satisfy you. You weren't that curious about your dad.'

'Have you still got photographs now?'

'In my bedroom.' She leaves the room and returns a minute or so later with a small tin box. 'There int many. We dint have no money for photographs.'

She holds up a picture of my father in his RAF uniform. A large, swarthy man, whose handsome smile is marred by a gap between his two front teeth. I stare at the face, trying to see something of my own, but all I see is a softer version of Agnes Ada's. In a wedding photo Mum looks much as I remember her when I was small. Here she wears a blue two-piece 'costume', as she and Agnes Ada would have called it. Dad stands beside her, awkwardly suited, his large frame somewhat bundled up in his new threads, hair Brylcreemed down, making the shape of his head like a seal's. She shows me one of him as a small boy, his last year at the village school, 1931 or '32 that would be. Two rows of children, my father dead centre of the front row. He looks just like Jake. The same jutting, confident jaw, the fair hair. His tie is askew but he stares confidently out at his future, looking forward to the rest of his life.

'Can I keep this one?'

'Take it. I don't need it no more. I was married to your dad for eight years. I've lived more than forty-five without him.'

'Shall I make some more tea?'

'No, thanks! Not unless you want one yourself. I'm up and down them lavatory steps all afternoon as it is. Any more and I might as well stay down there.'

I give her a hug. As we break apart her eyes well up with tears again. 'It weren't your fault, Michael. He shouldn't hev left a four-year-old on his own where there was a drain. You just did what any four-year-old would. He should hev known better.'

I squeeze her shoulder. She seems so small now, so child-sized herself, as if shrinking back to an earlier state. 'I know,' I say. 'I'm a father now myself. I know these things.'

When I get back to the car park, the Golf is empty. I walk along the lane beside it a little way, the one Agnes Ada and Aunt Clara took up to the town, but there's no sign of them. There's a rustle in the sycamore and I stand gazing up into its branches for a while, but then the grey form of a squirrel appears, staring back at me.

I get into the car and start the engine. Now I understand. It's no use looking for ghosts. I take out the photo Mum gave me and the small boy and I gape across the years at one another. If the dead could visit us, wouldn't the person in this picture have come with all the rest? Wouldn't he have been the main member of the party? He didn't, because my mind had no image of him to conjure up. I have my answer now about where the dead go.

I start the engine, turn my empty car round and commence the long, lonely journey home. The car smells comfortingly of bananas.

TWENTY-EIGHT

I can love both fair and brown,
Her whom abundance melts, and her whom want
    betrays,
Her who loves loneness best, and her who masks and
    plays,
  Her whom the country formed, and whom the town
    Her who believes, and her who tries,
    Her who still weeps with spongy eyes,
And her who is dry cork, and never cries;
I can love her, and her, and you and you,
I can love any, so she be not true.

                       The Indifferent

'I don't understand it, Tommo. It seems such an incredible piece of good fortune. He tossed the tape to his mate, which I have to say seemed a pretty innocuous thing to do, and it landed in the coffee cup. What are the odds against that happening?'

'Too high, for my liking. Not the kind of thing that should be left to chance.'

'You mean it wasn't chance?'

'Michael, what are you like? Of course it wasn't chance. Took quite a bit of skill to get that tape in that cup, if you ask me.' A fat grin opens up across Tommo's face. With his shaved head and uneven

339

teeth it makes him look like a Hallowe'en pumpkin.

'What do you mean?'

'Well, put it this way, Michael, I'm afraid you won't be seeing your three grand again. Policemen can be very greedy, you know.'

I take a minute to let this sink in. Three thousand pounds is a great deal of money to me, but on the other hand it's money well spent. It may have saved me from a prison sentence. It has definitely destroyed Tamsin's credibility as a witness. To be unable to provide one tape as evidence against me might seem possible, but for both the tape I'm supposed to have made of her and the one she made of me not to exist beggars belief. She won't press charges against me, anyway. Not now that I've come clean with her. I'm off the hook. My job is safe. Tomorrow I'll be giving the Kappelheim as planned.

'Let's get out of here, Michael. We should celebrate.'

'Here' is the gym, and Tommo's implication that this is not a suitable place to celebrate is strikingly correct. In one corner of the bar two of the Big Boys are bent over their drinks in close conversation. Ted the barman is chatting to one of his old boxing cronies, ducking and weaving from side to side, with the occasional left jab or right hook at the air.

'I don't know, Tommo, I have this lecture in the morning. I haven't even started writing it yet. It's very important. My whole career depends upon it.'

'Aw, come on, Michael, a couple of drinks won't hurt. After all, a few hours ago you didn't even have a career.'

'Well . . .' But even as I say it I know I will go along with Tommo and, heedless of the consequences, imbibe enough substances to get out of my mind. Why I would want to do this is hard to say. My mind, for once, is not an awful place to be in. It feels light and unfettered now that the burden I've carried all my life has been lifted. It may be the calm induced by the beta-blockers or the tingle of excitement from the two lines I did in the toilet while I was waiting for Tommo to arrive, but I'm less afraid of the future. I could even be looking forward to it. But there are things to celebrate: Tommo's freedom and the collapse of the case against me, the prospect of the promotion once again being in my grasp. And, of course, most of all that it's my birthday tomorrow and I have resolved to do as Donne did in later life: to abandon my libertine ways, to forgo drugs and alcohol, to devote myself to family and work. So tonight, the last night of my forties, will be a fitting last fling, a final farewell to my old way of life before I embrace the new puritanism of my future.

I make a quick call to Alison on my mobile. I explain I'll be home late as the lifting of my suspension means I have a lot of work to catch up on. 'Very late,' I say, then add, in imitation of Edward, 'It's a very lot of work.' I can almost see her smiling at the irony of my using our child's expression in this context. Its inappropriateness to cover what she'll (rightly) see as my intended debauchery. She doesn't know I'm about to change my life.

In the car park I offer to drive us. Tommo stares at my battered Golf as if I've invited him to roll in a dog turd. He doesn't say anything but walks towards a silver BMW and unlocks it.

We drive to the west side of town, down by the river, where most of the best pubs and the newest clubs are.

The first pub is dark and empty, apart from a couple of girls sitting at the bar. While Tommo approaches the bar to order our drinks, I slope off to the toilet to fix myself a couple of lines. It takes a while because the cistern top is shaped in a spectacular curve, a design mirrored in the loo seat cover, to prevent the preparation and use of chop. Luckily I have John Carey's biography of Donne in my jacket pocket. I have always thought it an indispensable work but just how indispensable I never knew until now when I chop a couple of lines on it. I roll up Her Majesty, take a toot and return to the bar, where Tommo is on a stool next to the girls, confidence already surging through me, altering both my mood and the way I walk into a strange kind of swagger, which I notice the girls have noticed.

I slide on to the bar stool on the opposite side of them from Tommo, so that we are flanking them. The girls are very young, eighteen or nineteen at most. Conveniently one is blonde and the other dark, making them easy to tell apart. I'm sitting next to the blonde. Not my hair colour of choice, really, but then, she is nearer.

'Who's this, then?' she says to Tommo, indicating me with a nod of her head. 'Your dad?'

Both the girls are wearing short skirts and on the high stool hers has risen to reveal most of her thighs. For a moment I contemplate dropping something on the floor as a way of enjoying a better view, but decide that might be a tad tacky. Being with Tommo is tacky enough; anything else might just push it over the edge. Besides, the memory of Tamsin Sharon-Stoning me is far too fresh to wish for a rerun.

'Nah, the Prof's not old,' says Tommo. 'He's just had a lot of worry lately.'

'Lived a lot,' I chip in.

'Lived a lot,' echoes Tommo, with a cryptic smile.

'Are you really a professor?' asks the dark one.

'It's just a nickname,' I lie.

'Only you see we're both at the university, Natasha and me. I'm doing a degree in catering because I want

342

to start my own wedding catering business. There's lots of opportunities in that field today. I'm going to offer a complete package, not just the food'

'What about you?' I ask the blonde.

'Catering.'

She takes a pull at her cigarette and mouths something to her friend – I can't see what because she has her back to me, but I know she's doing it because her friend shrugs. Tommo orders another round of drinks. The girls are drinking shorts and don't refuse.

The blonde turns to me. 'Just how old are you?'

I smile. 'Well, it's my birthday tomorrow and it's one of those that ends with a nought.'

'No! You're not! You're never *forty*?' She says it the way I might say ninety.

Strangely flattered, I shrug. 'I guess I just don't look it.'

'My dad's forty-two,' she confides.

'Does he look it?'

'Dunno. Haven't seen him for ten years.'

Tommo is draining his beer. 'Listen,' he says, 'I've got the Beemer outside. Why don't we go on to Cascades? I'll get you all in.'

The dark one is already slipping off her bar stool, by way of accepting the invitation, but Natasha puts a restraining hand on her arm. 'Here, hang on, I'm not sure I want to.'

'Oh, come on, it'll be fun.'

'But he's so old. I mean *forty*.'

Tommo leans across them confidentially. 'He may be a bit long in the tooth but he's got some very good blow.'

The blonde slides off her stool and we all head for the exit. The dark girl leans on me and says, 'Once she's had some Charlie she doesn't mind who she shags.'

I find myself mildly disgusted at this, but then I think, It's no different from me. Except I've never needed drugs to induce me to sleep with strangers. But this will be the very last time. Allow me just this one peccadillo, this last little sin, appropriately with someone as inappropriate as Natasha, a fittingly unfitting finale to my career as a serial adulterer. People make a lot of fuss about turning forty, but it's actually no big deal. At forty you might have as many years still to come as there are behind. People achieve in their forties. At fifty, assuming the average male lifespan of seventy-five, you have one year left for every two you've already had. Work it out on an annual basis, reckoning a lifespan as one year (as a number-obsessed, Type A person – me, for instance – might), and you've just hit September. Any day now the leaves will start to fall. Winter is already presaged by a chill in the morning air. There aren't many days left and still fewer sunny ones.

It's hard to think about all this in the car with the argument going on because Natasha and her friend, who's called Emma, want to sample the coke, but Tommo is adamant there will be no drug-taking in his car.

'For Christ's sake, I just got out of the nick for dealing, can you imagine what will happen if there's any trace of the stuff in my motor?'

At Cascades the doorman won't let me in because I'm wearing Levi's. He keeps saying, 'No jeans,' and is not even intimidated by Tommo's superior muscle bulge. Eventually Tommo puts his hand in his pocket, pulls out a wad of notes, peels off a couple of twenties and stuffs them into the man's hand, Frank Sinatra-style.

As soon as we're inside Natasha and Emma drag me off to the ladies' where the three of us cram into a cubicle. Natasha offers to do the honours and I hand over my stash and, since the loo furniture is all anti-coke here too, Carey's book. Natasha holds it up and gives it a disaparaging look, although it's obvious this is not meant as literary criticism but as a comment on its size, lack of gloss and general unsuitability as a chopping board.

Eventually we emerge into the club, whose dark cavern is being bombarded by horrendously loud music. I don't recognize the records. Not only that, I can't understand them, until at last I pick up a heavy thump-thump beat which seems to be coming from the floor and up through my legs. Then I realize that the people dancing are working to a completely different rhythm and decide the thump-thump must be my own blood beating after the coke. Tommo gets us another round of drinks and after a while Natasha, Emma and I repair to the ladies' to top up.

Coming out again I'm following the girls back to our table when a voice shouts, 'Hey, it's the stuntman!'

I stare through the gloom into the heaving throng of dancers. One – a man – is gesturing to me. I glide over to him. Somehow my feet don't seem to want to leave the floor so I have to slide them over as though on skates.

'What are you doing, my friend? Are you making a film here? Ah, no, stupid me!' He makes a big panto-mime of slapping his forehead. 'Of course, my mistake. Now I remember! But should you really be in here tonight when you have the *Nürburgring* coming up on Sunday? The Grand Prix? Isn't that a little risky?' He punches my arm playfully.

'Hello, Branko, fancy meeting you here. Somehow I didn't have you down as the clubbing sort.'

'Ah, yes, you're right. But once a month we have a meeting of the local Croatian Club. Third Thursday of every month. This is it.' He turns to speak to the girl he's dancing with, whom his body is blocking from my view. 'It's one of my patients,' he says. 'I am just beginning to realize why his blood pressure is so high.'

The woman dances round him to look at me. She gives me the warmest of smiles.

'Harriet!'

'Michael, what are you doing here?' Then she notices Natasha and Emma hovering in the background. 'Or shouldn't I ask?'

'Oh, they're just, well, some young friends.'

'Very young,' she interposes.

'But what about you? I had no idea you knew Branko.'

'Croatian Club.'

'You're Croatian? You don't have an accent. Aren't you supposed to roll your Rs and growl a lot?'

'I think that's Hollywood Transylvanian, actually. I was born and bred in this country. I'm only half Croatian. My mother's from Split.'

At this point Branko leans across and shouts confidentially in my ear above the sound of the music, 'We're going on to a Croatian restaurant where they have a folk singer from my country. You and your friends are welcome to join us.'

'Thanks, but I don't think it's my kind of scene somehow.' He starts to protest. I hold up my hand, traffic-cop style. 'No, really. Sorry.'

Harriet gives me one of her dark smiles.

In the car I sit in the front beside Tommo with Emma on my lap. Natasha and Harriet are in the back, either side of Branko. I suspect Natasha has insisted on this arrangement to prevent any foreplay on my part. Presumably she hasn't had enough Charlie yet and I suspect she has quite an appetite for it. I find myself wondering which will give out first, my modest stash or her septum.

Emma puts her face into mine in that way drunks have of zooming in on you. 'You married?' she asks.

I laugh, as though this is the most ridiculous suggestion anyone ever made. 'Do I look married?' I ask, very rhetorically.

'Well, if you was thinking of getting married, I could do you a lovely reception. I've started doing a few weddings already to pay my tuition fees. You can have it themed, you know. I do Indian, Mexican, kosher, anything you like. Or very traditional. You look traditional to me.'

'I do? Why?'

'Well, wearing Levi's and that jacket. Just like my dad. I bet you like traditional music, the Rolling Stones, REM, all that.'

'Listen,' I say, 'I may be old, but I'm not that old.' I quickly work out that I'm supposed to have been born in 1961. 'The Stones were already past it by the time I was your age.'

'Oh, really? Sorry, I never know that stuff. It all gets a blur before 1990.'

The restaurant is in the old part of town, the bit that wasn't flattened by bulldozers in the sixties and seventies. The walls are dado rail with varnished pine tongue-and-groove below. That's how old it is. A large mural of what looks to me like a Greek island set in a very blue sea dominates one wall. I look at Harriet and think how nice it would be to run away there, just the two of us. Can you get your old age pension paid to Croatia, I find myself wondering?

There's a tongue-and-groove bar on one side of the room and behind it, amid all the optics, is a picture of a football team. You can tell it's a foreign team because they have green shirts and red shorts. Only foreigners would play football dressed like Christmas trees. As we make our way in, Branko says, in a low voice, 'Just one thing, our community here has been swollen in recent years by the arrival of many who have suffered traumas in our homeland. So, please, it is best not to mention the war.'

'War?' hisses Natasha to me. 'Why would I want to talk about the war? I wasn't even born then.'

The rest of the Croatian Club has already arrived and the place is humming. On a little stage area a woman wearing jeans and a baggy, colourfully embroidered white shirt sits and tunes a guitar.

'Rosa Popic,' whispers Branko, his voice larded with awe. 'Probably the best Croatian folk singer outside Croatia.'

Our party take their seats around a large round table. I am between Harriet and Natasha. Tommo is on Natasha's other side with Emma next to him. Branko sits between Emma and Harriet. It's all quite cosy and conveniently arranged. I can chat up Harriet with Natasha for back-up if there's nothing doing. I'm just leaning across to Harriet when a large hairy hand is placed on my shoulder and I'm pushed away from her.

'Excuse me!' Suddenly my chair is being lifted and I'm transported a foot to my right so that I'm practically sitting in Natasha's lap.

'Here, what's going on?' she squawks. 'I don't want you all over me.'

I look up at the owner of the hairy hand, who is a monstrously tall, dark-complected man of around thirty. I suppose he might be called good-looking, if you go for that five-o'clock-shadow, hatchet-faced, Balkan look. I don't. He's shoving a chair between me and Harriet. 'Please, I am sitting next to Harriet,' he says.

'Hello, Luka,' she says, with a certain weary affection.

I tap him on his back, which he has placed squarely towards me, blotting out my view of Harriet. A total eclipse of the woman I love. He turns and regards me in much the way that Tommo looked at my car, that is to say, as if I were dog dirt.

'Excuse me, but I'm afraid you'll have to sit somewhere else. I was sitting next to Harriet.'

'Go fuck yourself,' he growls, and fixes me with a Charles Manson stare. A real one.

I lean round him to speak to Harriet. 'Who's your friend?'

'Luka? He's not exactly a friend.' She raises her eyebrows and points a finger at her temple, twirling it to indicate craziness. 'He's someone I met through the Croatian Club. This city has a large Croatian community – it's one reason I chose to work here.'

Luka places his elbow on the table and rests his large, sharply angled head upon it, a buttress it's impossible for me to see around: I have to make do with peeping and smiling at Harriet through the small triangle of space between his upper arm, his body and the table.

Suddenly there is a great deal of shushing, then silence. The woman with the guitar begins strumming it and singing something that sounds vaguely Oriental and a bit Italian too. She sings in a deep lugubrious voice. The melody, if it has one is flat, almost monotone, and certainly monotonous. The language sounds like Russian, only more guttural and as if it is impossible to pronounce correctly without a lot of spitting. Abruptly she stops singing and the whole room erupts into wild applause.

'You don't like?' Luka has pulled himself away from Harriet long enough to see that I'm not clapping.

'My Serbo-Croat's not quite up to it, I'm afraid.'

'Permit me to translate so you will understand why you should be applauding.' Luka talks, or rather growls in a monotone too. It must be a Croatian thing.

'When the grape hangs heavy on the vine we pluck it and it becomes wine. When the child is born we drink the wine to celebrate. It dribbles from our lips. We are drunk on joy. Later we drink the wine at his wedding. We praise the vintage of the year of his birth. We little think of winter when all things must die. We see only the little baby or the young man with his bride, not the old man he will be. One day we will drink wine at his funeral.'

'Hmm, cheerful.'

'If you want cheerful you should not come to Croatian restaurant.' He reaches out for one of the bottles of red wine that have appeared on the table and pours hefty glasses for himself and Harriet. He places the bottle out of my reach, drains his glass in one quaff and pours more. Fortunately Branko sees my plight and has another bottle sent over. The wine is dark as old blood and very fruity. I knock back a couple of glasses with ease.

The singer is off again. I notice Branko has a tear in his eye.

'What was that about?' I ask him, across the table.

'It is about a man who is in prison in a foreign land and can never return to Croatia. He is very unhappy and then he dies.' He breaks into a smile at my dismay. 'Don't worry, my friend, she also sings sad songs.'

While she is keening her way through another number food is served. Kebabs and rice and salad. I'm not hungry after all the Charlie so I push my plate aside. Luka turns to me again. His mouth is occupied with the kebab, which he is de-skewering with his teeth. He nods at my food and grunts interrogatively.

'Help yourself,' I say. He picks up my plate and tips its contents on to his own. He grunts again and waves a paw at Natasha's and Emma's plates, and we pass them along.

The singer has finished and while the restaurant applauds, Natasha pushes back her chair and stands. She totters over to the singer on her platform shoes and there's a moment or two's intense conversation between them. Natasha clumps back to my side.

'What did you say to her?' I ask, as she eases herself on to her chair.

'I just asked her to sing something English.'

The singer launches into 'Una Paloma Blanca'.

'Bloody hell,' says Natasha, 'I need some more Charlie.'

Luka's head swivels round. 'You have Charlie?' he asks, his spitting accent splattering the tablecloth with kebab shrapnel.

'He does.' Natasaha indicates me.

Luka hauls himself abruptly to his feet, so fast his chair topples over. He rights it then tugs my arm. 'Here, let's take a little walk.'

There's not much room in the cubicle with Luka. Once I've squeezed in enough to close the door behind me, out of habit, I reach into my pocket, take out John Carey and proffer it to Luka.

He stares at it dumbly. 'Fuck it, man, I don't want to read. Give me the Charlie.'

I take out my stash and hand it over. He kneels down before the loo and lays out the sacrament on the altar of its old-fashioned flat cover. He does two very long lines and snorts them both up. He does another couple, snorts one, and then hands the banknote to me. I'm quite proud to manage so long a line in one breath, as smug as Jake blowing out all four candles on his last birthday cake in one go.

When we return to the restaurant, music, disco music of the kind I recognize from the tongue-and-groove era, is playing and people are dancing. I have to take Natasha and Emma off to the ladies', not trusting them with my sadly depleted stash. Naturally I have to be sociable and have a toot myself, for otherwise what excuse could I have for accompanying them, other than mistrust?

When we return, Harriet is dancing with Luka. I grab Natasha and pull her towards the dance area. She makes a faint protest, probably because she's a person who would protest about anything, but I can see from her glazed expression that she's flying and definitely up for anything. Everyone seems pretty revved up. Myself, I'm on this weird cocktail of beta-blockers, coke and alcohol. The two former seem to be in some sort of equilibrium. It's as though I'm completely hyped up but I can't quite feel it. I wonder if I ought to take another beta-blocker. It's getting late and I always take my daily tab last thing before going to bed. I remember Branko warning me that if I stopped taking them the effect would wear off almost immediately and I'd be left with my dangerously high BP. The question is academic: the beta-blockers are at home because that's where I always take them.

I disco across to Harriet and Luka, who towers above her slight figure like a huge tree, an impression heightened by the fact that he doesn't move his feet beyond the odd shuffle or two, but confines his movement to rocking back and forth, as if he's bending in the breeze.

'Hi!' I give her a cheery wave. In front of me Natasha is bouncing around on a different planet.

Harriet rolls her eyes.

Should I cut in? I ask myself. Cutting in is something I've never experienced outside an American movie. It is definitely not a British way of taking someone else's girl. Briefly I wonder about Croatian etiquette. Then, coke piloting my brain, I think, What the hell?

'Excuse me,' I call up to Luka's head, which is somewhere high above me, around ceiling level. I take Harriet's arm and start to steer her away.

I've managed about half a step when there's a giant economy-sized hand on my arm. Luka twirls me round like a puppet. 'I'm dancing with her,' he says, spraying me Slavically with spit.

'You can have mine.' I nod to indicate Natasha, who is dancing on her own, out of it. 'She'll shag anything now.'

Luka grabs me by the lapels and – I swear it – lifts me bodily by them across the room. All I can think about is my jacket. I've had it years and it's a much-loved old friend. And it doesn't have Aunt Clara triple-stitched seams. Of course, there's a ripping sound and one lapel (only one – there are still, thank God, some standards) becomes partially detached, as Luka bundles me through the door of the men's loo. Inside he throws me against the opposite wall, which I hit hard, so I lose my breath and slide down its cold tiles. He crosses the room in a single lope and picks me up.

'Careful of my lapels!' I scream, but he takes no notice. Holding me by them in his left hand so that I can't slump again, he balls his right hand and smashes me in the nose. Tears fill my eyes so it's a moment or two before I can see the blood all over my arms as they reach up to protect my face as Luka pulls his fist back again. For a second all I can think is, How am I going to snort the rest of my very last stash of coke with my main drug-taking equipment busted like this?

'Wait, Luka, I'm on your side!' I scream. 'I always

said it was the Serbs who started it!' He takes no notice. I twist as the blow comes in and it strikes relatively harmlessly against my breast pocket with all the power of an elephant's kick. I shut my eyes, bracing myself for a third blow when I suddenly realize Luka has let me go.

I must be brain-damaged, I think, because although my eyes are open I still can't see. It's as though I'm surrounded by a white cloud. Then, through it, I see Luka standing still, transfixed by the vision too, like a child watching snow fall for the first time. All at once we realize what has happened.

'The coke, man!' he screams. 'I bust the coke bag!'

I feel in my pocket. His holding me must have worked it up so it was practically hanging out, which is what it's doing now, and his second punch burst it. I wonder how long Luka will watch it before he gets fed up and starts beating me up again, but then he puts his hand in his pocket, takes out a banknote and fashions it into a tube. In a second he's down on his knees, note up his nose, hoovering the floor for powder as it settles. He doesn't even look up as I step over him, dropping the bag beside him, and push out of the door.

There's quite a hubbub outside as Harriet has summoned the other members of the club to help. She and Branko are standing at the front of the throng.

'What happened?' asks Harriet. 'Where's Luka?'

'On duh floor,' I reply truthfully. 'Bud I dink he'll live.'

'You should let me take a look at that nose,' says Branko. 'It may be broken.'

'Id's OK.' I wave him away. 'Don't bodder.' I take Harriet's hand. 'Come on, led's ged oud od here. I don't want to go Round Two wid Luka when he comes out.

Ignoring Branko's protest, I pull Harriet towards the door. En route I notice Tommo dancing in a dark

354

corner with Emma, oblivious of the fight. A pity, I can't help feeling. A confrontation between him and Luka would have been interesting. I look around for Natasha. She's dancing with someone who, from the back, looks a bit like Uncle Frank. If it is my dead relative, he certainly seems a good deal more alive than she does, which come to think of it, wouldn't be difficult, even for a ghost. But I know it can't be him. We've already said our goodbyes. Besides, how can I still be having hallucinations? After all, I've given up the coke.

As Harriet and I push out through the doors, I hear Branko call something after me. 'I'd love,' he says, voice full of wistful concern, 'to take your blood pressure now.'

I hurry Harriet along the street, glancing behind for fear that a freshly coked Luka may be bounding after us. He's probably changed into a werewolf by now. Or isn't it Croatians that do that? Harriet hands me a wad of paper tissues and I press them to my nose, mainly because I don't want to leave a blood trail in case he comes after me with tracker dogs.

Eventually a couple of streets away from the restaurant we duck into a pub. Harriet steers me into the ladies', which appears empty until another couple emerges from one of the cubicles sniffing conspicuously.

Harriet runs some water and cleans my face with paper towels. She holds the bridge of my nose tight with two fingers. It's the closest we have ever come to an embrace. Suddenly I think of one of those old Hitchcock films where the wrongly accused guy is on the run and becomes handcuffed to this beautiful woman, Madeleine Carrol (blonde, not my type), who helps him. I think how nice it would be to be handcuffed to Harriet. I'm about to say as much when I realize this might sound too much like bondage sex, the *Sun* persona I want Harriet to forget about. Besides, that's the kind of perverted, abnormal behaviour I will be eschewing after tonight.

Now that it's stopped bleeding my nose is not too much of a problem. Harriet attempts to sponge my blood-spattered jacket but already the stains seem to have soaked into the material.

'Don't worry,' I say. 'From a distance id will jud look like a paddern.'

'Hmm,' she says, standing back to view it better. 'Not a cool look. If I were you, I'd stick with the bloodstain explanation.'

We go into the bar and have several drinks. Brandy for the shock I've had. Doubles because it was a big shock. After an hour I feel a warm sleepy glow from the alcohol and an aching tiredness as I come down from the coke. When we get up to leave I can hardly walk and certainly not in a straight line, which doesn't really matter because, as chance would have it, Harriet walks in exactly the same way. Outside I say, 'Where's your car parked?'

'Car? What car? I don't have a car. And if I did I wouldn't be driving it, I'm totally rat-arsed. We'll have to start walking and hope we find a cab.'

We begin to walk and we don't find a cab but the rain finds us. Within a minute we are drenched to the skin. We walk along like this for half an hour and I am now so wet that water is sloshing inside my shoes. Then I spot a minicab. I stagger into the road and hail it. It pulls up and the driver opens the passenger window.

'Can you take us to fourteen Hayston Terrace, please?' says Harriet.

The driver looks us up and down. 'Nah, I'm not taking you,' he says. 'You're all wet.'

'Of course we're fugging wed!' I scream. 'In case you habn't noticed it's fugging raining!'

He presses a button and the window starts to go up. 'No, wait!' I plead, jamming my fingers in the top to stop it closing. 'I'm sorry. Look, how about if I gib you dis?' I pull out my wallet, which is a pulp of sodden paper now. I extract a twenty, peeling it with difficulty from the lump of notes, and flap it through the remaining gap in the window.

'Yeah, OK, hop in,' he says. 'But try not to drip. I've just been re-upholstered.'

In the back seat I put my arm around Harriet, one wet person to another for warmth. She tips her face up to mine and folds her lips over my mouth. As our tongues meet I could almost weep with happiness. In fact I may actually be weeping, it's impossible to tell with all the rain running down my face from my hair. Eventually we pull apart.

'Ugh, you taste of blood,' she says.

'Dat's funny,' I reply, 'so do you.'

'That's all right, then.' She kisses me again for the longest time until we're interrupted.

'Here! Cut that out in the back, you two,' barks the cabbie, looking at us in his rear-view mirror. 'Sit still. All that moving about is making more drips.'

In Harriet's flat we stumble into the bedroom. 'Let's get you out of those wet clothes,' she says, an almost exact fulfilment (with the addition of only one word) of a fantasy line I've had her say many times. She slips off my jacket and begins pulling at my shirt, which is plastered to my hairy skin. There are few things more difficult than removing wet clothes and it is some time before I stand naked. Harriet throws me a towel, without looking at me. 'Here, give yourself a good dry.' Then, unselfconsciously, she takes off her own clothes, unzipping the black dress and letting it parachute to the floor. She smiles as she undoes her bra and when

357

her small breasts swing free I let out a little gasp. It's not so much that there's anything special about her breasts. It's just that they're hers and I'm seeing them.

'What?' she says. 'Is your nose hurting again?'

'No, id's nod by node, id's jud dat you're doh beaudiful.'

She laughs and sits on the bed to peel off her black tights. It's only when they're on the floor and I see the scrap of her underwear inside them that I realize she's naked. She pats the bed beside her.

I walk over and sit down. I put my arms around her. It makes each of us shiver to touch another body so cold. We kiss and fall backwards on to the bed together. Eventually I move down to press damp kisses upon her nipples. She attempts to run her fingers through my hair, but it's knotted from being damp and she has to make do with stroking me as if I were a dog. I reach between her legs and her fur is damp, but this time I feel sure it is not from the rain.

'If you knew how long I'b wanded you.' It comes out as a croak.

'Ditto,' she replies.

I pull back. 'Diddo? Why didn't you eber leb be know?'

'Lots of reasons. You're married. You have children. I was brought up to know that isn't right. Plus you never asked me and, from what I'd heard, if you'd been interested you would have. Plus I didn't want to be another notch on your bedpost. You've got us all now. Me and Karen.'

'She told you?'

'Of course. She said she felt sorry for you.'

'She piddy-fugged me.'

Harriet laughs. I'm still moving my hand between her legs. She moves from stroking my chest down through the thick fur (I'm my grandfather's grandson, after all!) across my stomach and into the action area.

'Oh!'

We both look down. The Old Soldier is definitely in mufti, disguised as a small pink shrimp. So tiny that if he weren't attached you could flick him clear across a restaurant. Harriet strokes him tenderly. She peels him delicately. She lifts him and caresses my balls, which now seem huge by comparison to their erstwhile commander.

'It must be the cold,' she says. 'Think we need a spot of mouth to mouth.'

For a moment the image of Edward lying on the riverbank flashes across my mind, which doesn't help, but by the time it's gone Harriet is down there. He is scarcely a mouthful, so shrivelled he keeps flopping out from between her lips. She works away manfully, so to speak, but after five minutes nothing has happened.

She raises her head and crawls up to lay it on my shoulder. She lifts the Old Soldier and lets him flop against my greying pubic hair.

'I think the trouble is he's drunk on duty,' she says, surprising me for a moment by her use of the military metaphor, almost as though she can read my thoughts. She holds him by the foreskin and shakes him with mock anger. 'Oh, why won't you stand up, you silly bastard cock? I so want you inside me.'

So I tell her everything. About the hypertension, the BP monitor, Tamsin, my dead relatives, the beta-blockers, everything, right up to this, the final irony. How my dissolute life has led me to this moment when the achievement of its very apex is denied as a result of its own corrupt nature.

At the end of it all, Harriet says, 'I'd quite like to meet your uncle Frank.'

'You wouldn't,' I say. 'Believe me, you wouldn't.'

And then, huddled in each other's arms, we fall asleep.

TWENTY-NINE

If we love things long sought, age is a thing
Which we are fifty years in compassing.

The Autumnal

I am driving the car with Alison beside me. Except it's not our car but a Mini like the one Uncle Frank had for a while, the Cooper S in which he used to roar along the straight bit of the Ely Road when he came to see my grandmother. The one in which he had his fatal crash. We're driving along the street I lived in all my childhood. The council estate of post-war, red-brick, semi-detached utility houses. Past number thirteen, Agnes Ada's house, where she lived with Aunt Clara and all those cats. It's a cul-de-sac and our old house, number twenty-eight, with its Siamese twin, squats across the end of the road, facing the rest of the street at right angles. I stop the car, get out, leaving Alison in it, and walk over to the house. I'm standing looking at it when a woman appears from round the back. She's youngish with blonde hair. She has a dog, a golden spaniel, which jumps up me, trying to lick me.

'Did you want something?' asks the woman.

'I used to live in your house. I was born in it, in that room up there. Fifty years ago.'

The woman smiles serenely. 'That's a long time.'

'I was wondering if some time I might come and have a look inside. You know, make an appointment when it's convenient. I'd be happy to pay you for your trouble.'

At this moment a man, slightly older than the woman, dressed in work overalls, appears from round the corner of the house, as she did.

'What's going on?' he asks. She explains. They exchange glances.

'You're welcome to come in and look round now,' says the man. 'It's no bother and we don't want paying.'

I step inside the back door and nothing is the same. The staircase is in the wrong place. 'We've made a few changes,' says the man.

I climb the staircase and at the top find myself outside a door. It has the same tortoiseshell bakelite handle I remember. I turn it and push open the door. It's my old room. Nothing has altered since I was a small child. The faded blue lino is still there, brittle and cracked with age in places like an old man's face; my bed is in the same position. Sunlight floods the room, leaching through the thin yellow curtains, which are closed. I walk over to the window, draw open the curtains and look down into the back garden. There's the familiar brick outside privy. And the lawn next to it. At the far end of the lawn is the old rose trellis, built from thick rough wooden poles. It used to spread across the whole width of the lawn but now only a portion of it remains. It's as though someone has taken a giant knife and cleanly sliced off more than half of it. What is left is as it was, undamaged.

'The rose trellis is still there. My father built it the year I was born,' I tell the couple. 'Isn't it wonderful? There's still a fair bit of it left.'

*   *   *

The sound of birds. The joyful song of a blackbird. Hardy's darkling thrush, I remember, lifter of his gloom. I open my eyes. Sunlight floods this room too. The significance of the dream strikes me. The morning of my fiftieth birthday. For a moment I expect to hear my children running to shout greetings and offer presents, to sing 'Happy Birthday'. And then, as the room gradually comes into focus, I realize that not only am I not in my childhood bedroom I'm not in my adult one either. This room too, like my first bedroom, is sparsely decorated and furnished. The walls are washed a pale yellow, with only a couple of small art prints inhabiting their emptiness. There's a big old pine mirror on the opposite wall. My birthday self stares anxiously at me from the depths of dark eye-sockets. Its hair is matted and there is a small Hitler moustache of dried blood upon its upper lip. Beside this other self is the rumple-sheeted shape of another body. I turn and find its mirror image next to me. The faint whistle of another's breathing trembles the sheet. As carefully as a child might move a leaf bearing a butterfly, I lift it. And see, to my wonder, a nest of black hair coiled upon the pillow, and on the creamy face beneath a tear-shaped smudge of mascara below the closed eye of Harriet Bright. I take a gulp of sun-warmed air. My mouth is dry and as furred as an old kettle. For a moment I almost gag on limescale and happiness. I am here, naked, beside the – I lift the sheet a little more to confirm this – naked form of Harriet Bright. I reflect that it does not matter that I can't remember how this miracle came to be or what the experience of it was like. It happened! I've slept with her! I have taken some kind of possession of her as, before I knew her even, I always dreamed I would.

But then I'm aware of a drumbeat in my head, crude and primitive, out of harmony with the quiet symphony I was constructing of the moment. With it come edited highlights of last night. Tommo. The two girls. A woman whose singing would break your heart if you understood her language. A fight. Blood and rain. A damp, futile attempt at coupling. And, over-laying it all, the vague unease of the hangover. The fear of what still lies unremembered.

Now the drums are pounding hard. It's one of those percussion groups who use only dustbin lids and whistles, stomping their booted feet inside my head. As if she, too, can hear them, Harriet's eyelids twitch and then open. The moment she sees me her face breaks into a smile. Oh, I think, not so drunk as me last night, then.

'Hello, you,' she says. 'What are you doing here?'

'Don't you remember last night?' I ask.

'I remember you getting bashed by Luka. You were awfully brave. I hope you didn't hurt him too much. He's quite sweet when he's sober.'

'What else do you remember?'

'Being drunk. Bringing you back here when I shouldn't have.'

'Nothing happened.'

'I remember that too.'

'What's the time?' She sits up to look at a digital clock on the bedside table and the sheet falls away from my loins. We both stare at the Old Soldier, who is not only stiff but pointing straight up, like a missile ready to launch itself into space.

'Wow!' she says. 'What happened to that?'

The pounding in my head, which is syncopating with a funny little skipping game my heart is playing in my chest, suddenly tells me. Of course, I wasn't home last night. I didn't take my beta-blocker. I think I will die if I move my head. But manfully I struggle to seize the moment. I know I must plant my flag in the dark, as yet unclaimed territory between Harriet Bright's legs. To requisition it for my own.

'Would you like to try again?' I ask.

Her mouth crinkles in a rueful smile. 'If it was going to happen, it should have happened last night. I'm sober now. I don't do this thing with other women's men. With somebody's father.'

'If it was OK last night, why isn't it OK now? What's changed, other than him?' I nod at the Old Soldier, who winks impudently back at us with his single eye. It occurs to me that it's his birthday too and I haven't wished him many happy returns yet.

'Don't you think all these things have a moment? Sometimes it's drink, or opportunity, or hormones or an evening of mutual loneliness or mutual horniness or shared madness. And then the moment passes and you know, you just know, that that was it and it will never come again.'

What can I do, the reformed and mature fifty-year-old Michael Cole, but nod in agreement? Except it hurts too much to do it. I do not, I know, have Donne's powers of persuasion. True, I have Carey's book in my pocket, razor-scarred and cocaine-dusted, but I know, in my heart of hearts, that it's time to have, well, done with my old accomplice. I can't go on dying like this.

'That's a description of life,' I say. 'I – oh, no, sweet Jesus, is that really the time?' I've caught sight of the bedside clock which reads ten thirty-five.

'Give or take a few minutes, why?'

I'm out of bed like a bullet and looking for my clothes, which I find lying on the floor, making, as chance would have it a two-dimensional picture, like the body map detectives draw after a murder. My underpants are still wearing my trousers and I pull them on together, hopping around on one foot to get the second leg in, incompetent with morning-after.

'What?' says Harriet. 'What's the rush?'

'The Kappelheim. I'm supposed to be delivering it at eleven o'clock.'

'Shit! You'll never make it.'

'I have to make it. It's my whole future. I can't just not turn up. The benefactors are going to be there. It's not just head of department, if I don't show I probably won't even have a job.'

Harriet's out of bed in a blink and in another has wriggled into a pair of jeans as if for a competition. Why is it, I find myself thinking, with that awful irrelevancy my mind so loves, that women can spend hours bathing, applying makeup, selecting clothes, snagging and replacing tights, *getting ready*, and yet, when the chips are down, as they most decidedly are now, they can do it in the time it takes a man to find his socks?

'Come *on!*' screeches Harriet. 'What are you doing?'

'I was just thinking, I was . . .' I was just thinking I'll never see you naked again, is what I want to say, but I don't have the words for it not to come out crude. I don't do *tender*. I'm out of practice on that.

'Well, don't think, just get a move on.'

'I'll have to go home and change.'

'You can't. You have twenty-five – no, twenty-three minutes. You'll be lucky to make it to campus in that time. Very lucky.'

I find my socks, two damp grey animals curled on the floor beneath my shirt. I sit on the bed and try to tug them on, but they are wet and unwilling.

'I'll get you a pair of mine!' cries Harriet, and hurriedly opens a bedside drawer.

'Don't be silly!' I gesticulate helplessly at her feet, whose size, or rather lack of it, is their beauty. I think how there is nothing that can break your heart like the size of a child's shoes.

I have my shirt on. It's wet and cold and sticky, as physically unlike the warm, prickly scratchiness of a hair-shirt as it's possible to be, yet equally effective in reminding me of my sins. A Nessus number, impregnated with the poison of regret. Fortunately, bearing in mind the formality of the occasion, it's also a white shirt. Unfortunately, it bears a scarlet splattering from last night. But in that respect, at least, it matches the jacket. Teamed and toned forensic evidence.

Harriet has a sponge in one hand and is trying to remove the blood from the jacket, but I wave her away. 'It's not doing any good, and you're just damaging the pile.'

'What about this lapel? It's hanging off. Here, let me try pinning it.'

She plants half a dozen pins in it, which at least removes the danger of it dropping off, though the ripped seam still shows. She gamely drags a brush through my hair, ignoring my pleas that she's hurting me. Now I know why Edward swears so much about it.

'I ought to shave, have you got a razor?'

'No, 'fraid not.'

'What about one of those for doing your legs?'

'Sorry, I use cream.'

'Damn!'

'Michael, I really wouldn't worry about it. Not having shaved is so low on the list of what's wrong with you . . .'

I squelch over to the mirror. I almost recoil from the figure who confronts me. For a moment I think he might be about to ask me for money. But, of course, it's me.

In spite of Harriet's best efforts, my hair is matted. My eyes glint out from sockets all too obviously darkened by debauchery. My cheeks are stubbled. My nostrils are hemmed with a crust of dried blood.

My jacket is soggy and the lapel torn. My jeans are wet and stick to my legs, tight and wrinkled, which makes them look like mediaeval hose and me, perhaps, a sad jester from those times. My brown brogues are dull with damp. They are connected to my dripping jeans by the white sticks of my bare legs. This is my second sockless public appearance. It's getting to be a habit.

I look across the room at Harriet, who's holding the phone. 'It's no good, I can't get a cab,' she says. 'Can't you just phone in sick?'

I shake my head. 'I have to do this.'

She grabs my hand. 'Seventeen minutes left. We can still make it if we're lucky with a bus. Let's go!'

We're out of the flat and down a couple of flights of stairs in record time – at least, for someone with wet shoes and no socks. Harriet flies down the street and I squelch gamely after her. The bus stop is about two hundred yards away. As we run towards it a bus overtakes us. Fortunately there's a guy at the stop, which means the bus will have to pull up. Harriet is going like the clappers, and my feet are squelching up the yards like there's no tomorrow. A hundred yards. Fifty. The percussion band in my head has moved outside it now. My heart is exploring ways of bursting through my chest, hurling itself against my ribcage. But it's OK, because there's a tight hoop of pain around my chest, keeping it in. Thirty yards, twenty, ten. We're there, just as the bus comes to rest. The door sighs open. The bus is packed.

'Room for one only!' shouts the driver.

I turn to kiss Harriet. 'Thanks for getting me this far.'

I turn back to the bus in time to see the guy who was waiting at the stop ascend the step. 'Hey, wait, I need that place,' I yell.

He's young. He has a shaven head, nose jewellery and a tattoo on his neck. Three of my four urban warning signs. And who knows? Just because he's not waving a loaded gun, it doesn't mean he hasn't got the fourth in his pocket.

He looks down at me. 'I was here first, Granddad.'

Granddad! God, I must look worse than I thought.

'Yes, I know, but I really have to catch this bus. If I don't I won't have a career.'

'Tough,' he says. 'I already don't have a career.'

'Come on,' says the driver. 'Move along so I can close the door.'

'Listen,' I fumble in my pocket and pull out a lump of papier-mâché with the Queen's head on it. 'I'll pay you. How much? Twenty? Fifty?'

'Piss off, mate,' he sneers, 'you can't buy me.' And he swings on to the bus. The door hisses shut and I watch my life disappear along the dual carriageway.

'Come on!' yells Harriet. 'You can still make it.'

'It's hopeless, there's no chance.'

'Don't give up.' She's pulling me by the sleeve.

'Hey, watch it, Aunt Clara hasn't been over it.'

'What? What do you mean?'

'Forget it.'

'Come on, stop talking, Michael, run!'

She slides her hand down to grasp mine and tugs me. Soon we're running again. The crazed drummers are at me once more and my heart is bouncing around. I don't know if it's from running, sheer panic or a combination of both but my breath won't come. I gulp down whole lungfuls of petroleum-flavoured air but it's still not enough. I'd give anything for a beta-blocker now.

Suddenly she stops and lets go my hand to consult her watch.

'How. Long. Left?' I pant.

'Nine minutes.'

In lieu of speech I give a dismissive wave of my

hand. I'm gulping for air like a fish out of water now, the way the eels used to when we pulled the reeds out of the Lark and they crawled on to dry land. The way Edward did, perhaps, in his dry balloon inside the womb.

Harriet's response is to give me a hefty shove so that I fall into a privet hedge, the border of a garden abutting the pavement. I'm trapped and can't see a thing. Suddenly the sound of a car slowing. Voices, one of them Harriet's. I can't catch what she's saying. The opening of a car door.

'Wait a minute!' It's Harriet. A hand grabs my arm and pulls me. I'm stuck and another hand joins the first and I'm being tugged now. Pins pop from my lapel. Twigs poke me in the head, the eye. The hedge is refusing to let me go. Another tug from behind. I feel myself being pulled backwards. Finally I'm free.

'My friend,' says Harriet and without further ado throws me on to the back seat of a car and jumps in after me.

'Never knew you had a friend,' says the middle-aged man driving. 'Might not've stopped if I had.' He glances round. 'Looks like he could do with a good meal, if you ask me. You want to watch yourself, love. You seem a nice girl. Schizophrenics, most of them dossers. You take my word for—'

'Can you please just hurry?' says Harriet.

The man turns back to look out of the windscreen and the car speeds up. 'Bloody hell,' he mutters, 'talk about ungrateful.'

'Who. Is. He?' I whisper. 'Taxi?'

'Nope. I hitched. Don't talk, try to get your breath back, you'll need it.'

'Oh, no. Can't! Can't. Run. Any. More!'

'Not for running, stupid. The lecture.'

'Lecture?'

369

'Yes, the one you're giving three minutes from now. Have you thought about what you're going to say?'

'Shit!' I cry.

'Now, now, less of that, if you don't mind,' says the man in the front. 'What did I tell you, young lady?'

The car draws up to the campus and the driver, for all his bad temper, takes us round to the front entrance, which is only a couple of hundred yards from the Great Hall.

Harriet bends over the seat and kisses the man hard on the lips. 'That's so you'll always pick up hitch-hikers.'

'I will!' says the man. 'I will!'

We're out of the car now and squelching along at one hell of a lick. How do you measure the speed of squelching? I find myself wondering. In m.p.h.? In knots? Then I glance up at the clock over the porter's lodge. Eleven-twenty. I should be finishing my lecture about now.

I screech to a halt. 'It's no good.' I nod at the clock. 'We're too late.'

'No, don't give up. These things often start a bit late. Come on, you never know.' We jog over to the hall.

We're just about to enter the large double doors at the rear of the hall when a familiar figure hoves into view. Jane.

'Michael!' she says. 'What happened to you? You look like you've been dragged through a hedge back-wards!'

'I – I'm sorry I'm late, Jane. Is everybody waiting for me?' Through the door I can see people are still there, still in their seats.

'No, they're not waiting for you. They're listening to Brady. When you didn't show up, I switched the order and put him on first. I slipped out a moment ago to see if there was any sign of you.'

A long sigh of relief escapes me. 'That's wonderful, I thought I'd missed it.'

I start for the doors, but Jane lays a restraining hand on my arm. 'You can't think you're going in there looking like that? You look like a derelict.'

'Thanks, Jane. I just had – a – well, a couple of, uh, mishaps.'

'It's not a couple. It's several years' worth. Michael, there's no point in going in there.'

'What do you mean? People are expecting me, it's my big chance. Head of dep—'

Jane is shaking her head. 'Michael, did you seriously think we'd appoint you? Even before this latest series of escapades you had only a small chance of tenure. The girls. The lack of any serious publication. The lazy self-absorption that has characterized you from the start. Did you think we'd promote you just because you couldn't shift your arse to find another job?'

'But Stanley—'

'In his day Stanley was a fine academic. He wrote novels. He appeared on TV. He published several definitive critical works.'

'But there's my book on Donne—'

'Ah, but there isn't.'

'Listen, Jane, give me one more chance, I beg you. Let me give my lecture, please.'

'Michael, you've had your last chance. You couldn't even turn up here on time in a presentable state.'

'Well, fuck you too, Jane! Anyway, since I'm here, I may as well say what I came to say.'

She tightens her grip on my arm, grimacing slightly as water squeezes from the soggy cloth. 'Michael, in spite of everything that's happened, there's a possibility you may still have a job. But if you go in there, you have my personal guarantee you won't have even that.'

'So be it!' I shake off her hand and stride towards the

371

doors from which, at that moment, issues the sound of rapturous applause, presumably marking the end of Tait's lecture.

'Wait, Michael!' It's Harriet. She trots after me. 'Do you know what you're going to say?'

There's a brief caesura in my anger, enough for me to smile. 'I'll think of something.' And into the hall I stride.

The place is packed. As I begin to walk along the centre aisle towards the stage at the far end, the last applause for Tait dies out. There is a faint hum of conversation, but that, too, dies as people become aware of my presence. A whisper spreads around the hall and in a trice every head is turned back to look at me. An amazed silence ensues, broken only by the rhythmical squelching of my sockless feet in their wet shoes. It's a very long walk, this one to my own personal Calvary. I straighten my figure, and pull at the cuffs of my jacket, attempting a dignity that belies my appearance. Eventually I reach the stage and stumble on the bottom step. Tait, who is sitting in the front row, shoots from his seat and catches hold of me, an offer of assistance I shrug off. As I climb the remaining steps I can hear the machine-gun staccato of Jane's high heels as she makes her way along one of the side aisles. I reach the lectern and turn to face my audience. Jane is below me, at the side of the platform, flanked by two security men. I grip the edges of the lectern, whose top is a carved piece of wood in the shape of a dove bearing an olive branch in its bill. I look down at my audience. They are all in their finery for the day: the women in bright summer frocks, sporting hats, as if at a wedding, the men in suits and ties. At the front, between Tait and an empty chair that I take to be the Dean's, sits a tiny, elderly man I recognize from photographs as Kappelheim himself, minnowed by the gigantic pink whale of a wife beside him, a former showgirl gone to fat, I seem to remember. The other side of Tait is another empty chair. Alison's, I realize with a stab of guilt. Suddenly, I haven't a thought in my head. But that has never been something to stop me speaking in the past. I am, after all, the master of the unprepared lecture, the champion of spontaneous bullshit. I clear my throat.

'Ladies and gentlemen, you see before you the thing itself, poor unaccommodated Cole, unadorned apart from a few rags and all of those torn, bloodstained and damp. It would take too long to tell you how this came to be and it is not, after all, important. My apologies if anyone here is so petty-minded as to be offended by dress; if so, there is no need for them to stay. They may leave now before I start.' I draw myself up over the lectern like some bird of prey on his mountain perch and glare at the audience. Nobody moves. 'Very well, then, I'll begin. For some twenty years, I have, as some of you will know, devoted myself to the study of the poet John Donne. Well, no more. The subject of my talk today is why I am done with Donne. Ladies and gentlemen, esteemed colleagues, security men,' a titter at this last and one makes as if to move towards the stage, but the Dean's hand restrains him, 'we live in a secular society. This might, in itself, be endurable. It is too soon to know. But not for my generation. Because for us it is also a post-religious society. That is to say, we were brought up on religion as well as white bread. We were endowed with all the expectations a belief in God offers: heaven, an afterlife, everlasting life. A money-back, good-for-eternity guarantee. So that now, for people of my age – and allow me to tell you that today is my fiftieth birthday,' slight applause, I hold up my hand deprecatingly, to subdue it, 'living in a secular age gives us a profound sense of disappointment. Worse even, of disbelief. We cannot accept – no, more than that, cannot comprehend the concept of annihilation. It is not the rosy end foretold in our childhood. We were promised angels, not the abyss. And yet accept it we must, for in the absence of God, any god, oblivion is what awaits us all. I wish I could preach a sermon to match Donne's last, his duel with death, which ended with a promise of resurrection. But even Donne, I suspect, would be hard pressed to claim one convert here today. I can offer you no reassurance. We are all, every last one of us in this hall, going to die. And then to rot and turn to dust and be blown to nowhere.' I have their attention now. One or two are moving uncomfortably. A woman in the second row looks around at her neighbours, flexing her shoulders as though to say, 'I don't know about you, but this isn't what I bought a new dress for.'

I resume speaking. 'And, cling to what we will, this is what we all know. Why else would we set so much store by material things? Why else do we make shopping malls our cathedrals? If we had even the slightest atom of belief in Christ or the afterlife, wouldn't we give everything away and devote our lives to the poor to secure a ticket? Could we sip our cocktails while the whole continent of Africa dies of Aids? Of course not. We have read the writing on the wall and we know what it means.'

I pause to take a sip of water from the glass thoughtfully provided on the lectern. There are faint mutterings from the audience now. I clear my throat.

'In the light of this new death, it follows therefore that we must find a new way to live.' I look meaningfully at my audience, yet in truth I'm straining for words. I have no idea what comes next. My head is thumping and the old pre-beta-blocker panic is back. But many of my listeners are looking at me with keen interest. There's a spark in Kappelheim's eye. I feel sure he's a shrewd little bastard. How else did he make all his money? And if he's not above crude materialism, why else would he give so much of it away? I sense his approval. I'm on to a winner here. But I have to be careful. Many more of my audience wear puzzled expressions, their brows pleated by doubt. Others consult their watches. In the front row Tait kicks the uppermost of his crossed legs restlessly.

'Listen,' I begin again, 'I've heard it said that as this new secularism seeps into our consciousness we will come to regard people as no more than ants and that serial killings and mass murders, high-school shootings and so on will proliferate. What will there be to prevent people doing this? What will be so wrong about destroying another set of molecules which merely happens to be arranged like your own?

'This brings us back to Donne. Donne had an ego even bigger than his prick.' A general gasp. The bejeaned figure of Harriet lurking at the back of the hall puts its head in its hands. 'As do I! Donne was the biggest and best at everything. He was the biggest womanizer! He fucked more than anyone else! He was the worst sinner! Even God couldn't reform him! Whatever Donne went in for, he was the greatest. He could scarcely defer to God. He could not, at heart, believe in his own death. He was too important to die! And it's this same faulty obsession with self that leads to all the talk of serial killings. Without God to give them a sense of proportion, the big egos go on killing sprees.' A general rustle of impatience now: people are openly talking to their neighbours. 'But if we can but lose the ego, and not as I have attempted to do in the momentary forgetfulness of the pursuit and consummation of random sex, or in the oblivion of alcohol and drugs, but in an appreciation of our own unimportance, then how much better might our lives be.' One or two people have risen from their seats now and are making for the exit. 'Listen! Wait a minute! This is important! We should revere the ant, as a small child does when he talks to it as an equal. The Judeo-Christian religion has left us with the idea of hierarchy. God is above us and He set us above the animals. But if we've lost the religion we should lose that idea too. Think dinosaurs! Think fossils! Compare your paltry three score years and ten with the dinosaurs. Millions and millions of years old! Here's the one my son Edward found on the beach. Forty million years old! Think of that, forty million years! And that's just a youngster. Most of us won't even be lucky enough to end up as fossils. But it's the best we can aspire to. Being waved about in a lecture hall aeons from now is our brightest future! We should respect the gift of life, which is all any of us has. If we can do this, lose the overweening idea of our own importance, then, and only then, will we begin to be happy.' More people are rising, whole droves of them pushing for the exit. 'No, wait! Listen! Where was I? Oh, yes, it's this. Once we appreciate the wonder of life, of all matter, then our own ceases to have significance and we can let go fears of its extinction. Jesus may not exist any more than our dead ancestors exist, except as an idea in our heads, perhaps, as not just a memory but as a set of moral precepts – wait! You have to listen!' I am shouting now. 'It's taken me half a century to work this out! Sit down! It's too important!' The Dean is coming up the steps of the platform, her high heels sounding like rifle shots so that one or two people at the back of the audience automatically duck, no doubt alarmed because of my earlier mention of high-school shootings. 'Listen to me! I am fifty years old today! I'm staring into the jaws of death! My willy won't work any more!'

The Dean has reached me and taken my arm, 'Michael, what do you think you're doing?' she says. 'You have to stop now! Come on, Michael!'

A security guard tugs at my other arm attempting to pull me away from the lectern. Dizziness hits me and I cling to it for support. But I have no strength in my arms and it topples from my grasp. I look up at the window high in the wall above the far doorway of the hall just in time to see a lightning bolt shoot through it, a bright white laser, coming right at me. The moment it hits me a supernova explodes inside my brain and everything is blasted white. White as a field of untrodden snow. White as a woman's breast. White as a virgin sheet of paper in an unwritten book.

THIRTY

Go, and catch a falling star,
Get with child a mandrake root,
Tell me, where all past years are,
Or who cleft the Devil's foot

Song

'No, no, no, Michael. It's not a firework. It's a Mr Tongue. Come on now, try again.'

'F-fought.'

'Thought.'

'Fought.'

'That's still a firework, Michael. Watch my mouth.' Her face looms into mine, which I always find alarming. It's because of the right eye being so blurry and useless. You can't judge distances with only one eye and things seem to zoom towards you. 'Come on, now,' she continues. 'I know it's tricky but you're doing ever so well. Now you're putting your top lip over the bottom one, like this. That's making a firework. I want you to push the tip of your tongue forward, like so. Come on now, one last try, just for Rebecca. Thought.'

'Th-thought.'

'Well done! You see? Rebecca knew you could do it all along, didn't she? OK, I think that's enough for today.'

She walks over to the door, opens it and calls, 'We're all through in here.'

I hear footsteps coming and the one I can't remember what she's called, the one who lives here with me, comes in. She's blonde and pretty with very long legs.

'How did it go this morning?'

'Oh, very well, really. He's making real progress.'

'Do you think so, Rebecca? Do you really think so? I find it so hard to tell. And the aphasia – his entire world was words and now he can't remember even the simplest ones.'

'Yes,' says Rebecca, with that friendly thing you do with your lips, 'I know, it's just like teaching a child.'

'Worse. Children begin by saying the names of everything and all you have to do is fill in the verbs and grammar. It's the nouns that give him most trouble. He can't remember the names of even the most basic things.'

'I know, Mrs Cole,' ah, that's it, she's called Mrs Cole, 'but it's not that long since the stroke, is it?'

'Six weeks.'

'Well, there you are, then. If he wasn't talking at all by this stage, I'd be worried, but the fact that he's started means it will all come back eventually.'

'Do you think so? It's hard to believe. I mean, done was his whole life, but he doesn't remember a single word of it now.'

'He will. You just have to keep stimulating him. Bombard him with his favourite things. Sounds corny, I know, but believe me, I've seen it work.'

Rebecca sits down and takes out a whatsit and lays it on the thing you eat off. She opens the whatsit and now Mrs Cole has one and she opens hers too and each looks into her own. 'Next Tuesday, three o'clock, OK?' says Rebecca, and Mrs Cole nods and they each stroke their whatsits with writing sticks.

'Bye-bye, Michael, see you next week.' Rebecca's face zooms in on mine and out again. I feel her hand in my hair. Mrs Cole opens the door and she follows Rebecca out. I'm left alone, thinking about what Mrs Cole said.

'Done was his life and now he doesn't remember any of it.' 'Done was his life'? What can this mean? First, although I have trouble remembering how to say things myself, I feel sure this is not right. Something is wrong. Surely it should be 'His life was done'? And what about what it means? How could my life have been over before this thing they call the stroke attacked me? I'm still here even now. And, while it's true I do not remember much of my life, *any* is not right. I remember some things. For example, I remember a red bathing-suit for a not-man to swim in. Why, I don't know. But if I shut my eyes I can see it.

The door opens again and Mrs Cole comes in. 'Rebecca says you're doing very well, darling.' She does the friendly mouth thing. 'You're doing swear words next week.' She looks at me, as though waiting for something. 'Only joking,' she says. 'Now, I have a few little chores to do, but I'll be back in a while. Why don't you listen to some music?' She walks across the place where we are and I hear a noise. The buzzing music starts up, and I try to tell her to make it stop but it's so noisy she can't hear my not very noisy saying.

'Enjoy it, see you in a while.'

She's gone and once again I try to make sense of the music. After the buzzing a man's voice sings that a storm drove him here, and then a not-man sings about the water she has brought him. She wants him to drink. 'Cool water,' she sings. The music is heavy and makes me feel something not-good will happen to me. I try to lift the working hand to the hearing ear, but it won't go that far up. I am desperate for the music to stop.

The door bursts open and the two little ones come in, the whatsits, the boys.

'Hello, Daddy,' shouts the big blond one. 'We've come to see you.'

I try to think of their names because I know that I know them. Jack? Jack and . . . ? That's it, Jack and Edmund. No, not right, but nearly.

'This music is very loud,' says Jake. Ah, yes, that's it! Jake. Jake and Edward. 'I'll turn it off, shall I, Daddy?'

'Mmm.' I can't remember that word to agree. It's one of the ones I know, but it's gone away for now.

Jake takes a thing you sit on from under the thing you sit at and walks across the place where we are and then gets on the sitting thing, only standing, and reaches his hand up and immediately the music stops. I turn my head and try to do the friendly thing with my mouth but I don't know if it works.

'I'm a pirate,' says Edward. I see he has a something over one eye, tied there by a string round his head and at first I am worried he's hurt his eye, but it is obviously just something they are playing. He climbs on to my lap and hugs me. 'Lovely Daddy,' he says, stroking my head with his hand.

'Right, come on, the enemy are upstairs,' shouts Jake. ''Bye, Daddy!' He runs out of the door. Edward follows him but turns at the door, lifts his leg up and points to the bottom of it.

'Foot,' he says. Jake and Edward have been teaching me words. We've been doing parts of the body. I know nearly all my body parts now. He's gone with a slam of the door and I mouth the new word to myself.

'F-foot.' Luckily it's a firework, which makes it easier. 'Foot.'

Then I remember that although Edward is a very good speaker – he knows a very lot of words more than me – he can't do a Mr Tongue. It always comes out as a 'f—'.

I try the word again using Mr Tongue. 'Th-thoot. Th-oot. Thoot.' Yes, that's it. I seem to remember that all right. 'Thoot.'

It's all so difficult, especially Mr Tongue, and Rebecca is always telling me off for using fireworks by mistake. Just like someone else always used to say, 'Don't mention the F-word, Michael,' though I don't remember who. Anyway, I have to learn to talk again for the boys. I don't need to know all the words there are, but I need to learn enough to pass on what I have learned in my life before it is quite over (if it is not over already – 'Done was his life,' she said, after all).

It is this: do not chase shadows – you will never catch them unless the sun is overhead and then they will chase you. And do not spend your life chasing after things to own. One day you may not even be able to remember their names. Do not worry about being happy all the time. Bad men know freedom comes in interludes between prison sentences. Happiness is the same. Grab it when it comes. Do not fret over its loss; with luck it may come again. Do not fear being dead, for you won't be there when you are. Fear of death is all about not being me. I know something about that, as I am not me any more. I have lost who I was. And it's not so bad. Whoever he was, this Michael, he was not so special. The world can get along without him very well and he doesn't mind because he is no longer here. And, anyway, maybe he can be rebuilt. Maybe better next time. Snap his head off and swop it for another. Break him in the middle and switch the bottom half with someone else's. Change him around a bit. And when all's said and done, what's death but another kind of change? So do not think about ever after, but make now better. Keep busy. Consider ants. How they rush around, getting on with their lives, doing whatever it is they do, not sitting around wondering why they are here and worrying how one day they won't be. Oh, and one more thing, the most important of all: learn to swim.

I have just finished composing this message to my sons when the door opens and Mrs Cole comes in. She is carrying under her arm the big red thing you open-and-read. She pulls a chair over to mine and sits down facing me, our knees (we did that word last day, and also 'willy', the floppy thing you wee with) touching so she can look into my eyes.

'Hello, darling, thought we'd read for a bit,' she says. She holds up the thing that you open and read but I don't understand the squiggles on it. 'Your favourite.'

I almost let out a groan but I don't partly because I'm not sure I can and partly because her mouth is doing the friendly thing because she is so happy to be doing this.

' "Go, and catch a falling star," ' she reads and something stirs inside me. I know these words! They are part of a song. Suddenly the name Perry Como leaps into my mind. I don't know who it is or even if it's a man or a not-man. But I can hear the song inside my head! 'What?' says Mrs Cole, her mouth doing a big friendly thing now. 'You remember it? That's wonderful.' She carries on reading, her voice trembling with excitement.

' "Get with child a mandrake root . . ." ' I am puzzled. This is not how it should be. The song is inside me. Something about putting the star in your pocket. And then saving it for a rainy day. My face must look troubled because Mrs Cole's mouth is no longer doing the friendly thing. She puts a hand on my knee. 'Don't worry, darling, it won't all come back at once. But it's a start. You're starting to remember.'

She picks up the open-and-read again. ' "Tell me where all past years are, or who cleft the Devil's foot, teach me to hear mermaids singing, or to keep off . . ." '

On and on she drones and the words seem so strange I find it impossible to understand any of them. I detest this open-and-read so much I could scream, except that I can't. Instead I close my eyes and try to make the half of my mouth that works do the friendly thing. With luck, as long as I do not snore, Mrs Cole will never even know I'm asleep.

THE END